THE PRISONER'S GOLD

BY CHRIS KUZNESKI

CHRIS KUZNESKI

THE PRISONER'S GOLD

headline

First published in 2015 by
HEADLINE PUBLISHING GROUP

1

Cataloguing in Publication Data is
available from the British Library

Hardback ISBN 978 0 7553 8659 8
Trade paperback ISBN 978 0 7553 8660 4

Typeset in Garamond MT
by Palimpsest Book Production Limited, Falkirk, Stirlingshire

Printed and bound in Great Britain by Clays Ltd, St Ives plc

Headline's policy is to use papers that are natural, renewable and
recyclable products and made from wood grown in well-managed
forests and other controlled sources. The logging and manufacturing
processes are expected to conform to the environmental
regulations of the country of origin.

HEADLINE PUBLISHING GROUP
An Hachette UK Company
Carmelite House
50 Victoria Embankment
London EC4Y 0DZ

www.headline.co.uk
www.hachette.co.uk

Acknowledgements

Here are some of the amazing people I'd like to thank:

Scott Miller, Claire Roberts, and the whole gang at Trident Media. They sold this series long before it was written. That's the sign of a great agency!

Vicki Mellor, Emily Griffin, Darcy Nicholson, Jo Liddiard, Ben Willis, Mari Evans, and everyone at Headline/Hachette UK. They bought this series when it was nothing but an outline, then they helped me bring it to life. Thanks for believing in me and the Hunters.

Ian Harper, my longtime friend/editor/consigliere. He reads my words before anyone else – and then tweaks them until they're perfect. One of these days, you'll see his name on a book of his own, and when you do, I urge you to buy it!

Kane Gilmour, who has traveled more than Polo himself. In addition to being a talented writer, he actually visited most of the locations in this book. His time in Asia and Italy helped me get things right. Thanks for all of your help.

All the fans, librarians, booksellers, and critics who have enjoyed my thrillers and have recommended them to others. If you keep reading, I'll keep writing.

Last but not least, I'd like to thank my family for their unwavering support. At some point, I'll actually take some time off and get to thank you in person.

Okay, I think that just about does it. It's finally time for my favorite part of the book. Without further ado, please sit back, relax, and let me tell you a story . . .

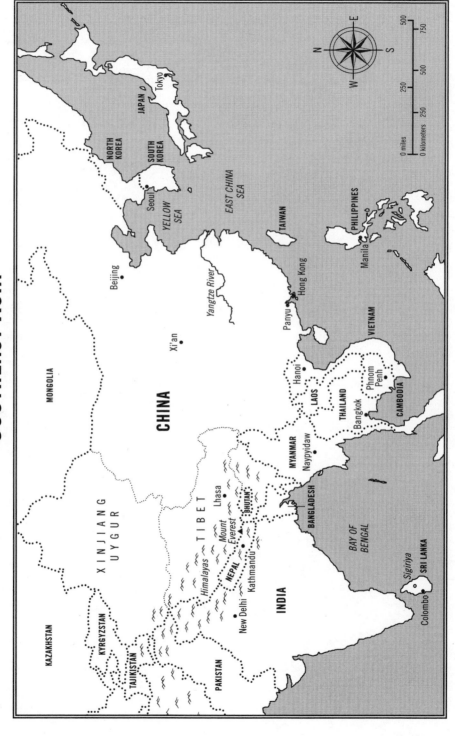

SOUTHEAST ASIA

Prologue

Metal creaked and groaned, startling Rustichello da Pisa from his restless sleep. Even in the fog of slumber, he knew the horrific sound of a cell door opening. Anytime he heard it, he would snap awake to the pounding in his chest – even after all these years.

His senses on full alert, he strained to hear every rustle and scrape on the other side of the wall. He knew the Genoese guards were returning his neighbor after yet another round of torture. With any luck, they were done for the day and wouldn't be coming for him next.

He would find out soon enough.

The uniformed guards moved into the adjacent cell and dumped their day's entertainment on the floor with a wet splat. Then they quickly closed the door behind them and left without a word. Only then did Rustichello let out the breath that he had been holding.

He didn't move until he heard the guards' heavy footsteps recede down the dark corridor. He always did his best to avoid their notice, unless they were coming for him. On those occasions there was nothing to do but submit. He was too weak and frail to fight them anymore.

There was no sense in making them mad.

He slowly stood from the loose straw on the floor that served as his bed and brushed away the pieces that were tangled in his hair. Then he slipped a hand into his ragged linen trousers and scratched at the fungal infection on the right side of his groin. Thanks to the humid air in the city of Genoa, everything in the dungeon was damp. The walls, the ceiling, the floor, his clothes. Molds and lichens grew over every surface of his cell. Some patches were so large that they looked like broccoli.

On the bright side, at least he hadn't started eating them.

Or naming them.

Confident that the guards were gone, he moved over to the wall and peered through the small window into the next cell. It was little more than a missing stone that had been dug out by a previous occupant, but the rectangular gap served a monumental purpose. Rustichello and his neighbor used the empty space to chat, to pass the long hours well into the night.

Their *window* provided meaningful human interaction.

But today, he couldn't see his friend through the hole.

Suddenly worried, Rustichello lay on the damp floor where it met the moss-covered wall and glanced through an even smaller gap. This one at floor level and designed for drainage. The stench of dried urine in the gutter near the hole was overpowering, but he needed to check on his neighbor, who was deadly silent in his cell.

'My friend,' Rustichello said in Venetian, 'do you need water?'

He knew better than to ask if the man was all right. Both had been to the chamber where the Genoese slapped them around. When they left there, they were *never* all right.

The beaten merchant blinked at him a few times, trying to regain his bearings, then coughed up some blood from his broken ribs. Though he was far younger and hardier than Rustichello, the constant beatings were taking their toll.

'If you can spare some,' he croaked.

Their daily rations were minimal at best, but Rustichello would gladly share his water. His neighbor had done the same for him on his own return trips from abuse. He grabbed his tin cup and scooped some murky water from the stone bowl he was given each morning. Then he carefully positioned the cup in the tiny drainage hole on the floor and nudged it through the tunnel, careful not to tip it or touch the drinking rim to the top of the tunnel's roof.

With a trembling hand, the merchant grasped the thin handle and dragged the cup along the floor until it was right next to his face. He pressed it to his swollen lips and sipped cautiously, pleased when swallowing did not add to his pain.

'I don't think they are after information anymore . . . I'm not even sure they still enjoy the beatings. It feels more like routine now – for them as well.'

'Must not have been Guillermo, then. That sack of shit enjoys it every time.'

The merchant smiled at the eye on the other side of the wall. They would frequently curse their captors in private, but never loud enough to be heard by the guards or other inmates.

'No. Not the ogre,' he muttered. He finished the water in small sips, quietly thankful that Guillermo hadn't been to work in nearly a week.

It was a small blessing in his current hell.

The merchant had been captured during Venice's war with Genoa when his ship had run aground on a sandbar near the Anatolian coast. Enemy soldiers had taken him in chains on one of their boats back to the Republic of Genoa – one of the last places a Venetian ever hoped to find himself. Of course, it probably hadn't helped matters that during the fighting he had fired the severed heads of Genoese sailors from a massive catapult in between the volleys of rough iron balls designed to plunge through the decks of enemy ships.

The merchant had spent the last few years paying for his hubris.

'So,' Rustichello whispered, 'do you need to rest for today, or shall we continue?'

The merchant smiled and slowly clambered to his feet. 'I think we can continue.'

He moved to the gap in the wall at eye level, grateful to no longer smell the latrine. Rustichello's smiling face quickly appeared on the other side of the opening. The merchant handed him the empty cup through the hole. 'Thank you, my friend.'

Rustichello took the cup and nodded.

He was only in his fifties, but he looked at least seventy – his hair white, his skin pale, his eyes sunken. He had been captured in an earlier naval defeat, and as a result he had already languished in the dungeon for a decade by the time the merchant had been imprisoned. Everything about him was thin and haggard, the look of a man who was nearly defeated.

The one thing that would return life to Rustichello's face was story. It didn't matter whether the tale was told or received, he thrived on sending his mind to other places. At first, the elder man had impressed the merchant with tales of King Arthur, but once Rustichello had heard some of the details of the merchant's travels to the far edges of Tartary it was the only subject that he wanted to talk about.

And write about.

Amazingly, on the night of his imprisonment – before the pouches on his clothing had been properly searched – Rustichello had discovered a small nook under a loose stone in his cell and had managed to hide a book, a broken quill, a small inkpot, and a pair of spectacles.

Not much, but enough to keep him sane.

The book, a stained and worn copy of Herodotus's history, had seen better days, but it was serving a different purpose now. The

Venetian would talk about his journeys, and Rustichello would carefully write down each word in French in the spaces between the lines of existing Greek text. He was defacing one of the greatest historians who ever lived so that the merchant's adventures might one day lead Rustichello on a journey of his own.

That is, if the guards never found his hiding place.

And if he lived long enough to be released.

And if he could grab the book before he departed.

Everything, it seemed, came down to that one small word.

If.

'Shall we begin?' Rustichello asked.

The merchant turned his back to their window and slowly slid down the wall in his cell. Rustichello did the same. It was their custom to sit with their backs to the wall between them. The Venetian would speak for a few hours each day, until his voice felt dry, while Rustichello scribbled and scratched his quill on the paper of the book, always attempting to tease out more information on the hidden wealth of Asia and the treasures that his friend might have left behind.

'Where were we?' the merchant asked through the wall.

'You were about to describe the people of Tebeth.'

'Ah yes,' he said, remembering, as he closed his eyes and left the cell in his mind. 'The province of Tebeth was terribly devastated at the time of our arrival . . .'

The merchant had no problem recalling the most trivial details of his journeys abroad, and yet there were some aspects of his travels that he refused to share with anyone. Though he was extremely grateful for the kindness that Rustichello had shown him over the years, he wasn't ready to trust his neighbor with his greatest secret: the location of his family's fortune.

That was a secret that Marco Polo would keep for himself.

I

Present Day
Saturday, March 15
Denver, Colorado

Hector Garcia couldn't have cared less about the view.

He was there to hack.

Garcia was oblivious to the panoramic landscape of the Rocky Mountains outside the windows of the suite he had leased on the upper floor of the CenturyLink Tower. He hadn't rented the office for the scenery but for its proximity to the roof of the second tallest building in Denver – and its array of antennas, satellite dishes, and telecommunications equipment. As it was, he had covered most of the windows with thick tinting to reduce the glare on his monitors and to regulate the temperature inside the suite.

The room was kept at a perfect sixty degrees from the industrial-strength air conditioning unit that constantly battled the heat output of the room's vast collection of computing hardware. Three racks of enterprise-grade servers and switches from Juniper Networks, Cisco, and half a dozen other vendors filled one wall of the room. An adjacent office held the rest of his system in row after row of next-generation devices that resembled stacks in a public library.

The wood floor of the main room was littered with overlapping power cords and network cables, and Garcia lived in the middle like a spider in its web. A collection of tables was configured in a circle, with a small gap to access his comfortable office chair in the center. A total of twenty-four screens – two rings of twelve monitors – encircled the single seat like the walls of a fortress.

In front of the monitors was an assortment of wireless keyboards, mice, track pads, web cameras, and other peripherals, plus an unopened package of Twinkies. Garcia would save the snack cakes for later. He never ate or drank at the desk, preferring to eat in the kitchen down the hall or on the mattress he had thrown in the corner. He'd seen too many people ruin a good system with a spilled can of Mountain Dew. The Twinkies were only there to remind him to get up once in a while to eat.

In his early years as a hacker, Garcia often went to bed hungry because he had spent all of his money on computer equipment instead of food, but money was no longer a problem since he had been hired by an enigmatic Frenchman named Jean-Marc Papineau to assist a team of specialists in finding the world's most famous treasures.

The first mission had taken the team to the Carpathian Mountains in search of a missing Romanian train. Then they were asked to find the tomb of Alexander the Great in the vast Egyptian desert. After a devastating tragedy on the mission, Papineau had reluctantly paid the surviving team members a portion (twenty percent) of their agreed-upon fee (five million dollars each) while placing the rest of their money in separate trust funds that they couldn't touch as long as they continued to work on his team. They still hadn't received payment for their second mission, but Garcia wasn't the least bit concerned about the money.

In a matter of seconds, he would be forty million dollars richer.

As his eyes skimmed financial transactions on twelve of the monitors, he watched as funds simply disappeared from the accounts of several would-be dictators in Africa, a Ukrainian mobster, and a few corrupt politicians in America before reappearing in an offshore account of his own. To Garcia, it was blood money that none of them deserved, and he was one of the few people in the world who could do anything about it. He would keep two of the forty million as working capital and anonymously donate the rest to charities. The only thing money got him personally was the promise of more computing power, but as long as he maintained his association with Papineau and his team, that would never be a problem.

Five of his monitors were hooked into a quantum computer manufactured by Payne Industries and maintained by Papineau in the team's headquarters in Florida. Each of the five connections had been established through a back door that Garcia had installed into the quantum. Papineau was aware of and occasionally tracked one of these connections, but the other four would remain undetected as long as Garcia had access to a keyboard.

Once the money had been moved, Garcia shifted his focus to the monitors that he used to keep tabs on his team. They had been on vacation since the last mission had ended in November, but he kept track of their whereabouts through a combination of facial recognition software, Papineau's super-computer, and ubiquitous camera feeds. Garcia could pull footage from a variety of sources from cell phones to security systems. This gave him almost constant supervision of his targets, as long as they didn't stray too far into the wilderness.

And for those times there were NSA satellites.

He knew Jack Cobb, the team's leader, had entered the United Kingdom at London's Heathrow airport, but once he had left the terminal, he had slipped off Garcia's grid. Cobb wasn't aware that Garcia was spying on him, but he was quite familiar with facial recognition software and was cagey about cameras all the time.

Papineau was also good at avoiding cameras, but in the Frenchman's case he knew he was being followed – not only by Garcia but by his employer as well.

The other team members, Sarah Ellis and Josh McNutt, were far easier to catch on screen. Sarah had spent some of her money decorating a small apartment in San Francisco. And one in Dallas. And another one in Toronto. Garcia wasn't sure why she had so many places, but he assumed it had something to do with her career as a world-class thief.

Or rather, a world-class 'acquisitions specialist'.

Sarah hated when people called her a thief.

Meanwhile, McNutt had surprised everyone with his recent purchase. The former Marine sniper had spent half of his funds on a beachside bar in Key West, Florida. He lived on the second floor and mostly kept to himself, unless his biker buddies stopped by. Garcia had expected wild orgies with hookers and drugs and more hookers, but McNutt was laying low as Cobb had recommended. Today he was snoozing in a hammock near the shore.

A transaction on one of his monitors completed with a soft ping, and Garcia swiveled his chair around to see the money that he had looted from the son of the former Nigerian president, who had swindled billions from his government's coffers. The former leader had died in office, but his son was living a cushy life in the south of France. Every month, Garcia lightened his fortune by a few million. No one in his family had yet to even notice.

A second ping confirmed the stolen funds had been sent to fifteen NGOs in Nigeria. Garcia smiled at the transactions, just as his cell phone started to ring. He glanced at the screen and saw it was Papineau calling. He leaned forward in his chair, muted the master volume on his system, and answered the phone.

'Good afternoon, Jean-Marc. What can I do for you today?'

'I have another job for the team. Can you please call them in for me?'

'Right now?'

'Yes, Hector, right now. It's time to get back to work.'

'Yes, sir. But just so you know, Sarah isn't going to be happy.'

'Why not?'

Garcia glanced at one of his monitors and grimaced. 'Right now, she's kind of busy.'

2

Pittsfield, Vermont
(132 miles northwest of Boston)

Sarah Ellis wiped a swath of mud from her face and flung it to the ground. In her left hand she held a plastic bucket filled with rocks. The rope handle was thick and rough. If not for the numbness in her hands and fingers, she would have felt the fibers digging into her flesh.

Just like the rope she used to climb in gym class.

Towering above her, a waterfall surged over a thirty-foot cliff. The clear mountain water splashed and sprayed in the air with a roar of white noise. It took her a moment to gather her senses. She wasn't sure if she should admire its beauty or curse at it for being in her way.

She ended up doing both.

Although it was a perfect day for skiing, she hadn't come to Vermont to enjoy the fresh powder. She was there to compete in the PEAK Winter Death Race, a form of hell that combined endurance racing, obstacle courses, and mental acuity exams. It was a competition designed to push contestants to their breaking points . . . and then dare them to keep going. The race was so grueling and the racers so determined that it was common for competitors to leave behind torn flesh – and even the occasional fingertip – and never break stride.

Snow covered most of the course, and the air temperature was hovering around forty degrees. Brisk, but not devastatingly cold. Despite the chill, Sarah wore only a tight-fitting black sports outfit that was now so encrusted in mud that her shapely figure had transformed into a bulbous blob of browns and grays, like a corpse buried in the woods.

She had already run several miles up and down the mountainside, stopping only to complete the challenges. It had begun with quartering logs with an ax before swimming to the bottom of a muck-filled pond to retrieve a bag of LEGO. Per instruction, she had carried the pouch to the next station where she had used the tiny bricks to construct a toy motorcycle while reciting the names of all fifty US states. Once she had completed that task, she had stacked a thousand pounds worth of sandbags into a ten-foot pyramid while shouting the list of states again – only this time in reverse alphabetical order.

The hardest parts for her weren't the tasks themselves but the complete uncertainty about the length of the race or what drudgery might be lurking around the next corner. In her line of work, having a plan was crucial; failing to think ahead could get her captured or killed. But at PEAK, she never knew what to expect next. There was no way to train for this event. She just had to be in good enough shape to handle anything that they threw at her, no matter how long it lasted.

Thankfully, the next task was right up her alley.

She had to climb the waterfall.

In the summer when the stream was barely trickling, the rock face would have presented little difficulty for an expert climber like Sarah. But with the spring thaw in full effect, the wall was protected by a thick layer of bubbling whitewater that was so cold it was one step away from being ice. To make the task harder, she had to carry the bucket of rocks to the top without using her hands. For her, that meant placing the bucket behind her head and shoving the rope handle into her mouth.

A field marshal inspected her every move. 'You know, you don't have to do this. Just say the word, and I'll give you a warm blanket, a thermos of hot chocolate, and a ride back to the lodge.'

'Fuuuu youuuuu!' she said through clenched teeth.

He laughed at the vulgarity and backed away.

Sarah stepped into the frigid pool at the foot of the falls and felt her legs go completely numb. As she trudged toward the falling water, her mind drifted far from Vermont. Mentally she was no longer in the icy froth but on a warm beach at the team compound in Fort Lauderdale.

During the past year, she had learned a lot about herself. She used to prefer to work alone, but now the isolation of it was less thrilling. After working with a team of highly skilled experts on a pair of high-stakes missions, she had discovered the value of team-work. Not only had she come to recognize the talents of others but she saw how they could complement her own abilities. And this realization had slowly carried over into other aspects of her life.

Including the Death Race.

Two tasks back, she had convinced other contestants that the only way up a steep mudslide was to form a human chain. Many of the others had refused to accept that the obstacle required collaboration, but Sarah had figured it out immediately. After becoming a part of a 'Barrel of Monkeys' chain with five mud-coated competitors, she had succeeded in reaching the top.

Everyone who insisted on doing it alone had failed.

Champing down on the rope handle of the bucket – with its heavy cargo of river stones nestled behind her damp head – she felt like she was wearing some kind of torture device. She stepped into the downpour and was immediately drenched. The water felt like needles piercing her skin. With the rope jammed in her teeth, she couldn't close her lips. The cascade of icy water flooded her mouth, making her teeth ache and breathing difficult. All she could do was try to close off her throat as she looked up under the falls to see the next hold.

Fortunately, the rock wall was merely damp from spray and not fully soaked from the surging water, which arched out from the ledge above and mostly hit the bucket of rocks behind her head as she tried to find her grip. This made the bucket heavier and the task that much harder. Although the challenge was devious, she quickly figured out how to defeat it.

Sarah noticed two thin crevices up the back of the cliff. She jammed her fingers inside the left crack and placed her boots inside the right. Then by pulling her hands in one direction and pushing with her feet in the other, she was able to anchor herself against the wall. From there, she simply had to adjust her pressure as she inched her way up the rock face. The technique was called a *layback*: an advanced maneuver that was difficult to master. But with a low center of gravity, most women climbers found it easier to do than men did.

Once she found her rhythm, she made her way up the cliff with relative ease. As long as she kept her head turned to the right or left, the water passed harmlessly behind her and missed the bucket entirely. At the top of the rock, right below the apex of the surging waterfall, she found a horizontal crevice that allowed her to slide completely to a rocky ledge past the edge of the water. From there, she climbed around the frigid stream and made her way to a different field marshal who was there to make sure her bucket of rocks was still intact.

He gave her a thumbs-up and pointed her toward the finish line.

A short jog through the snow, and she would be the winner of the event.

The first female ever to capture the main prize.

Just then, she heard her cell phone start to ring. Attached to her arm in a bulletproof case capable of withstanding water, mud, rock, and LEGO, the phone blasted out a verse from Oingo Boingo's *Weird Science*. It was her ringtone for Hector Garcia.

If the geek was calling, it could mean only one thing.

There was another mission for the team.

Sarah smiled as she reached for her phone, which was buried under a layer of mud. She had balked at first when Cobb had requested each team member be available at all times, but it truly didn't bother her. In fact, she actually looked forward to the next call. She had quickly come to realize that she only felt truly alive when on a mission with the team.

Sure, she would pretend to be annoyed and put on a huge show of bitching and complaining that she had been called in during the middle of the race, but the truth was she couldn't wait to fly to Florida to get back in the game.

Besides, she had no intention of winning the race.

Not with TV coverage at the finish line.

The team didn't need that kind of attention.

Still smiling, Sarah put the phone to her ear and hissed, 'What?'

3

Normally Lim Bao would take his time as he strolled through the plush lobby of the high-rise hotel where his boss lived. He would admire the shiny marble floors, the expensive artwork on the walls, and the attractive hostesses behind the front desk.

But today wasn't an ordinary day.

Today someone was chained to a chair in the parking garage.

Waiting for the elevator, Lim impatiently tapped his leather shoe on the carpet until he heard the chime indicating the car had arrived. He stepped inside, slid his keycard into the slot, then entered his security code for the 117th floor. An elderly couple with their grandson stepped toward the car as the doors began to close, but he glared at them and shook his head.

They quickly got the hint and backed away.

A moment later, the doors sealed shut and the elevator rocketed skyward as Lim's stomach leaped into his throat. Though he hated the nausea that always accompanied him to the penthouse, he knew it could have been much worse.

At least it wasn't a *glass* elevator.

On the *outside* of the building.

Whoever invented those was an asshole.

The hotel occupied the top sixteen floors of the International Commerce Centre, which was the tallest building in Hong Kong and the seventh tallest in the world. Roughly two hundred feet shorter than the One World Trade Center in New York, the ICC would have been higher on the list if the number of stories was the determining factor instead of raw height – since many of the world's tallest buildings added massive antennas for no other reason than to be taller.

A soft ding signaled the car's arrival, and the elevator slid open with a quiet whoosh. Waiting on the other side were Chang and Lang, the identical twins hired to guard the door during the day shift. They looked like trolls comically stuffed into black Armani suits. Rippling with muscles and bulk, the men were also highly flexible, lending far more function to their heft than was typical of bodybuilders. As Lim passed, each raised a fist diagonally across his chest in salute. He barely noticed as he raced down the corridor to his mentor's room.

Another two guards stood at the double doors to the Presidential Suite, but they allowed him to pass without being frisked. He was the only one permitted to do so. Once inside, Lim ignored the breathtaking/nauseating view and went straight to the exercise room where he found his middle-aged mentor face down on a rubberized mat, working through his daily calisthenics. Wearing only dark sweat pants, the man was effortlessly raising himself in a one-thumbed push-up. His rippled torso glistened with so much sweat under the harsh lights that he almost seemed to glow.

Feng He was the present-day leader of the Righteous and Harmonious Fists. The brotherhood had existed in secrecy for centuries but had risen to fame at the start of the twentieth century when they had fought off the British imperialists who they believed were plundering the wealth and resources of China. The members of the brotherhood were still vehemently opposed to any and all foreign interference in China, but it had taken Feng's leadership over the past decade to bring the organization out of the shadows and into the world of high finance.

Lim was constantly amazed at the financial support that the brotherhood received. He couldn't actually remember the last time he had seen Feng pay for anything – not only in Hong Kong, but anywhere they went. And with a rising tide of Chinese nationalism, that sort of respect would only continue to grow in the future.

Feng leaned back on the downthrust of his push-up, then sprang forward with his legs. The lunge launched his body upward at a forty-five-degree angle. He deftly landed on his feet and continued forward to the ballet bar mounted across the wall of windows. Feng grabbed a plush towel off the wooden bar and gently patted the perspiration from his face. Then he breathed in and out a few times, exaggerating the action with his arms, as if the heavy breaths completed his exercise.

Lim said nothing as he waited for his boss to acknowledge his presence.

Eventually Feng turned and smiled broadly, showing perfect white teeth. Then he spoke in Mandarin to his second-in-command. 'What has you in such a rush today?'

'The brothers have captured a smuggler,' answered Lim, who was standing at attention as if he were reporting to an emperor.

'And why should I care?' Feng asked, amused. In a district the size of Hong Kong, there were literally thousands of crimes per day, most of which had nothing to do with the Fists.

'The smuggler is Australian. We caught him at the Tsim Sha Tsui marketplace.'

'What was he smuggling?'

'Jade figurines from the Ming Dynasty.'

Feng's smile vanished, and a scowl furrowed his brow. He took notice whenever foreigners committed any crime in China – from small slights to massive drug deals – but he took particular interest when a foreigner tried to rob his country's heritage. He moved across the room, grabbed a thin black T-shirt, and slipped it over his powerful torso. 'Where is he?'

'We have him downstairs. Should I have him brought up for you?'

'No,' Feng growled. 'We will go down.'

They rode silently to the hotel lobby and switched elevators to descend the entire distance to the sub-basement's parking level.

The elevator opened to a clean, brightly lit lot with thick yellow lines on the ground and walls. The building had several lots, but this level was closed off for the Fists. Diagonally across from the elevator was a private office where the smuggler was being kept.

Inside the office there were three large guards in tailored suits, all standing silently around a wooden desk and chair. Chained to the desk was a scruffy Australian of nearly thirty. His eyes were sky blue and his hair an unruly mop of dirty blond curls. He was big – more than two hundred pounds of meat – although his body lacked definition.

'Good afternoon,' Feng said in English.

Relief filled the tourist's face as he looked up at Feng and Lim.

'Oh, thank God! Someone who speaks English. Listen, mate, I'm not sure what these boys have told you, but I didn't do anything wrong. My business partner assured me that the items were paid for and our shipping permits were up to date. Obviously I can't read the damn forms – they're written in symbols or whatever you call those squiggly things – but I swear to you, I thought everything was legal.'

'Is that so?' Feng said, pondering his next move.

'I'm telling you, mate, it's nothing but a misunderstanding.'

Feng nodded and stuck out his hand. 'Yes. A big misunderstanding.'

The Aussie smiled and leaned forward to shake hands with Feng, hoping upon hope that Feng was dumb enough to believe his lie, but it wasn't meant to be. Feng struck with lightning speed, grasping the man's wrist and twisting it with so much force that bones cracked.

The man dropped face first onto the desk, wailing in agony.

Feng continued, 'You believed you could come to my country and steal our history. You misunderstood who the Chinese people are. We are not your playthings, your servants, your inferiors. Then again, your people descended from criminals, so I should expect no better.'

Between shouts of pain and gasps for breath, the Aussie tried to explain himself. 'I'm sorry . . . I didn't mean to disrespect you . . . Ahhhh! Look, just call the embassy, I'll give everything back . . .'

'You'd like us to contact your country's consul general? To send him a message?' Feng twisted the hand harder, and the young man screamed. Tears were literally shooting from the man's eyes, and a thick band of yellowish snot stretched from his nostril to his mouth. Meanwhile, the rest of his face had turned a brilliant crimson from the rush of blood.

'Yes! Please! Send him a message!'

Feng slammed the Aussie's arm flat on the desktop and held out his free hand. One of the guards placed a gleaming meat cleaver in it without missing a beat. Then he stepped back to enjoy what he knew would happen next.

With one perfectly executed swipe, Feng brought the blade down, embedding it almost an inch into the scarred wooden desktop, separating the foreigner's hand from his wrist. The Aussie's choked tears sounded like a drowning victim trying to spit out seawater, as the table and floor were coated with a viscous puddle of gushing blood.

Feng picked up the severed hand and dangled it in front of the

Aussie's face. 'I will gladly send him a message. Your hand, along with a note reminding him that foreigners are no longer welcome in the new China. You will all leave immediately – whether whole or in pieces.'

Then Feng tossed the hand to Lim as he turned for the door.

4

Hay-on-Wye, Wales
(134 miles west of London)

Jack Cobb stepped into the small café and inhaled deeply, enjoying the rich aroma of freshly baked bread that had caught his attention outside on the sidewalk. The place was tiny, but there was an open table near the bay window that overlooked the street.

His seat, much like the area itself, was perfect for his needs.

Hay was a small market town straddling the border of England and Wales. It was known far and wide as a Mecca for book lovers. With over two dozen bookshops, there was one in nearly every building in town. Additionally, every spring the community hosted the Hay Festival, a major writing event that attracted authors from around the world.

Although Cobb enjoyed reading in his downtime, it wasn't the reason he had picked this place. He had chosen Hay because it was so far off the beaten track that it barely had any CCTV cameras on the streets, which was a rarity in the UK. Cobb always did his best to avoid cameras whenever he could, but privacy was particularly important for today's meeting.

It needed to be confidential.

During the past year, Cobb had grown more and more suspicious of Papineau. Whether it was seeing through his lies and half-truths or doubting his real motivation for finding these treasures, Cobb knew that Papineau wasn't the free-spending billionaire that he pretended to be. He sensed that Papineau was working for someone else – someone who preferred to stay in the shadows – and that didn't sit well with Cobb. If he was going to continue to risk his life and the lives of his squad, he needed to know who was calling the shots.

And he needed to know now.

Cobb ordered tea and toast, then looked outside through his own reflection in the glass. He was a shade over six feet tall with short brown hair and a handsome face. For some reason, women always told him that he looked like a racecar driver. He didn't know what that meant, but he was assured it was a compliment. Chiseled, but not bulky; people often underestimated his strength until he rolled up his sleeves and they saw the muscular definition of his forearms, with veins so thick it looked like snakes had crawled under his skin.

And yet that wasn't his most distinguishing feature.

What stood out the most were his eyes.

They were gun-gray and piercing, so distinct that he was often forced to wear colored contacts on covert missions for fear of recognition. When he landed at Heathrow, they had been brown. Now they were hazel. After this meeting, he would wear aviator sunglasses to hide his eyes completely. Sometimes it was a pain in the ass, but he wouldn't trade his eyes for anything.

They were his favorite feature.

As the waitress arrived with his order, Cobb saw the man he was waiting for.

Seymour Duggan ambled along the cobbled street, jauntily whistling a tune as if he were on his way to work in one of the local bookstores. Thin and nearly bald, he wore a tweed jacket with patches on the elbows. The lone splash of color in his outfit was his bright-yellow bow tie, which matched the canary-colored suspenders that were hidden under his coat.

Cobb stood as the man entered the café. 'Good morning, Seymour.'

Duggan smiled warmly. 'Same to you, Jack. It's been a while.'

They shook hands like old friends before settling in at the table. 'Would you like something to eat or drink?'

Duggan nodded. 'Same as you. Tea and toast.'

'Actually,' Cobb said, 'I ate earlier. I ordered these for you.'

Duggan broke into a wide grin. 'I see you've done your homework.'

Cobb shrugged. 'I like to be prepared.'

'So do I,' Duggan said as he poured himself some tea. 'Which is why I left my wallet at home. I naturally assumed you were going to buy me breakfast to curry favor.'

Cobb smiled. 'Touché.'

The New Zealander laughed loudly. It was a snorting kind of laugh that grated on most people's nerves, but Cobb was the kind of man who would tolerate such things as long as Duggan could deliver when it mattered most.

In the spy game, Duggan was known as a *bloodhound* – a specialist at finding people who didn't want to be found. For years, he had rented out his services to governmental agencies like MI6 or the CIA, which was where Sarah Ellis had met him on one of her undercover missions with the Agency. Based on her recommendation, Cobb had hired him to find a missing professor during their search for Alexander the Great's tomb, and Duggan had performed brilliantly.

So brilliantly, in fact, that Cobb wanted to hire him again.

Duggan sipped his tea. 'I have to admit that your invitation caught me off guard. So did the first-class ticket from Cairo. It wasn't necessary, but much appreciated.'

Cobb nodded but said nothing.

'Do you know, in all the years I lived in England I hadn't even *heard* of this town.'

'Good. Let's hope no one else has either.'

'So, why are we here, Jack?'

'I'll get right to it. I need your expertise; or the expertise of someone you recommend, if you don't think you're the man for the job.'

Duggan leaned forward. 'You have my attention, sir.'

'Based on our last conversations in Egypt and the assistance you were able to provide, I won't insult you by assuming you don't know who I'm working for.'

Duggan smiled coyly. 'That would be a great start, because of course, I do. Monsieur Papineau not only paid me for that service, but he tried to recruit me after your adventure.'

That last bit was news to Cobb. 'And you turned him down?'

'Despite what Sarah might have told you, I don't work strictly for the money. I have enough of it now that I can pick and choose my clients. Oh, I told Jean-Marc that I was already embroiled in another issue, but the truth was I just didn't like the cut of his jib.'

'But you were still willing to meet with me . . .'

'Yes. My curiosity has got the better of me.' Duggan raised an eyebrow. 'I have an idea what it is you want me to work on, but I'd like to hear it from you.'

Cobb obliged. 'I need someone to perform the work that I can't do when I'm on a mission. I want someone on my side. A resource I can call who can find anyone or anything for me.'

Duggan sat back and straightened his bow tie. 'I couldn't possibly recommend anyone else for the job. This sort of thing requires international work, which happens to be my specialty.'

'I know.'

'And international work is *quite* expensive.'

Cobb nodded. 'You're obviously aware of what went down in the desert. Prior to that mission, we located a lost train in Romania.'

Duggan's face showed that he'd heard about the train full of gold.

Cobb went on. 'Jean-Marc – or rather his employer – is paying each member of my team a nice chunk of change. The implication is that there might be several more jobs ahead. I will pay you a quarter million per job. Retroactively. So you'll get a half-million signing bonus.'

Duggan had just taken a sip of his tea when he heard the amount. He sputtered and coughed, having snorted some of the hot liquid up his nose. The other customers looked over briefly, but Cobb waved them off as Duggan whipped out his handkerchief and coughed into it.

Cobb continued. 'From this point on, you'll only get paid on successful missions – just like me. But I'll cover your expenses up until that point, naturally.'

'Dear God,' Duggan whispered, once he had recovered his ability to speak. 'That's bloody generous, mate. You understand that's far beyond my typical salary, right?'

'I do,' Cobb said, leaning forward. 'But I require absolute silence for it. The truth is I don't need the money. The money I have now will keep me for the rest of my days. What I need is to live long enough to enjoy it. I don't like being in the dark.'

'No one does.'

'Plus, I need your complete loyalty on this. You wouldn't be Sarah's asset anymore. You'd be mine. I'll need you to drop all your other clients and work for me full time.'

'Understood,' Duggan said with a nod. 'My experience with these sorts of things has shown me that you might not like what I uncover . . .'

'Let me worry about that. The team will be in Florida today or tomorrow. That seems like a good time to start – if you like the cut of *my* jib, that is.'

'I like the cut of every sail on your sloop, Jack.' Duggan leaned across the table and shook Cobb's hand. 'I'll have my people begin immediately. Just tell me who you're looking for.'

'Wait. Your people?' Cobb said, suddenly wary.

'Relax, Jack. This sort of work can't be done with a single man anymore. I have agents who are highly skilled and loyal to me. In addition to their loyalty, there are *several* layers of protection between us. These days I don't meet these people in person, but I still keep tabs on them, as any employer should. There's a reason I've managed to reach this age in my profession.'

'That's fine,' Cobb said with a nod, 'as long as there's no direct connection from them to me. I know you, and I think I can trust you. But I'm not really comfortable trusting other people. So do me a favor and keep those layers intact. Or this relationship will end real quick.'

5

The concrete stucco and simple tiled roof of the team's headquarters gave the impression of an industrial compound rather than a lavish house. Built with practicality in mind, not prestige, the building looked more like a bunker than a beach home. The squat architecture, perfect for withstanding the tropical storms and powerful hurricanes that threatened the Florida coast each year, was unassuming in almost every way.

From the outside, it reeked of modesty, not money.

But inside was a different story.

Nicknamed '*La Trésorerie*' – the Treasure House – by Papineau, the four-thousand-square-foot home was adorned by the trappings of wealth. Exotic rugs, valuable paintings, and expensive chandeliers decorated the interior of nearly every room. Although the building was designed to keep them safe and included air filtration and water purification systems, as well as walls that could withstand a missile assault, the Frenchman saw no reason to sacrifice comfort.

Ironically, the team couldn't have cared less about such opulence. As long as they had beds to sleep in, couches to sit on, and food in the refrigerator, everything else was unnecessary. They were here to train, not entertain guests.

Gaudy works of art meant nothing to them.

Unless they were part of a mission.

The morning had been relatively quiet at the team's headquarters when Sarah Ellis burst through the front door like an angry bull. 'Where is he? I know he's here somewhere!'

Sprawled in a wingback chair in the living room, McNutt froze when Sarah stormed into the house. He didn't think he had done anything to piss her off in the past three months, but he braced for impact just in case. Thankfully, she blew right past him without so much as a glance. McNutt merely shrugged and went back to reading the latest issue of *Guns and Ammo*, as if this type of thing happened every day.

Meanwhile, Garcia had a much different reaction. Dressed in a *Skyfall* T-shirt, knee-length shorts, and sandals, he grabbed his laptop and retreated to the opposite side of the dining room table from where he had been working. Behind him was a huge picture window that looked out on a magnificent terrace interspersed with interlocking swimming pools and palm trees. He figured Sarah was less likely to throw something at him if he was standing in front of glass.

'It wasn't my fault,' Garcia shouted in his defense.

Sarah glared at him. 'Not you, Hector. You were just the messenger boy. I'm looking for Papi. I know he's here. I saw his yacht in the marina.'

At that moment, a short Chinese woman in her early forties entered the room from the kitchen. She carried a plate of steaming scrambled eggs and bacon, which she set down in front of Garcia as if she was a waitress at his favorite diner.

Garcia thanked the woman quietly, then sat down to eat.

Stunned, Sarah rocked back on her heels and examined the stranger.

She had a flat nose, black hair pinned back behind her head, and bright red lipstick. Her outfit was a dark exercise suit partially covered by a white apron.

She smiled at Sarah. 'Mr Papineau assured me he would be here for breakfast.'

'Um . . . thanks.'

'You're welcome,' the woman said before slipping back into the kitchen.

Sarah remained frozen. 'Who the hell was that?'

Garcia shrugged and mumbled, 'Looks like Papi's got himself a maid.' Then he shoveled some eggs into his mouth, grateful to be eating something other than Twinkies.

'A maid? How do we know we can trust—'

Before Sarah could finish her question, the woman came sweeping out of the kitchen again, this time with a bowl of spiced beef and rice in one hand and a pair of silver-tipped ebony chopsticks in the other. She set them down on a side table next to McNutt.

He smiled and bowed politely. 'Xièxiè.'

Sarah's mouth hung open as the woman scurried back to the kitchen again without a wasted step. Somehow she appeared to glide rather than walk. Sarah looked from the doorway to the kitchen, back to McNutt, then over to Garcia, then back to McNutt.

'What did you say to her?' she demanded.

McNutt picked up a piece of beef with the chopsticks. 'I said, "Thank you".'

Garcia stopped eating. 'You speak Chinese?'

'Hell no. Learning Putonghua is like trying to herd cats in the nude. You can do it, but you're gonna hurt yourself.'

Garcia was confused. 'Wait. But you just said—'

'I can say "thanks" and order beer in a bunch of languages. I can also say "How much for the girl with the donkey" in Tagalog, but that's a loooong story with lots of graphic details.'

Sarah rubbed her eyes in frustration. 'Dear God, please don't tell it.'

A moment later, Sarah sensed someone behind her. She opened her eyes, and the Chinese woman was standing a foot away. Somehow she had slipped back into the room without the whisper of a sound. Sarah jolted back away from her.

'Would you care for some breakfast?' the woman asked. Up close, her face was smooth, with just the hint of laugh lines around her eyes.

'Uh . . . no, thanks,' Sarah managed. She was about to ask the woman's name, but before she could the woman flitted across the room to McNutt's chair.

'You like the Naxi beef, Joshua?'

He smiled. 'Yes, ma'am. It's delicious.'

She beamed with pride. 'It is, isn't it?'

Then she zoomed off to the kitchen again.

Sarah turned and glared at McNutt. '*Ma'am?* Did you say *ma'am?* Wow. It looks like someone's been taking his medication.'

McNutt put the bowl up to his face and shoveled in some rice. 'What?' he said with a mouthful of food. 'I have great manners.'

Sarah walked over to him and placed her hand on his forehead. 'No, really. Are you okay? Maybe you have a fever.'

He smiled and poked her in the stomach with a chopstick. 'Just because I'm not being rude like Fernando doesn't mean—'

'The name is *Hector.*' To emphasize his point, Garcia stood and pointed his fork at McNutt. 'And I wasn't being rude. I said thanks, too. Just not in Chinese.'

McNutt continued to eat. 'You called her the maid, nerd. That's rude.'

Garcia's eyes opened wide, the full gravity of his faux pas suddenly dawning on him. His face turned bright red. 'Wait! You said she was the maid!'

McNutt looked like he'd swallowed a cockroach. 'No, I didn't!'

Sarah watched the exchange in silence, trying to make sense

of things. *Wow, that race must have messed with my mind more than I thought.*

'Yes, you did!' Garcia argued as he stamped his foot like a three year old. 'I said I was hungry when I got up, and you said, "Why don't you ask the maid to get you something?"'

McNutt rolled his eyes. 'I was being sarcastic, genius.'

Sarah caught movement out of the corner of her eye and jolted again. The Chinese woman was standing behind her. 'Gah! I'm going to tie a bell on you or something.'

A dark look fell over the woman's face. 'I'd like to see you try.'

'Wait,' Sarah said. 'If you aren't the maid, who the hell are you?'

'I'm guessing she's our new historian,' said a new voice.

All eyes turned to the doorway to see Cobb walk in, carrying a green duffel bag that looked like it had survived several wars. He dropped the bag on the soft rug covering the entryway and looked past the others, toward the far end of the room. 'Isn't that right, Papi?'

All heads swung the other way to see Jean-Marc Papineau standing in the archway to the library. Garcia was sure the room had been empty a moment before. He made a mental note to search for a secret door when he had the chance.

Papineau wore a light-colored linen suit with an expensive tie. His gray hair and mustache were perfectly styled as usual. 'You are correct, Jack,' he said as he stepped toward the woman. 'Allow me to present Miss Maggie Liu of the People's Republic of China. If you are going to find the next treasure, you will most certainly require her assistance. And while she is a first-class chef among other things, I can assure you that she is *not* the maid.'

The focus of the room shifted to Maggie, who didn't flinch in the white-hot glare of the spotlight. Instead, she remained composed and confident; two traits that Jasmine lacked when she had first joined the team. 'It's nice to officially meet everyone. I am truly honored to be here. Jean-Marc told me about your last mission. I am deeply sorry for your loss. Just so you know, I am not trying to replace Miss Park, but, if you're willing, I want to become a part of this group.'

Cobb studied his team to see how they took the news. Although three months had passed since Jasmine Park's funeral – a somber affair where they had met her family and were forced to lie about her cause of death because of the secrecy of their mission – this was the first time the team had met in the house without their historian. He knew there would be some emotions early on, but he figured they would work through them together as they considered their options.

Never one for subtlety, Papineau had wasted no time with the hire.

Not only had he found an Asian woman to replace Jasmine, as if the team was made up of interchangeable parts that could simply be plugged in, but he had done so without consulting the team leader who would ultimately be in charge of the mission.

In Cobb's mind, it was a major misstep on Papineau's part.

Thankfully, the team took the announcement in stride. Maggie had already won over McNutt with her cooking skills, and Garcia was still so embarrassed about the maid comment that he would do anything to make up for it. Even Sarah, who had been slow to warm to Jasmine's charms but had eventually taken her death the hardest, seemed willing to give Maggie a chance.

All in all, the group's reaction was much better than Cobb had expected.

6

After the brief introduction, Papineau moved the conversation from the dining room to a more appropriate location. The upstairs portion of the house was fine for everyday conversations, but it didn't cultivate the sense of focus he demanded when the topic turned to team objectives. So he led them to an underground room that had been specifically designed to host such discussions.

The group took the back stairs past the entrance to the indoor swimming pool, which seemed like overkill since there were two pools and an ocean outside, before they descended an additional level to the 'war room' in the sub-basement of the compound. The thick door that guarded the space was identical to the one that protected the White House Situation Room. When properly sealed, it would keep out water, toxins, and McNutt when he had too much to drink.

The interior of the room was also modeled after the president's command center, but this one was slightly more luxurious. Climate-controlled to museum standards, the lavish room was decorated with fine art and thick tapestries. Despite these regal trappings, the space had a decidedly serene feel. Recent additions included a variety of low-light houseplants, an ionizer, and lighting that mimicked the outside sun.

A railing separated the room into two different meeting areas: a casual section with leather couches and plush easy chairs, and a formal space with a state-of-the-art computer table.

Papineau surprised everyone by heading to the casual side of the subterranean lair. This was a markedly different approach than for their previous missions when he had been nothing but business during their initial briefings. He encouraged everyone to find a seat while he stood with his back against the far wall like a professor waiting for his students to arrive.

Instinctively, Maggie chose one of the armchairs by herself.

The decision was not lost on Cobb, who sat on a couch next to Sarah.

Maggie doesn't feel like she's part of the team yet, Cobb thought. *Papi might have hired her, but she knows she still needs to prove herself.*

Cobb decided to speed the process along.

'Jean-Marc, why don't we jump right into Maggie's qualifications?' Cobb said it like a challenge, but he knew that a quick review of her résumé would do wonders for the team's confidence. After all, Papineau wouldn't have hired her if she wasn't the best of the best.

Papineau nodded, understanding the request for what it was. He had seen Cobb efficiently slice through group dynamics and tension on more than one occasion. 'Sarah, Jack, Hector, Josh – this is Miss Maggie Liu. She's worked in China as an elite tour guide for nearly two decades, which is a much greater undertaking than it may seem. More than handing out maps and reciting trivia, her position demanded an encyclopedic knowledge of anything and everything about the region. She has an extensive knowledge of Chinese and Asian history, speaks a dozen languages fluently, and has an academic knowledge of two dozen more lingua francas.'

McNutt whispered to Sarah. 'What the hell are "lingua francas?"'

'I think it's French linguine,' she whispered back.

'Sweet! I'm eating that for lunch.'

Garcia ignored their whispering while tapping away on his ever-present laptop. 'Miss Liu is also accomplished at wing chun, one of the more mysterious Chinese martial arts.' He looked up from his screen and smiled a sheepish grin. 'My apologies for earlier, Miss Liu.'

Maggie nodded at him. All was forgiven. 'While Chinese names are traditionally surname first, many of us choose Western names for ourselves because we prefer them – so please call me Maggie. In addition to competitive-level wing chun, I've also studied tai chi and kung fu since I was a small girl. That came in handy when dealing with some of my free-spirited clients. I needed to protect them when we went into dangerous areas along our way.'

She sat erect in her chair, her posture perfect.

'Why did you take them to sketchy areas?' Cobb wondered.

'My job was to lead them where they wanted to go, no questions asked. For many people, the adventure does not begin until after you've left the beaten trail.'

Cobb knew from experience that she was right.

He was one of those people.

'So who did you work for?'

'I can't mention any names, but you would be impressed with my client list.'

'Billionaires?' Garcia asked.

'Definitely.'

'Royalty?' Sarah asked.

'Undoubtedly.'

'Rock stars?' McNutt asked.

'Unfortunately.'

'In any case,' Papineau said, 'Maggie is talented both academically and physically. She has book smarts *and* street smarts, plus a wide swath of experience in unusual situations, which I'm confident will work to your advantage on this mission.'

'Which is where?' Cobb wondered.

Papineau glanced at him. 'I honestly do not know.'

'But Asia is a good guess, right?'

'Yes.'

'What are we looking for?'

'That,' the Frenchman said, 'is also a mystery.'

Cobb scowled. He was about to lay into Papineau when Maggie spoke up first.

'There's only one thing it could be,' she said.

Papineau's mouth hung open in surprise.

So did Cobb's.

'Don't worry, Jack. You didn't miss anything. *I'm* the other variable in this equation,' she assured him. 'Based on my range of expertise and my knowledge of Chinese history, I feel there is only one treasure that might fit the bill. Jean-Marc is speaking of the merchant.'

'What merchant?' Cobb asked.

Papineau smiled at Maggie. 'Please continue.'

She was happy to oblige. 'He was just a youngster when his adventure began in 1271 AD. He traveled with his father and his uncle across the whole of Asia, to Dadu, which is present-day Beijing. But rather than just sightseeing or seeking their own fortunes, the boy's family was on a mission of utmost importance. You see, on a previous journey they had met Kublai Khan, the grandson of Genghis Khan, and had been welcomed to his court. While there, he had tasked them with bringing a special item back from the Vatican.'

'What was it?' McNutt wondered.

'Oil.'

'Couldn't they get that from Kazakhstan in those days?'

'Not that kind of oil,' she said kindly. 'He wanted special oil from a lamp in the Church of the Holy Sepulcher, which was rumored to be the resting place of Jesus Christ. In addition, the Khan also wanted the brothers to return with a hundred Christian scholars from the Vatican who could bring the teachings of the Bible to China.'

Garcia continued to type on his laptop. 'According to these

figures, that didn't turn out well. Christians comprise only around three percent of the populace.'

'It's actually closer to four percent, but that is today. Would it surprise all of you to know that, at one time, nearly half of China was a Christian kingdom?'

'Really? When?' Sarah asked.

'America was busy with its Civil War when interest in Christianity peaked in my homeland.' She turned her attention back to Garcia. 'China has had a long, complicated history with Christianity – the citizens are both fascinated by it and repelled by it in equal measure.'

Cobb had already figured out who Maggie was talking about when she mentioned Kublai Khan, but he could tell that Sarah and McNutt were still in the dark. After several months of studying the members of his team, he could read their behavior. Sarah's arms were crossed in frustration, and she looked like she was about to start complaining. Meanwhile, McNutt sat quietly and refrained from his usual silliness.

'So,' Cobb asked, 'the brothers brought the scholars back to Beijing?'

'Yes and no,' she said. 'Their mission was complicated by the *sede vacante.*'

'I am not familiar with that term,' Cobb admitted.

'It was a period of vacancy between Pope Clement IV's death in 1268 and his successor, Pope Gregory X, taking over three years later. Niccolò and Maffeo – the brothers – managed to bring the oil to the Khan, but the date of their arrival is uncertain. They also tried to bring some Dominican monks with them, but the men were terrified and turned back long before the group reached China. Along with Niccolò's son, the brothers stayed in China for another seventeen years before they returned to Europe. During that time they amassed an immense fortune, yet when they returned to Italy the riches that they had with them paled in comparison.'

'In other words,' Sarah suggested, 'they hid the bulk of their treasure before they reached home.'

Maggie smiled. 'Perhaps. There are certainly those who believe that is what happened. The brothers were not stupid. They knew upon their return that the government and the church would seize most of their wealth, and that is precisely what occurred.'

'So,' McNutt said, 'what happened to Nico and Muffy?'

'Niccolò and Maffeo,' she corrected gently. 'Very little is known about what happened to the brothers. Most assume they died shortly after they returned to Italy because the legend no longer focused on them. Instead, it shifted to Niccolò's son. Now a man, the son went to war in a conflict between Venice and Genoa. He was captured by the Genoese and imprisoned for nearly four years. During that time, he told a fellow prisoner of his adventures.'

Sarah grinned. 'And the prisoner wrote a book about him.'

Maggie nodded. 'Yes. You have it.'

McNutt grimaced. 'Am I the only one who doesn't know this story? What was the title of the book?'

'The book has several names,' Maggie explained. 'Its author called it *Livre des Merveilles du Monde.*'

Papineau translated the French. '*Book of the Wonders of the World.*'

'In Italy, it was called *Il Milione* – which means "*The Million*".'

'Now we're talking,' Sarah said as visions of treasure danced in her head. 'The Million *Dollars*? The Million *Diamonds*?'

'Nope. The Million *Lies*.'

'Ugh. I'm guessing the Italians didn't believe his story.'

'Many of them did not,' Maggie admitted.

McNutt stared at her, waiting for the punchline. 'And what do we call it in English?'

Maggie smiled. '*The Travels of Marco Polo.*'

7

FBI Field Office
New York City

Special Agent Rudy Callahan stared at his calendar and groaned.

It was a torturous routine that played out every morning when he reached his desk and several times throughout the course of the day. Like a prisoner scratching lines on a wall, he was obsessed with the length of his confinement. Only instead of a cell, Callahan was trapped in a windowless office at the Jacob K. Javits Federal Building.

The previous August he had been doing what he loved most: chasing down leads on the streets of New York. Now he wondered if he would ever see that type of action again. He realized that his last assignment had ended poorly, but he also knew that he wasn't to blame. Unfortunately, his superiors viewed the episode as a colossal failure and decided to make an example out of him and his partner, Special Agent Jason Koontz.

Seven months later, they were still paying the price.

All because of a single incident in Brooklyn.

While conducting surveillance on the waterfront estate of Vladimir Kozlov – a Russian criminal who ran a local syndicate known as the Brighton Beach Bratva – Callahan had gotten caught in the middle of a firefight. On one side were Kozlov's guards. On the other, a team of highly skilled thieves who were trying to escape the mansion under a torrent of gunfire and a series of well-placed explosives. The skirmish had left several gunmen dead, even more wounded, and the neighborhood engulfed in flames. Yet, for some reason, the thieves had gone out of their way – even returning for him at one point during their escape – to make sure that Callahan was okay.

It didn't make sense then, and it didn't make sense now.

Not that he was complaining.

Though his superiors were thrilled that he had survived, they had been furious to learn that neither he nor his partner, who had been parked outside the mansion in a high-tech surveillance van that was able to detect a mouse fart from over a mile away, had recorded anything but static during the confrontation.

No thieves. No gunmen. No crimes of any kind.

Both men had sworn that the equipment had been functioning perfectly throughout the evening, and each was at a loss to explain what had happened. Their best guess was that someone had scrubbed the signals to cover the incident. Their bosses had laughed at the notion, claiming that it would have taken an elite hacker with inside knowledge of the FBI's technology to access their surveillance feeds, much less alter them.

Little did they know, that was exactly what had happened.

Hector Garcia had worked his magic and erased everything.

Regardless of the cause, the result was inexcusable. For their efforts, or, more accurately, the lack thereof, Callahan and Koontz had been pulled from the streets for the last seven months. Assigned to a drab office in Federal Plaza, they were forced to watch old recordings of news from around the world, while writing tedious reports that explained how the events might be relevant to the FBI: a government agency that had no authority outside the United States.

It was the Bureau's version of busy work.

And it was wearing Callahan down.

Even though his shift was just starting, he grabbed a black magic marker from his desk and drew a giant X through the seventeenth day of the month. Then he sat back and admired the string of identical markings that covered the previous blocks in March. 'Two more months. Just two more months until I'm free.'

'Talking to yourself again?' Koontz asked from the office doorway. 'My grandfather used to do that, too, right before we had him committed.'

Callahan defended himself. 'I'm not senile. I just want this torture to end. Only two more months, then we can get the hell out of here.'

'No,' Koontz said, 'in two more months we're *eligible* to leave here. There's no guarantee of anything. We might be stuck here for the rest of the year. Besides, there are a million other assignments that they could give us that don't involve fieldwork. Given their take on things, they might send us back to the academy to teach the cadets how *not* to do surveillance.'

Callahan couldn't bear the thought. 'They wouldn't do that . . . would they?'

'I doubt it. They hate us a lot more than that.'

Callahan groaned and rubbed the back of his neck. His day was just starting, and the stress was already taking root in his shoulders. If he wasn't careful, he would be incapacitated by a migraine before lunch.

'Two more months,' he mumbled again. 'Just two more months.'

Koontz laughed as he tossed his jacket onto the floor in the corner of the room. Unlike his partner, he didn't mind their current assignment. The Bureau's 'punishment' allowed him to watch television for several hours a day, only now he was getting paid for it. 'Speaking of our superiors, I shared an elevator with the bald, fat one this morning.'

'You mean the Assistant Director in Charge?'

'Yeah, that's the prick. Anyway, he said he was so impressed with our recent reports that he was giving us an extra special case to work on today, one with – and I quote: "international significance".'

Callahan hoped for the best. 'Really?'

Koontz nodded. 'Unfortunately, he was *laughing* when he said it, so you should probably temper your enthusiasm a little bit. On the bright side, at least he's talking to me again. That has to mean something.'

'Yeah, it means he doesn't know that you call him "a bald, fat prick" behind his back.'

'That's nothing. You should hear what I say about you when you're not around. It's a lot worse than that.'

'I can only imagine,' Callahan said with a smile. 'So, the suspense is killing me. What are we working on today? The Nazis invading Poland? Melting glaciers in the Arctic? Or is it something closer to home?'

'Nope. Today's assignment is the bombing in Alexandria.'

'Egypt? You mean the incident from four months ago?'

'Yep. That's the one.'

Callahan cursed under his breath. All things considered, he would rather watch videos on global warming than media coverage of a terrorist attack. As someone who had survived 9/11, he certainly didn't want to relive that nightmare by watching footage of a bombing that was far from the Bureau's jurisdiction. Even if they found something in the video footage, they couldn't take action. And it was an *old* bombing. Stale, as far as investigations went. Much of the damage had already been rebuilt. He'd seen a story about it in the *Times*.

'You've got to be joking! They already know what happened over there. The block was blown to hell with Semtex. What else do they expect us to tell them?'

Koontz shrugged. 'You're preaching to the choir. It's not like we can do anything about it anyway. If the CIA wants to know

44

something about the bombing, let their trolls figure it out. Just because we're the ones with *Investigation* in our name doesn't mean we should do all the research.'

Despite their situation, Callahan laughed. He had been in the Bureau for over twenty years and had never heard that line. He'd be sure to use it the next time he was stonewalled by someone at the Agency – which happened way more often than it should. 'Let's be honest: it's not like anyone actually reads our reports anyway.'

Koontz nodded. 'I know I don't.'

8

The Travels of Marco Polo.

McNutt smiled when he heard the title. 'Marco Polo had a treasure?'

Maggie nodded. 'Supposedly, yes.'

He whistled softly. 'Holy hell, that has to be huge! He invented polo *and* that game where people call out his name.'

Garcia stared at him. 'Actually, he did neither.'

'Really? What about Polo cologne?'

'Nope.'

'Are you positive? Double-check that on your computer.'

'I don't have to. Marco Polo died in 1324. Polo cologne came out in the 1970s.'

'Exactly. So they owe him, like, six hundred years of royalties!'

Sarah grinned. This was the McNutt she remembered from their previous missions, not the polite ass-kisser from upstairs. 'It's about freakin' time. Where have you been?'

McNutt glanced at her. 'When did I leave?'

'Anyway,' said Papineau, who rolled his eyes at McNutt's antics, 'the book is a good place to start, but it is merely an introduction to the subject matter. On his deathbed, Polo himself said that he had only revealed half the story.'

'Let me guess,' Cobb said. 'Our job is to figure out the other half.'

Papineau nodded. 'Don't worry, Jack. I have something to help your cause.'

Without saying another word, Papineau strolled past the railing that separated the room into two and sat at the head of the computer table. The others got the hint and followed his lead. Within seconds they had taken their normal seats around the hi-tech device.

Still worried about fitting in, Maggie stared at the lone empty chair – the one where Jasmine used to sit – but opted to remain standing off to the side out of respect.

That is, until Sarah spoke up.

'What's wrong? Not used to sitting in chairs? You can sit on the floor if you'd like.'

'Actually,' Maggie said, 'I'm Chinese, not Japanese. We're big fans of chairs. In fact, we probably built most of the furniture in this house.'

McNutt laughed. 'You're probably right!'

Sarah pointed at the chair. 'Then what are you waiting for?'

Maggie nodded and took her seat.

Papineau tapped a few keys on his virtual keyboard. 'Hector, I've just sent you the name of a file on our server. Please project it on the wall behind me.'

Garcia did what he was told, and the video screen came to life. But unlike the large maps of Eastern Europe and Ancient Egypt that the team had studied in previous briefings, the only thing that appeared on the screen was the name of a single file: UA11273_MP.

Cobb recognized the UA prefix as belonging to the Ulster Archives, a private facility in Küsendorf, Switzerland, that had aided their efforts in the past. He rightly assumed the MP was for Marco Polo, but he wasn't quite sure about the numbers.

Garcia clicked on the file, and the first page appeared on the screen. It was a scanned copy of a worn and yellowed document, with cramped writing in a foreign language that the team struggled to translate. That is, everyone except Maggie.

She gasped as soon as she saw it. 'Wait. Is that . . . ?'

Papineau smiled but did not reply.

Sarah showed her frustration. 'What are we looking at? Polo's book?'

'I don't understand,' McNutt said. 'I know we have his book in the library upstairs. I've seen it. Why don't we just look through that one? It's typed *and* in English.'

Maggie shook her head. 'That one is most likely a compilation of over fifty manuscripts, each edited by different publishers and editors over the centuries, and based on multitudes of sources, notes, and ideas.' She stared at the image on the screen. 'What we're looking at is something different. This appears to be penned by Rustichello da Pisa himself: the man who wrote the original version of the book.'

'The prison mate?' Cobb asked.

Maggie nodded as she struggled to translate the document on a notepad.

Sarah opted to fill the silence. 'I have to admit I'm kind of impressed. Who knew that Josh had been in the library – let alone looked at the books?'

'Hey, I read. Not the so-called "classics" and literary novels. That stuff is crap. I was looking for the latest Kuzneski.'

Sarah stared at him. 'Who the hell is that?'

'Some Polack. Medium talent. Anyway, given our adventures over the past year, I've taken an interest in history. And his books are easier to read than the encyclopedia.'

'It's better than nothing,' Cobb said, although he knew McNutt was reading more than just thrillers. He had tasked the sniper with researching several historical eras and had asked him to write reports on a number of lost treasures. Cobb had sensed there would be more missions, and he wanted to familiarize himself with what was out there. To that end, Garcia had been told to study various legends and stories about South America while Sarah had been assigned Europe. Cobb had figured they would eventually obtain a new historian, but he wanted each member of the group to be well rounded.

'So,' Cobb said as he focused on Papineau, 'how did we get this manuscript from the Ulster Archives? And what does it tell us about the treasure?'

'Actually, Jack, I was the one who *gave* it to the Archives for authentication and preservation, not the other way around. As for your second question, I was just getting to that.'

Papineau double-tapped the table's hi-tech surface and a copy of the document on the main screen appeared under the glass. Then, by pushing his hand toward the team members in turn, he digitally slid the documents to their individual workstations. Now each of them could flip through the document at their own pace.

'As Maggie pointed out, this document seems to have been written by Rustichello da Pisa. Though he only had it for a few days, Petr Ulster is reasonably certain it is authentic. The document is written in a mixture of Italian dialects, along with Old French and Latin. Curiously, it also contains some words and phrases in Asian languages, which is what convinced Petr of the manuscript's authenticity. That and carbon dating.'

Cobb knew that Ulster wasn't just the head of the archives; he was also its most revered scholar. Cobb trusted his opinion implicitly. 'So what does it say?'

'We can't answer that yet,' Papineau admitted. 'Maggie will need to spend some time deciphering it.'

'And once she does?'

Papineau smiled. 'Your mission is to locate and retrieve Marco Polo's treasure.'

'If it exists,' McNutt said.

'Yes.'

'And in exchange?' Cobb asked.

'Our standard arrangement. Five million dollars each.'

'You still need to pay us for the second mission,' Sarah complained. 'I don't start on this one until you pay up for the last one.'

'Me, too,' Garcia said.

McNutt looked to Cobb for his opinion on the matter, but Cobb just sat there, silently watching Papineau.

The Frenchman put on a show of considering the request, but Cobb could tell he had already anticipated the complaint and planned to acquiesce. 'Very well. Those of you who participated in the last mission will each be paid for it before you leave for Asia, or Europe, or wherever the trail leads. But you will need to begin researching now. Agreed?'

'Yep,' Sarah said.

Garcia and McNutt both nodded. Maggie remained quiet.

All eyes turned to Cobb.

He looked at Papineau for a long moment, and at first the Frenchman gazed back impassively. But then his resolve began to crack as he realized what was about to happen.

'Sorry,' Cobb said. 'No deal.'

9

McNutt twisted his finger in his ear with a dramatic flourish. 'I think I misheard you, chief. Did you just say "no" to five million dollars?'

Cobb continued to stare at Papineau. After a tense moment of silence, he finally spoke. 'That is correct, Josh. I said no.'

Papineau looked disappointed, but not really shocked. 'May I ask why?'

'Why?' he said in a mocking tone. 'I get the distinct feeling that you're holding back pertinent information from us again because it doesn't suit your agenda. That didn't work out so well for Jasmine the last time, did it? Yet here you are, asking me to lead this team into the field on another adventure, and you're still keeping secrets.'

'Jack—'

'Truth be told, it's my fault for letting it get *this* far. You coerced Hector into spying on us during the first mission, yet I let the incident slide. I should've quit then and there, and the fact that I didn't has been bugging me ever since.'

'Come on, Jack. That isn't fair, and you know it.'

'Do I? I'm not so sure.'

Although it wasn't Cobb's intent to embarrass Garcia, the computer genius hung his head in shame. Upon being hired, Garcia had been ordered by Papineau to secretly keep tabs on the team – a task that he had performed without question until Cobb had discovered his efforts and put a stop to them. During the team's initial bonding, Garcia had felt like an outsider, the geek trying to fit in at the cool kids' table. But the group's dynamic had changed significantly since then. Garcia was now fully accepted by the team, which was why he felt so guilty about his transgression on the first adventure.

Cobb went on. 'You've also interfered with my command of the team during both missions. This isn't a game. It's life or death in the field. I told you from day one that I needed absolute authority once we left this building, and you agreed to stay out of my way. Unfortunately, you've been unwilling to uphold your end of the bargain, so it's time for me to walk.'

'Don't be hasty, Jack. I know we've had some rough patches during the past year, but it's nothing we can't overcome.'

'Says who? The wealthy guy in the linen suit who sips champagne on his yacht? Spend some time in the trenches with a gun in your hand, and then you'll understand: minor issues for you are a major problem for us.'

McNutt, Garcia, and Sarah nodded in support.

Despite Cobb's posturing, Papineau sensed that the team leader would eventually come around. The Frenchman knew there would be a condition or two – or possibly several – tied to his return, but he also realized that if Cobb had intended to quit, he could have done so by phone. 'Come on, Jack. There must be something I can do to convince you to stay.'

Cobb's eyes never left Papineau. He didn't blink, or flinch, or look away. He just continued to stare for several seconds.

The others, realizing this was a pivotal moment for the team, sat transfixed.

Eventually, Papineau broke the silence.

'Enough of this foolishness. Tell me what you want.'

'You don't say another word as leader once we leave this facility. I will be in charge from the moment we pass the front gate until the moment we find the treasure. You will finance everything we ask for, and you'll be happy to do it. In addition, you'll pay everyone for the Egypt mission *now* – not before we leave. And you'll also pay us the first half of the five million for the Polo job whether we succeed or fail. The money can be placed in trust, per our original agreement, but it gets transferred before we risk our lives in the field.'

'Oh, is that all?' Papineau asked, his face growing red in anger.

'Actually, no. There's one more condition; and it's non-negotiable. If any of us die during the mission, our heirs receive a bonus of ten million dollars.'

'You've changed, Jack. And not for the better.'

Cobb stood slowly. His demeanor was calm. He knew he had the upper hand. 'Josh is one of the finest snipers in the world, and you know it.'

All eyes turned to McNutt.

'What did I do?' he asked, confused.

Cobb pointed to the others, one by one. 'Sarah is the best infiltration and extraction expert out there, and Hector is one of the finest hackers on the planet. And though I just met her, I'll bet Maggie is incredibly gifted, too, or you wouldn't have hired her.'

Cobb turned back to look at Papineau.

'You've spared no expense in obtaining the best specialists for this squad. And let's be honest: we work pretty well as a team. So let's not pretend, Jean-Marc. If you got the best of the best for each of their roles, then what does that make me?'

Papineau grimaced. He knew he had been beaten.

'I'll give you a hint. The word you're looking for isn't "replaceable."'

Cobb paused briefly before he continued. 'I know time is precious and this is a lot to consider, so I'm going to do you a favor. While you stew over my demands and slowly come to the realization that you'll meet them – all of them – I'm going to start prepping my team. Unless I hear otherwise before midnight tonight, I'm going to assume that we're good to go.'

Papineau grunted but said nothing.

'Excellent,' Cobb said as he shifted his focus to Garcia. 'Hector, we're going to need something from you before any of us can get started.'

Garcia sat up straight in his chair. 'Name it.'

'Get your hands on a map of Polo's travels. Then compile a list for every team member of every place he supposedly visited. I'm talking about all the locations in the commonly accepted versions of the original book, not the new manuscript.'

Garcia nodded and started tapping at the glass of the tabletop.

'Josh,' Cobb said, 'I'm hoping we'll only need to visit a few places on that list, but until we know which ones, I want you to figure out the logistics for every single site.'

'Damn, chief. That's a lot of equipment,' McNutt said.

'Someone died on our last mission. No one dies on this one.'

'Got it, chief. Lasers and wing suits for everyone.'

Cobb ignored the comment and faced Maggie. 'How are your translation skills?'

'Depends on the language,' she admitted. 'The Rustichello manuscript is written primarily in Latin, Old French, and Venetian – a Romance language spoken in the Veneto region of Italy. It's similar to Italian, but different. I also noticed a few phrases in Ottoman Turkish, Mongolian, and Arabic. I can handle most of those, but I might need some help from time to time.'

Cobb paused in thought before he glanced at Garcia. 'Hector, do we still have access to the language software from the Ulster Archives?'

'Definitely.'

'Good,' Cobb said as he altered his plan of attack. 'In that case, let's go about this a different way. Since the document has already been scanned by the Archives, let's use the computer to translate it. Once it's done, we'll have Maggie go back through and make any corrections. The software is a huge timesaver, but it isn't perfect, especially when it comes to names and idioms. You'll need to print up a version that has the original text under the translation, line for line, so Maggie can do a thorough analysis.'

Garcia kept typing. 'No problemo.'

'Speak English!' McNutt shouted from across the room.

'That was English!'

Maggie smiled at the team's chemistry. 'What can I do in the meantime?'

Cobb had anticipated her question. 'According to your résumé, you're highly skilled in hand-to-hand combat. Is that correct?'

'Yes, sir. I'm quite proficient in several disciplines.'

'Actually,' Cobb said, 'I'll be the judge of that. We'll spar tomorrow. If I find your fighting skills lacking, you're off the team. I need people I can trust.'

Maggie nodded. 'Fair enough.'

Cobb continued. 'How are you with weapons?'

'What kind?'

'Firearms.'

'I've done some skeet shooting with clients, and I've held – but not fired – an assault rifle during mandatory military training in China.'

'Josh will teach you the basics when you aren't sparring or trans-lating. With your martial arts training, you should already know breath control. I expect safety and mechanical proficiency in two days. Target precision within a week.'

McNutt shouted out, 'That's gonna be a lot of rounds, chief.'

'Got anything better to do?'

'Well, I was going to wax my bikini line, but that can wait.'

Cobb tuned him out and addressed Sarah. 'Once Hector is done with his list, I need you to figure out what we'd need to extract a treasure the size of the one in Egypt. I know Papi has handled that in the past, but I would prefer if we were in charge of this extraction.'

Sarah nodded. 'Consider it done.'

'I also want you to completely re-envision our personal gear. We need to be prepared for anything, but we also need to be able to cross borders without arousing suspicion. Feel free to think outside the box. Use Hector to brainstorm new comms and personal computing. I don't want a situation like in Alexandria where we lost contact. Our bodies might glow green from radiation, but I want to be able to talk to everyone through tons of rock and metal.'

'I already have some ideas,' she said.

Cobb returned his focus to Maggie. 'Once you've translated the manuscript, I want your opinion on possible locations for the treasure.'

Maggie was about to offer a theory, but before she could say a word Cobb's eyes darted toward his left shoulder and to Papineau, who sat beyond it. Cobb followed the glance with an almost imperceptible shake of his head, warning her that this wasn't the time or place to discuss her thoughts on the matter.

To her credit, she picked up on the signal instantly.

'As soon as you know something, we'll make our move,' Cobb said, loud enough for the others to hear. 'In the meantime, while Hector gets the computer translation ready, why don't you come with me and Sarah for a quick tour of the house and grounds?'

10

Sarah acted as a tour guide, pointing out features of the compound to Maggie, while Cobb silently accompanied them. They eventually wandered out toward the pier, past the palm trees and the interlocking swimming pools, while Sarah told Maggie some details about the *Trésor de la Mer*, the four-level-high, sixty-five-foot yacht that Papineau usually arrived on.

'Let's take a stroll on the beach,' Cobb said. 'We need to give Hector time to work, and I'd like to hear more about Maggie's life.'

Sarah looked at him and knew exactly what he was suggesting.

They angled away from the house and headed toward a small private beach along the edge of the property. As they passed behind a small concrete structure that served both as a storage shed for the pool equipment and a shower to wash off saltwater and sand from the sea, Cobb signaled for them to stop.

Maggie did so without complaint or concern.

She sensed the tour had been for show.

Sarah pulled out a small black device from her pocket. She activated the sensor with a flick of its switch, then moved it around the three of them in a slow arc, as if she were holding up a cell phone and trying to find a single bar of service. When the LED light didn't illuminate, she knew that they were clean.

'We're good,' she said to Cobb.

'What is that?' Maggie asked.

'It picks up any directed transmissions on a number of frequencies. If there were a bug or a camera anywhere near here, this would detect it.'

'What about a directional microphone pointed at us from the yacht?' Cobb asked.

Sarah grinned. 'I followed your lead and did a rekky on the boat before I stormed into the house like a mad woman looking for Papi. We're clear.'

'Good job,' he said with a smile.

'I have my moments.'

Cobb nodded and shifted his focus to Maggie. 'I'm sure you realized that there are a lot of things going on in this group. This spot, for now, is the only place on the compound where you can speak without being filmed or recorded. The next time Sarah and I come out here, if we find it bugged, we'll know we can't trust you and you'll be gone.'

'I understand,' Maggie said. 'I have to earn your trust.'

'Actually, you already have my trust. The key is not to lose it.'

Maggie smiled. 'I'll do my best.'

'Good. In the meantime, tell us what you found.'

'You found something already?' Sarah asked.

'Maybe,' Maggie said, not wanting to seem too confident. 'The last page of the journal had a sentence which loosely translates to: "Soon I will begin my search for the lake that cannot be found." Obviously I didn't have a chance to read the entire manuscript, but I got the sense that Rustichello had gathered some clues from Polo and hoped to travel to Asia to find Polo's treasure for himself. Based on that line alone, I think the lake is a possible location.'

Sarah studied her closely, looking for anything that seemed off. Thanks to years of fieldwork with the CIA, Sarah was a pretty quick judge of character. She assumed that was the main reason that Cobb had asked her to tag along during the tour of the grounds: to get a read on Maggie.

Although Cobb had told Maggie that he trusted her, Sarah knew better. There was no way that Cobb would take her into the field until she was cleared by the team. Garcia had already started digging into Maggie's background, and McNutt would determine if she could handle herself at the gun range. Meanwhile, Sarah and Cobb would study her every act and comment, probing for anything that might put them at risk. They knew they needed a historian in the field, but they wouldn't tolerate a liability. If their evaluation produced any red flags, Maggie would be sent back to Asia before Papineau could prevent it.

'And you know where that is?' Sarah asked.

Maggie nodded. 'Lop Nor is a dried-up salt lake in Luozhong in northwest China. It is a former nuclear test site known for the mining operation presently located there.'

'What do they mine?' Cobb asked.

'Potash – for salt and fertilizers,' Maggie explained. 'But the lake was famous in antiquity for something else entirely.'

'And what was that?' Sarah wondered.

'The lake moved.'

'Wait. It did *what*?'

'The Tarim River, the body of water that feeds the lake, changes its course periodically. When that happens, the lake itself changes locations while the previous lake dries up. This phenomenon confounded explorers and mapmakers for years until a Swede, Sven Hedin, sorted out the puzzle at the beginning of the twentieth century. Perhaps Marco Polo knew about the wandering lake in the thirteenth century. For all we know, it might have been common knowledge back then and was somehow forgotten along the way.'

'Like the location of a lost tomb.'

Maggie nodded. 'Exactly.'

'And what do you think we'll find at the lake?' Cobb asked.

'I honestly don't know,' she admitted. 'But if it's okay with you, I was hoping you could ask Hector to use his computer skills to search for satellite coverage of Luozhong. Or is that beyond his capabilities?'

Cobb laughed at the thought. 'No, that's definitely in his wheelhouse.'

'That, and a whole lot more,' Sarah mumbled.

'But instead of me asking him,' Cobb said, 'I think you should ask him yourself. Not only will he be flattered that you need his help, but it will also give him a chance to make amends.'

'Amends for what?' Maggie wondered.

Cobb smiled. 'For calling you the maid.'

I I

Two hours and three cups of coffee later, Special Agent Callahan stood from his chair and stretched his aching back. As expected, the footage of the bombing in Egypt had been hard to watch, and nothing of value had been gained. He was nearly ready to give up on the process when something unexpected popped up on the screen. It was so surprising that he thought he was seeing things.

'Hold on! Run that back for me!'

Koontz, who was half asleep in front of the computer, blinked a few times before he emerged from his trance. 'Why? Is she hot?'

Callahan pushed his partner aside and scrolled back through the last few minutes of footage before he let it play again. Shot by a witness with a cell phone, the video was remarkably clear. The camera panned across the scene of destruction before settling on a man who was bravely helping those trapped underneath the wreckage. As the bystander zoomed in, the hero's blood-caked face filled the screen.

Callahan quickly pressed PAUSE. 'I'll be damned. Will you look at that?'

Koontz stared at the man, confused. 'Um . . . that's a *dude*.'

Callahan nodded, completely oblivious to his partner's innuendo. 'You're not going to believe this, but I've seen that guy before.'

'Where? *Playgirl?*'

'No, asshole, that's the guy who saved my life in Brooklyn.'

Koontz glanced at his partner, then back at the screen, then back at his partner. 'And on that note, I think it's time for a break. Just how much coffee have you had today?'

'Jason, I'm serious!'

'I'm serious, too. This is footage from a crime scene in Africa, *not* Brooklyn. Granted, both are filled with black people, but—'

'Listen,' he blurted, interrupting the racist remark, 'I know what I'm saying sounds crazy – I *know* it does – but I'm telling you: that's the guy who saved my life.'

'And?'

'And I need to know why.'

Koontz, who had been trapped inside the surveillance van during the firefight, hadn't seen the man in question, but based on the tactics involved and the number of guards who had been eliminated, they had always suspected that the man had received extensive military training. If so, he was bound to be in their system.

'Fine!' he grumbled, as he copied the man's face from the paused footage and fed it into the FBI's facial-recognition database. 'This doesn't mean that I believe you. It only means that I want you to shut the fuck up.'

'Trust me, I know the feeling.'

Koontz took the insult in stride. 'I hope you realize that you can't put any of this in your report, or we'll be teased more than we are right now.'

Callahan nodded. 'I know.'

As the program processed the face from the video, Callahan paced around the room like an expectant father. He knew the system could take hours to find a match, but there was no way he would be able to focus on anything else until the search was done.

Surprisingly, he received his answer less than ten minutes later.

'I'll be damned,' Koontz muttered as he stared at the file that had popped up on his screen. 'It looks like you were right.'

The black-and-white photo had been taken long ago, but it was definitely the same man from the video. His face had been slightly more rounded and vibrant in his youth, before the rigors of life had taken their toll, but his piercing gray eyes hadn't changed. His stare was unmistakable.

Callahan read the accompanying information. 'Jackson Cobb, Junior. US Army, Special Forces. Military record: classified.'

Koontz glanced at his partner, concerned. 'Classified? Why would it be classified? You don't think that . . . ?'

'I don't think *what*?'

'Do you think he's the one who blew up Alexandria? Maybe this was some sort of Black Op that went wrong.' The blood drained from his face as he considered the ramifications. 'Son of a bitch! What the hell did you get us into?'

'Me?' Callahan teased. 'You're the one who ran his face through the system.'

'Because you wouldn't shut up about him!' Koontz shook his head in frustration. 'Look, we're in enough trouble as it is. I don't need the Pentagon getting involved with my personal life. I have more skeletons in my closet than Jeffrey Dahmer.'

'Relax,' Callahan said. 'The guy was digging people out of the rubble. If his mission was to blow up the city, he wouldn't have stuck around to help survivors. I think it's safe to assume that he wasn't responsible for the blast.'

'Really?' Koontz argued. 'Because if I remember correctly, his team blew up half of Brighton Beach, then he stuck around to help you.'

'True, but that was different. The only people who got hurt in Brooklyn were Kozlov's men. Not me, not you, and certainly no civilians. Meanwhile, the bomb in Alexandria killed hundreds of innocents.' Callahan shook his head at the thought. 'Trust me, the two assaults were *nothing* alike.'

'On the surface, no. But let's be honest: Egypt hasn't been the best place for tourists for a while. If he wasn't there to see the sights, why the hell *was* he there?'

'Beats me,' Callahan answered.

Over the past several months, his passion had been waning as his talents were wasted in this windowless purgatory, but thanks to Cobb's mysterious reappearance the gleam had suddenly returned to Callahan's eye. After all this time, he finally had a reason to be excited about work again.

'But I intend to find out.'

12

After spending the last few days immersed in their tasks, the group reconvened in the war room for a short briefing. It had only been three days, but everyone looked noticeably tired.

Papineau had been locked away in his office for most of the time. He claimed he still had a business to run and needed to check on several deals so he could finance the mission. Cobb suspected the man had other ambitions, but he allowed the Frenchman his privacy.

Sarah had been looking into escape routes and shipping options throughout most of the Pacific Rim. If they located the treasure inland, she would have it moved on trucks, which were more versatile than trains and less regulated than planes. All they would need to do was transport the trove to the coast, and from there she could get it out of Asia on a freighter.

McNutt had been on the phone almost constantly, joking and laughing with his overseas connections one minute and then speaking so softly he couldn't be overheard the next. He was paving the way for possible weapons deals in several countries, and that required a certain amount of finesse. Even though he was frustrated that he couldn't complete any of the deals without a destination, he told the team that laying the groundwork would be fruitful.

Once the team was seated around the computer table, Cobb

addressed the group. 'I know these last few days have been a grind for all of us – particularly for Maggie and Hector, who have lived in this room since Monday. Thankfully, our hard work is about to pay off.'

Cobb nodded at Maggie, who was still sore from their sparring session. He had worked her over pretty well, but she had managed to pass his test. She stood up slowly and made her way to the front of the table. Then she gestured to the massive screen that filled the wall behind her.

'With Hector's assistance, I was able to translate and analyze Rustichello's journal,' she said as a drawing of Rustichello appeared on the screen. 'He was obsessed with ferreting out details of Polo's treasure and, even though he was an older man at the time of their imprisonment, he planned to mount an expedition of his own to recover the Polo fortune. According to his notes, he subtly prodded Polo for details about the riches the merchant had accumulated on his journey. But Polo was cagey. Sometimes he would feign exhaustion to avoid answering certain questions. Other times he would talk in riddles that could be interpreted in multiple ways. Still, Rustichello gleaned some things from their four years together.'

'Enough to find the treasure himself?' Sarah wondered.

'Yes and no,' Maggie answered. 'Rustichello narrowed down the possible locations of the treasure, but after being released from prison he fell down a flight of stairs and broke his leg. He never got around to mounting his expedition.'

'So the treasure might still be untouched,' Garcia added.

Maggie nodded. 'Unfortunately, the location that Rustichello suspected is rather vague. It's a lake called Lop Nor in northwest China.'

Garcia tapped a key on his keyboard. The drawing of Rustichello shrank in size and was bumped to the corner of the screen by a large map of China.

Maggie continued her lecture. 'Although "Lop Nor" is not mentioned by name in the manuscript, Polo referred to it as the "lake that cannot be found". Thankfully, this was a phenomenon that I was familiar with. The river that feeds Lop Nor has been known to change positions, so the lake has literally moved over time. Polo repeatedly described Loulan – an ancient city near the lake that was abandoned several hundred years before his arrival – to Rustichello in amazing detail. For some reason it had a special place in Polo's heart, but he refused to mention why. At first Rustichello was annoyed by Polo's repeated tales about this abandoned city in the desert, but after a while he began to suspect there was a reason for them.'

'Rustichello thought the treasure was buried there,' Sarah said.

Maggie nodded. 'It was at the top of his list.'

'Then what are we waiting for?' McNutt asked.

'Two reasons,' Garcia answered. 'Number one, it's located in a remote part of China with virtually no passable roads. The terrain is barely navigable, plus the area is subjected to frequent wind and sandstorms. It's so grim it's known as a "dead zone".'

'Sounds like Cleveland.'

'The area used to be a nuclear test site ages ago, but the military has long since abandoned it. The only thing out there now is a mining operation, and that's twenty miles away. Any satellite intel that I have is several years old. Nothing military has bothered to pass over this region in a decade.'

McNutt grimaced. 'All of that was *one* reason? What the hell is number two?'

'The second reason is even worse,' Maggie admitted. 'The Chinese sent an archaeological team to Loulan in 1979, and they thoroughly excavated the site.'

'Well that sucks,' Sarah grumbled.

Papineau tried to lift her spirits. 'It's not the kiss of death, though.

The city of Alexandria had been picked clean for centuries, but we still found what we were looking for.'

Sarah nodded. 'Good point.'

Cobb glanced at Maggie. 'Any other potential leads from the manuscript?'

'Unfortunately, no. Rustichello never got specific details on the size of the treasure, why Polo didn't return with it, or exactly where Polo left it. All we have are his suspicions, probabilities, and guesses. But he liked Loulan as the site.'

Cobb had been led to believe that this meeting was necessary because they had encountered some good news. Now he wasn't so sure. 'That doesn't leave us much to go on.'

'Not from the manuscript,' Maggie admitted. 'But there is more – thanks to Hector.'

Garcia puffed up slightly at the praise, then ran his fingers across his keyboard as the giant screen came to life. It showed an overhead view of Genoa on the northern coast of Italy. The satellite view resembled a plot of concrete acting as a barrier between the blue of the sea and the green of the foothills to the north that marched up to the Alps.

'As you know,' Garcia said, 'Polo and Rustichello were held captive in Genoa for four years, but little is mentioned of their imprisonment in *The Travels*. Most publishers rightfully assumed that people would be far more interested in Polo's journey to Asia than his time in prison. And yet a few editors disagreed. One bit of trivia that appeared in a few translations of the book was the names of their captors.'

'And that helps us how?' Papineau wondered.

'Go on, Hector. Tell them what you found,' Maggie said.

Garcia beamed with pride. 'I learned that two of the guards were illiterate, but the third was decidedly not. While Rustichello was recording the details of Polo's adventures, the third guard, Giovanni Ravio, spent much of this time compiling an elaborate diary of his thoughts. His son, Luca Ravio, became a poet of some note at the time. And Luca's collection, including his father's journal from the days he worked at the prison, made its way to a private collector, and eventually to a museum in Florence.'

Garcia touched a key, and the display scrolled southeast, a third of the length of Italy from Genoa to Florence, then it blurred briefly before zooming in on the red-tiled roof of a U-shaped museum building between a river and a cobbled plaza.

Sarah recognized it at once. 'That's the Uffizi Gallery. It's one of the most celebrated galleries in the world. If Luca's collection is displayed there, he really was famous.'

'Maybe so,' Garcia said. 'But as far as we can tell, no one has ever connected the poet's father with Marco Polo.'

Cobb smiled. 'You think Giovanni wrote down information we could use?'

'The guards were torturing Polo,' Maggie stressed. 'According to Rustichello, Polo's muffled screams could be heard throughout the building. It stands to reason if Polo ever slipped up and declared the location of the treasure, it would have been under duress.'

Cobb nodded in agreement.

He was familiar with the effects of torture.

'Okay,' Cobb said, 'we'll need time to prepare for either possibility. Sarah, you're in charge of the Italian job. Figure out what you need to retrieve the journal.'

'I saw that movie,' McNutt joked. 'All she needs is Mini Coopers.'

Sarah laughed at the reference.

'Meanwhile,' Cobb said, 'Josh and I will take a rekky to Loulan. We need some boots on the ground to determine the feasibility of the site. While we're gone, everyone should continue to prep for both countries: Italy and China. Regardless of what we find in Loulan – *unless* we find the treasure itself – we'll go to Florence first, so Sarah can steal the guard's memoirs.'

'*Steal?* I don't *steal,*' Sarah argued. 'I'm not a thief!'

'But you can get the book, right?' McNutt asked.

Sarah nodded, but concern filled her face. 'Truth be told, I'm one of the few people in the world who can. But this is going to be tough.'

'Tough?' McNutt blurted. 'You're going to a *museum* in Florence. I'm going to a former nuclear test site in China called "the dead zone". Would you like to trade?'

Sarah smiled and patted him on the back. 'When you put it like that . . .'

McNutt growled softly. 'Yeah. Didn't think so.'

13

Cobb was on the verge of falling asleep in the passenger seat of the Toyota Land Cruiser when he spotted a camel in the distance. Since it was the first living thing he had seen in the desert in two days, he asked McNutt to steer closer so they could get a better view.

So far, this had been the highlight of their trip.

The camel was wandering aimlessly through the sand on the south side of a long strip of endless gray tarmac that seemingly touched the horizon. The animal looked sickly and thin, its two humps sallow and dull as it lumbered over the arid turf.

McNutt didn't want to spook it, so he slowed as he approached the beast. 'Do you know how to tell the difference between a Bactrian camel and a dromedary?'

Cobb was prepared for most things, but not that question. 'Nope.'

McNutt pointed at the animal's back. 'Bactrian camels have two humps and dromedaries have one. To help you remember, imagine the capital letters for B and D and turn them on their sides. This camel looks like a B, which means it's a Bactrian.'

'How the hell do you know that?'

'A BBC documentary. Can't get enough of them. Plus it helps to know what animals might trample on you when you're in a hide,

71

sweating your ass off for days in the desert, waiting to put a bullet through a terrorist's face.'

'Been there,' Cobb admitted.

'Done that,' McNutt added as he waved goodbye to the camel. Then they lapsed into silence for another hour.

Cobb was increasingly impressed with McNutt, who, without the audience of the rest of the team, had kept his typical zaniness to a minimum. They had left Florida separately before meeting up in Bishkek, Kyrgyzstan, where McNutt had arranged for them to travel to the border. Cobb had been surprised to find a small group of Marines waiting for them with forged passports bearing phony visa stamps; as far as he knew, no US forces were stationed in Kyrgyzstan at all. From there, the men had smuggled him and McNutt down to the bustling city of Kashgar in western China.

After their Marine escorts departed, McNutt had secured the Land Cruiser, an Uyghur guide, and a few weapons. They had set out on an actual highway, which loosely followed the Silk Road of old, but quickly discovered how little time they would spend on blacktop. They had frequently encountered areas of the road in such disrepair that they had been forced to travel for miles on the shoulder. Many of the construction projects they had passed – if that's what they could be called – were often little more than mountains of gravel dumped into the middle of the road for later renovations. More than once they had seen billboards proclaiming that the work would be done on schedule . . . in December of 2004.

In this part of China, travel wasn't measured in miles.

It was measured in days.

Maggie, who remained in Florida to research other aspects of Polo's life, had warned them of this concept, but it didn't really sink in until they got here. She had also explained the bleak terrain they would encounter. While the remnants of the Loulan kingdom had still been of note during Polo's time, the city itself had been abandoned after a natural disaster more than a thousand years ago. In the millennium since, the area had been all but forgotten.

One look was all it took.

It was obvious why no one returned.

Identifying Loulan as ruins was an insult to good ruins everywhere. Sandy brown soil stretched for miles in every direction. Without the aid of their guide and their GPS, they wouldn't have known they had reached their destination.

As recently as the 1980s, archeologists had found man-made evidence of a former settlement including canals, burial domes, and hundreds of ancient objects. Now there were virtually no signs of life except for an occasional polished rock or hand-cut fragment of petrified wood.

They were driving on top of the former salt lake, which wandered no more thanks to multiple dams on the Tarim River. The lake had dried up completely, leaving only patches of sand that looked smoother and lighter than the pebbly ground.

'Might as well stop here,' Cobb said.

'Why?' McNutt asked as he slowed the vehicle to a halt. 'This rekky is going to be as useful as a helicopter with an ejection seat.'

Cobb understood McNutt's frustration. It had been a difficult journey, one that seemed likely to produce no leads. 'Well, we're here now, so let's look around for a bit.'

McNutt climbed out of the vehicle and spat on the arid ground. It was the only moisture in sight. 'If it's okay with you, I'll let you handle the archeological shit. I'm more concerned with checking out the potash setup. I don't want to get caught with our pants down.'

Cobb eyed the distant facility, glimmering in the desert heat several miles away. He knew McNutt wasn't being lazy. Rather, he was being security-conscious. If anyone would detect their presence here, it would be the guards at the mine. 'Suit yourself.'

'What are you going to do?'

'Now that I've seen the terrain, I'm going to call Maggie and find out exactly what we're supposed to be searching for.'

'Before you do that, maybe you should look at the truck.'

Cobb raised an eyebrow. 'Why? What's wrong?'

McNutt pointed at one of the tires. 'It's been feeling sluggish in the turns. I thought it was just the terrain, but it looks like we have a slow leak.'

'No worries,' Cobb said as he glanced at the tire. It was extremely low on air. 'I'll have Ali work on it. It will give him something to do while we look around.'

Mashuq Ali, their guide, had spent the bulk of the journey sleeping in the back seat. He would occasionally wake to eat and he insisted on stopping five times a day so he could get out of the truck and pray toward Mecca, but other than that he barely said a word.

McNutt lowered his voice to a whisper. 'About time he did something other than eat, pray, and sleep. Who does he think he is: Julia Roberts?'

McNutt walked away laughing as Cobb stayed behind to explain what needed to be done. Ali assured him that he would handle it as soon as he finished praying. Cobb was tempted to stay behind and fix the tire himself but ultimately decided he had better things to do. Their goal was to get in and out as quickly as possible, and that meant starting their search immediately.

Cobb pulled out his satellite phone and called Maggie, who was in the war room with Garcia. They were expecting his call sometime that day. 'Well, we made it here safely, but there isn't much to see. Not even a deserted site.'

'Really?' Garcia said. 'Are you sure you're in the right place?'

'Did you give me the correct coordinates?'

'Definitely.'

'Then we're in the right place.'

Maggie chimed in. 'Unfortunately, we knew this was a possibility. The weather there is notoriously bad. I've heard stories where the temperature has fallen over sixty degrees in less than an hour. When the temperature drops, the wind sweeps in and covers everything with sand.'

'And that's what I'm looking at: *sand.*'

'Not us,' Garcia said, 'we're looking at static. Are you wearing your glasses? Because right now we aren't getting your feed.'

On previous missions, the team had used high-tech flashlights that recorded and transmitted video, but for this journey Garcia had given Cobb aviator-style sunglasses that would accomplish the same task. Meanwhile, McNutt had chosen yellow-tinted shooting lenses. The glasses sent video signals via Bluetooth to a laptop in the vehicle, and it forwarded that information back to Florida.

'Hang on,' Cobb said as he turned on his glasses. 'We just arrived on site. I didn't want to set up the broadcast link until I touched base with you. Give me a minute.'

Cobb pulled a small satellite dish out of the vehicle and set it up on a tripod. Then he ran a line to his laptop that allowed video files to be transmitted at an incredible rate of speed. Within seconds, Maggie and Garcia were seeing a live broadcast from Loulan.

'Much better,' Garcia said as he tweaked some settings on his end. 'We can see everything that you're seeing – which isn't much. You weren't kidding about the sand.'

Cobb slowly turned in a circle to give them a view of everything. Other than the Land Cruiser and McNutt walking in the distance, they saw nothing but desolation.

'Jack,' Maggie asked, 'do you see anything resembling the site?'

'You're joking, right?'

'I don't mean an actual town. I mean remnants of the Chinese excavation. Perhaps a section of wall that is barely visible in the sand or a landmark of any kind?'

'I'm afraid not,' Cobb said as he walked away from the SUV. 'As I mentioned, we just got here. The place is so barren I didn't know where to start.'

'Unfortunately,' Maggie said, 'neither did Rustichello. He felt confident that the treasure had something to do with Loulan, but if you can't even find the deserted city, I honestly don't know what to tell you. We were hoping that you might stumble upon a clue of some kind – a carving on a wall or perhaps a geographic feature that matches a note in the manuscript – but the truth is there's very little we can do with sand.'

Cobb grimaced. 'Yeah. Didn't think so.'

'Jack,' Garcia said, 'why don't you walk around the site with your glasses turned on? Just record as much as possible, and we can analyze it later.'

'Why? Do you have something better to do?'

'Actually,' Garcia said, unsure if Cobb was mad at him for being dismissive or if he was simply interested in the latest findings, 'Sarah needed our help with the Italian job. I'm trying to find the latest schematics for the gallery's security system, and Maggie is helping with some translations. Of course, we can do that later if you prefer.'

'Nah,' Cobb said. 'That sounds more promising than what we're doing here. I'll record anything I find that isn't sand, and if I spot something interesting I'll use the GPR to take some underground images. Other than that, there's not much we can do.'

Garcia breathed a sigh of relief, glad that Cobb wasn't angry at him. 'Sounds like a plan. Call back if you need anything.'

After hanging up, Cobb spent the next hour probing the sand with ground-penetrating radar, or GPR. The briefcase-sized device couldn't detect objects covered by solid rock – for that he would have needed a much larger, much more powerful version of the technology – but it was perfect for studying the sandy soil. If there was anything important buried beneath his feet, Cobb would see its outline on the video screen.

He walked the nearby desert in a grid, similar to the pattern they had used in Egypt. He marked the periphery with tiny wooden posts and used string to organize the rows of his search. Using his glasses, he filmed the rocks and rubble on the ground, occasionally making out a faint line in the sand that might have been a former wall. He marked those with tiny ribbons that he tied to the nearest string.

All in all, it was the most boring hour of his life.

When he was done, he turned to find McNutt. He quickly realized that McNutt had climbed the rear-mounted metal ladder to the luggage rack on the roof of the SUV. Lying on his stomach, the sniper was now checking out the distant mine with a telescope since the facility was beyond the range of his riflescope. The Marine obviously didn't care that the vehicle was still up on a jack. He knew it was strong enough to handle his weight, too.

Cobb ignored him and focused on Ali instead. The guide had abandoned the tire-changing operation and was now sipping on a water bottle while sitting in the shade of the SUV. They hadn't really needed the man much – occasionally for interpreting and twice to bribe officials – but this was the first time he had disobeyed a direct order.

Daily prayers were one thing.

Laziness was something different.

Cobb headed over to give the man a piece of his mind.

But before he had a chance to say anything, his thoughts were interrupted by McNutt, who had sprung off his stomach and onto his knees as if he had been stung by a scorpion.

'Chief,' McNutt shouted from the roof of the vehicle. 'You're not going to believe this, but there's a convoy of Vikings coming this way.'

'What?' Cobb blurted.

Even Ali seemed surprised. 'Vikings? What are Vikings?'

'Three BvS 10s – tracked troop transports. Bastards can go over anything and don't have to stop a tread to turn. Looks like a fifty-cal mounted on the lead Viking, but hard to tell at this distance.' McNutt started to climb down the rear ladder. 'We've been spotted.'

Cobb swore under his breath as he tossed his gear onto the back seat. Then he ran to help Ali, who had suddenly found the motivation to put the spare tire on the Land Cruiser.

None of this made any sense to them.

They were parked in the middle of the desert.

With nothing but sand and rock for miles.

Why in the world were they being attacked?

14

Cobb and Ali worked frantically to tighten the new wheel on the Land Cruiser while McNutt readied his weapon. The Barrett M82 semi-automatic rifle had been fitted with a Leopold Mark 4 scope – a combination that could do serious damage at close range. The gun was still effective at nearly two thousand yards, but the convoy from the mine was still fifteen miles away.

At the moment, distance wasn't McNutt's main concern.

Speed was.

The Land Cruiser had been great on the paved road, but the asphalt was far behind them. The bouncing and jostling over uneven sand and stone would make for a slow retreat. The trip back toward civilization would take them an hour; maybe more.

'What are our chances?' Cobb asked the sniper.

McNutt loaded the weapon as he considered their situation. 'If we make the road, they have no chance of catching us. But we haven't started moving yet, and they're already on the way. There's no point in me shooting until they're within a mile or two of our position, but by the time they're within range we won't be able to outrun them.'

'So what are you saying?'

'Tell Ali to hurry the fuck up.'

From that point on, Cobb took over the operation himself. Once the last lug nut was fastened on the new wheel, he lowered the vehicle off the jack. The instant the tire touched the ground, McNutt climbed the ladder again. 'I'll ride topside. Try to find higher ground when you can. If I slap the roof two times, stop immediately.'

Ali tossed the tools into the back of the Toyota and climbed inside. This time there was no mention of his need to pray. The guide sensed the danger they were in.

Cobb climbed behind the wheel and started the engine.

Then he drove the truck as fast as the terrain would allow.

They had gone no more than two miles and were just cresting a rise when the roof boomed twice from McNutt's loud slaps. Cobb stomped on the brakes and threw the gear into park before he ran to the back of the SUV and leaped to the third rung on the ladder.

McNutt was already lying prone and lining up his rifle.

Cobb turned and saw the dust plume from the vehicles in pursuit, but they were so far away that he could barely see them. 'Why did we stop?'

'We aren't going to make it,' McNutt said coolly.

Cobb cursed under his breath. 'Any good news?'

'Yeah,' he mumbled. 'I'm on your team.'

To calculate his shot, McNutt needed to consider many things: the distance to his targets, their speed, and the difference in their altitudes. He instinctively processed variables such as the dry weather, the direction and velocity of the wind, and even the gravitational pull of the earth. Based on his experience, he knew the transports were almost in range, but not quite.

Unfortunately, none of that really mattered.

McNutt didn't have the artillery to finish the job.

The Vikings were so heavily armored that even if McNutt managed to find his mark, the chance of a round from the Barrett penetrating the thick metal plates was minimal. To kill the men inside he would need something with a little more kick, like . . . a rocket launcher.

Regrettably, he kept those under his bed in Florida.

McNutt adjusted his scope one click at a time before speaking again. 'They're not military. Color schemes on the vehicles are all wrong for PLA. I'm guessing private contractors who play by their own rules. I bet it's like the Wild West out here.'

Cobb squinted his eyes, but he saw nothing but specks at the bottom of the billowing plume of dust rising into the sky. 'What else?'

'They have more than Vikings. That's why I stopped you. They have one . . . no, make that *two* Light Strike Vehicles.'

Cobb was familiar with the LSVs. They were dune-buggy-type vehicles that could be outfitted with anything from M60 machine guns to anti-tank missiles. Agile and light, they were the perfect fast-attack vehicles for the local terrain.

'They're hanging back at the end of the convoy,' McNutt said, his eye still in the scope. 'Trying to stay hidden until the last minute. We'll never outrun those things, and we won't find a better rise. I'll take the LSVs when they make their move. Then we'll haul ass away from the bigger Vikings.'

'Okay. What do you need from me?'

'Just lie down and keep me company.'

Cobb didn't move.

'Your weight, chief. It balances out the truck, gives me a level position.'

'Right,' Cobb replied as he stretched out next to the sniper.

McNutt chuckled. 'Relax, chief. You're not exactly my type.'

'Yeah, like you have a type.'

'Fair point.'

As McNutt regained his focus, Cobb started thinking about the men approaching them and wondered if there was any way that they might be aware of his mission, but he rejected that idea quickly. No one knew he and McNutt were here or what they were doing. Only members of his team knew about this rekky – and Garcia had vetted Maggie before they left.

No, these men are only upset that we're trespassing near the mine.

Still, that's a lot of hardware just to scare someone off.

Cobb turned his attention back to the silent sniper. The jokes had stopped, and McNutt had steadied himself in anticipation.

'Still with us?' Cobb asked.

'Mmm-hmm,' was his only response. A full minute later, McNutt started mumbling to himself. 'Still pretty far off. But we have height, and the wind is minimal . . . It's dry . . . Air density . . . forty-eight angular units. Make that forty-nine. Harrison was almost twenty-five hundred meters out. Two kills from there. That's badass. This'll be close.'

Just then Cobb heard a distant boom. He was about to ask McNutt about it, but the sniper mumbled an answer before he could.

'Yeah, they started shooting already. Morons. Still two miles out. That fifty-cal can't reach us for another few minutes.'

Then he lapsed into silence again.

'Chief,' McNutt suddenly whispered, 'I'm going to shoot now, and it's going to be loud. You might want to cover your ears.'

Cobb covered his ears with the palms of his hands.

A moment later, McNutt pulled the trigger.

The Barrett boomed, echoing across the sandy expanse.

Cobb grabbed McNutt's telescope and checked the lead vehicle for damage, but he couldn't see anything. He guessed the trucks were still too far out of range.

McNutt nudged the barrel of the rifle left – away from the target, and up a few inches.

Cobb watched, fascinated. He had the utmost respect for McNutt's skills. The trucks were still roughly two miles away, and the sniper was raising the barrel of his rifle like an English long-bowman, aiming high and hoping for the arc of an arrow to impale his opponent.

The weapon boomed again, startling Cobb.

Given the distance, he really hadn't thought McNutt would take that shot.

Cobb studied the lead Viking through the telescope. A second later, it ground to a halt. He didn't see any damage, and he knew the armored plating would hold up against a single .50 BMG round at this distance. He was no sniper, but he knew the round would have lost most of its velocity by the time it reached the truck – if it had reached that far at all.

Still, the caravan had stopped.

He scanned the truck and then lowered his gaze down to the vehicle's base. The tread had split, and the track had slid right off its wheels.

Holy shit, Cobb thought. *That's incredible.*

Just then the Barrett boomed again.

The second Viking had been forced to stop because of its proximity to the first in the convoy. Now its tread was shattered, too; just like that of the lead transport.

Cobb was about to compliment the Marine when something blurred past his field of vision through the telescope. He pulled his face back and saw both LSVs tearing around the sand in front of the disabled Vikings.

McNutt didn't flinch at the new development.

The Barrett cracked again, and the lead LSV's front left tire exploded. The wheel smashed into a rocky dip, launching the rear of the vehicle skyward. The car flipped, bouncing end over end, disintegrating from the force of repeated impacts with the ground. The devastating somersault kicked up a plume of dust, momentarily hiding the other LSV.

McNutt waited patiently for his target to reappear.

When it did, he put an end to the pursuit.

Cobb watched through the telescope as McNutt pulled the trigger. An instant later, blood poured from the driver's chest as if someone had opened the tap of a faucet. He slumped forward in his restraint harness, the life quickly draining out of him.

McNutt smiled from nearly two miles away.

After the first treasure mission in Romania, Cobb had looked up the longest confirmed sniper kills. He knew an Australian had an unconfirmed kill at around 2,500 meters. The shot he had just witnessed was nearly two hundred meters longer. Even more remarkable, McNutt had hit a target that was moving at high speed in a jouncing vehicle.

Cobb patted him on the back. 'I might have to call Guinness.'

McNutt laughed. 'I might have to drink one.'

15

Chen Jie spat on the arid ground and cursed the foreigners who had so effortlessly halted his attack. He cursed his luck further since he had been the one to spot the intruders in the first place. He had been on his security rounds on the roof of the mine's main building and had seen them and their four-wheel-drive vehicle in a secluded area of the desert.

He knew what was out there.

The Loulan ruins and nothing else.

His bosses were very protective of Chinese culture and history, which is why he went after the foreigners with everything at his disposal. Unfortunately, his effort had failed miserably. Now he had no choice but to report this incident to his superiors in Hong Kong.

But first he needed to assess the damage.

Two of his three tracked Vikings had been disabled by their sniper. Both of his light strike vehicles had been halted as well. One was so badly demolished in a rolling, flipping crash that he doubted it would be good for anything but scrap – and the driver had been in more pieces than the vehicle. As it was, his guards still hadn't found the man's head.

Chen glanced down at the second LSV. It was undamaged and had rolled to a distant stop after the driver, Chen's best friend, Zhang Min, had taken a round from the deadly sniper. Zhang's body was slumped forward in the restraining harness of the vehicle, as if he were taking a nap. But the dark blood that covered the lower half of his body disproved that notion.

Chen considered pulling the body upright, so he could see his friend's face one last time, but he decided against it. He would have to live with the loss regardless, but for the time being he could lie to himself and pretend that the death had been quick and painless. If he raised Zhang's head, he might see a grimace of eternal pain, and that would be too much to bear.

He stepped back and shook his head.

I'll live with the lie. And I will avenge his death.

'Goodbye, my brother. I will find them. I give you my solemn vow.'

Chen walked away from the vehicle and back to the still-functioning Viking. The treaded vehicle was packed with those men who had left the immobile transports behind. They would all need a ride back to the mine, and it would be a grim affair for those riding inside. The transport had no air conditioning. While it was chilly outdoors at this time of year, the temperature would soar with so many sweaty bodies crammed inside.

Chen would ride on the roof next to the gunner's turret instead.

He climbed the metal grill that covered the outside of the armored vehicle and stepped onto the flat roof. The gunner stared at him, waiting for further instructions.

'Get us back, and then come out for the wreckage and the dead,' Chen said.

The gunner, a young man of twenty-two, turned and relayed the command into the microphone attached to his military-grade helmet. He wasn't a soldier, though. Owned by the Righteous and Harmonious Fists, the Jiu Quan Mining Company had hired the private security guards from the local population and had trained the men themselves.

It was much cheaper than paying for mercenaries.

And they were much more loyal to the cause.

The orders transmitted, the Viking's diesel engine growled to life, making the metal roof vibrate with restrained horsepower. With a jolt the vehicle lurched forward in a wide-arcing turn back toward the mine. One of Chen's men followed them in the still-functional LSV, Zhang's body carefully relocated to the passenger seat.

The entire mission was a failure, and Chen knew Lim would ask him why.

His life would depend on his answer.

It was true that the gunner on the lead Viking had opened fire ridiculously early, and he had berated the man for that. His machine gun wouldn't have been in range for a few more minutes. But beyond that point, did his men do anything wrong?

Chen pondered the question for a few minutes but came to the same conclusion each time: there was nothing they should have done differently. They hadn't known the foreigners would be armed, and there was no way they could have guessed the enemy sniper could shoot targets with deadly accuracy from nearly two miles away. Chen wondered if he was using a next-generation sniper rifle. Though he was far from an expert, he had never heard of such range before.

Hopefully Lim hadn't, either.

Chen pulled out his black satellite phone and dialed Hong Kong.

Lim picked up on the second ring. 'Chen, it has been a long time. Something interesting to report, or did you merely miss my voice?'

Chen breathed a sigh of relief. At least his boss was in a good mood.

Chen quickly reported the events of the last half-hour, stressing the stunning abilities of the foreign sniper. He finished by requesting permission to pursue the intruders out on the open road, hoping that would restore Lim's faith in him.

'Are you sure about the distance?' Lim asked.

'At least one-point-five miles. Probably less than two, but not by much.'

'You know that Brother Feng doesn't like foreigners. He especially frowns on foreigners who try to loot our great nation. But the sniper you described must be military, which is far worse. Yes, do chase them down. And before they die, find out what they were looking for.'

Chen smiled at the opportunity to make up for his earlier failure and the chance to claim vengeance for his fallen friend.

'And Chen,' Lim said, before ending the call, 'get some video of them *before* the shooting starts. Just in case they get the best of you again.'

16

John Sylvester was a talented detective; so talented, in fact, that he had been on Seymour Duggan's payroll for nearly three years, which was pretty much the biggest compliment that someone in his profession could get. Based in Orlando, a tourist city in the middle of Florida, Sylvester's area covered the entire length of the Sunshine State.

Shortly after being hired by Cobb in Wales, Duggan had arranged for Sylvester to track Jean-Marc Papineau upon his arrival at his coastal compound in Florida. The property itself was practically untouchable – the private drive from the gate to the house was covered by surveillance and protected by an electric fence – so Sylvester had focused his efforts elsewhere.

He had placed cameras in the trees along the main road, allowing him to monitor the turnoff that led through the swampy marsh to the mansion. He had rented a fishing boat to take him a mile down shore from the compound's small stretch of beach, and he had planted a camera there too. A few of the more pliable locals had informed him that the yacht parked on Papineau's pier was mostly for show; it had barely left its slip in more than a year. That meant that if his target needed to travel somewhere, he would most likely fly out of the Fort Lauderdale–Hollywood International Airport, which was only a few miles away.

Knowing this, Sylvester set up shop in a nearby diner.

He watched his camera feeds from there.

The diner was a little on the grubby side for Sylvester's taste, but he had seen worse. Despite the grime and the terrible coffee, the diner was perfect for his needs: the food was tasty, the Wi-Fi was free, and the location was perfect. Anyone driving from the compound toward the airport would need to use the road out front, and he would see them coming from far away. This would give him enough time to hop in his sedan and pull out ahead of them. People always suspected a tail when a car pulled out behind them, but they would hardly think twice about a car that was on the road up ahead – even if it ended up tailing them for miles.

Sylvester knew this from experience.

He had just finished soaking up his last bit of grits with a home-made biscuit when he noticed movement on his beloved laptop. A nondescript, white Hyundai hatchback had turned off the dirt road and was headed his way.

'Is that you, Frenchie? What, no limo today?'

He stared at his camera feeds until he was positive it was Papineau. 'A Korean rental? How disappointing! You could have done so much better and still remained incognito.'

Sylvester laid a crumpled twenty on the table, wiped his mouth with a paper napkin, and closed his computer. He paused by a mirror near the front door and admired his square jaw and thick brown hair. For a man in his forties, he still looked to be in his twenties, and he often used those good looks to his advantage. Sylvester exited the blissfully cool air-conditioned diner, trading it for the thick, soupy air of south Florida. He started his sedan, which had built-in Wi-Fi, and opened the laptop on the passenger seat.

He cranked the vehicle's AC to high and relaxed, knowing it would be a few minutes, even if Papineau was speeding. When the Hyundai showed up on the video feed in the lower right corner of the laptop's screen – the final camera that Sylvester had placed along the road before the diner – he shifted into DRIVE and eased his sedan onto the road. He headed south with a constant eye on his rearview mirror. The Hyundai finally appeared a minute later. The small car followed him for a mile before passing him, steering west onto highway A1A toward the airport.

'Where ya headed?' Sylvester asked aloud as he turned to follow.

As if in response, Papineau suddenly spun around and drove back in the opposite direction.

The U-turn both surprised and impressed Sylvester. It was called a Surveillance Detection Route, or SDR. He knew that the Frenchman would perform a series of seemingly random turns, attempting to notice any vehicles following him. An SDR might only amount to a few minutes of detour, or it could take hours. In any case, Sylvester couldn't turn to follow or he would be spotted. He had no choice but to continue west toward the city.

Fortunately for him, Sylvester had planned ahead.

He had cameras positioned along every road that led to the airport.

If that's where Papineau was headed, he would see him again soon.

A mile later Sylvester pulled into a gas station to wait. He parked in front of one of the pumps, but didn't get out. Instead, he simply sat there, flipping through the feeds on his laptop until he caught sight of the Frenchman nearly twenty minutes later.

'There you are.'

Having completed the unpredictable driving of his SDR, Papineau felt confident enough to approach his final destination. Sylvester quickly caught up to his target and watched Papineau pull off a busy street and head toward a private terminal for small aircraft. Lacking the appropriate gate pass, Sylvester continued on toward the cargo terminal before circling back with a cover story to gain access to the private facility.

He told the guard at the gate that he was interested in renting a private hangar for one of his Learjets, and the hint of money prompted a call to the general manager. Sylvester had long ago discovered his clean-cut good looks lent themselves to role-playing a wealthy young businessman. A few minutes later, a paunchy man named Wilson was giving him a tour.

During their twenty-minute conversation, the general manager explained the operations at the small terminal and spoke convincingly about the obnoxious aspects of commercial air travel and security – all in an attempt to lure prospective business. But the only thing that Sylvester cared about was the tour of the hangers. All it took was a fleeting glimpse of Papineau's private jet and the lone security guard standing by it for Sylvester to memorize the aircraft registration number on the tail of the plane. With that, he could determine where the plane had been, where it was scheduled to go, and the name of the registered owner.

In short, he had everything he needed.

After thanking his host and indicating that he might be back to tour the facility again, Sylvester excused himself on the pretense of a business meeting in Miami. He promised to have his accountant get in touch within a week.

Instead, he returned to his rental car and pulled up the online database for FAA registration. He entered the tail number that was fresh in his mind and began his trace of the aircraft's ownership. It took him ten minutes to sort through the layers of shell companies, and ten minutes more to scour the log of flight plans, but he eventually found what he was looking for.

He pulled out his phone and dialed Duggan.

Seymour picked up on the first ring. 'Yes?'

'I have a destination.'

* * *

Eight hours later, Duggan's phone rang again in his opulent room in the Corinthia Palace Hotel & Spa in Malta. He checked the display and saw it was another of his operatives: Jerry Westbrook.

'Tell me you found him,' Duggan said calmly.

After receiving the tip from Sylvester in Florida, Duggan had phoned Westbrook, his best man in California, to drive to San Diego to tail Papineau from the airport to his final destination. Duggan had used Westbrook, a part-time actor and full-time private investigator, on a number of cases in the past. They had never met face-to-face and Westbrook, like Sylvester, knew Duggan only by the alias of 'Harry Reynolds'.

In Duggan's line of work, it paid to keep things close to the vest.

He liked Westbrook, but that was no reason to compromise his own security.

'Yep. I got him, Mr Reynolds. A private limo picked him up at the airport and took him up to a swanky estate in Castillo. Big security. I had to park about a mile away to make sure I wasn't made. Nothing but sprawling estates out there. Place looks like a damn castle. Want me to keep on him when he leaves?'

'Hmm,' Duggan said, thinking it over. 'I'd head down the road a ways. He'll most likely be going back to the airport tomorrow. It would be nice to confirm.'

'No problem.'

'In the meantime, why don't you ask around a bit? Maybe one of the locals will know the name of the man who owns the estate. At the very least, get me a street. I can do quite a bit with a mailing address.'

'Consider it done,' Westbrook bragged.

Duggan smiled, glad that everything was going so smoothly.

Unfortunately, it was the last thing Duggan would ever hear him say.

17

Castillo, California
(22 miles north of San Diego)

Papineau took a small bite of the succulent crab cake, swallowed, then wiped his mouth with a fine linen napkin. 'You knew this would happen, sir. You planned for it.'

Maurice Copeland nodded, chewing his food with the grace of a camel.

Papineau smiled and marveled at his apparent new stature in his boss's organization. On his last visit, Copeland had hinted none too subtly that Papineau might soon find himself out of work – or worse – but on this visit, he had been treated regally. Copeland had sent a limo to bring his guest from the airport to the fortified home. For the first time ever, Papineau had enjoyed the scenic ride to the private hilltop community. He had paid no attention to the electrified gate that momentarily blocked their path or any of the other security measures that protected the land from intruders.

Instead, he admired the house and the distant Pacific Ocean.

When Papineau had reached the residence, Copeland had welcomed him warmly at the front door. In the past, Copeland's beautiful-but-broken wife had always greeted him, but she was nowhere to be found. He couldn't help but wonder if she had finally found the courage to leave Copeland, or if his boss had killed her and buried her somewhere on his spacious estate.

Papineau knew that the second option was far more likely.

'Yeah, I planned for it,' Copeland said, taking a swig from a bottle of Dos Equis. Papineau watched as the lime slice the man had shoved down the neck of the brown bottle jammed in its throat, flavoring the Mexican beer. 'He surprised me, though. I didn't think Cobb would have the stones to dig deeper into who was pulling the strings until the fourth mission.'

While his face showed nothing, inside Papineau raised a mental eyebrow. His boss – the man who had ruined him in the world of business and then offered him a lifeline of servitude – had let it slip that there would be another mission after the Polo treasure.

That is, of course, if they were successful.

For all his own private investigations, Papineau had failed to discover why Copeland was so intent on discovering these treasures. The man was already fabulously wealthy, and he didn't really seem to want them. He had repatriated a good portion of the Romanian treasure to Bucharest and had allowed the Ulster Archives to examine the findings in the tomb of Alexander before the treasure was carefully packaged and shipped to Cairo. Copeland's only desire had been to visit the burial site before Papineau had notified anyone else of its location.

Copeland took another sip of beer. 'Obviously you can agree to all of Cobb's terms. Let's also throw him a small bone; something that will get him to slow down his search for me. You can confirm that you work for a nameless benefactor. Tell him I prefer to remain anonymous for the time being, but if the team is successful on this mission I'll reveal myself to him and him alone. The others must never know my name.'

Copeland smiled, but it did little to improve his bulldog looks. With a cauliflower ear and a nose that had been broken many times, his grin only made him look constipated.

'I don't think he will accept those terms,' Papineau said with just the right hint of uncertainty in his voice. He looked out past the massive swimming pool to the expansive view, feigning uncertainty as to how he might sell Cobb on the idea.

He knew full well that Cobb would accept the terms.

He was merely playing to Copeland's ego.

'He'll agree to it,' Copeland assured him. 'And in the meantime, he'll still be hunting me. So we'll throw him a bone there, too. Something that makes him feel like he's getting closer.'

Copeland inhaled his last crab cake in one giant bite and started speaking again before he was finished chewing. 'Where is the team on Polo?'

Papineau hid his disgust. 'Hector has finished the computer translation of the Rustichello manuscript, and Maggie is done with her contrastive analysis. Jack and Joshua are in northwest China while Sarah and the others are planning a trip to Florence to retrieve a different manuscript that might have some leads.'

Copeland leaned forward in his wrought-iron chair. He was a short man with an even shorter fuse. 'In other words, you have nothing.'

Papineau was prepared for Copeland's reaction. 'You knew this one would be tougher than the others. They are working with very thin leads. The manuscript you procured is full of Rustichello's suspicions, not maps. There is no "X marks the spot".'

'Then why is Cobb in Asia?'

'They are performing reconnaissance in Xinjiang. Obviously, they've stumbled upon a clue of some sort. It's in Cobb's M.O. to investigate a location before bringing the team in. He calls these trips "rekkys".'

'But this time he's done it without telling you the reason why,' Copeland goaded.

'Or so he believes. It's all part of my calculated management style. I've actually been taking pointers from you.'

Copeland leaned back. 'Are you trying to flatter me, Jean-Marc?'

'Never, sir.'

Copeland let loose a throaty laugh, then stood and began to walk around the infinity pool set into the side of the verdant hill. Papineau stood and followed the man without being told.

The immense estate might have looked like just another lavish home in yet another exclusive neighborhood, but Papineau knew that it was actually the centerpiece of a sprawling collective. All of the surrounding mansions were also owned by his employer, making the entire hilltop his personal dominion. It was an act of both convenience and arrogance. While he loved a good fight, he was uninterested in spending any time with adversarial neighbors he considered beneath him – at least not when victory could be bought instead of battled for. To ensure his complete control over both his property and his privacy, Copeland had convinced the local zoning board to declare the land outside of the township's authority. It had been money well spent.

He not only owned the land, he ruled it.

It was his kingdom.

The estate was surrounded by a low stone wall and landscaping that was so perfect it looked like it had been planted by a robot. The compound made the security at the house in Fort Lauderdale look primitive. The house itself resembled a reinforced castle piercing skyward out of the soil of the hilltop. The stones had been quarried from all over the country and presented a tapestry of shades of gray against the piercing blue of the California sky. The inside of the home was just as impressive, with tasteful artwork, handcrafted furniture, and multitudes of skylights to fill the place with natural light. Despite all the man-made luxury, the thing that Papineau liked best about the home was the view.

He walked in silence as he absorbed the transcendent vista of the Pacific Ocean.

'Just be sure he's still on mission,' Copeland said, shattering the moment. 'I need him hunting for me, not hunting *for* me. Understand?'

Papineau understood the distinction. 'Yes, sir.'

'One more thing, Jean-Marc. I may not want him looking for me, but it is the only acceptable alternative. If you ever sense that he's lost interest in the treasures *and* my identity, I need to know immediately.'

'May I ask why?'

Copeland stopped walking and stared at Papineau. 'Because if he's no longer trying to find a treasure or find out who I am, it'll be because he's figured out what I'm doing. And once he does that, I'll be forced to kill him . . . and his whole fucking team.'

18

Sarah paced the floor of the swank living room, asking herself the same question over and over again for the last several hours. 'Where the hell are they?'

She knew Cobb had touched base earlier in the day, but the data from the ground-penetrating radar had stopped suddenly and all attempts to contact him since had been unsuccessful. Normally she wouldn't be worried about Cobb, who tended to be very focused when he was on a rekky, but thanks to the volatile weather in Loulan, she couldn't help but wonder if a giant sandstorm had ravaged their communications gear, their vehicle, or them.

If so, they could be stranded in the dead zone.

She walked irregular patterns through the Doric columns of the living room, ignoring the crystal chandeliers overhead and the gorgeous hardwood and marble floors beneath her feet. She eventually noticed that she had been subconsciously avoiding the exotic Turkish rugs and was instead weaving a path around on the parts of the floors that were uncovered.

Even lost in thought she was cognizant of the treasures around her.

She changed her course and headed into the compound's vast library to speak with Maggie. Lined with dark wood shelves that stretched up into the alcoves of the loft ceiling, the room contained close to 5,000 volumes, many of which were leather-bound first editions.

All were meticulously free of dust.

Sarah wondered briefly who performed the actual dusting. She guessed that Papineau had a professional cleaning crew come in once a week or so. Even the most perfectly constructed homes in Florida required constant maintenance. And if the air conditioning went out for even a week, every volume in the spacious library would be crawling with mold.

Surrounded by sheaves of loose paper and piles of open books, Maggie sat at a long table, completely focused on her work. Sarah stood in the doorway for a moment, hoping to be noticed. When that didn't happen, she pulled out a wooden chair and sat at the table across from Maggie, who welcomed her with a smile.

'Any more leads?' Sarah asked.

Maggie nodded. 'Actually, yes. It's a bit complicated, but I think if we follow—' She caught herself and smiled. 'I'm sorry. I was about to start a long historical explanation. Do you actually want to hear it, or were you just interested in the end result?'

Sarah was surprised by the question. It was one that Jasmine had *never* asked – even when they were in the field under fire. Bullets would be flying, and Jasmine would launch into a graduate-level thesis on a historical tangent that had nothing to do with the original query because she felt it was a teaching moment.

It was annoying as hell, but part of her charm.

And one of many things that Sarah missed about her.

'Please,' Sarah said, 'regale me with details. I need to understand everything anyway, and I need to keep occupied. I've already procured new gear for the team, and I really can't move much further in my preparations for extraction if I don't even have any clue as to what the treasure is, how much there might be, or where in the world we might find it. Right now all I have to go on is: treasure . . . somewhere in Asia. That's a hell of a big haystack, especially when you don't even know what the needle looks like.'

Maggie laughed. 'Well, let's see if we can narrow things down a bit. The first thing you need to know is that even though the Polos logged thousands of miles on their travels, they weren't exactly trailblazers. Most of the paths that they followed were established trade routes of the indigenous population. What made the Polos special were the places they went and the people they met. They did things that no Europeans had ever done before.'

'Like Columbus "discovering" America.'

'Exactly,' Maggie said. 'Niccolò and Maffeo left Istanbul around 1259. They traveled to Uzbekistan and traded there for a few years. They then joined up with a caravan that was on its way from Persia to Dadu. That trip took roughly two years, but the members of the caravan had made the trip before. They were emissaries for Hulagu Khan and Kublai Khan.'

'And who were the Khans?' Sarah asked.

'They were brothers – grandchildren of Genghis Khan, former supreme ruler of the Mongol Empire. At that time, Hulagu ruled everything from Turkey to the Baluchistan province of Pakistan. Kublai held Mongolia and the west and northern parts of China. The point is, the members of the caravan knew their way.'

'Got it,' Sarah said.

'The brothers were received warmly in Dadu, which is modern-day Beijing. As I mentioned in my initial briefing, Kublai Khan sent them back to Europe with two tasks. Do you remember what they were?'

'Oil from the Holy Sepulcher and one hundred Christian scholars.'

Maggie nodded. 'When they returned to Dadu, they were now covering the same ground a third time – only this time with young Marco.'

'So,' Sarah said, understanding the significance of the story, 'Marco would be experiencing the route for the first time, but to his father and uncle—'

'Correct. The route was becoming more and more familiar to

them. Along the way, they shared all their knowledge with Marco and showed him the sights that impressed them the most. Marco would almost certainly have passed through Loulan at this point, but it would have been the third time for his father and uncle. It took them roughly three years to reach Beijing, and they remained there for seventeen more. During that time, Marco took several voyages for Kublai Khan to various locations around the empire.'

'And then the Khan finally let them go home?' Sarah asked.

'Not exactly. He sent them on a mission to escort a princess to her betrothed in Ilkhanate, part of Hulagu's empire.'

'Ilkhanate? Where's that?'

'Modern-day Iran,' Maggie answered. 'That trip was primarily by sea, and it may have taken as long as three years before the Polos finally parted ways with the rest of their group. There were some six hundred people with them on the return journey. Only eighteen made it to their destination. The official accounts don't say much about why. Neither does Rustichello's manuscript. The description of the return journey is sketchy at best, but I can tell you for sure that the Polos left the wedding party at the Strait of Hormuz and headed home.'

'And Marco found himself in jail shortly thereafter,' Sarah concluded.

'Yes. And here is an interesting bit. After narrating his tale to Rustichello in Genoa, Marco was released from incarceration and made a small fortune as a merchant in Venice. Rustichello's book on Marco's travels was a huge success. But then, ten full years later, Marco himself spent years writing a new version of the book, this time in Italian.' Maggie whispered the last part, as if it were scandalous information.

'What language was Rustichello's version?'

'Old French,' Maggie answered. 'My point is, I wonder whether Marco's version was written to obscure certain details that might lead people toward the treasure. So I've been comparing the extant versions of the manuscript, of which there are one hundred and fifty-two, to be precise. I'm looking for places where the memoirs from Rustichello differ from the other accounts by even the slightest detail.'

'And what are you finding?'

'Well, here is where it gets difficult. The versions of the book that we have today are all written like travel guides. It is likely Marco and Rustichello were hoping the book would act as a manual for future traders who were brave enough to head east. The accounts are big on practical detail and shy on personal depth.'

'So no, "Dear Diary, today we ate yak meat . . . *again*,"' Sarah joked.

'Exactly. There's nothing like that. You end up comparing details against details without the aid of anyone's actual viewpoint. It's all the same perspective without any individual thought.'

'Sounds like we're shooting in the dark,' Sarah said.

'I wouldn't say that just yet. We know that Rustichello believed Polo had visited Loulan multiple times. That's at least something to go on. This kind of research is all about making connections between the bits of information you have and the ones you acquire along the way. We don't have the guard's account yet, and Hector is still cross-referencing all the versions of the published editions of *The Travels* on his computer.'

'Actually,' Hector said from the doorway, 'I still have nothing on that front, but I do have something important to talk about.'

Sarah flinched from the sound of his voice. 'Is it about Jack?'

Garcia shook his head. 'No. It's about me.'

19

Xinjiang Autonomous Region, China
(101 miles east of Kashgar)

Cobb pressed on toward the market city of Kashgar as the sun slowly rose behind him. They needed to dump the Land Cruiser and rid themselves of their sleeping guide, whose body odor was now an exercise in masochism. This early in the day, Cobb was able to drive with the windows down, but he was still looking forward to saying goodbye to their snoozing companion.

After hours of silence, Cobb heard movement in the seat behind him. 'Can't wait to see those pals of yours again at the border.'

'You and me both,' McNutt yawned. When he wasn't taking his turn behind the wheel, he had preferred to ride in the back seat – closer to the stash of weapons in the vehicle's rear cargo area. 'I could go for some coffee, too.'

Cobb nodded in agreement. 'You know, I try not to pry too much into how you do what you do, but I've got to ask: how did you get those guys at the border to come through for us? Is that just some Marines-for-life stuff, or did you actively save their lives in Afghanistan?'

'No, nothing like that. They all work at the embassy in Bishkek.'

'Wait. Those guys were diplomatic security?'

'How do you think they were able to get us fake passports and visas so easily?' McNutt said with a laugh. 'Anyway, they want a Marine Corps Ball this year, but the ambassador didn't want to shell out the cash for it. He said they'd have to raise the funds themselves. What a douche. You can always spot the political appointees in an embassy. They're the assholes.'

Cobb nodded in agreement. He had noticed that, too.

'Anyway,' McNutt said, 'they were throwing parties at the Marine House every weekend to raise funds, but the money coming in from selling cold hot dogs and warm soda just wasn't cutting it. So I offered to pay for the ball for the next three years.'

Cobb smiled. He imagined the bond between Marines was a much larger part of the story than what McNutt was telling, but he also understood that sometimes the smallest of gestures was enough to grease the wheels in the armed forces. He remembered a few 'scratch my back' stories from his army days. He was about to share one with McNutt when he noticed a sudden change in their surroundings.

They lapsed into silence when they realized what was happening; they were about to be swallowed by a sandstorm. Even on the outskirts of the dead zone, the violent winds could whip up a cloud of sand more than a mile long in a matter of seconds. This one was at least forty feet high with an unknown depth. Although neither man said a word, they both knew Cobb would need his full concentration to drive through the violent haze.

And then things got worse.

The bulbous nose of a Russian Mil Mi-171E helicopter burst through the cloud and ripped out over the road. As the chopper closed in from two hundred yards, Cobb watched as the transport's side door opened and a Chinese Type 56 assault rifle emerged.

'Hang on,' Cobb said. It was the only warning he could offer before the man on the chopper opened fire.

Cobb swerved to the left shoulder of the road as a hail of bullets tore into the Land Cruiser's roof. He pressed the accelerator to the floor and barreled into the dust storm, praying that the helicopter didn't have any ground support on the other side of the cloud. It wouldn't do Cobb much good if he slammed into a roadblock of big trucks at sixty-five miles per hour.

Thankfully, the cloud wasn't as deep as Cobb had expected, and the Toyota sliced through it and into fresh air before he realized he hadn't closed the windows to keep out dust.

'Josh,' Cobb yelled, 'what do you have to take down a chopper?'

The Marine didn't answer.

Cobb glanced in the rearview mirror and nearly panicked.

The Land Cruiser fishtailed wildly across the road as Cobb slammed on the brakes. Once the vehicle finally stopped, he threw the transmission into PARK and whipped around to make sense of the scene behind him. McNutt and Ali were both slumped over with their eyes closed. The entire back seat was covered in a mixture of blood and guts, and everything was coated with so much sand that they looked like they had been dipped in breadcrumbs.

'Josh!' Cobb yelled as he ripped off his seatbelt. Fearing the loss of another team member, he started to climb into the back seat to check for vitals. 'Stay with me, Josh!'

McNutt's eyes popped open. 'Where the hell am I gonna go?'

Cobb leaped backward, startled to find McNutt alive under the blanket of gore. 'Holy shit! I thought you were dead!'

'Nah,' McNutt said, partially dazed. He turned his head and noticed the guide's entrails spilled upon the floor. Much of his torso was leaking, too. 'Just this guy.'

Cobb grabbed the wheel of the Land Cruiser, then yanked the transmission back into DRIVE. His first order of business was locating the chopper again.

'Chief,' McNutt said as he examined the guide, 'you're not going to believe this.'

'What now?' Cobb blurted, fearing the worst.

McNutt took a deep whiff. 'This joker actually smells better dead.'

20

Cobb stomped on the accelerator as McNutt climbed into the rear storage compartment of the SUV. He had plenty of weapons to choose from, but one in particular caught his eye.

'Hurry up!' Cobb shouted. 'The chopper's coming back around!'

'Weave or something! I need a little time!'

Cobb jerked the wheel back and forth while McNutt flipped back over the seat and landed in a puddle of blood and guts that had pooled on the leather. The middle third of the vehicle looked like a slaughterhouse, and McNutt, coated from head to toe in Ali's innards, looked like something that had crawled out of Hell and planned to attack Gotham City. He shoved the dead man aside to make room for the artillery he had just dragged from his arsenal.

Cobb swung the SUV wide, taking it completely off the asphalt and onto the hard-packed dirt shoulder to avoid yet another mountain of abandoned construction gravel left in the middle of the road. The conditions were taxing the Land Cruiser's shocks, but Cobb was forced to increase his speed to outrun the helicopter.

A few seconds later the road cleared and Cobb yanked the wheel back to the right. The Land Cruiser bounced onto the asphalt just as a line of bullets tore into the dirt on the side of the road. Cobb checked his side-view mirror and caught a glimpse of the gray Mi-171E. It was charging after them close behind, trying to get the shooter the best angle of fire.

'Hold on,' Cobb yelled, dragging the wheel hard.

The SUV careened to the other side of the road as yet another stream of metallic death chewed into the blacktop where the vehicle had just been. The truck bounced across the hard, rocky soil, then off the shoulder completely and down a small embankment. The dead guide flew into the air like a prop from *Weekend at Bernie's*, bouncing off the roof and landing face-first on McNutt's lap.

'What the fuck!' McNutt screamed as he shoved the dead body again.

'Sorry!' Cobb yelled.

'I wasn't talking to you! I was talking to Ali! He keeps touching me!'

Cobb didn't question it. He was too busy driving.

Once he regained his composure, McNutt kicked open his door – and then he kicked it again and again until the whole thing ripped off the hinges and went tumbling away. His renovation left a gaping hole in the right side of the Land Cruiser. 'Gimme a little more warning before you do that again! I need to set this up!'

'Who are you talking to now?' Cobb asked.

'You!' McNutt shouted. 'I'm talking to you!'

Cobb's eyes darted to the rearview for a second, trying to figure out what McNutt was doing. He turned his attention back to the countryside just in time to avoid a large stretch of boulders in the terrain. 'Right! Turning right!'

McNutt braced for the turn.

Unfortunately, Ali did not.

The leaking corpse attacked yet again, this time flopping its arm over McNutt's shoulder as if the dead guide was trying to hug him from behind. Making matters worse, the centrifugal force of the sudden turn pushed liquid from the bullet holes in Ali's chest. Blood and other bodily fluids squirted onto McNutt's neck and ran down the back of his shirt.

'Aaaaaagggghhhhhh!' McNutt screamed.

'What's wrong? What happened?'

'First he tried to blow me. Now he tried to bang me!'

Enraged and disgusted by the offense, McNutt turned around and punched the dead guide in his face to teach him a lesson. Instead, the force of the blow popped the corpse's eyes wide open, startling McNutt so much that he actually believed Ali had come back to life. Worried for his own life and the survival of the human race, McNutt instinctively pushed the body out of the moving truck before the zombie transformation could take full effect.

Meanwhile, Cobb hit the edge of the road as fast as he dared. The Land Cruiser caught air for just a second before smashing down again onto the embankment. He straightened the vehicle and poured on the speed while he could. When Cobb hazarded a glance back, McNutt was finishing the installation of a swivel mount that clamped to the bottom of the doorframe and would hold his M60 machine gun in place when he fired. Otherwise, the recoil would be tough to control.

'Nice!' Cobb shouted.

McNutt connected the rifle to the mount and the ammunition belt he had placed on the floor of the SUV. Then he wrapped his finger around the trigger. 'Ready when you are, chief!'

Cobb turned to find the chopper, which was now flying low on their right rear flank. He jerked the wheel to the right, cutting across the road on a nearly perpendicular path. The maneuver sent them bounding across the uneven soil, but it also gave McNutt and his weapon a direct line of sight.

The sniper zeroed in on his target and squeezed.

The M60 let loose with the distinctive *chuff-chuff-chuff* noise of the massive weapon's 600-rounds-a-minute rate of fire. Both men watched as the pilot swung the helicopter upward into a vertical position, trying to avoid the onslaught. Never in his wildest dreams could he have expected such firepower from *inside* a vehicle, and now it was already too late. The fuel tank ruptured, showering a spray of glistening gas all over the road only moments before the tail smashed to the ground. The fuselage crumpled and then burst entirely, encasing the occupants in a grave of twisted metal and broken glass.

But it was the rotors that sealed their fate.

The blades striking asphalt kicked up sparks, quickly igniting the growing pool of aviation fuel. The flames started slowly, running around the crash like a corona until they completely surrounded the wreckage. As expected, there was no huge explosion – fuel tanks caught fire; they didn't usually explode – and this one had lost most of its fuel to the ground before the flame had climbed. But the inferno quickly consumed those trapped inside.

Just to be sure, McNutt armed himself with an Uzi that he had pulled from the back of the vehicle as Cobb brought the truck to a stop. The Marine limped down the road toward the wreck, looking for survivors. Cobb followed closely behind with a rifle of his own.

The men reached the edge of the blaze just as the fire on the pavement was going out, but the interior of the chopper still burned. Smoke billowed out of the shattered windows, filling the air with the scent of charred flesh that was eerily similar to the tang of a good steak.

McNutt caught a whiff. 'Smells like ribs.'

Cobb blocked the thought from his mind and focused on the remains instead. He could see that the helicopter wasn't military, which meant that it was most likely more security guards from back in Loulan. Cobb didn't know why their opponents from the mine had been so tenacious, but he was just glad the pursuit was over . . . for now.

He glanced across the rocky soil and the craggy hills of the distant landscape. They needed to get out of the country in a hurry, before reinforcements showed up. And hopefully before the Chinese Army caught their scent. The only thing they had going for them was the sheer remoteness of the region. If they got a move on, no one would be able to connect them with the mess here.

'Let's go.'

'You know,' McNutt mumbled, 'we should probably—'

Before he could finish, he collapsed to the ground in a heap.

Cobb rushed to the man's side. He quickly realized that the Marine had a bullet wound in his left thigh that was gushing thick arterial blood. He looked up and followed the trail of dark brown fluid smeared across the asphalt, winding its way back to the abused SUV. He hadn't noticed the bleeding before, and McNutt hadn't said a word. Given the rush of adrenaline that came with being attacked, he wondered if the soldier had even noticed.

Cobb tore off his shirt and stuffed it into the gaping wound. Then he ripped off the bloody shirt on McNutt's torso and quickly wrapped it around the man's leg, holding the makeshift bandage into place over the injury. After tending to the wound, Cobb set about dragging McNutt away from the smoke and fumes of the sizzling helicopter.

Cobb lifted him in a fireman's carry, then turned toward the distant Land Cruiser. Three hundred yards away never looked so far.

He began to curse in his head.

Everything that could have gone wrong on this rekky had. Now he desperately needed medical attention for McNutt. After which he would have to get himself and his wounded companion out of the country – all without an interpreter and while evading any connection with the turmoil here and back at the mine. Cobb didn't even know how to find the Marine escorts that would smuggle them back across the border.

After a moment of self-pity, he berated himself for drifting into negative thinking and refocused on the task at hand. Cobb felt sure he could find a small doctor's office in Kashgar and get help. He just needed to stay calm and focused.

Then he saw the smoke billowing from the front of the SUV. The Land Cruiser's engine had been hit.

They weren't driving anywhere, and McNutt was dying.

21

Garcia walked into the library wearing a T-shirt with an Atari 2600 joystick icon, a pair of battered tan cargo shorts, flip-flops, and a huge grin. He pulled out the chair next to Maggie and sat down across from Sarah, who seemed perturbed about the interruption.

'Don't worry,' he assured the women, 'there are no listening devices active in this room. I hacked the feed and put it on a silent loop so we could speak in private.'

'What are you talking about?' Sarah asked with a straight face.

'Come on, Sarah. Don't play dumb. I *know* you know about the bugs. And I know that Papi is the one who put them there. It doesn't take a genius like me to figure that out.'

'Genius?' Sarah said with a laugh as she secretly pulled the bug detector from her pocket and activated it under the table. A quick glance down at its darkened LED confirmed that the listening devices that were normally present in the room were not recording, just as Garcia had said. 'Aren't you the same guy who mistook our translator for the maid?'

Garcia blushed but didn't take the bait. 'I want in on the search for Papi's employer.'

'What search?' she demanded.

'Come on, Sarah. I know you and Jack are trying to figure out why this house is bugged and why Papi's keeping us in the dark about his funding. I want to help.'

'Help?' Sarah blurted. 'If I remember correctly, you were involved with spying once before – but you were doing it *for* Papi and *against* us.'

Garcia groaned. He knew she was going to bring up the incident on the train. 'How many times do I have to tell you: I didn't betray anyone. He was paying me. Back then you were total strangers, and I was merely doing my job. Things are different now, and you know it.'

'Maybe so,' she said, reluctantly acknowledging the loyalty Garcia had shown ever since. 'But there's nothing to tell you. Maggie and I were just talking about history.'

'Relax,' Garcia said, 'I looped the bugs in the next room, too. Even if you shout, no one will hear you.'

'Why do I get the feeling that you've said that to women before?' Sarah teased.

Maggie put her hand over her mouth and tried to stifle her laugh. She had been completely quiet up to this point in the discussion, but the line was just too funny to ignore. 'Sorry.'

Garcia remained focused on Sarah. 'Tease me all you want, but the truth is I watch your backs all the time – even when you don't know I'm doing it.'

Sarah leaped to her feet. 'So you *are* a perv, just like Josh said!'

'What?' Garcia blurted.

'I swear to God, if I find out that you've been watching me in the shower—'

'No!' he shouted as he stood to defend his honor. 'Nothing like that! I swear! All I do is make sure you're safe. That's it. That's all I do. I make sure the team is safe.'

'Safe, how?' Sarah demanded.

'For instance, I ran a thorough check on Maggie as soon as I knew she was joining the team – even before you and Jack asked me to.'

Maggie stopped laughing and stared at Garcia. She knew that they were going to check up on her, but she was surprised that they were going to reveal the results with her in the room.

'And?' Sarah asked.

'She is who she says she is: a high-end travel guide based in China. I thoroughly checked her credentials, and there's nothing weird in her history. And she's not reporting to Papi, either. As far as I can tell, the two of them first spoke earlier this month. No prior connection.'

Sarah stared at Maggie. 'And since then?'

Garcia answered. 'One phone call, two emails, and three texts; all *before* she was introduced to the team. Nothing since.'

Maggie simply nodded.

Garcia took a deep breath. 'Seriously, Sarah. I'm here to help. Just tell me what to do.'

Sarah reluctantly sat down again and signaled for him to do the same. Thanks to a rocky childhood and many years of undercover work with the CIA, she found it difficult to trust people – especially those who had wronged her in the past. Even so, she realized that sometimes a second chance was warranted, and she sensed this was one of those times.

Of course, she wasn't going to make it easy on him.

That wasn't Sarah's way.

'Look,' Maggie said to break the icy silence, 'I came to this party a little late, but if it's okay with you, I'd like to speak on the matter.'

'Go ahead,' Sarah said.

'As I understand it, we were hired by Jean-Marc to find a treasure. We were selected for our abilities and our willingness to step outside the law to accomplish that goal. I don't find it the least bit surprising that he might have some skeletons in his closet. And considering the amount of money that he's paying the team, I understand his desire to keep tabs on us.'

Sarah and Garcia nodded grudgingly.

Maggie continued. 'I can see where Jack might want to have more information about Jean-Marc's motivation, but how exactly does that help us accomplish our goal? I mean, all that matters right now is that Jean-Marc *does* want us to succeed on this mission, right?'

Sarah sighed. 'Yes, but the thing is, we were hired on the understanding that Papi was in charge. It was all presented as a scenario where we were working for *him* and spending *his* money, but we sense that isn't the case. And that makes us very uncomfortable.'

'Why?' Maggie wondered.

'Why?' Sarah echoed. 'Because I'd prefer not to be working for the Russian mob. Or a Mexican cartel. Or any of the million or so criminal organizations in the world.'

Maggie conceded the point.

'Plus,' Sarah continued, 'why is Papi – or our *real* employer – spending millions of dollars to find these ancient treasures if they just give them away?'

Garcia nodded. 'That's been bugging me, too.'

Sarah glanced at him. 'Hector, I'm going to ask you an important question, and I need you to be upfront with me. No bragging. No exaggerations. Only the honest truth.'

'Go ahead. Ask me anything.'

She stared at him. 'How good a hacker are you?'

'I'm very good. Why?'

She shook her head. 'I mean, if you were to rank yourself compared to all the other hackers in the world, where would you fall?'

Garcia gave the question some consideration. 'Probably near the top ten, if not in it. It's hard to say. There are a lot of us out there who don't exactly advertise.'

'You're that good?' Maggie asked.

Garcia tapped briefly on the small tablet he'd brought into the room. In less than a minute, he had the information he was searching for. 'You have precisely $107,123.11 in your numbered account in

Liechtenstein.' He smiled at Maggie. 'You shouldn't have set that up online.'

Maggie grimaced. 'Hector, if I forgive you for calling me the cleaning lady and for snooping on me, will you show me how to hide those funds better?'

Garcia nodded. Then he turned back to Sarah, who was waiting patiently. 'Why did you ask about my ranking?'

'Two reasons,' she answered. 'The first is obvious: if we're going to get more information on Papi and what he's really up to, we'll need your help. The truth is Jack was always going to bring you in, but I asked him to hold off until you and I had a chance to talk. Now that we've cleared the air, I think it's time to prove your worth.'

'Just tell me how.'

'We know that Papi has access to millions of dollars to pay for us, this compound, his yacht, and everything that we need on our missions, and yet we've gotten absolutely nowhere on his background and business holdings. So we have to assume that he's got some incredible cyber power on his side.'

Garcia was surprised. 'You think he's hired someone better than me?'

Sarah nodded. 'I think he *thinks* he has. Now it's up to you to find a way past his defenses and prove him wrong.'

Garcia grimaced. All this time he had been thinking that the reason he couldn't find anything on Papi was because he was clean. He had honestly never considered that someone better than he was responsible for hiding the Frenchman's dirt.

'It'll be easier said than done,' Garcia replied. 'Don't get me wrong, I can do it. I'll just need some time.'

'How much?' Sarah asked.

'A few days. Maybe a few weeks.'

'Weeks?' Sarah groaned. 'Why so long?'

'If someone else *is* protecting Papineau's digital footprint, then I can't just bombard his accounts with everything in my arsenal – they'll pick up on that and know we're up to something. I'll have to come at this from another direction, something they'll never see coming.'

'But you've got something in mind?' Maggie asked.

Garcia nodded. 'Yeah, I think I have something that'll work.'

'Good,' Sarah said. 'Get to it.' She didn't need to know the specifics of his plan; she just needed it to do what he said it could.

'Will do,' Garcia said as he grabbed his tablet and stood.

'Wait,' Sarah said. 'We're not done.'

'Right. You said there were two reasons you wanted to know my worldwide ranking as a hacker, and you only named one. What was the second?'

'You have to double-check all your protocols.'

Garcia flashed a look of confusion. 'I'm not following.'

Sarah stood and walked around the table to place her hand on Garcia's shoulder. Though he had the highest IQ on the team, his lack of street smarts was sometimes disconcerting. 'Think about it, Hector. If Papi hired a hacker who is better than you, what do you think his first assignment was? Here's a hint: I guarantee it wasn't *me.*'

Garcia's face went pale when he realized her point. Everything he had established might already be compromised. Until he had rechecked his system, he had to assume that all of his work was unsecure. The thought sickened him.

The team was vulnerable, and it was all his fault.

Garcia nodded. 'I'll start right now.'

22

Cobb dragged McNutt the last few yards back to the ravaged Land Cruiser, then laid his unconscious form on the ground. Steam was still hissing from the engine when Cobb climbed over the gore-splattered back seat and accessed the cargo area of the vehicle. He quickly found the first aid kit that he'd brought along and tore it open.

The bullet had ripped through McNutt's leg and come out the other side, leaving two external wounds to close and a multitude of blood vessels to plug internally. Unfortunately, the kit was designed with superficial lacerations in mind; McNutt's injuries were simply too severe for gauze and tape. Even with the military-issue, quick-hardening bandages and next-generation spray-on skin, there wasn't much Cobb could do.

Then he had an idea.

Cobb threw the first aid kit aside and scrambled for the backpack that contained his laptop. Rummaging through the case, he quickly laid his hands on the cylinder he was seeking then returned to his fallen friend.

He dropped to McNutt's side and slid a folding serrated knife out of his pocket. He used the blade to cut off McNutt's T-shirt, some of which he'd already used as a makeshift tourniquet. Next he ran a long slit up the leg of McNutt's trousers to expose the wound.

The hole was to the side of McNutt's thigh and just larger than an American quarter. Blood formed a perfect half-sphere as it bubbled up out of the puncture before seeping down the Marine's leg. Cobb used McNutt's sliced shirt to swab away at the bulk of the fluid and then brought up the cylinder that he'd retrieved from his computer case.

He pointed the aerosol can at the wound and began to spray. A thick, black, gelatinous substance squirted out of the can and into the hole. Cobb laid it on heavy, then he pulled back and watched. In just a few seconds he could see the dark gel hardening. A moment later, the blood around the edges of the wound stopped flowing entirely.

Miraculously, the spray had saved McNutt's life.

But Cobb had no way of knowing if the substance would eventually kill him.

The thick gel was filled with colloidal quantum dots: microscopic semiconductor particles designed to function like solar cells. The US military was constantly field-testing stuff like this. A soldier could spray it on a rock and shove in the plug of a power cord – or even just the frayed wires where the plug used to be. The black ooze would harden in seconds and collect enough solar energy to power an electronic device in a pinch.

In this case, Cobb simply used it for its quick-hardening property and hoped like hell that none of the small particles would be swept through McNutt's system and cause an embolism. He also had no idea if the material was toxic; the military wasn't big on warning labels.

At least it did the job for the time being.

Cobb rolled the sniper onto his stomach and applied more spray to the exit wound. Once the bleeding stopped, Cobb wrapped the leg with the quick-hardening bandages from the first aid kit, then moved the unconscious man to the front passenger seat to get him out of the sun. He would have laid him down in the back seat, but there was so much blood and gore back there he was concerned about infections.

Next Cobb went to take a look at the engine. He didn't have any spare parts, but he hoped there was something he could do to fix it. Instead, just as he rounded the front of the vehicle, he caught a glimpse of something down the road. Way past the remains of the burning helicopter, far off in the distance, a trail of dust was rising.

Someone was coming.

Cobb cursed loudly as he retrieved the telescope that McNutt had used earlier and then climbed to the roof's luggage rack for a better view. As he focused on the billowing stream of dust in the distance, he slowly breathed a sigh of relief.

It wasn't reinforcements.

It was a commercial truck.

With massive wooden boards surrounding the bed, the Pakistani rig was painted in brilliant reds, greens, and blues. The front of the cab was decorated with more superfluous crap than Cobb had ever seen on a vehicle that wasn't in a parade: lights, fringe, beads, fluttering fabrics, and carvings in the shape of peacocks. He could also see that the bed was crowded with Muslim men – their beards and *taqiyah* skullcaps announcing their faith. He reasoned the truck was most likely headed for Kashgar, and then probably on to Gilgit, and maybe even Peshawar.

As far as he was concerned, any of those cities was better than here.

Cobb climbed down and grabbed the M60 from the rear of the Land Cruiser. He stepped onto the asphalt and hoisted the barrel of the machine gun skyward with a single arm, allowing the weight of the weapon to pin his elbow to his side. The pose was meant as a display, not as a threat, and it freed his left arm to flag down the approaching visitors.

Cobb stopped in the middle of the road and waited.

He could clearly see the vehicle speeding toward the ruins of the helicopter. Moments later the truck slowly picked its way around the wreckage and approached the human blockade.

Cobb didn't move.

He simply stood there and stared.

The driver stopped the truck a hundred feet away. From this distance, the Pakistani was the only man that Cobb could see. All the others were hunkered down in the back, completely out of sight. Were they praying? Getting weapons? Planning an attack?

Cobb didn't know, but he kept his cool.

He slowly moved his finger to the trigger, just in case.

The driver, who didn't know what to make of the scary man with the M60, started to whisper to his brothers behind him. At their urging, he called out in his Uyghur dialect.

Cobb countered with a single word. 'English?'

'Ah! I can speak!' a different voice yelled out.

A man's head popped up in the rear of the truck. He wore a white and blue skullcap over black hair, and his face sported a short beard. Cobb put him at no more than twenty-five.

'I speak the English good! What you are needing?'

'I need transport to Kashgar. My friend is hurt.'

The young man's face darkened as his eyes darted lower, toward where McNutt sat slumped in the interior of the SUV. Cobb could hear the others mumbling to the man in Uyghur and Urdu, but not loudly enough for Cobb to make out any words.

'Okay,' the young man said. 'One moment.'

Then he ducked his head back down behind the headboard of the truck. A heated discussion arose, and occasionally a loud voice would bark something out for the driver's attention. He routinely answered in monosyllabic grunts or with the word 'acha', which Cobb knew to mean 'good' in both Hindi and Urdu.

Finally the man popped his head up above the board again. He looked a little sheepish when he spoke, as if bargaining hadn't been his idea. 'How much?'

Cobb had been prepared for this. Haggling was a way of life in western Asia, and it stretched well into the interior of China too. 'I have two hundred American. It's yours if you get us to Kashgar – but no police or army . . . Two hundred. That's all I have.'

Of course, that wasn't true. Cobb had a few thousand in hundred-dollar bills stashed in watertight bags on his body and a few thousand more in the SUV, but he knew he'd need most of that for a back-alley doctor who wouldn't ask questions and the rest to cross the border back into Kyrgyzstan.

The negotiator ducked his head down and informed the others of the deal. There was some thoughtful bickering, but no more outright arguing. Cobb took that to mean they would accept the deal. One lone voice still sounded like it wanted more.

There was always a greedy one.

Then he raised his head above the barrier with a sad look. 'Two hundred? Is all you have? Nothing else? They are wanting *baksheesh*.'

Cobb knew the word meant 'gift', but in practice it was more like a bribe.

He slapped his free hand on the M60. 'You get the machine gun, too – *after* you get us to where we need to go.'

The young man's face erupted into a wide grin, full of genuine joy. He only had a few teeth left, but the smile was the best thing Cobb had seen all day.

23

Saturday, March 29

Papineau was worried about Cobb and McNutt. As far as he could tell, it had been a few days since anyone had heard from them. Their last communication was Wednesday, right before the transmission of their GPR data had stopped abruptly.

Based on his conversations with the team, he sensed they were worried too.

Particularly Sarah. He had never seen her so uptight.

It made him wonder if she had fallen for Cobb.

Though it pained him to admit it, Papineau realized his presence at the compound only added to the tension of the team, so he decided to give them some space. Upon returning from California on Thursday night, he had boarded his yacht and set a course for the blue-green waters of the Atlantic. Normally a few days at sea would melt his tensions away, but not this time. He had been too wrapped up in his thoughts to enjoy the scenery.

His trips out west to see Copeland always made his blood boil. His hatred for the man was extraordinary, so much so that he often stayed up late thinking of ways to knock him from his perch. As it was, his best plan involved Cobb and his treasure-hunting team. If the team leader had gotten himself killed on his advance fieldwork in Asia, everything would be lost.

As the yacht gently nuzzled against the private pier, Papineau pulled his mind into the present. He stood from his lounge chair and donned his linen jacket, waiting for the captain to finish with the lines and the gangplank. After stepping ashore, he strolled through the grounds of his estate, studiously avoiding direct looks into any of the cameras. He knew the others must have detected some or even most of them by now – he'd have been disappointed if they hadn't – but he didn't want to tip them off to any they might have missed. Instead, he breezed past the palms and assorted flowers without a glance, moving directly into the living room through the sliding glass doors off the patio.

Not surprisingly, Garcia was nowhere to be seen. He would be secluded down below in the room that Papineau had dubbed the Control Center, but which the members of the team insisted on calling the War Room. Even without the cameras secreted around the compound, Papineau knew he would find Garcia there.

He also knew Maggie would most likely be in the library. She seemed to have staked out that space as her primary working area, spreading her printouts and documents across the surface of the large antique table. Unlike the others on the team who had fully embraced the digital world, she worked almost exclusively with paper. Maybe that was a generational thing as she was slightly older than the others, or maybe it was her field of study.

Papineau was well enough versed in the subject of Marco Polo to understand that not only were there multitudes of varying accounts but, in some cases, scholars had even taken to adding copious notes in the margins of different versions of the tale. The *marginalia*, as they were called, despite being anonymous in many cases, were often deemed by scholars to be as useful as the main document. In fact, many of the most well-known theories concerning the Venetian's travels had come from these additions.

Papineau made a mental note to ask Maggie if she had discovered anything useful in the marginalia of any of the copies of the book she had obtained.

But he would do it later.

Right now, he needed to speak with Garcia.

Unfortunately, Sarah was in his way. She was pacing in the kitchen, wearing low-rise shorts and a bikini top while eating a piece of fruit. Her skin was a deep tan and her blond hair was lighter than it had been before his trip. Her small, bare feet slapped on the marble floor as she walked. Despite the elaborate swimming pools out on the patio, he realized this was the first time he had seen her in an actual swimming suit.

'Sarah,' he said, startling her from her thoughts. 'Finally enjoying the pool? I hope you've been getting some work done as well.'

Instead of responding with her typical defensiveness, she looked relieved to see him. 'I'm actually going a little stir crazy without the others here. Hector's locked himself in with the computer, doing God knows what. Maggie's busy with her books. I've already done as much of the advance prep work that I can without knowing exactly where we're going. Do you know how hard it is to devise an exit strategy from a dozen different nations for a treasure of indeterminate size?'

Papineau smiled with compassion. He had been in charge of that same task on the previous two missions. 'I cannot imagine, my dear.'

'Let's just say it isn't easy. But I did it, plus I acquired some new equipment for the team as well. Now I'm left wondering what to do with myself. Do you want to look over some of the new gear? I'd be happy to show you.'

Papineau wondered if she was acting or if she was really bored. He suspected a bit of both. 'That would be fabulous, but first I need to speak with young Hector. If you'll excuse me.'

'Sure,' she replied. 'I'll be around.'

As he made for the stairway that led down to the War Room, Sarah pulled her cell phone out of the tight back pocket of her shorts and sent an emergency text message.

*   *   *

Garcia's phone emitted a soft tweeting noise, and he leaped up from underneath the tabletop computer where he had been planting his own listening device. He jumped into his usual chair, which had an array of empty snack packets in front of it, and quickly tapped the tabletop touchscreen, activating five different windows on the glass surface of the table.

Now, when Papineau walked into the War Room, he would see the hacker embroiled in research, coding, and reports from three different international news stations on events in China and India. The empty wrappers for the Twinkies and Snickers candy bars – consumed over the past few days – were just set dressing to make it appear he'd been at work for hours.

To complete the illusion, Garcia began tapping at the virtual keyboard displayed on the table's surface just as the Frenchman entered the room.

'Good morning, Hector,' Papineau said.

Garcia made a show of acting startled. 'Papi! You're back.'

The man frowned. 'Please, don't call me "Papi".'

'Are the others back, too?' Garcia asked.

Papineau slid into a chair at the table, opposite Garcia. 'Actually, I was hoping you could tell me where they are and when they'll return.'

Garcia felt a quick moment of fear. He'd started as the Frenchman's informant, but now his allegiance had shifted to the team. He was afraid Papineau was about to ask him to spy again and he wasn't sure he could act as a triple agent.

As it was he'd been busy ferreting out the cyber intrusions into his own systems, which he assumed were the work of Papineau's people. The snoops were definitely there, as evidenced by the malware they had placed in his Denver system. He'd spotted it covertly, and it was enough for him to know that he would need to write off the whole facility and all the hard work he had done there.

'I wish I knew where they are, but I don't.'

The Frenchman just stared at him, unsure if he was telling the truth.

Garcia opted to change the topic. 'Did you speak to Maggie? She said my computer translations were incredibly helpful. I think she's done with her own translations, and now she's just sifting through the information. She said most of what was in the original document echoes the account in the first third of most copies of the book we have today: descriptions of the Middle East, the journey to China, and the meeting with Kublai Khan.'

The Frenchman rubbed the bridge of his nose and took in a deep breath of the basil-scented air. The other plants in the room had been his idea, increasing oxygen and making the space homier, but Garcia had added the basil, knowing the scent increased mental acuity and also had anti-viral properties. Plus he liked the rich smell.

'Are we closer to a location?'

'Yes, sir. We're getting there. Any day now.'

'Good,' Papineau said as he stood up. 'I'd like to have a destination ready to go as soon as we obtain a new team leader.'

Garcia did a double take. 'A new team leader? You're firing Jack? I know he was a little demanding in the last meeting, but—'

'No, Hector. It isn't that. He's long overdue from wherever he's gone. We cannot wait on him any longer. Once we have a location, we must proceed without him.'

'Well, I'm waiting on him,' a voice said from behind.

Papineau and Garcia turned and saw McNutt standing in the doorway with an aluminum crutch under one beefy arm. He was wearing a black T-shirt with the slogan THE HELL WITH YOUR MOUNTAINS, SHOW ME YOUR BUSCH on it, with a can of beer superimposed against a distant mountain range. His blue jeans were faded, and his beard hadn't been shaved since he had left Florida. He was starting to look very much like the biker he was.

Both men noted the crutch.

'What happened to you?' Garcia blurted.

'And where have you been?' Papineau demanded.

'Nice to see you guys, too.'

Garcia ignored the sarcasm. 'Seriously, Josh, are you okay?'

'Yes, Penelope, I'm fine. Just a minor accident. I met this really hot Asian chick during the rekky, and I got sooooo excited my boner actually pierced my leg. Doc says I need to use this damn crutch for a while, but I should be up and running by summer.'

'Summer?' Papineau shrieked.

McNutt laughed as he limped into the room. He loved messing with Papi. 'Don't worry, if we need to mobilize, I'll ditch this sucker and keep up. Oh, and as for where I've been, I was doing what I was supposed to be doing: checking out China and arranging supplies for our mission. Jack and I separated a few days ago in Kashgar. I haven't heard from him since . . . Why? Is he missing?'

'Yes,' Papineau said. 'For some time now.'

'And you don't think we should wait for Jack?'

'What?' Sarah said as she entered the room. 'Who's not waiting for Jack?'

Papineau took a deep breath. 'I merely mentioned the possibility of moving forward without him. This mission is time-sensitive, and our leader is nowhere to be found. If I don't hear from him soon, well, I'll have no choice but to move in a different direction.'

Although this was merely a bluff – he hoped that someone on the team would contact Cobb and get him to return – he sensed that time was of the essence with Maurice Copeland's plans for the treasure. That meant time was crucial to Papineau as well. And if Cobb didn't return soon, Papineau really would need to find another man to lead the team.

Surprisingly, Garcia was the first one to draw a line in the sand. 'Sorry, sir. I'm not going on this mission without Jack.'

Sarah smiled. 'That might be the first thing you've said that I completely agree with.'

McNutt nodded at Garcia, then turned his focus to Papineau. 'You heard the team. None of us are going anywhere without the chief.'

Papineau stepped around the others and started up the stairs.

'Where are you going?' Sarah demanded.

'I'm tired of these little mutinies,' he called over his shoulder. 'In addition to finding a new team leader, it appears I need a new hacker, weapons expert, and thief.'

24

San Diego, California

Jerry Westbrook was running for his life.

But he didn't know why.

He had first spotted the tail as he left the airport on Thursday. The black SUV with the tinted windows had followed him for several miles, careful to never get too close. When it disappeared thirty minutes later, Westbrook had begun to wonder if he had only been imagining things. For all he knew, Jean-Marc Papineau was nothing more than an unscrupulous businessman. Surely nothing in his investigation would warrant this type of attention.

His opinion had changed earlier that night.

That's when the same SUV had reappeared.

Westbrook had driven all around the city for hours trying to lose them; but each time he'd been successful at slipping a tail, a new follow vehicle would appear. With each new tail, he was able to eliminate another possibility. Amateurs wouldn't be so coordinated. Gangsters, mobsters, and other unsavory types would have been more brazen and reckless. A military or government agency could have taken him anytime, anywhere – they didn't need to fool around with car chases.

He couldn't say who they were, but he definitely knew the type.

They were private contractors and extremely well funded.

With his sedan running low on gas, Westbrook made a last-ditch gambit. He sped up, putting some distance between himself and the nearest car, and headed toward the San Diego Zoo: one of the largest wildlife parks in the world. The main entrance was barricaded with wooden sawhorses painted in cheerful orange and white stripes, but he had no problem smashing through them with his car.

He shot across the empty parking lot and hastily parked in the row nearest the grounds. From the glove box he grabbed the vehicle's registration card and his proof of insurance – papers that listed both his name and current address. He stuffed them in his pocket as he leaped out and sprinted for the closest point of access. After scaling a wall and dropping to the ground beyond, he crept off into the zoo.

He could hear the squeal of tires behind him as his pursuers gave chase.

Westbrook had been to the zoo dozens of times but never when it was deserted. Without the steady murmur of the usual crowds, the sound of his shoes slapping on the asphalt pathways rang out like gunshots in his ears. To limit the noise, he slipped off the track and onto the sandy soil at the side of it. He darted between trees, vaulted over obstacles, and ducked under low-hanging branches. He deliberately careened through the landscaping off the beaten trail, hoping the others wouldn't be able to follow.

Out of breath, he stopped and took cover behind a huge bush. The shrub easily concealed his frame, giving him a moment to consider his predicament. He wiped the sweat from his forehead and looked around, peering intently at the dark shadows pooling between the far-too-distant street lamps that lit the trails. One thing was clear: the zoo had not been designed for a nighttime audience.

The heat of the night was stifling. He wondered if it was just unseasonably warm or whether he was badly out of shape. In either case, the random scents of animals – both those free to wander their paddocks and those caged in more confining containers – filled the night air like the cologne of the damned. It was a rich, meaty stink. Westbrook had never experienced allergies before, but now he found it difficult to breathe in the stench.

After a minute of silence, he pushed deeper into the park. There were exits at each end, and exits meant roads. With any luck he could flag someone down and hitch a ride. He rehearsed a convincing story as he ran, but he never had a chance to use it.

The six-seat golf cart, used to transport employees and customers around the park, bore down on him like a runaway train. The powerful electric motor propelled the vehicle silently on its collision course until it made contact with the unsuspecting jogger. The first thing Westbrook heard was the sound of the cart hitting him.

The hit wasn't lethal, but it was hard enough to send him flying through the air. He barely had time to see the darkened world flutter past him in slow motion before time sped up and his body slammed into the ground. He rolled a few times, and then started to get up, marveling that the only injuries he noticed were small patches of road rash on his wrists and palms.

Unfortunately, the worst was yet to come.

Suddenly rough hands were grabbing him and dragging him to his feet. He could hear questions, but the voices sounded blurred, like adults in a Charlie Brown special.

Despite the dull throbbing in his head, Westbrook opened his eyes as his three assailants tossed him up against a fence. They slapped him across the face a few times to ensure that they had his full attention. As his senses returned, Westbrook realized that only one man was talking.

'Who paid you?' the man demanded. He wore a dark suit, and his head seemed to shimmer in the moonlight.

As Westbrook's vision adjusted to the darkness, he could see that his interrogator was not simply bald, he was completely hairless.

'Hey man, relax.' Westbrook's own voice sounded strange to him; it was thick and slurring. He realized something was wrong with his ear when he touched it and felt blood. 'I'll tell you anything you want to know. The money wasn't that good.'

The man moved uncomfortably close to Westbrook. Without lashes, his jet-black eyes took on a hollow, vacant stare. Instead of eyebrows, he had only the thick, bony protrusions of his orbital ridge. He looked like a skeletal ghoul, wrapped in barely enough flesh to pass for human.

His face wasn't just menacing, it was haunting.

'Give me a name,' the demon demanded.

Westbrook sensed this was a man who plowed through every obstacle in life, rather than using finesse. 'Harry Reynolds . . . I think he's English or something.' Westbrook started to wobble on his feet. His balance suddenly gone, the world started spinning upward and to his left. 'I think . . . I think I might need some help.'

'Give him a hand,' the man said as he turned and walked away. The other two men, similarly dressed and shorn with military-style crew cuts, stepped forward at his command. One grabbed Westbrook's arms, the other Westbrook's legs, and with a single easy motion they tossed him over the fence.

His body hit a grassy slope and slid down sideways until he landed in a shallow pool. He sputtered and thrashed in the water for a moment until he realized that the pool wasn't deep. He stood up and then immediately fell down again. His balance was shot.

Vertigo was making his stomach queasy.

Then, even through his shattered eardrum, he registered the roar.

The bass of it reverberated in his sternum. The hair on his arms stood on end, his body reacting with primal fear to the new life-threatening menace. He turned slowly in the water to see the approaching behemoth.

Jerry Westbrook screamed long and loud.

He was still screaming when the polar bear began to eat him.

25

Sunday, March 30

McNutt rested his leg on a pile of pillows at the end of his chaise longue. He was wearing pajama pants to cover his bandages, but his shirt was off and his sunglasses were on as he sipped a can of beer next to the pool. He had told the rest of the team what had really happened in China, but Cobb had asked him to keep Papineau guessing for a while. The Cheshire-cat grin on McNutt's face was the giveaway that he was truly enjoying his task.

'Oh, be reasonable,' Papineau said, his voice close to pleading.

'Not a chance,' Sarah replied. 'There was nothing in our original contract that said we needed to share our research with you in the event that you decided to sack us.'

After Papineau's threat the previous day, Garcia had conveniently 'lost' the passwords to the mainframe computer. Though they had tried all night, Papineau and his people couldn't get back into the system. While Sarah and Garcia had threatened to leave, McNutt had insisted on moving in as part of his injury settlement. He remained armed at all times and dared Papineau to remove him from the compound. Meanwhile, Maggie allowed Papineau to confiscate her handwritten notes, but she refused to translate her personal shorthand or Chinese scrawl for him.

Dressed in a linen suit, Papineau stood fuming by the pool. The thin veneer of civility that he wore like a badge of honor was finally cracking. 'Miss Ellis, the Rustichello document is not yours to withhold. I urge you to return it at once.'

Sarah looked up at him from the water. Her red bikini matched the color of Papineau's flustered face. '*Urge?* Did you say *urge?* What did you mean by that? Is that a threat?'

'Sounded like a threat to me,' McNutt called out as he patted his Glock. 'And I should know, I threaten people all the time.'

'No,' Papineau assured her, 'it wasn't a threat of bodily harm. I wouldn't stoop that low – unlike some of you. It was merely to let you know that you're crossing a boundary. Your recent behavior will forever taint our professional relationship.'

'You mean the relationship that ended last night when you fired us?' She paused briefly to slick back her blond hair, which seemed to glow in the sun. 'Why don't you just get another copy from the Ulster Archives? Isn't that where it's being stored?'

Papineau had tried that already, but Petr Ulster claimed he had temporarily misplaced the original. 'Be reasonable, Ms Ellis. I've paid you fairly for the work you've performed. I've even offered to pay you for the time you've put in on this aborted mission. Now kindly return the digital copy of the Rustichello manuscript, and we shall part on friendly terms.'

'I'm sorry to say I don't have a digital copy of the manuscript anymore. None of us do. Hector kept all of the copies for security purposes. He's inside right now trying to find them.'

'And you expect me to believe that?'

Sarah smiled at him. 'Why would I lie?'

In addition to the truth about his injured leg, McNutt had also passed along a request from Cobb: he needed the team to buy him some time. He was fine, and he planned to return to Florida soon, but he hoped to talk to some of his sources in Asia before he left. He needed to figure out who had tried to kill them on their rekky.

The decision to lock out Papineau was actually Sarah's. She knew it would infuriate the man, but she felt he deserved it after he had threatened to fire the entire team even though Cobb and McNutt had just risked their lives in China. Ultimately, she knew that Papineau had the resources to replace the team, but she figured he wouldn't do it if he didn't have access to their work.

Papineau sensed he wasn't getting anywhere with Sarah, so he turned his attention to Maggie, who was sitting quietly in the shade of a palm tree. 'Ms Liu, please be reasonable.'

Maggie simply shook her head. Despite the nervous tension she felt inside, her face was calm. This had been a dream job for her, and although she wanted to show solidarity with her team members, she really wanted Cobb to return so the mission could continue.

'But why?' Papineau asked.

'Because *you* put Jack in charge of the team, and he wouldn't want me to.'

McNutt laughed. 'Woman has a point, Papi. You did hire Jack.'

Papineau cursed in French and wheeled back toward Sarah. 'This is all your fault! You have turned them against me. And what did I ever do to you? I paid you a fortune for two simple jobs and asked you to do a third job for an equal fortune. And you treat me like this?'

Just then a man walked out of the trees on the far side of the patio. He held a small backpack in one hand while he strolled casually across the concrete. When he spoke, his voice was soft and level, and it doused the fire in everyone like a bucket of ice water.

'Jean-Marc,' Cobb said calmly, 'you can stand here yelling at my team all day, or we can go inside and get to work. Obviously I'd prefer the latter.'

* * *

Maggie was the first one to follow Cobb into the house and down to the War Room. She wanted to speak to Cobb before the others started bombarding him with questions.

'Mister Cobb,' she said softly as she caught up with him on the stairs that led to the War Room. 'I wanted to apologize for the events in Loulan. If I had known the security guards at the mine would be that aggressive, I would have warned you not to go.'

He smiled at her. 'Relax, Maggie. It wasn't your fault. Even the local guide was surprised by the attention we received. That's one of the reasons that I like to take these rekkys. We get all the bad surprises out of the way early to make it safer for the team when we're in country.'

'So you're not mad at me? Sarah implied you would be furious.'

Cobb laughed as he continued down the stairs. 'Rookie hazing. That's her way of welcoming you to the team.'

Maggie breathed a sigh of relief and followed him into the room below. Cobb nodded at Garcia, who had suddenly 'found' the passwords to the computer system and was getting everything ready for the briefing. Cobb took a seat next to him as Maggie sat across from them. Sarah entered the room next and sat beside Maggie. The two exchanged a quick laugh about the hazing incident, which made Maggie feel even more welcomed.

Somehow McNutt had made it to the stairs before Papineau, and it was clear to the team that he was going slower than he needed to. He even took extra time at the doorway to fumble with his crutch and shoot Sarah a wink before ambling toward the table.

The moment Papineau entered the room, he started speaking. 'Where have you been, Jack?'

'Working,' Cobb answered. 'I take it everyone else has been doing their share of that while I've been gone, right? Or did you spend all of your time at the pool?'

McNutt groaned as he sat down, then gently set his injured leg on the only remaining empty chair, right before Papineau was about to sit in it. He looked up at the Frenchman with a sheepish grin. 'You don't mind, do you? This sucker is starting to itch like

Vietnamese crotch rot. I'm gonna need to get at it . . . unless you're volunteering.'

Papineau's face crumpled with disgust, as if the visual might be enough to make him vomit. He stepped back and waved his hand at the chair as if to say, 'I'll never sit in that chair again.' Then he turned his focus to Cobb, who was staring at him once more.

Cobb sat calmly at the head of the table. The message had been sent. There was no more power struggle. These were his people now. He turned his attention from Papineau and looked at each member of the team, one by one.

They were ready to get back to work.

'Let's hear what you've got,' he said to Maggie.

'The Rustichello document is remarkably similar in content – if not in wording – to the surviving texts. There's a line at the end of the journal that described Lop Nor in China. From that and Rustichello's own theories, we deduced that the Loulan ruins must have been where Polo had hidden something; whether a clue or the treasure, we weren't sure. Unfortunately, the radar images you sent back were all negative.'

Garcia touched a button on his virtual keyboard, and a series of grainy black and white images filled the main video screen. 'I know these won't mean much to you guys, but trust me, what these images show is a bunch of sand and natural rock. Absolutely no treasure.'

'What about the relics that have been removed from the site?' Cobb asked.

Maggie answered. 'They were scattered to different museums and universities, most of which have no online presence. There's a chance the relics were never properly documented and photo-graphed, or – and my money's on this one – the people who did the cataloging are all still in the pre-internet age. If you'd like, I could make some calls to China, but after what happened in Loulan I think it would be best if we didn't announce our interest.'

'Agreed,' McNutt said. 'At least until I'm healthy.'

Cobb nodded. 'Unfortunately, we have to start somewhere. Where are we with the guard's journal?'

'Better news on that front,' Sarah said as a picture of the gallery and a map of Florence appeared on the screen. 'The Uffizi Gallery is no slouch when it comes to security, but I think Hector and I have figured out how to get the manuscript. We just have one small problem . . .'

Cobb stared at her. 'Which is?'

Garcia answered before she could explain. 'We're confident she can acquire the book, but once she's outside we have no idea how to get her out of Florence. The police and museum security will be on her in about thirty seconds after she grabs the book. I've run simulations, and we can't get her past a half-mile away from the gallery before she'll be caught.'

McNutt spoke up. 'Have we considered just buying the book from the gallery? I mean, Papi's got some big pockets. Hell, so do I for that matter. How much is it? I'll put it on my credit card and earn some air miles.'

'We don't want anyone to know we're interested in the journal,' Sarah said. 'And the sale would likely take longer than tracking down all those Loulan relics. Art sales have more red tape than real estate deals.'

'Okay,' McNutt said, looking up at the rooftop of the U-shaped gallery adjacent to the Arno River in Florence. 'Why don't we just meet her out front with a car?'

'We'd be cut off for sure,' Garcia assured him. 'The city has started putting in automated bollards. We wouldn't get very far.'

'How in the hell are a bunch of robot ducks gonna stop us? I'll just shoot the fuckers.'

Garcia shook his head in disbelief. 'I said "bollards", not "mallards", you moron. *Bollards* are metal posts that stick out of the ground.'

McNutt glared at Garcia. 'Call me "moron"' again, and there will be something else buried in the ground – and the only post in sight will be my crutch sticking out of your ass.'

'Anyway,' Sarah said with a laugh, 'the museum is located in a very crowded part of the city. We considered motorcycles, but we're afraid a road pursuit could possibly result in civilian injuries or deaths. That's a risk I'm not willing to take.'

'What about the sewers?' Cobb asked.

'Ewww,' Sarah said. 'Definitely not. I'd smell like shit for a week. Besides, the ancient system underneath the city is flooded with water and debris, so it just isn't safe.'

'What about the river?' McNutt asked, pointing to the big screen.

'What about it?' Sarah countered.

'You're a good swimmer. We can stash some gear, and you can escape underwater.'

'Believe it or not, that's actually been tried before. The security team at the gallery now has scuba equipment on hand in case someone tries it again.'

Cobb stared at the screen, noting some renovations that were being done to the exterior of the museum. 'How current is this picture?'

'It's from earlier today,' Garcia answered.

'And the construction, is it scheduled to end anytime soon?'

'Nope. Not for another month.'

'Good,' Cobb said with a smile. 'Then I have an idea that just might work.'

26

Monday, March 31

Special Agent Rudy Callahan was thrilled to be out of his private dungeon at the Jacob K. Javits Federal Building in New York – even if that meant flying to Florida at roughly the same time that half of the state's population was flying to New York.

Or at least it seemed that way.

Most of the snowbirds left Florida right after baseball spring training, returning to their main homes in Pennsylvania, Michigan, Canada, or wherever else they might have come from. The temperature and the humidity would steadily increase in the next few months until the summer weather became oppressive, and they had no desire to experience it.

But Callahan didn't mind the heat.

After all, he had spent the last several months in Hell.

Thankfully all of that ended with a strategic move on his part. Although he was still on the FBI's shit list after the fiasco in Brighton Beach, he had taken his findings about Jack Cobb straight to the Assistant Director of Counterintelligence in Washington, bypassing several key people in the chain of command in New York: a serious violation of Bureau protocol. He'd kept his partner's name out of it initially, just in case the blowback destroyed his career.

Luckily, the Assistant Director's political aspirations took priority over everything else. She was thrilled with the connection that Callahan had made between the mess in New York and the bombing in Egypt and had praised him for his tenacity and his initiative in bringing the case straight to her. She immediately took Callahan and his partner Jason Koontz off probation, pulled them out of the New York office, and reassigned them to her department in Washington where they would delve deeper into the mysterious former soldier in the video.

No more endless days of torture.

No more agents making fun of their past blunder.

Things got even better when Callahan's request to place Cobb on the Transportation Security Administration's watch list had paid off immediately. In a stroke of luck, Callahan had received a phone call from an agent at the Fort Lauderdale–Hollywood International Airport who remembered seeing a man who looked like Cobb before the alert had posted. The TSA didn't have any clear photos of the man but, based on the way that the suspect avoided the airport's cameras, Callahan was positive that it was Cobb.

Koontz wasn't quite as confident as his partner, but he had been more than willing to join him in Florida. Not only was Callahan responsible for getting them out of the doghouse, but Koontz was also looking forward to some sunshine. He wondered if Cobb was a regular at any of the local beaches where models and strippers worked on their tans.

He would have to interview them all, just to be sure.

Callahan drank his morning coffee at their hotel near the Fort Lauderdale airport while waiting for his partner's arrival. The plan was to track down some leads and interview the TSA agent before he and Koontz headed south to work temporarily out of the Miami field office. He looked around the empty dining room with its fading white paint and wallpaper borders of palm trees and dolphins and couldn't help but smile. The room hadn't seen an overhaul since the early 1990s, but at least he wasn't in the windowless office in New York.

While Callahan ate a bowl of freshly picked fruit salad – the most satisfying breakfast he'd had in months – Koontz came rushing into the dining room. His dress shirt was half buttoned, and his tie was draped around his neck.

'Rudy! We got him,' Koontz shouted.

'Got who?' Callahan asked.

'Cobb! He's at the airport right now.'

Callahan snagged his jacket from the back of his chair and bolted toward the parking lot. He had figured it would take weeks, if not months, to spot Cobb again.

Somehow they had found him in less than a day.

*   *   *

Callahan revved the engine of the Jeep Grand Cherokee as they sped toward the airport while Koontz continued to get dressed in the passenger seat.

'Who spotted him?' Callahan demanded.

'The AFSD called the Miami office—'

'That's what again?'

'Um . . . A Fucking Short Detective,' Koontz guessed as he tucked in his shirt. 'Anyway, he placed the TSA agent who originally spotted Cobb on surveillance duty. You know, monitoring the main airport entrance cameras, the gates, and parking structures. I guess they figured if Cobb returned, that guy might spot him easier than anyone else.'

'Huh,' Callahan grunted. 'I always thought TSA just did the security check and airport employees manned the cameras.'

'Don't be stupid. They're too busy stealing shit from the luggage to do anything else.'

Callahan laughed. 'You're probably right.'

'Anyway, the guy spots Cobb in a van with a few other people. They were headed for the private plane terminal. We don't have permission to ground their plane, but TSA said they would try to stall them for as long as they can.'

'Good. That's good.'

'Still,' Koontz said, 'it would probably help if you drove a little bit faster. Just because you're a senior citizen doesn't mean you have to drive like one.'

'Screw you, Jason.'

'Only if I can be on top.'

Then the two of them laughed.

After months of boredom, they were finally enjoying their jobs again.

When they reached the security gate, Callahan held his badge out the window and the uniformed security officer opened the boom barrier. Callahan sped directly across the tarmac, swerving around a fuel truck and heading straight for a dark gray hangar. He stomped on the brakes in front of the metal building and threw the SUV in park.

Koontz was already leaping out of the vehicle when a man in a TSA windbreaker approached them from the open mouth of the hanger. He was holding a cell phone in his hand.

'You the FBI?' he asked.

'Special Agents Callahan and Koontz,' Callahan said, showing his badge.

'Rob Gillespie, TSA.'

'So . . .' Callahan said, looking around. 'Where is he?'

'Sorry guys, you just missed him.'

'Fuck!' Koontz screamed as he kicked an imaginary dog. 'How is that possible? We just got the fucking call ten minutes ago!'

'Sorry,' Gillespie said as he pointed in the air to a sleek private jet that had left the ground no less than a minute earlier. The plane performed a slow semicircle around the airport before heading north. 'I tried to stop them – I really did – but I got a phone call from my supervisor saying I had to let them go. I think the owner of the jet complained about harassment.'

Callahan took the news in stride. 'Who's the plane registered to?'

'We've got that info for you inside.'

'Thanks,' he said to Gillespie. He knew it was the Bureau's fault, not the TSA agent's. The FBI hadn't sent the order to detain the flight like they should have. He knew how reluctant they were to inconvenience the upper one percent, and the private plane implied wealth.

Koontz took a deep breath and regained his cool. 'Sorry about my outburst. Completely unprofessional on my part.'

'No problem,' Gillespie said. 'Sometimes I'm an asshole, too.'

Callahan smiled. 'Any idea where they were going?'

'Yeah. They were going to Italy.'

*　　*　　*

Much to their chagrin, the paperwork in the office was a dead end. The jet was registered to a shell company based in the Cayman Islands, a territory in the Caribbean Sea that had no income tax, capital gains tax, or corporation tax, and was known for banking policies that attracted criminal organizations and tax-evading millionaires from around the globe. Even with their FBI credentials, Callahan and Koontz would get nowhere with the plane.

Thankfully, the agents had more luck with the surveillance footage.

The last several months of punishment had honed their abilities to spot even the slightest clue, but this time would be much easier. Here they were looking for something specific.

Gillespie cued up the video before giving them some privacy.

Callahan anxiously sat in front of the computer screen while Koontz pulled up a second chair next to the metal desk. Once Koontz was ready, Callahan pressed PLAY.

Filmed from the rafters of the hangar, the overhead video showed a limousine with tinted windows pulling up next to the private jet. Six people got out of the car, and four of them – two men and two women – headed up the steps of the plane without turning toward the camera.

Based on the height of the limo, the agents were able to estimate the height of the passengers. They also took note of their shapes and sizes, hair colors, clothing styles, and anything else that might help them down the line.

Callahan and Koontz watched as the two remaining travelers, both athletic men, walked to the rear of the limo and pulled out several large bags from the spacious trunk before carrying them onto the plane. Neither of them faced the camera, but their profiles could be seen on the screen.

One of them was Jack Cobb.

The other was the sniper from Brighton Beach.

27

Tuesday, April 1
Florence, Italy

Hector Garcia lifted a succulent slice of Neapolitan pizza out of the box and savored the aroma. The team was staying in a small hotel just down the street from one of the best pizzerias in all of Italy, a charming restaurant called La Grotta di Leo on the via della Scala. More importantly, the hotel was just a mile away from the Uffizi Gallery.

They had checked into the hotel the previous night, and now Sarah and Maggie sat on the bed as Garcia took a moment to eat while going over last-minute details. Cobb and McNutt were already out in the city, ready to begin their respective parts of the plan.

The museum sat in the heart of the crowded central district of Florence. The massive building was several stories in height, and the closed end of the U-shaped structure looked out over the scenic Arno River. Housing artwork from Michelangelo, Raphael, Rembrandt, Caravaggio, and Botticelli, the Uffizi was one of the most famous museums in Europe.

Thankfully, the guard's journal hadn't been recognized by historians as having anything to do with Marco Polo; if it had, it would have been a featured attraction. Instead, it was a small part of a 'slice of life' exhibit showcasing random artifacts from thirteenth-century Italy. Since there were no items of considerable value, the collection was displayed on a glass-covered desk the size of a dinner table in one of the hallways between two marble statues.

Most tourists ignored the display completely.

Maggie had cased the gallery earlier in the day, following directions that Sarah had fed to her through an earpiece. Sarah would have preferred to do the legwork herself, but she couldn't risk being spotted on security cameras the day of the heist.

Although photography was strictly forbidden in the museum, Maggie filmed everything with a pair of Garcia's high-tech glasses. She paused briefly in front of the journal itself, hoping to glean information about Polo, but the book was opened to a page that had nothing to do with him. She also pretended to examine the statues across the hallway from the display while slipping a small magnet next to a contact switch at the base of a nearby window. Garcia had given her the device and said it would prevent an alarm, even if the circuit were disrupted.

'Let's go through this one more time,' he said before blowing on the piping hot pizza that was about to ravage the roof of his mouth.

Sarah nodded. 'The plan is ridiculously simple for a museum of this caliber. Their security is relatively lax in the hallway because the most valuable items – the paintings and such – are inside the well-guarded galleries. The floor in the hall has no pressure plates, or lasers, or cages. Just the cameras, which you'll cut right before I go in. Maggie already placed the magnet, so I should be able to break the case, grab the book, slip out the window, and run to the river.'

'And if anything goes wrong . . .' Maggie said.

Sarah finished the thought. 'I go up.'

* * *

Four hours later, just after sunset, Sarah slipped along the crowded alleys toward the Uffizi. She wore a brunette wig and a locally purchased, leopard-spotted coat-and-scarf combination that made her look like any number of Italian women in the area.

She passed some graffiti on an alleyway wall that loosely translated to: *Italy. Go. Fuck. Party.* She smiled at the message, thinking of the drunken locals who were already starting their revelry despite the fact that it was barely dark on a weekday.

That type of chaos would only aid her escape.

Under her wig and scarf, Sarah had an earpiece that allowed her to communicate with the rest of the team. 'Approaching the gallery now.'

'Copy that,' Garcia said as he adjusted her feed.

The museum would be open for an extra two hours to accommodate Dr Maria Pelati, a guest lecturer who would be talking about her recent discoveries in Orvieto, Italy, and Cholula, Mexico. Though her family was very well known in the region, she rarely made local appearances, so the gallery was expecting a huge crowd.

The fortified stone walls of the building gave the appearance of strength, but the outside plaza located between the wings of the building was designed to attract visitors, not scare them away. Each side of the building had terraced steps up to numerous doors and lit windows. Sarah could see that the hallways behind them were no longer packed, but they were still flowing with tourists who would be attending the lecture.

It wasn't the only thing she noticed.

A construction crane being used to restore the terracotta tiles that covered the building's roof had been parked near the closed end of the U-shaped plaza. The broad, bright orange base of the vehicle was surrounded by a six-foot-high chain-link fence that had been hastily erected around it. Two of the sandbags that anchored the fence in place were ripped open and leaking damp sand onto the cobblestones.

On the river side of the building was a fluorescent-yellow debris chute that ran up to the roof. Sarah wondered how long the roof repair had been going on. She mused that if she had needed to get into one of the more heavily guarded exhibits, the construction crane provided a ludicrous amount of exposure to the building's roof. For the time being, she hoped they hadn't increased security on the roof to counter that flaw.

'Ready,' she whispered.

A second later, she heard Cobb's voice. 'I'm good.'

Then McNutt's. 'I'm better.'

Then Maggie's. 'All clear.'

Garcia spoke last. 'Just say the word, and I'll kill the cameras.'

Sarah nodded and stepped inside the museum.

28

Sarah walked through the gallery, pretending to admire the works of art on the walls while making her way to the slice-of-life display in the mostly empty hallway. The entire operation hinged on crackerjack timing, and Garcia was in charge of the clock.

The long wooden table was filled with an assortment of items from the thirteenth century: a few cups and bowls, a nicked sword, a small shield that looked more ornamental than battle-tested, and a swath of fabric from a shirt supposedly worn during that era. The book was there as well, tucked in the back corner of the display like an afterthought – even though it was the most interesting item in the case. Unlike the dishware that looked remarkably similar to modern china, the journal didn't look like a modern book. Instead, a twelve-inch long slat of wood held together long sheets of parchment that had been folded like an accordion. Roughly six inches wide, every fold made up two pages of the codex.

Sarah ignored the table and continued down the hallway toward the gallery where the lecture was about to start. One of the larger rooms in the museum, it displayed mostly Christian artwork, which would be the main focus of Dr Pelati's presentation. In the center of the cavernous gallery, a thick slab of dark mahogany served as a bench for weary patrons. It was currently occupied by a portly Italian man, who looked like he might nod off at any moment.

If he did, they would have to work around him.

Sarah breathed a sigh of relief when he stood and walked to the other side of the room. This cleared a spot for her on the bench. A waiter strolled past with a tray of champagne, but he barely glanced at Sarah, who kept her head down as she looked at her phone. Out of the corner of her eye, she noted one lone security guard by the doorway through which she had entered.

He seemed even less attentive than the waiter.

Sarah put her phone to her ear and pretended to speak into it. In reality, she was talking to Garcia over the comm. 'I'm ready when you are.'

'You're good. I've looped the camera in the gallery.'

Sarah leaned forward and stealthily slipped her hand under the bench. Her fingertips coated with latex, she wasn't the least bit concerned about leaving prints on the small device that she anchored to the wood with double-sided tape. To complete her charade, she casually adjusted the black laces on her shoes before she stood up. She strolled around the room for a few minutes, looking with interest at the paintings on the wall.

No one paid her any mind.

'Device is in place,' she whispered. 'I'm ready to move.'

Garcia acknowledged her comment. 'Okay, people. It's show time. Everyone set your watches on my command. Three . . . two . . . one . . . mark.'

Sarah started the timer on her digital watch. They had planned how long everything would take under perfect circumstances. If things went poorly, they knew how long it would be until the local police arrived.

She took a deep breath and waited for the watch to hit fifteen seconds, then slipped out of the lecture hall, past the bored guard, and into the hallway with the glass display case. At the thirty-second mark, Garcia pressed a button on his laptop.

An instant later, the fun really started.

The high-tech device she had planted underneath the bench emitted an intense burst of ultrasound beyond the range of human hearing. It was the perfect pitch to shatter all of the glass in the lecture hall. The cases didn't explode outward – flying glass would have been too dangerous – they ruptured inward with a frightening crack that startled the nearby patrons.

One person screamed, followed by another, and another.

Before long, everyone was shouting and running.

The display case in the hallway shattered as well. As Sarah walked by, she swept up the book and slid it into a waterproof sack strapped against her side and underneath her long coat. Multiple security guards rushed into the gallery to calm the chaos inside while Sarah blended in with the rush of people surging toward her in the hallway. As expected, stainless steel bars slowly began to descend from the top of the hall's arched entryway to prevent possible thievery and limit damage to other parts of the museum. But in this case, all the bars really did was trap multiple guards inside, just like Sarah had planned.

She knew that a heist in a highly secure facility was practically impossible when it was closed and the guards were on high alert. But something going wrong during an event was more likely to be viewed as an accident or even a prank. There were plenty of disgruntled groups in Italy forever setting off smoke bombs and trash can fires to draw public attention to their causes. It wouldn't be a stretch for the guards to picture such protestors attacking a simple lecture. Sarah hoped to use the panicked crowds and the guards' desire to get everyone out of the building as cover for the theft. With any luck, they wouldn't realize the book was even missing until the following day when they were picking up all the shards of glass.

Then something happened that Sarah didn't expect.

According to her research, a simple fire alarm should have sounded that would direct patrons to the nearest exits, but that's all that should have happened since no paintings had been pulled from the walls. Instead, a hideous piercing noise that sounded like an air-raid warning started blaring. Then the rest of the museum's alarm systems went off inside the gallery. Loud klaxons rang outside the museum, and pre-recorded messages announced in a variety of languages that tourists should step a respectful distance away from the building.

Sarah cursed at the development.

Things were about to get crazy.

*　*　*

Inside the sealed lecture hall, Dr Maria Pelati shook her head in amazement as she took in the scene. She leaned close to her traveling companion, a muscular man with mocha skin, and whispered, 'I can't stand this country. Every time I come here, something bad happens.'

'Quit complaining,' David Jones blurted as he held his hands in the air. 'You know damn well who the guards are gonna blame. That's right – the black guy.'

*　*　*

Outside the south end of the building, Cobb piloted an inflatable Zodiac with an outboard motor up to the quay. A nearby dock was home to a red-and-white pedal boat that could be rented by tourists who wanted to splash around the river, as well as two crew-style rowing boats with seating for eight. Just inland was a twenty-foot-high concrete wall that bordered the road and led to the south wall of the museum.

A few people milled about, looking at the building and wondering what was happening. None of them noticed Cobb as he moored the boat then casually strolled up the road behind the Uffizi.

*　*　*

Sarah moved toward the window where Maggie had disabled the alarm earlier in the day, but it was no longer a viable escape route. She watched as a heavy metal grate descended from recessed housings above the framing, sliding down on greased tracks and silently sealing in place. She glanced down the corridor, hoping to spot another option – with the sirens already wailing throughout the museum, she wasn't worried about security sensors – but the other windows were blocked as well, all the way down the hall.

'Shit,' she cursed as the guests in the hallway went from panicked to frenzied. 'Hector, I'm trapped. The windows are sealed.'

'What do you mean? The device should've worked. It should've prevented the windows' electromagnetic locks from engaging.'

'Maybe so, but bars slid down to cover them before I had a chance to find out.'

'Bars? What bars? There were no bars on the schematics. They have to be new,' Garcia complained as he tried to make sense of things. 'What do they look like?'

'What do they look like?' Sarah snapped at him. 'Holy shit, Hector! I have more important things to worry about!'

'Yeah, dumb question. Sorry about that.' Back at the hotel, he scanned all of the camera feeds from the museum, looking for a way out. 'I guess we'll just have to improvise.'

'*Improvise?*' Cobb nearly choked on the word. 'There's no need to *improvise*. We planned for this possibility. The team is in place. Move to Plan B.'

29

As frantic patrons raced and pushed for the main entrance, Sarah lowered her head and calmly walked in the opposite direction until she reached the nearest stairs. The instant the stairwell door closed behind her, she sprinted upward to the second floor.

She knew she would have to run the length of the building to reach the roof as there was no access on this side of the museum, but she expected an easy jog through an empty corridor. Instead, she emerged from the stairwell to find the hallway in the midst of extensive renovations.

'Shit,' she mumbled.

'Now what?' Garcia asked in her ear.

'They're remodeling a lot more than I thought,' Sarah answered as she pushed through a curtain of plastic sheeting designed to confine the dust to the construction site. She could see piles of flooring tiles and stacks of drywall panels, as well as all the other materials and tools that the job would require. Picking her way through the mess would slow her down, but it wasn't cause for alarm.

That honor fell to the guard chasing after her.

'Stop!' he yelled in Italian from the hallway behind her.

'Double shit,' she cursed as the lone guard rushed at her.

If this had been a solo mission, Sarah would have reacted differently. She would have attacked the man, taking him out with a well-placed kick to the groin before continuing on like nothing had happened. As part of a team, though, she had to rethink her behavior. Everyone else was counting on her to stick to the plan, so she did what she was supposed to do.

She ignored the guard and charged forward.

She darted through the piles of building supplies, moving steadily toward the door at the opposite end of the hall. She could hear the guard give chase behind her. A moment later, his shouts were joined by a pair of new voices.

Instead of one pursuer, she now had three.

In her mind, this was actually a positive development.

She was the fox and they were the hounds.

She wanted all of them to give chase.

'Talk to me,' Cobb said from outside the museum.

'Heading for the roof,' was all she said as she ran under scaffolding and past abandoned cans of paint. The floor was covered with thick drop cloths and a series of wide planks that created an obvious walkway to the back stairs and the roof access.

She heard at least one of the guards trip on something and crash to the floor behind her. The hallway echoed with Italian profanity and the clang of metal on marble.

At the end of the hall, Sarah rushed up the last set of stairs to the welcome sight of an unbarred door. She barreled into it at full speed and the door popped open onto an improvised platform of plywood panels. She skidded to a halt as she tried to regain her bearings.

'Where?' she shouted, knowing the guards were gaining fast.

'Straight ahead,' Cobb replied calmly.

Sarah could see a metal girder dangling from a steel cable attached to the arm of the construction crane she had noticed earlier. She knew Cobb was in the cab of the crane right now, preparing to lift her off the roof the moment her feet hit the girder.

Sarah ran for the beam as the door swung open behind her.

'Stop!' yelled the lead guard.

'Go!' she shouted into her microphone.

The six-foot beam began to spin as Cobb lifted it from the

rooftop. Sarah leaped up and grabbed hold of the rough cable with her hands, her feet scrabbling for footing on the metal beneath. The lights of the surrounding city glinted off the river and reflected back up at her, allowing her to see the braided thread of the cable, but it was still a challenge to keep her grip and firm stance while the beam was spinning.

The beam rose higher and higher into the night as Cobb swung it toward the river. A few seconds more and Sarah would have been suspended alone in the darkness, beyond the reach of the guards. But just as the beam cleared the edge of the roof, the closest of the trio launched himself out into space and tried to grab her. The guard missed her completely but somehow nabbed the edge of the I-beam, which tipped the girder down like an unbalanced scale.

Suddenly, he was hanging on for his life.

Holding the cable from the center of the beam, Sarah realized the poor guy was going to slide off the end and plunge nearly four stories to the pavement below. To stop that from happening, she quickly shifted her weight to the other end of the beam to stabilize it.

Cobb pulled the beam and its two passengers higher, swinging them away from the building and toward the river. Sarah stood with her feet planted on the end of the beam while keeping both hands on the cable to steady herself. At the height of the beam's arc, she could see past the road and over the retaining wall, clear down to the murky green Arno.

As the I-beam swung out well over the river, Sarah caught sight of the black Zodiac that was waiting for her at the water's edge. She was running out of time.

She had to ditch her passenger.

While still holding the cable with both hands, she simply pulled her feet off the beam. Without her counterweight, it tipped suddenly into a near-vertical position. The guard immediately lost his grip and plummeted forty feet into the dark water below. Had it been summer, the plunge would most likely have killed him; but Sarah knew that the spring run-off had swollen the river and made the water deep enough to break the man's fall.

'Are you okay?' Cobb asked as he lowered the beam.

'I'm fine. Just enjoying the ride.'

The beam rocked violently until she used her feet to steady it.

A few seconds later, she was bracing for impact.

Five feet from the ground, she sprang away from the beam and toward the dock. She landed in a full crouch and rolled forward to dissipate the force of her fall. Behind her, the beam and cable smashed into the concrete wall that led up to the gallery. Not because Cobb had lost control – he simply didn't have time for a smooth landing.

'That was fun,' she said with a smile.

But her amusement was short-lived.

A shot suddenly erupted from the gallery, and a tuft of concrete ripped upward from the ground near her feet. A moment later, another shot rang out.

And then another.

And another.

Just as she had hoped, most of the guards were now stuck on the roof. They couldn't follow her over the edge, and they didn't have time to race back down.

'Jesus!' she yelled as she ran for the Zodiac.

'Keep going,' McNutt said softly in her ear. He was perched in a tree across the river, following the action on the roof through the hi-tech scope he had attached to a WWII-era US M1 carbine. It was the only weapon he could find on short notice, but he assured her it was fine, considering the short distance between the museum and his hide.

Sarah heard an echoing boom, followed by an explosion of terra cotta tiles on the roof behind her. The guards screamed in the night as they dove for cover.

McNutt grinned. 'Calm down, Luigi. It was just a warning shot.'

Sarah continued to run. 'Am I clear?'

'For now,' he answered.

The wooden slats of the codex dug into her side as she cleared a low, decorative fence. The bystanders from earlier were nowhere to be found, scared off by the gunfire. The only person in sight was the guard from the beam. He was far downstream, breast-stroking through the murky water for the shore.

She hopped into the inflatable boat, started the motor, and tossed the lines away before pulling away from the dock and speeding toward the nearby Ponte Vecchio.

'I'm at the piazza,' Maggie said.

'I'll be there soon,' Cobb assured her.

Sarah raced the boat west on the algae-covered river. Behind her, the swimming security guard reached the shore. Meanwhile, his comrades from the Uffizi's roof were nowhere to be seen. Most of them were headed back down to the ground level – and a few had decided to sit this one out. Three additional guards from the museum raced out of the building and sprinted down the long walkway to the river's edge.

Thirty feet from the Ponte Vecchio – Florence's famous arched bridge – Sarah hunkered down in the belly of the craft, practically hidden from view. The bollards at both ends of the pedestrian bridge prevented vehicle traffic, so police cars were forced to continue on to the next one, which was several hundred feet down the river.

The black Alfa Romeo with its flashing blue lights raced ahead and turned onto the Ponte Santa Trinità. Two *carabinieri* – military policemen – scrambled out of the car, wearing their traditional black uniforms with red piping. Both men rushed to the edge of the bridge, just in time to see Sarah's boat zoom under the distant Ponte Vecchio.

The *carabinieri* watched as the boat came rushing out from beneath it at a ridiculous speed.

They could see her leopard-spotted coat in the belly of the boat.

She showed no signs of stopping.

So they raised their guns and opened fire.

30

The Ponte Vecchio ('old bridge' in Italian) spans the Arno at its narrowest point. The famous three-arched span is believed to date back to the Roman period and has always had a variety of vendors, stalls, and tables along its length. Once known for its butcher shops, the bridge now features mostly high-end jewelers that cater to tourists.

The 'back shops', as they are called, were added in the seventeenth century and consist of actual stores that were built out past the sides of the bridge to dangle over the river. Metal and wooden struts support their undersides like stanchions on an observation deck.

Hidden in darkness, Sarah clung to one of them.

Moments earlier, while concealed in the bridge's shadows, she had tossed her coat on top of a duffel bag stuffed with newspaper before propelling herself at the bottom of the Ponte Vecchio. The Zodiac had continued at top speed toward the next bridge where the cops had mistaken the duffel bag as their suspect and had opened fire on the coat.

It would take them a few minutes to realize their mistake.

Meanwhile, Sarah grabbed one of the damp beams and started her climb. She pulled on the closest strut with her hands and pushed against the stone foundation with her feet until she reached the bottom of a back shop. There she found a crack and lodged her fingers in it while she adjusted her footing.

A few feet away, she noticed a metal drainpipe held in place by thick metal anchors. She was confident that it could handle her weight. To reach it, she swung her legs back and forth like a gymnast on the uneven bars until she generated enough momentum to launch herself from the crack. She snagged the pipe with one hand, then started her ascent.

Thirty seconds later, she was crouched on the roof of a back shop.

'Halfway there,' she said, slightly out of breath.

'Roger that,' said Cobb as he scrambled into position.

No longer worried about blending in with the crowd at the museum, she tossed her scarf and brunette wig into the river before she pulled her skin-tight black pants from above her knees to below her ankles. Her matte-black bodysuit absorbed light, leaving no trace of reflection. To complete her outfit, she slipped on a pair of black gloves and pulled a hood and blank mask over her head.

It wasn't just black; it was actually *blank*.

No eyes, no nose, and no mouth.

The effect was beyond creepy.

Still sheltered from view by the taller roof that covered the bridge itself, she ran on top of the back shops for forty feet, completely hidden from the oblivious police on the next bridge. But she knew as soon as she ascended to the main roof – which would give her access to the buildings to the south – she would stand out as a silhouette against the well-lit river. Her outfit would help for a while, but she figured someone would eventually spot her.

Sarah climbed the next drainpipe to the main roof before sprinting all the way to the end of the bridge. In the distance she could hear shouting, but she didn't know if she had been seen. She didn't dare take her eyes off the slippery terra cotta tiles under her feet. It was like running on ice. She could do it, but she had to be perfect or she would go flying. Roof tiles shot out from under her feet like flicked marbles, skidding down the slope of the roof and into the river below.

Just before she hit the end of the span, a spotlight from the squad car on the distant bridge illuminated her sprint. The military policemen who had fired at her coat had finally realized that they had been duped, and that didn't sit well with their Italian machismo. Instead of radioing in her position, they tried to hit her with a lucky shot.

Cobb spoke in her ear. 'The police have blocked off the bridge. We have to keep going to get across to you. We'll be there soon.'

'Mmm-hmm,' was all Sarah replied as she grabbed the next drainpipe. This one took her off the roof and up the side of the tallest building on the south end of the bridge.

As she made her way up, she heard a shot.

Five feet away, a tile shattered, the fragments scattering in all directions.

She kept her cool and scrambled over the edge of the roof. The next rooftop was fifteen feet lower than her current position and six feet away. She ran down the slope of the roof and jumped over the gap to the next building. Then it was over the rise of that roof and down a drainpipe on the other side before her feet hit the solid ground of a narrow alleyway.

Dressed in black, she was virtually invisible in the shadows.

After that, she ran as fast as she could, hoping to conceal herself in the maze of alleys between the Ponte Vecchio and the next nearest bridge on the south of the river. She was aiming for the Boboli Gardens, a scenic park filled with sculptures and trees and plenty of places to hide.

She heard the shrill piercing of a hand-held whistle and realized her getaway wouldn't be that clean. Police or Uffizi guards, she didn't know which, had followed her across the Ponte Vecchio and spotted her landing in the alleyway. She didn't have time to look back, but she guessed she was hearing no more than two sets of footsteps chasing her.

'Ummm . . . maybe a distraction?' she said as she ran, turning the corner and opting for Via de' Bardi. She knew she could make better time on the asphalt than on the older cobbled lanes.

'Josh is approaching your position,' Garcia said. He was monitoring the chase from the CCTV cameras in the area. Eighty feet later, Sarah darted right into another alleyway, this one leading toward the gardens.

'They're almost on you,' McNutt said. His voice was soft, as if he was afraid of being overheard. 'On my mark, you leap high like you're an Olympic hurdler. Understand?'

'Yep,' was all she could muster between breaths.

The security guards were less than ten feet behind her now. She was in great shape, but they were actually gaining on her.

Must be soccer players, she thought.

As she approached an alley on her left, she heard McNutt's voice.

'Now!' he blurted.

She leaped like a track star, and as she did she saw McNutt tumbling below her. A slim black case was strapped to his back, and his aluminum crutch went flailing.

The timing couldn't have been more perfect.

To the pursuing guards, the suspect had just knocked over a crippled man, who tumbled to the ground with a shriek of pain. Worse still, they ran headlong into the crash so they had no time or space to avoid him. They collided with him at full speed: arms, legs, and crutch all tangled in a frenzied dance of calamity.

McNutt grunted and groaned but did not speak – words would reveal that he was not Italian. The guards rapidly disentangled themselves, blurting apologies in their native tongue before darting off down the lane. But the damage was done. The suspect's lead was too great now.

Of course, Sarah didn't know that.

After taking one for the team, McNutt decided to have some

fun with her. 'Sarah! It didn't work! They're gaining fast! Oh my God, run faster!'

'What?' she blurted. 'Where are they? I don't see them.'

'Neither do I,' Garcia said as he stared at his CCTV feed.

'Sweet lord, they must have wings. They're actually flying!'

'They're airborne?' Garcia shouted, his voice filled with confused panic. 'How are they airborne?'

McNutt started to laugh. 'I'm just kidding! I got you both. April Fools!'

'April Fools?' Sarah shouted. 'I'm running for my life, and you're pulling a prank?'

'That's the best time to pull one. No way you expected it.'

'I know I didn't,' Garcia said, laughing. 'That was awesome!'

Still smiling, McNutt grabbed his crutch and limped down the alley even though he didn't really need the support anymore. He'd brought it mostly for camouflage. People tended to avert their eyes from injured and disabled people. The crutch made him nearly invisible.

'Josh,' Garcia said. 'End of the alley, turn left.'

A few minutes later, a car slowed next to him. He tossed the crutch and the bag with the rifle into the trunk and slammed it shut. Then he slipped into the back seat next to Sarah, who was wearing a white blouse over her black catsuit. She smiled at him sweetly, and then punched him in the arm as hard as she could.

'That's for messing with me,' she said.

He laughed it off. It was totally worth it.

As the car drove back toward the Ponte Vecchio, they passed the Uffizi security guards, walking dejectedly along the side of the road.

They didn't give the attractive blonde more than a glance.

The brunette they were after had escaped.

31

Thursday, April 3
Hong Kong International Airport
People's Republic of China

The team arrived in China on the private jet after a grueling fifteen-hour trip across Europe and Asia, made two hours longer by a refueling stop in Bahrain. They had all slept in varying amounts on the way over, but none of them felt well rested when Papineau handed their passports to the customs officer. The man barely glanced at the documents before stamping them and handing them back – not that anyone was surprised.

Papineau had connections all over the world.

'What's first?' asked McNutt, who had convinced the team it would be much easier to procure weapons in the smuggler's haven of Hong Kong than mainland China.

'We check into our hotel and try to sleep,' Cobb said. 'Tomorrow we pick up our supplies. Tomorrow night we fly to Beijing. So get some rest tonight.'

Papineau nodded his approval. 'I am relieved to hear you say that. I think we could all do with some time off.'

During their long flight, Maggie had translated the journal that they had acquired from the gallery. The guard's notes painted a detailed picture of his torture sessions with Marco Polo, but nothing in his narrative stood out except for a reference to 'a crumbling barrier that stretched across the land for as far as the eye could see.'

To a layman, the description would seem trivial.

Thankfully, Maggie understood its true importance.

Many of Polo's harshest critics believed his tales of the Far East were fabricated because he never mentioned the Great Wall in any of his writings, but this quote would change everything. Finally, there was evidence that would silence his skeptics forever.

Still, something bothered Maggie about the quote.

If Polo found the Wall to be so impressive, why did he never speak of it again?

Eventually, she came up with a theory on her own.

Maybe the Wall played a vital role in the location of the treasure.

* * *

As expected, Maggie led the group outside to the limousine that Papineau had arranged. Unlike during her two weeks in Florida where she sometimes struggled to fit in with the team dynamic, her confidence was soaring now that she was back on familiar turf.

'Hector, is this your first time in Hong Kong?' she asked.

Garcia nodded. 'I don't travel much. I work best in an air-conditioned room with tons of computing power.'

'Then I'm sure you'll feel right at home while we visit the Great Wall. The hotel in Beijing is world-class.'

Garcia raised his eyebrows in surprise. 'You're going with them? I figured you'd hang back with me. You know, doing the academic thing.'

She shook her head. 'The man we're meeting is an old friend of mine. He'll be much more forthright with his answers if I'm asking the questions.'

As the team climbed into the limo, the driver glanced in the rearview mirror. 'Your destination?'

Papineau answered. 'The Peninsula Hotel, please.'

Garcia's eyes lit up. 'We're staying at the Peninsula?'

'Yes,' Papineau said. 'Why? Is there a problem?'

'No, sir. Great choice,' Garcia said with a smile. Unlike the rest of the group, Garcia knew the Peninsula Hotel and its fleet of Rolls Royce courtesy cars had been featured in *The Man with the Golden Gun*, one of his favorite James Bond films. 'Couldn't be happier.'

'Thank you,' Papineau said warmly. 'I'm glad *someone* appreciates my effort.'

Sarah rolled her eyes and changed the subject. 'Maggie, I don't mean to be nosy, but what were you telling Hector about your friend in Beijing?'

'His name is Dr Chu Shen, and he is a leading authority on the Great Wall of China.'

'And you think he'll be able to shed some light on Polo's travels?' she asked.

Maggie nodded. 'In addition to being an expert on the Great Wall, he's an expert on Chinese history. If anyone can tell us about the connection between Polo and the Wall, it is Professor Chu.'

After that, the ride along the North Lantau Highway was quiet for a while. Each jet-lagged passenger took in the relatively dull sights of the vegetation covering the retaining walls on one side of the road and the scenic mountains of Lantau Island on the other. Occasionally they would catch a glimpse of the sea.

Eventually, McNutt spoke. 'Where are all the skyscrapers?'

Maggie answered. 'They are all on Hong Kong Island. We are on Lantau Island now. We'll cross the Ma Wan channel to the mainland and then swing around south toward Tsim Sha Tsui. You'll see all the buildings then. The view from the hotel is quite amazing.'

McNutt grinned. He was wide awake while Cobb and Garcia were fast asleep. Sarah was nodding off with glazed slits for eyes. 'Say that name again.'

'Which one?'

'Chim Cha Choi. What's that?'

Maggie corrected him. 'Tsim Sha Tsui. It's an area of Kowloon.'

'Cow-loon? Is that where mad-cow disease comes from? If so, I need to stay away from that place. I like a good burger, but I don't get along with farm animals. They sense my hatred, I think. Or maybe they smell burgers on my breath. Whatever the case, no cows for me.'

Maggie smiled at McNutt's rambling and gently patted him on the knee like a Victorian schoolmistress correcting a wayward student. 'Hong Kong is actually a collection of a few places: Hong Kong Island; the peninsula of Kowloon, which points downward toward the island; and an area known as the New Territories. There are also two hundred other islands that fall under the collective name of Hong Kong.'

'So the Peninsula Hotel – that's on Kowloon?' McNutt asked.

'Correct. It is at the very southern tip of the peninsula, hence the name. So your view of the harbor between Kowloon and Hong Kong Island will be impressive.'

'And the Tsim place?'

'The southern portion of the Kowloon peninsula, where the best shopping is located.'

McNutt pulled a small piece of paper from his pocket and read the name he had scribbled earlier. 'And where is . . . Wan Chai? I need to head there, later today.'

'Wan Chai? It's the business district, right across the harbor from the hotel. You can take a ferryboat across the water, if you'd like. What do you need in Wan Chai?'

'Something special . . . just for me.'

The grin on his face told her it was a weapon.

'Would you like me to come with you? I know the area quite well.'

'No thanks,' McNutt said. 'These guys will only deal with me.'

32

Hong Kong Harbor

Designed to look like a Ming Dynasty junk, the triple-masted ship's square, maroon sails billowed in the breeze. Despite its historical appearance, the boat was powered by propellers and filled with the latest technology. Like its owner, the yacht honored the old traditions of Ancient China but embraced the modern world.

Feng He leaned forward in his deck chair and smiled his best smile.

The man across from Feng was an American named Harold Ledner. He was proposing the sale of Mobility, his telecommunications company, to China Mobile, the world's number one telecom, for an exceedingly reasonable price of $130 billion. Although Feng wasn't the actual buyer – China Mobile was – Feng would get the credit in his homeland even though the world media would never hear his name.

That was just how Feng preferred things.

Ledner wanted assurances about a variety of things, none of which Feng actually intended to deliver on. He just had to put on a good show. Drinks, women, the ship's sail – it was all a part of his sales pitch. Yet another attempt to convince a decadent Westerner into giving up something valuable for much less than it was worth.

Feng had dealt with hundreds like him before.

He knew what buttons to push.

The acquisition of Ledner's company would do wonders for Feng in political circles, but unlike some businessmen who focused only on the bottom line, this transaction had little to do with money. Feng's chief goal was securing China for the Chinese. Telecommunications was a booming business, and even though China Mobile had the number one spot, Verizon and AT&T were constantly eyeing China as the new frontier. The way to stop them was simple: Feng would acquire all of the smaller companies – like Ledner's and his closest competitors – then he would use the increased revenue to buy out Verizon. After that, if AT&T didn't get the hint to stay out of China, he would gun for them, too.

Ledner took a sip of his single malt Scotch, savoring the 40-year-old limited edition Bunnahabhain. Feng swirled the similarly colored liquid in his own glass: nothing more than apple juice over ice: the same trick Elvis Presley used to employ.

'Let's get down to brass tacks, Mr Feng. If China Mobile buys out Mobility, it'll put you in a perfect place to take on the competition in America. What are your plans for the US?'

Feng smiled while seething inside.

Why did Americans always assume that everything revolved around their country?

Feng couldn't care less about economic development in America. He only cared about the 1.4 billion people in China. Ledner still thought the whims of the market were dictated by what Americans bought and sold. Instead, it would be the rising Chinese middle and upper classes that would sway the world.

'I have no plans to take on AT&T. They would crush us. The same with Verizon. No, we'll be happy to keep your European clients and our hold on the Asian market.' Feng leaned closer, as if sharing a secret. 'We're actually focusing on Africa. If the sub-Saharan countries ever get their acts together, the market will be huge.'

Ledner laughed. 'You know what they say about fixing Africa. Can't be done — internally or externally.'

'Perhaps. But with money thrown at agriculture and education, instead of pointless NGOs and unstable petty warlords, a company like China Mobile might have a chance.'

'Good luck with that,' Ledner said with a laugh. 'So, no interest in the US?'

Ledner seemed surprised, but Feng knew it was exactly what the man wanted to hear. He was happy to make a fortune selling to China, so long as the Chinese didn't make further inroads into his country.

'None,' Feng lied. 'The competition is too tough. You know how Asians are. We'll sit back and wait until the competition shoots itself in the foot. Then we'll offer a helping hand when AT&T is dying — if it ever comes to that. But we don't want to walk in the door. The American people will gladly buy foreign TVs from Wal-Mart, but they'll never pay a monthly bill to a Chinese telecom.'

Ledner laughed again. 'Truer words, my friend, truer words.'

I am not your friend, you overweight slug, Feng thought, yet he managed to keep the disgust from his face. They hadn't signed the papers yet, but the deal was done.

Just then Lim Bao appeared at Feng's side. While Feng had more athletic ability and raw power than Lim did, the smaller man was stealthier than a cat.

He leaned down and whispered into Feng's ear.

'A situation, sir,' he said in Cantonese. While Ledner might be familiar with the Chinese Mandarin language, it was extremely unlikely he could speak Cantonese, a far more complex one, with eight 'tones' to Mandarin's four.

Feng stood slowly. 'Excuse me, please. I'll just be a moment. Should I send the girl up with something to eat?'

Ledner had been staring at the serving girl all night. His leer consisted of one part lust and one part awe. She was the most beautiful woman that he had ever seen. He would gladly sign away his fortune just to taste her. 'Definitely. She can serve me all night long.'

Feng ignored the remark and followed Lim below deck for a private conversation.

'What is it?' Feng demanded.

'Remember the two foreigners from the Loulan ruins?'

'Of course. The only reason I didn't have Chen killed was because of the sheer range of the sniper's attack. I still don't know how he killed a man from that distance.'

'It took us a while, but we were finally able to recover the hi-res video from the helicopter's camera system. We identified him as a former US Marine. His name is Joshua McNutt.'

Feng stroked his chin in thought. 'An American soldier in Xinjiang. Very interesting indeed. But surely you didn't call me out of the meeting just for that.'

'No, sir,' Lim said. 'You know me better than that. The Marine and the other man were spotted arriving on a private plane in Hong Kong earlier today.'

Feng was stunned. 'They're here?'

Lim nodded.

'Outstanding. I assume our brothers are watching them?'

'They just checked into the Peninsula with another two men and two women.'

'All military?' Feng asked with a hungry gleam in his own eyes.

Lim could tell that his boss was already envisioning how he would punish the foreign intruders. 'No. That's the strange thing, sir. One man is French. A businessman. The others we couldn't identify, although one woman is Chinese.'

Feng wondered about her ethnicity. 'Han?'

'She appears so.'

Feng thought about the information and fell into silence.

'Should we pick them up?' Lim asked.

'No, not yet. Let's see what they're up to first.'

'Of course, sir.'

'One more thing,' Feng said, 'when Ledner is done signing the papers, make sure his trip home meets with some kind of horrible tragedy. His manners are atrocious.'

Lim smiled. 'Perhaps a mugging on his layover in Singapore? That city is getting so dangerous these days.'

Feng nodded. 'Perfect.'

33

The Great Wall stretched for as far as Cobb could see. It marched up and down hills, twisting and turning as it went, giving the impression it could still keep the barbarian hordes out today.

In reality the Mutianyu section of the Wall stretched for only 2.5 kilometers, but it was dotted with twenty-two watchtowers that helped to achieve the illusion of endless security. The hills around it were lush and green, a picture postcard come to life.

But that was where the touristic glory ended.

The day was bitterly cold, with a brutal wind ripping down from the Mongolian steppe to the north. The bite of the frigid air seeped through Cobb's coat. The relative scarcity of tourists on the Wall was explained by the season and the fact that Mutianyu was off the beaten path. Other nearby spots had the expected infrastructure of gift shops and eateries, but not here.

This place was like a ghost town.

McNutt kept an eye on things in the nearly empty parking lot while Cobb and Maggie met Professor Chu Shen up above. He was an extremely short man with a ridiculously long white beard. A lecturer from the International Centre for Chinese Heritage and Archaeology at Peking University, he looked old enough to have actually built the wall.

'Thank you for taking the time to speak with us,' Maggie said.

'It is my pleasure, Ms Liu. It has been quite some time.' The small man strolled across the path on the top of the Wall as if he owned the place. With no one around, Cobb could understand how he felt that way. 'It is also very nice to meet you, Mr Cobb.'

'Likewise, sir.'

'Maggie tells me you are interested in details about the Great Wall. Things that I alone might know.' The man smiled, flashing teeth stained from a lifetime of coffee consumption. 'You have me quite intrigued.'

'If it's okay with you, I'll let Maggie tell the tale. I'd only mess it up.'

The old man nodded and, when he did, his beard flapped in the breeze.

'Professor,' she said, 'we are interested in what you can tell us about the Wall during the Yuan Dynasty.'

The strolling man stopped in his tracks and turned to her, eyebrows raised. 'The Mongol period? Very interesting. It is a time that much of the world no longer cares about – and one that most Chinese would like to forget. What aspect of this period interests you?'

Maggie exchanged a look with Cobb, who nodded his approval.

Then she turned back to Chu and whispered, 'The Venetian.'

Chu's face darkened. 'Ahhh, I see.' He walked down a flight of steps on the Wall's top, heading for the nearest watchtower. 'I come here every week to walk the length of this section, and I've visited all the other sections as well. I've studied this structure my entire life. In all my decades investigating the Great Wall, you are the first person to ask me about Marco Polo.'

Maggie remained silent, fearing they had offended Chu.

The truth was far from it.

Chu smiled. 'I am not a Polo scholar, of course, but I am one of the foremost experts on the Wall. And since the Wall stretches back to the Qin Dynasty and before, I'm naturally well versed in the history of China. I have to be. You see, the Wall *is* China, and China *is* the Wall.'

Cobb remained silent. He knew the man was just getting started.

'This part of the Wall was restored and built in the early Ming Dynasty – 1368 on toward the seventeenth century. That was less than a hundred years after Marco Polo would have passed this way on his journey to meet Kublai Khan. Of course, his narrative is famous for many things in the West, primarily for him being the first Westerner to visit and describe so much of Asia. Although he certainly did the latter, he was hardly the first European to make the journey. Can you tell me about the connection you are seeking between Polo and the Wall?'

Maggie nodded. 'We've come across a few documents that imply he did, in fact, see the Wall during his time in China. What's more, these writings insinuate that the Wall held some special place for him, even though it was mostly ruins by the time of the Tang Dynasty.'

Maggie gave away as much as she could without coming right out and saying they were seeking Polo's treasure. Not that it mattered much. She had known Chu for many years, and she realized that he had probably guessed their true intention as soon as she had mentioned Polo.

The man was as sharp as a scalpel.

'The ruins were featured widely in the poetry of the Tang,' Chu said, and then he abruptly turned to Cobb. '618 to 907 AD.'

Cobb nodded his thanks. As Chu had guessed, Cobb was not familiar with all the various dynastic periods of China's long history.

'The Tang was a memory some four hundred years before Polo arrived, so you can imagine the state of the ruins back then. But there still would have been segments of it standing at that time, circa 1275. As you know, Polo's account is notable for his omission of any mention of the Wall. Many scholars have even posited that Polo couldn't have visited China, all based on that omission. They say any Westerner visiting China would certainly have mentioned the Wall.'

The old man lapsed into silence as they walked along the deserted battlements.

Cobb glanced out through the parapet to the wilderness beyond. 'We were aware of such theories.'

'People always want to challenge antiquity,' Chu said with frustration in his voice. 'The notion that someone like Polo could get so much right, and yet, because of one simple omission, his entire tale is suspect? Ridiculous.'

Chu shook his head before continuing. 'Of course Polo visited China, and all the other places that he mentioned. Back then, there was a scarcity of knowledge about Asia in the West. The level of detail in the book alone suggests he must have visited. No merchant, even one who collected tales from Asian travelers for decades, could have included such detail in his account.'

'I agree,' Maggie said with confidence.

'Besides,' Chu said, 'there are several Chinese sources that confirm his presence as well. After all, the Great Wall was where Marco Polo met the love of his life.'

34

Maggie was stunned by the professor's claim. In all of her years as a tour guide, this was the first time she had heard it mentioned. 'Marco Polo had a woman in China?'

'Not just a woman,' Chu stressed, 'Yangchen was the love of his life.'

He glanced at Cobb and smiled. 'Her name means *the sacred one* – and she certainly was to him. Marco met the young Yangchen, a Chinese girl, on his way into China from the Silk Road. This was way out by the western end of the Wall near Lanzhou.' The man pointed vaguely west, but it was understood he was talking about the other side of China.

'Why have we never heard of this before?' Cobb asked.

'Why indeed, Mr Cobb. Western scholars are so fond of congratulating themselves for their accomplishments and so busy reinforcing their imperialistic viewpoints that they forget there was a "rest of the world" before they discovered it. The written histories in China go back more than thirty-five hundred years. Yet from the Middle Ages onwards, Western scholars interested in Marco Polo – and anything else for that matter – have been content to dig through musty libraries and monasteries in Europe while pretending that the Chinese and the Arabs were so underdeveloped that they couldn't read or write. The truth, of course, is very different. While successive wars and invasions decimated libraries in the Middle East, China's history has been preserved. Unfortunately, there is one major problem with it.'

'And what is that?' Cobb asked.

'There is too bloody much of it,' Chu said with a laugh.

Cobb smiled in understanding.

Compared to China, America was just a baby.

'Too bloody much,' Chu repeated. 'Several thousand years of history recorded by several thousand bureaucrats, who note every little detail that happens in government on the national and local levels. Combine that with folklore, superstition, songs, poetry, and the like, and it quickly gets overwhelming.' The old man stopped walking and turned to face them. 'It's just too much information for any one person to consume in a single lifetime.'

'I don't understand,' Cobb admitted.

'In the not-too-distant past, you had to study everything to be a scholar. But somewhere along the line, people began to specialize – just as I have with my studies of the Wall. But you see, the folly in that is you don't see the big picture. Are you familiar with the story of the blind men describing an elephant? One touches its leg and says it feels like a tree stump. One touches its tail and says it feels like a rope. The last one touches its ear and says it feels like a fan. Eventually the three men come to blows over their wildly different perspectives, and yet none of them are technically wrong. The problem is they can't see the whole animal.'

Cobb was familiar with the parable, but smiled nonetheless.

Chu continued. 'Scholars are like that now. Polo specialists read the early editions of his book, and they argue over silly things like whether or not he came to China. But how many of *them* ever did so? How many of them took the time to track down imperial court records from the time of Kublai Khan to confirm Polo's stories? Maybe a handful. And those that did were expecting Polo's appearance to be likened to the arrival of a foreign king – described with pageantry and grandeur. When they found nothing matching their preconceived Western notions, they returned home and claimed that Polo never set foot in China.'

'But . . .' Cobb said.

'But the truth was Marco was simply a merchant when he arrived; barely a footnote in the eyes of China. He was not the figure that he is today.'

'But *still* a footnote, right? I mean, he *was* mentioned, wasn't he?'

Chu smiled. 'Yes, he was. Many times.'

'In what context?' Maggie asked.

'In many contexts,' Chu assured her, 'though not always by name. To find evidence of him in China, a researcher would have to focus on Polo, *and* the time period, *and* the bureaucracy of the day. I only know about it from reading up on the Wall during that era.'

Maggie pressed the issue. 'What can you tell us about his connection with the Wall? Or this woman?'

'Only that the two were intertwined. Beyond that, I'm afraid the details escape me. I came across Polo several decades ago, but I wasn't particularly interested in him at the time.' He tapped his temple with his index finger. 'Luckily for you, I do remember that the records I was looking at were from the court of Kublai Khan.'

'Any records in particular?' Cobb asked.

'Unfortunately, no. But the time period you are concerned with is fairly small. Less than twenty years. And the other details were mostly dull observations. Ledgers declaring how much grain was being stored for the winter. That sort of thing. I suspect you'll be able to find what you are after – if you can get to the records.'

'If?' Maggie asked.

'The records passed from Peking University to the State Administration for Cultural Heritage sometime in the 1980s. They're not on display at any museums, or I would have heard about it. Most likely they are in storage somewhere.'

'Somewhere? Could you narrow that down for us at all?' Cobb asked.

'I'm afraid not,' the old man said. 'There are hundreds of storage facilities all over China, which is one of the biggest problems facing researchers today. Remember, we are talking about thousands of years of history packed away in boxes and crates. To know which documents are being kept where, you'd have to be a genius.'

'Thankfully,' Cobb said, 'I have one of those on retainer.'

35

Despite the fertile soil of the Pearl River Delta, Panyu is known more for factories than farming. A former suburb of Guangzhou, the expansive urban sprawl has effectively consumed Panyu, folding it into a megalopolis that continues to grow. More than sixty million people reside in the region, making it one of the most densely urbanized areas in the world.

The tightly packed population of the delta was a double-edged sword. Cobb knew that people in large cities often kept to themselves, but he also realized that distinct faces stood out in a crowd. Here, his chiseled American features would stick out like a sore thumb – especially if he visited the same spot twice.

In his mind, a rekky was simply too risky.

'Lorenzo, are you *sure* this is the right place?' McNutt asked as he peered down at the warehouse from a hillside overlooking the industrial neighborhood.

Garcia grinned from the safety of his suite at the Westin a few miles away. McNutt had yet to call the computer whiz by his proper name, and he had all but given up correcting him. At this point, the teasing actually made Garcia feel more accepted.

'I'm sure,' Garcia replied.

Garcia had found the facility, and a brief description of the artifacts housed inside, by hacking into the database of the State Administration for Cultural Heritage. The SACH, as it was known, was a subsidiary of the Ministry of Culture responsible for the management of China's museums, including the cataloging of the country's historical relics.

'Well, I'm *pretty* sure,' Garcia continued. 'The site didn't list the exact info we were looking for, but Maggie agreed that it's our best target.'

'Pretty sure?' McNutt repeated. 'Now he tells us.'

McNutt wasn't complaining. He had covered countless incursions, and as far as vantage points were concerned the warehouse was nearly perfect. It had been built at the base of one of the few protected nature parks that remained in the city and from his hiding place on the wooded slope McNutt had full view of the warehouse, the surrounding neighborhood, and the highway that encircled both. He could protect the team's entrance and their escape, just as long as they stayed within the two-thousand-yard range of his custom-made EDM Arms Windrunner: the present he had purchased for himself during their visit to Hong Kong.

Cobb interrupted them. 'Josh, are you in position?'

'Affirmative,' McNutt replied.

They were using a sophisticated communications set that utilized tiny buds placed in the inner-ear canal and a thin film with an embedded microphone that had been attached to each team member's molars. Garcia had tweaked the software to filter out both mouth noises and background hiss, and he had boosted the level of encryption to such degree that every hacker at the NSA would grow old and die before cracking it – or so he claimed. As a result, Cobb felt comfortable using their real names on the operation.

'And ladies,' Cobb said, encouraging Sarah and Maggie to finish the radio check, 'how are you doing tonight?'

'Reading you loud and clear,' Sarah said.

'Me, too,' Maggie added.

'Last chance for "no-go",' Cobb instructed. It was military-speak to let them know that any of them could call off the mission if they felt that something was wrong. All they had to do was speak up.

The radio channel was silent.

'We're go on Sarah's lead,' Cobb said.

'Approaching now,' Sarah replied.

McNutt dropped the binoculars and pressed the scope of his rifle to his face. He didn't have eyes on Cobb, but he took that as a good sign. He reasoned that if he couldn't see Cobb, it was unlikely anyone else could either.

Sarah and Maggie drove to the warehouse in an inconspicuous Mercedes A-class hatchback that Papineau had chosen because of its ubiquity throughout the region. They parked the Mercedes behind a small outbuilding across the street from the main warehouse and immediately exited the vehicle. The pair walked purposefully toward the building, their confident strides giving off an air that they belonged there. Even their attire failed to attract attention.

The women were both dressed in the new dark uniforms Sarah had put together. The fabric was designed to absorb light, but the material could pass as eveningwear instead of tactical clothing. Despite their chic appearance, the trousers concealed several hidden pockets that held first aid and survival gear. Their tops had been constructed with built-in holsters for their 9 mm handguns and sheaths for their ceramic, T-handled knives. The outfits were complemented with all-purpose boots that also fit the style of well-moneyed tourists.

'Going in,' Sarah said.

McNutt watched as she made short work of the front door's lock. A moment later, the women disappeared into the warehouse.

He turned his attention to the facility grounds, then continued outward to the surrounding buildings. It was his job to warn the others if anyone approached. He switched his scope to night-vision mode, hoping to illuminate the shadows. When he still saw nothing, he activated the scope's infrared capabilities and looked for the heat signatures of anyone who might be lurking nearby.

He spotted Cobb for the first time that night.

The team leader was resting against the wall of a bus stop canopy roughly one hundred feet from the warehouse entrance, on the other side of the street. He held a map of Guangdong in one hand, keeping the other hand free for the Glock that McNutt knew he had strapped under his shirt. If anyone approached the warehouse from his direction, it was Cobb's job to run interference.

McNutt watched as Cobb subtly adjusted the bud in his ear.

'How we doing in there?' Cobb asked.

'This place is pathetic,' Sarah answered. 'I opened the lock on the front door in two seconds, and that's the only security we've found. No cameras. No guards. Nothing. Maggie could have kicked in the door and done this job without me. The place is all boxes on shelves with Chinese characters and numbers. You know that last scene in *Raiders of the Lost Ark*? It's like that. The shelves run on forever.'

'Stay cautious,' Cobb warned. 'You never know what's around the next corner. Until you find the manifest, stay radio silent—'

'I found the manifest,' Maggie interrupted.

Garcia chuckled at the timing. 'Can you translate it?'

This time, Garcia didn't have access to a live feed of what they were seeing. That would've required an active laptop to stream the Bluetooth connection from the cameras in their eyewear, and Garcia didn't want to risk leaving a computer in the car unattended.

'Yes,' Maggie answered. 'It's all numbered descriptions. Just give me a few minutes.'

She fell silent as she flipped through the pages of the printed ledger, which were filled with cramped Chinese characters etched in a careful scrawl.

The book was over five hundred pages thick.

She had her work cut out for her.

*   *   *

After nearly ten minutes of silence, Papineau's patience was wearing thin. Like Garcia, he had been listening from the hotel suite, but even in his posh surroundings he was growing uncomfortable.

'Anything?' he asked.

Maggie finally filled them in. 'We're looking for two boxes. I've got the identification numbers; we just need to find them.'

'Easier said than done,' Sarah added.

Cobb knew she was talking about the seemingly endless rows of shelving that she had described earlier. 'How much time?'

'No way to say for sure,' she admitted. 'Ten minutes? Maybe fifteen?'

Cobb watched as a patrol car cruised down the road toward him. It slowed slightly as it neared the outbuilding, then came to a stop as the men inside noticed the parked Mercedes.

'Sorry ladies,' Cobb said, 'but you don't have that much time.'

36

Sarah and Maggie moved quickly through the warehouse, checking the markers for each row as they ran. Fortunately, what the facility lacked in modernization was more than made up for in organization. Each section of the space had been assigned a numeric label, and each box within that space had been further identified with a unique stamp. Every object was perfectly catalogued, with a place for everything and everything in its place.

Sarah wondered if the artifacts themselves had been tagged with barcodes.

She would find out soon enough.

Maggie suddenly stopped dead in her tracks. 'There,' she said as she pointed at a pair of boxes collecting dust on a shelf. 'That's what we're after.'

'Jack, did you copy?' Sarah asked. 'Maggie found the boxes.'

'How big are they?' Cobb asked.

Sarah stepped forward and took note of the size. 'A little bigger than a shoebox. Why?'

Cobb didn't give her an answer.

*   *   *

Cobb watched as the two men from the patrol car stepped out of their vehicle and walked cautiously toward the Mercedes. 'Hector, talk to me.'

'I'm not getting any radio chatter from the police band,' Garcia said in his ear. 'Looks like a genuine patrol. They're not responding to a call, at least. I can't understand what they're saying on the radio, but the voices are all calm and bored.'

'Stand down, Josh,' Cobb instructed. 'Let me see if I can work this out.' Cobb didn't want anyone to get shot just for doing his job, but he knew that McNutt wouldn't hesitate to drop the unexpected visitors if it meant protecting the team.

'Copy that, chief. But I'm here if you need me.'

Cobb knew his sniper was zeroed in, the crosshairs of his scope tracking the patrolmen's every move. He stepped away from the bus stop and waved his map like a flag. 'Hey there! Hey, officers!' Cobb called out with a phony drunken slur to his voice. He ambled across the road toward the warehouse, staggering like a drunkard.

The men abandoned the Mercedes and headed straight for him.

'Jack just bought you some extra time,' McNutt informed the women.

'How?' Sarah wondered.

McNutt watched closely. 'I think he's pretending to be me.'

Cobb spread the map on the ground in the middle of the street, luring the patrolmen in for a closer look. 'You're just who I was looking for. Can you give a guy directions? I think there's something wrong with my map. It's in *Chinese*.'

He wobbled as he spoke, then flailed his arms wildly as he pretended to catch his balance. In actuality, he used the move to lift his shirt and expose the grip of the semi-automatic pistol he had holstered in the rear of his waistband.

Just in case.

*   *   *

Sarah peeled open the seal on the first box with one of the tools in her burglary arsenal. Some girls never left home without lip gloss; Sarah rarely went anywhere without lock picks and a pocket knife. She lifted the lid and peeked inside.

'Loose-leaf documents, a couple of bound notebooks, and a book,' she announced. She opened the second box and reported its contents as well. 'More of the same.'

Maggie rifled through the collection. 'I can't translate all of this right now. Even if I hurried, I might not catch what we're looking for. I need to be thorough.'

'Just take it,' Papineau ordered. 'Take all of it.'

Sarah didn't need to be told twice. From one of her pockets she withdrew a small folded piece of fabric. With a snap of her wrist, the compact square unfurled into a pouch. After dumping the entire contents of the first box into the bag, she threw her arms through the handles and swung the satchel over her shoulders like a backpack.

When she was done, she pulled an identical bag from Maggie's pocket and emptied the second box. In less than a minute, the haul was secured and the boxes resealed. The missing layer of dust was the only evidence that anyone had tampered with the collection.

'Done and done,' Sarah announced. 'We're on the move.'

*   *   *

As the men from the patrol car drew closer, they started shouting in Cantonese.

'Sorry, fellas,' Cobb replied, 'I have no idea what you're saying. I'm just trying to find my way back to Guangzee . . . Guangzow? . . . Gesundheit?'

Maggie translated their response in his ear. 'They said, "What are you doing here? Show us your papers. You have no right to be here."'

'Chief,' McNutt said, 'this party's about to get crowded. I have a car approaching from the north. He'll be on you in twenty . . . nineteen . . . eighteen.'

Cobb could see the headlights of the new arrival in the distance.

The patrolmen saw it, too. The first turned to the second and quickly argued his point.

Maggie translated. '"Shit! They're already here. Let's just kill him and get this over with. We'll get all the credit."'

Cobb pulled his weapon before Maggie had even finished.

It was kill or be killed.

Cobb squeezed his trigger twice, burying a hollow-point round into each of the men's foreheads. The backs of their skulls burst open like overripe cantaloupe. As their bodies hit the ground, their weapons clattered harmlessly to the pavement.

McNutt saw everything through his scope. 'Nice shootin', chief. By the way, those are Czech machine pistols. Definitely not military or police issue. Not around here.'

'They weren't cops,' Cobb agreed as he took out his phone and snapped their pictures for possible identification. Then he turned his gaze toward the car that was bearing down on him. 'And neither are they. A little help here, Josh?'

'Already on it,' McNutt replied as he steadied his aim. 'Three . . . two . . . one . . .'

A second later the .50 caliber slug from McNutt's rifle tore through the engine of the approaching sedan as if the car was made of Jell-O. Smoke and steam billowed from under the hood as the driver jerked the steering wheel and slammed on the brakes. The car came to a stop a mere twenty feet from where Cobb stood, but none of the goons inside leaped out to confront him.

'Wrong move, fellas,' McNutt said with a grin. Moving objects at least made things interesting – though not much of a challenge to a marksman with McNutt's skill – but a stationary target was child's play. The next time he fired, the gas tank ruptured and the sedan exploded in a magnificent shower of flames.

'Sorry, chief, didn't mean to singe your whiskers.'

Cobb had bigger concerns than a few burned hairs.

'More from the west,' Cobb shouted as he spotted two more cars barreling in his direction. 'Sarah, get Maggie out of there. Evac plan *beta*. Josh, light 'em up!'

'With pleasure,' McNutt announced.

Cobb broke for the Mercedes as McNutt opened fire. The modification the sniper had purchased for his rifle allowed for semi-automatic fire; he didn't need to chamber each round; all he needed to do was tap the trigger.

It didn't just make things easier, it made things fun.

Cobb started the engine with his spare key and threw the gear into DRIVE as thunder boomed from the hillside. McNutt squeezed off round after round, each roar from his rifle leaving his enemy more damaged than the last. But it wasn't enough. He had already destroyed the first car and disabled the next two, but three more vehicles suddenly appeared.

'More party-crashers headed your way,' McNutt informed the others. 'And I've only got two shots left. I was never strong in math, but—'

'I can handle the last one,' Cobb assured him. 'Just make your shots count.'

'Copy that.'

Cobb floored the accelerator and sped toward the rear of the warehouse.

* * *

Maggie glanced in all directions, but the only exits she saw were the oversized garage doors of the loading bays. She was sure that Sarah couldn't pick her way through it because there were no locks to be picked. Nor were there mechanical overrides. The doors were opened electronically or not at all.

'Where are we going?' Maggie asked.

Sarah ran toward the garage doors. 'Through there.'

Maggie didn't understand. 'How do we raise it?'

'Who said anything about raising it?' Sarah replied. As she spoke, she reached into her suit and produced a small aerosol bottle that had been labeled as designer perfume.

It wasn't.

'Stand back,' Sarah warned. 'You really don't want to inhale this stuff.'

She drew a three-foot arch near the door's base.

Maggie watched with fascination as the colorless liquid that Sarah sprayed on the metal panel began to bubble. By the time Sarah stood back to admire her artwork, the fluid had transformed into a thick arc of foam.

Sarah pressed a breath-mint-sized receiver into the goo and stood back.

'Open sesame,' she said as she pressed the detonator.

Maggie instinctively covered her ears, but there was no explosion. Instead, the receiver ignited like a white-hot ember. In a flash of sparks and smoke the foam incinerated, cutting cleanly through the metal door as it burned. When the fire was out, all that remained was a hole.

'Careful,' Sarah said. 'The edges are still hot. Like, *really* hot.'

Given what she had just seen, Maggie had no trouble believing that the rim of their escape tunnel was still too hot to touch.

*   *   *

Cobb arrived at the delivery zone just as Sarah crawled through the improvised exit. Maggie stood beside her, clutching her own pack as if it held the meaning of life.

'We good?' Cobb asked.

'We're great,' Sarah answered as she and Maggie jumped into the car.

'Josh?' Cobb said.

'The highway,' McNutt replied in his ear.

Given the location of the warehouse, the team had multiple escape routes. They could work their way through the residential neighborhoods to the east to the subway line that serviced this section of Panyu. Or they could head south to the crisscrossing waterways of the delta. But their best option – the one that McNutt was recommending – was north on the adjacent highway. If they could get to the thoroughfare, they would have a straight shot toward the relative safety of Guangzhou.

'Can we make it?' Cobb asked.

'Yes,' McNutt answered. 'Go to Plan D.'

Cobb turned to Maggie as he gunned the engine. 'You better buckle up.'

As the Mercedes bounced up the road toward the highway, Maggie hunkered low in her seat. When Cobb cranked the wheel, the centrifugal force pinned her against the side of the car. Tires squealed and a horn blared from behind as the last remaining sedan gave chase.

'What's Plan D?' Maggie asked. 'I only heard about A and B.'

'D stands for "demolition",' Sarah explained. 'That means Josh gets to blow some shit up.'

Cobb pushed the pedal to the floor, trying to put some distance between his team and their pursuers. *Why aren't they shooting at us? Why do they need us alive?*

Then the real reason came to him.

They can't risk damaging what we took.

'Hey, chief,' McNutt said, 'see the construction barrels?'

Cobb saw a row of bright yellow barrels just ahead of him, lining each side of the road. 'Affirmative. I see them.'

'Yeah, whatever you do, *don't* run into them. Seriously, that would be . . . not good.'

Cobb understood the message. 'Everyone, hang on.'

As he drove past the barrels, Cobb braced for the fireworks.

McNutt laughed in his ear. 'Boom.'

No sooner had the word left his mouth than a huge fireball erupted behind the Mercedes. The charges he had concealed in the plastic drums not only flipped the approaching sedan, they destroyed the road entirely. The asphalt that the team had driven on only moments before was now a smoldering crater in the earth.

The shockwave shattered the rear window of the Mercedes as it sped off into the distance. Through Maggie's screams of confusion and Sarah's shouts of excitement, Cobb could still make out the chuckling of his sniper over the comms.

'Is everyone okay?' Garcia shouted.

He knew better than to press for updates throughout the chaos, but the explosion had sounded like an atomic blast. For all he knew, he was listening to the death knell of his dying teammates.

'You're clear,' McNutt said to Cobb. 'No one on your six. Actually, *nothing* on your six. See you at the rendezvous.'

'Thanks, Josh. See you soon.' Cobb turned his attention to Garcia. 'Yes, Hector, we're fine. Tell Papi we're coming home.'

Cobb pulled onto the highway as real police cars, legitimate cruisers this time, raced past them in the opposite direction, sirens blaring and lights flashing.

'And the package?' Papi asked impatiently. 'Do you have it?'

Cobb glanced at the backpack on Sarah's lap. 'Yeah, we've got it.'

Maggie held her satchel with both hands. 'I hope Polo ends up being worth it. We might have just started World War III.'

37

The team abandoned their beat-up Mercedes at the edge of downtown Guangzhou and walked a few blocks through the alleys before Papineau pulled up alongside them in a limo. They all piled in, and he took them back to the Westin hotel in silence. Cobb had instructed each of them to remain quiet until they reached their suite, which had been swept for listening devices.

Once safely inside the room, all hell broke loose.

'Well, that was a clusterfuck of epic proportions,' McNutt said. 'Someone please tell me there's treasure in those bags. Not descriptions of treasure, but *actual* treasure.'

Maggie shook her head. 'It will take some time to—'

'The treasure can wait,' Cobb growled, anger flushing his cheeks. 'I want to know who the hell that was back there. That wasn't a fluke, people. That was an *ambush*. Those men came prepared for us. They knew we would be there.'

In the limo, Cobb had considered the possibility that the attack at the warehouse was related to the security men from Loulan who had tenaciously followed him and McNutt on the rekky, but he had quickly rejected the notion. Besides the prize that Cobb's team was after, the dead zone in Xinjiang had no connections with the warehouse in Guangzhou.

Garcia was sitting at a desk, typing away. 'I'm already looking into it, but I haven't found much yet. The men who attacked you were clearly not cops, but the real police are investigating the incident now. The bombs threw the whole thing into chaos.'

'Didn't have a choice,' McNutt said with a shrug. 'No way they escape without it.'

Cobb glared at Papineau. 'What about you, Jean-Marc? Is there any chance these guys found us through you? Maybe they were upset about a business deal of yours gone bad?'

Papineau gave the question some thought. 'I haven't done any deals in China in over a year. It has to be something else.'

'Even if this did trace back to Jean-Marc,' Maggie added, 'how could they have even known we would be arriving in Guangzhou? We'd only gotten into town a few hours earlier.'

'That's what I was wondering,' Sarah said. 'No way anyone gets an ambush together that quickly. They weren't following us. They were *ahead* of us.'

'Which means somebody tipped them off,' Cobb stated.

Sarah shook her head. 'I didn't talk to any contacts about extraction from Guangzhou – there were just too many conventional ways out of the city with trains, boats, and cars. Plus we weren't looking to move a haul this time; just the books. So the leak didn't come from my end.'

McNutt chimed in. 'I met a contact in Hong Kong to collect weapons, but there's no way those guys were involved. I've known a few of them for years. They're unsavory types, I'll grant you that, but there's no reason they'd want to ambush us. They get a lot of business from referrals. Something like this would be bad for business. So it wasn't me.'

Cobb turned to Garcia. 'Hector?'

'I don't have any contacts in this part of the world. And there wasn't even a computer network for me to hack at the site. Everything was pre-Y2K. Paper records and filing cabinets. I listened in on the police band, but that was it. The rest of the time I was waiting for something to do.'

Cobb glanced at Maggie but said nothing.

'I contacted no one,' she assured him, 'and Professor Chu didn't know where we were headed after our meeting. Obviously I know many people in the area – both in Hong Kong and Guangzhou – but I saw no one I recognized. I just assumed this was something from one of the team's previous missions. Revenge, perhaps? These men were quite determined.'

McNutt nodded. 'You can say that again. They sent in a lot of support to take us out. Did you get a visual on your guys, Jack?'

'Both Chinese. I had no reason to suspect them until the second car arrived, and the two men started arguing. Maggie's translation saved my life. No doubt about it.'

Maggie smiled with pride.

'So where does that leave us?' Papineau asked.

'With an unknown enemy hunting us,' Cobb said. 'But at least we know they're out there now. We need to be extra careful wherever we go. We have to assume they know our faces. We need to get out of the area, and we need to do so very carefully.'

Sarah stared at him. 'Do you think they're after the treasure – or just us?'

'That's the million-dollar question,' Cobb admitted.

'*Five-million*, actually,' McNutt added.

Cobb nodded his acknowledgment. 'For the time being, I'm only sure about two things. If they're not after the Polo treasure, they will be once they find out about it.'

'What's the other thing?' Papineau asked.

'They won't be getting it.'

* * *

The team started to pack their gear immediately and were out of the hotel before dawn. They boarded a battered commercial fishing boat and headed down the river to Hong Kong.

When the boat pulled into the familiar docks in Victoria Harbor, the team didn't head toward a limo or a fancy hotel. They walked off in different directions, per Cobb's instructions, before making their way to their accommodations.

They separately checked into budget guesthouse rooms at the infamous Chunking Mansions, a block of small, gray apartments renowned as a hotbed of backpacker activity. None of the team contacted any of the others, and they all had removed their communications gear and dropped it in the river on the way into Hong Kong.

They had ditched every weapon as well, retaining only their first aid and survival kits, which could easily be explained as backpacker gear. As an extra precaution, the documents from the warehouse were divvied up between team members.

At a predetermined time, they each wandered out of their rooms. Some of them had checked in for just a single night, while McNutt had requested three. None of them intended to spend an evening in Hong Kong, though. They returned separately to the docks and boarded the hydrofoil to the gambling city of Macau. They ignored each other on the boat and continued to do so once they had arrived.

They headed separately to the airport via taxis, but they all wound up on the same Japan Airlines flight to Tokyo. Although they each had connecting flights to different destinations, they reconvened in the terminal and exited the airport together, heading to the Imperial Hotel.

Only after showering and changing their clothes did they meet up in Papineau's suite.

It was time to plan their next move.

38

Lim Bao had been at the warehouse for several hours, trying to figure out what had gone wrong. What should have been an ambush had turned into a bloodbath.

And his team was on the losing side.

Despite the presence of his men, the foreigners had infiltrated the warehouse, pulled down two boxes from the storage shelves, emptied the contents, then put the two boxes back on the shelves. If not for footprints on the dusty floor, Lim wouldn't have known even that much. According to the ledger, the boxes contained records of the Great Wall of China during the Mongol era.

Lim had no idea why the Westerners wanted the ancient records, and neither had the old professor from Peking University. The man had been quite forthcoming when questioned – especially when his grandchildren had been threatened. The Fists had informed Lim that the Westerners would be searching for records from the Mongol era pertaining to the Wall, but the old man had been unable to shed any light on what specific questions the group hoped to answer.

Given the Fists' connections in China, it hadn't taken long to figure out which warehouse the foreigners would be visiting. Unfortunately, business in Hong Kong had kept Lim from personally supervising the ambush.

Now he had no choice but to visit Panyu himself.

He needed to know why his men had failed.

Local law enforcement was not a problem for Lim. No one questioned him or even asked to see his identification. They'd simply given him a cup of coffee and asked if he needed anything, then they had left him alone at the scene. They knew who he represented, and that was enough.

They dared not interfere with the Fists' investigation.

McNutt had destroyed all of their vehicles, but he hadn't killed every man. Those who had survived the assault had removed the bodies of their deceased brothers before the police had arrived. Having cleaned the scene of evidence, they had provided Lim with a detailed account of the incident. Feng was dealing with them and their failures while Lim examined the site.

He knew what had happened.

It was his job to figure out why.

When he was certain nothing else had been disturbed besides the boxes, he left the warehouse and asked a uniformed officer to take him to the hillside where the sniper had been perched. He didn't expect to learn much over there, but if Feng questioned him he wanted to be able to respond that he'd been thorough.

An hour later he phoned Feng, who was out of breath when he answered the call. In the background, Lim could hear a noise that sounded like a whimper.

'Yes?' Feng said.

'Sir, I've examined the site. They were after something specific, and it appears they found it. Two boxes of records were removed. And as the professor told us, those records concerned the Wall.'

'Anything special about them?'

'They are normal governmental records from the Mongol period. Information about the Wall's restoration efforts, information about payments and taxes. Ordinary things. Unfortunately the records had yet to be scanned, so we don't know the exact details of what they contained.'

'Very interesting. First the Loulan ruins, and now this . . .'

Lim could tell when his boss was thinking aloud, so he didn't respond.

'The Loulan ruins were from when again?'

'Some estimates say as early as 1800 BCE, sir.'

'Goodness,' Feng said. 'Eighteen hundred years before the current era.'

Lim noted his boss's use of 'current era' instead of 'Christian era' with pleasure. Even though Lim wasn't a believer in Jesus, at times he still found himself using Christian terminology to describe things. The long reign of the Christian church was so very embedded in modern language. Feng, however, had eliminated all Christian references from his vocabulary.

'Which part of the Mongol era are the missing records from?' Feng asked.

'The last quarter of the thirteenth century,' Lim answered.

'That's three thousand years apart! What is the connection between them?'

'I'm not sure, sir. It will take some researching, but we'll figure out what the foreigners are after.'

'You better, Lim. They have killed several of our people and made us look like fools. We will *not* let that stand. I want you on this issue full time now. Find out who they are, and find out what they want. Bring them all to me – dead or alive. *Preferably in pain.*'

*   *   *

Five hours later Lim was back in Hong Kong, rushing through the lobby of the hotel where he and Feng lived. Only now he was heading to the basement to find his leader. He'd heard that Feng was still downstairs after all this time. He pitied the men who had botched the job in Guangzhou and hoped never to find himself on the receiving end of Feng's wrath.

Lim had spent the duration of his train ride searching the web for information on Loulan, the Great Wall, and the reign of the Mongols. By the time he had arrived at his destination, he had put together a theory. He still didn't know everything, but he was certain he had enough to convince Feng.

Lim had the elevator to himself. The bell chimed and the doors opened on the concrete space of the empty parking level. Lim always liked that this level was closed off for the Fists. He made his way diagonally across from the elevator toward the small office in the corner. It was the same place where his leader had chopped off the Australian's hand.

Lim entered the office to find Feng seated at the desk. He was covered from head to toe in blood, his eyes wide open and staring at nothing. If Lim hadn't seen the man's chest rising and falling, he would have thought he was dead. The guards that were typically around on this level were nowhere to be seen – which meant they hadn't been able to stomach the afternoon's festivities. Or Feng had sent them away. Or the leader's rage had overwhelmed him completely, and he had killed them as well.

Lim knew each scenario was just as likely as the others.

'Sir?' he asked gently.

Feng stirred out of his trance and glanced at Lim.

'Can I get you anything, sir?'

As if finally registering where he was and what he looked like, Feng shook his head. The scent in the room was one of slaughter, but Lim had smelled worse.

'I've done some research, sir. I might have an answer.'

A hungry light appeared in Feng's eyes. One that still needed to be fed. 'Already? Well done, Lim. What have you learned?'

'Because of the drastically different time periods, I started looking into people who might have passed through Loulan during the Mongol era. Armies. Emperors. Explorers. I started thinking outside the box while trying to connect the two locations, and I realized that only one well-known traveler was in that region during that particular timeframe.'

Feng caught on instantly. 'You don't mean the Venetian?'

'I called some historians and a few other experts in Asia who specialize in the Mongols. I also called a professor in Oxford. They all had the same thing to say: there's been a rash of recent inquiries into all things related to Marco Polo. These are people who are not used to having outside interest in their work, but in the last month they have been contacted by the Ulster Archives and a Chinese woman who claimed to be studying Polo for a graduate thesis.'

'The Han woman?'

'My thoughts, sir.'

'So Marco Polo connects Loulan with the Great Wall somehow, and these Americans . . .' Feng's voice trailed off.

Lim waited. He preferred Feng to make the connection for himself.

Finally, Feng smiled. 'They are searching for Marco Polo's fabled lost treasure!'

Lim nodded but said nothing.

Feng stood, excited. 'We need to find them at once.'

'Yes, sir.'

'But do not intervene. Let them solve the mystery. Once the treasure is found, it goes to Beijing – where most of it undoubtedly originated.'

'Yes, sir.'

'Forget what I said about dead or alive. As soon as that treasure is located, I want you to bring them to me.'

Lim didn't understand. 'Sir?'

Feng grinned like a wolf. 'I want to kill them myself.'

39

Tuesday, April 8
Imperial Hotel
Tokyo, Japan

After a day of rest, the pressure the team had felt in Guangzhou had eased considerably.

Garcia was waiting outside the fitness center after Cobb's early morning workout. Garcia wore blue jeans, paired with a T-shirt with an image of a TIE fighter from *Star Wars* on it. Cobb wore black shorts and a gray T-shirt soaked with sweat. One of the hotel's white towels was wrapped around his neck, soaking up the perspiration that dripped from his head.

'Been meaning to tell you, I love how you fixed Josh's wound,' Garcia said. 'That was good thinking with the solar goop. Last night I trickle-charged my laptop on his leg.'

Cobb stared at him. 'You guys are consenting adults. What you do in the privacy of your room is none of my business.'

Garcia blushed. 'What? No, wait, you misunderstood me! I charged my *computer* laptop in his hole . . . In his *leg*. The *hole* in his *leg* . . . Oh my God, this is ridiculous.'

Cobb smiled. 'Hector. Relax. I knew what you meant. I was kidding.'

'Me, too! I was kidding about his hole. I swear I didn't touch it.'

Cobb let that one slide. 'Why are you here?'

'The photo,' Garcia said as he held up his tablet. 'I still can't believe you took a photo of the fake cops after you shot them. That took a lot of nerve.'

'I wanted to have something on them.'

'Well, I struck out on the first guy,' Garcia said as he pointed at one of the dead men. 'But the other guy was named Wu Bai. He used to be a low-level criminal.'

'What kind of criminal?'

Garcia accessed a second photo. It was a grainy picture in a Chinese newspaper of a shooting at a restaurant. There were several bodies on the floor amidst upturned tables and chairs.

'He grew up in Shanghai and joined a local gang called the Strengthened Dragons, or something to that effect. They mostly dabbled in petty crimes until the shooting at this restaurant over two years ago. Rumor has it that he was the main gunman, but he was never charged. After that, I can't find anything on him until he turned up at the warehouse.'

'Shanghai's a thousand miles from Panyu. That's too damn far for a local gang.'

'I know,' Garcia said. 'Unfortunately, that's all I have. Again, as I said last night after the others had left, if we involve Maggie in this, we might get places faster.'

'I don't want to do that,' Cobb whispered. 'I trust you more, and she's got her own work to do with all those documents that we acquired from the warehouse. For now, I want you to work on this gangster lead alone. And whatever you do, don't let Jean-Marc know about it.'

'You still think the leak came from us?' Garcia asked.

'It's likely – even if one of us didn't realize it. For all I know, it could have been me. The only other option is they were watching us since we got to Hong Kong. If that's the case, then they were definitely connected to the rekky in Loulan.'

Cobb thought for a moment as he wiped the sweat from his

face. 'If you can't find anything else on Wu Bai, see what you can uncover about the people killed at the restaurant. Maybe the Dragons had a rival gang. If so, maybe we can contact them for information about Wu Bai.'

'You want to talk to a gang?'

'Not particularly, but I'm willing to if it points us toward the people Wu Bai was working for at the warehouse.'

Garcia nodded. 'You got it.'

'Also, start digging into the mining operation in Xinjiang. Find out who owns it and who the security people were that chased us. Basically, get everything you can. They might not be connected to the attack at the warehouse, but if they are, we need to know about it.'

Garcia nodded and took his tablet to breakfast.

Meanwhile, Cobb headed for the elevator to go back to his room.

Sarah emerged seemingly from nowhere and sidled next to him. 'Nicely handled.'

'I'm not sure what you mean,' Cobb replied. He took a gulp from the bottle of Fiji water that he had been given in the exercise room.

'You know exactly what I mean,' she said as the elevator arrived.

They stepped into the empty car together.

The doors closed before Cobb spoke again.

'You overheard the assignment I gave Hector.'

'You said it yourself: you're the best qualified person to lead this team – and I continually see why. I told you Hector wanted to be more involved in our plans, and you found a way to involve him deeper. Not only that, you *showed* him we trust him completely instead of simply telling him that his stint as a spy for Papi has been forgiven.'

'Maybe,' Cobb said. 'Or maybe you're giving me too much credit, and I just gave him an assignment to keep things going. We're nowhere yet. We still don't have a location for the treasure, and until Maggie tells us otherwise we're running out of leads.'

'We know a few things, though,' Sarah said. 'Polo was definitely in China. He did see the Wall. And there was a girl involved. That's a lot more than we had a week ago. Hopefully, Maggie will be able to point us in a specific direction with the new documents.'

The elevator opened on Cobb's floor, and they both walked out.

He wondered if she realized this wasn't her floor.

Either way, she kept talking.

'There's certainly more waiting on this mission than I'm used to, but we're making progress. Now all we have to do is figure out who's hunting us.'

'That would be nice.'

When they reached the door to his room, Cobb unlocked it with his plastic keycard.

She walked in first, still talking. 'Where are we with that other matter?'

'What other matter?' he asked as he closed the door.

'Have you found anything on Papi yet?'

Cobb stepped deeper into the room, past the mini-bar and the closet, and stood adjacent to the bathroom door. 'I've got someone looking into things. So far all I know is that Jean-Marc met with someone in California. Our bigger concern right now is this group that tried to kill us. I'm pretty sure they're not connected with Papi or his mysterious partner.'

Sarah turned casually, glancing out the window at the greenery of Hibiya Park, which sprawled out just below them. Farther north, she could see the Imperial Palace, the main residence of the Emperor of Japan, in the Chiyoda section of the city.

'Do you want me to reach out to some of my contacts? Maybe a bloodhound like Seymour Duggan could get a fix on these people?' she asked.

'No thanks. I've got it covered.' Cobb took off his soaking wet T-shirt and flung it to the bathroom floor. It landed with a noticeable splat.

Sarah turned at the sound. When she saw him shirtless – his muscles coated in sweat – she couldn't help but stare. 'Yeah, well . . . you don't look covered to me.'

'Sorry. The shirt needed to go.'

'Um . . . why?' she said, blushing.

Cobb suddenly remembered how uncomfortable she had been when they had needed to shed their clothes on Brighton Beach to disguise themselves as normal beachgoers during their first mission. He silently chastised himself for not waiting until she had left the room.

'I need to take a shower,' he said as straightforwardly as he could manage. He hoped she didn't see his embarrassment, and that the comment would set her at ease.

'Oh,' she stammered. 'Of course. I'll, uh, I'll go check on Maggie.'

'Great,' he said, sliding into the doorway of the bathroom so she could pass behind him.

Sarah left without saying another word.

40

Later in the day, they all gathered in Papineau's room for another briefing.

They all wore variations on their 'uniforms', the specialized outfits Sarah had designed with the first aid kits and survival gear tucked into various pockets. Cobb had told everyone to be prepared to leave the hotel at a moment's notice, so they had dressed accordingly.

To avoid looking like a team, they all wore shirts of different colors. McNutt wore a gray T-shirt with an Indian motorcycle logo. Papineau selected a beige safari shirt with buttons, long sleeves, and multiple pockets. Maggie wore a colorful blouse that helped her blend in with the locals. Sarah opted for the black, long sleeve jacket that came with the pants. Meanwhile, Garcia's shirt, which looked one wash away from completely falling apart, had HASBRO emblazoned across the chest.

Dressed in a black T-shirt, Cobb started the meeting. 'Okay Maggie, what did you find in the documents? Any mentions of Polo?'

'I haven't had time to read all of the records yet. They were written with an ancient flair that has been tough to decipher. That said, Marco Polo *is* mentioned – but not by name.'

'That's a relief,' McNutt said while sprawled on Papi's bed. 'It would have sucked if those books were just full of egg roll recipes.'

Maggie glanced at him. 'Joshua . . .'

He immediately sat up straight against the headboard. 'Sorry, ma'am.'

Sarah stared in awe, envious of Maggie's way with him. 'I'm not sure how you were able to train him, but can you teach me?'

Cobb ignored the comment. 'If Polo isn't named, how do you know it's him?'

Maggie answered. 'He is referred to as *bakgwei*, which means "white ghost". There couldn't have been that many Caucasians in the area at the time. As I told you yesterday, most of what was recorded in those ledgers was a long list of boring facts scribbled by government underlings – and absolutely nothing about egg rolls.'

McNutt lowered his head in shame.

She continued. 'So when something out of the ordinary came along, it was usually written about in great detail. In this case, a Caucasian man carrying a *paiza* and acting as an emissary of Kublai Khan? That's certainly going to be mentioned.'

'Maggie,' McNutt said, 'if I can't joke about egg rolls, you can't joke about pizza.'

Maggie shook her head. 'Not pizza, Josh. He was carrying a *paiza*.'

'What's that?' Sarah asked before McNutt could.

'A *paiza* – or a *gerege* in Mongolian – was a foot-long, three-inch-wide golden tablet. It was engraved with a message that read: "By the strength of the eternal Heaven, holy be the Khan's name. Let him that pays him not reverence be killed."'

She glanced around the room to emphasize her point. 'This tablet was essentially a passport, a foreign ambassador's ID, and an American Express Black Card all rolled into one. It told everyone in the empire that they were to assist Polo on his mission, or they would be put to death. That meant free food, free lodging, free women, free soldiers . . . whatever he desired.'

'I have something like that in *World of Warcraft*. It's awesome!' Garcia bragged.

Everyone in the room just stared at him.

He quickly got the point and pulled up an artist's rendering of Polo's tablet. Gold in color, it had a number of etchings at the top and two columns of Chinese characters running vertically down the middle. With a few keystrokes, the image appeared on the flat-screen TV that was mounted on the wall.

'What was his mission?' Cobb asked.

'It wasn't described – most likely because it was confidential. He did fondly mention the Loulan Kingdom and asked several questions about that area, but it wasn't clear whether he was heading there after he left.'

'And where was this?' Papineau asked.

'It was in the town of Lanzhou in Gansu province,' Maggie answered.

A few seconds later, a map of modern-day China appeared on the TV. A red dot indicating Lanzhou was blinking in the middle of the landmass.

Maggie glanced at the map and shook her head. 'I'm afraid this map is a little misleading. Remember, most of what is western China today was not a part of China then. At the time, Lanzhou was one of the last outposts of civilization and a gateway toward the frontier of the west.'

'Sorry,' Garcia said as he typed furiously. A moment later, a neon-green outline of Ancient China was superimposed over the modern map. 'This was China during Polo's time.'

Maggie smiled. 'Thank you, Hector.'

'Is that important?' Papineau wondered.

'I think so,' she said. 'I'm reading between the lines a lot, but I think by the time Marco traveled to Lanzhou, the three Polos were already planning to leave China.'

'What makes you think that?' Cobb asked.

'Intuition, really. Things said, things left unsaid. It's the way Polo is described by the government scribes. It seems that after a while he had become accustomed to the privilege of the golden tablet. Some of Marco's actions . . . it's hard to put into words.'

Maggie, still finding her footing, paused to gather her thoughts.

Sarah found her indecision troubling. 'Is it possible that you're seeing things that aren't actually there? I'm not trying to accuse you of anything, but I know from our previous missions that treasure has a way of messing with your head. Trust me, all of us have been there. You start making up crazy theories to fit the facts, all in hopes of finding the pot of gold.'

Sarah glanced at Cobb, who subtly shook his head.

Now wasn't the time to add more pressure.

Maggie considered the question for an uncomfortable moment while the others remained silent. 'Yes, I guess it is possible. Remember, I'm giving my opinion here. We don't have a clear roadmap to follow, so all we're left with are my impressions and interpretation of events. That said, I have a possible location after my reading – but all I have to back it up is a hunch.'

'I'll be honest,' Sarah said, 'I'm happier putting my faith in your hunch than on all the guesses that the rest of us could come up with. As far as I'm concerned, you're the expert.'

Cobb smiled warmly at Sarah.

It was the right thing to say, whether she meant it or not.

Maggie beamed. 'Thank you, Sarah. I appreciate your confidence in me. Unfortunately, the area that I'm thinking of is one of the most politically turbulent areas in Asia. We can get in, but we are sure to face several issues with security.'

Papineau opened a bottle of water and poured some into a glass.

He didn't like the sound of her initial warning.

She continued. 'Polo mentioned – and the scribes recorded – many of the travels he undertook as a diplomat for the Khan. He traveled far and wide across China and the neighboring kingdoms. He claimed he was always impressed by the people and the cultures he encountered, and the scribes recorded his enthusiasm. He is recognized as being very progressive for the time, keeping an open mind about the unusual sights and practices he encountered. Still, by this point in his journey, I feel Polo was evaluating potential hiding places for the wealth he had accumulated. Of all the places Polo mentioned in Lanzhou, he seemed most impressed with the people he found in the region we call Xizang today. Besides Taiwan, it's the biggest cauldron of raw feelings and political animosity in all of China.'

'And where is Xizang?' Cobb asked.

Garcia's fingers were a blur on his laptop. As soon as Maggie mentioned the name, he had started looking for a map of the region to put on the TV. But his efforts screeched to a halt when he realized which part of China she was talking about it.

'Oh crap,' he said as all eyes turned to him.

'What's wrong?' Cobb demanded.

'Xizang is the Chinese name for Tibet.'

41

Papineau stood quietly and opened the window for some fresh air. The sounds of Tokyo drifted up into the room as a chaotic but subdued din. It was raining outside, but the balcony from the room above kept any water from coming into the suite.

'What's the problem with Tibet anyway?' McNutt asked. 'Monks, yaks, mountains. I saw a documentary once. Buddhist people. What's not to like?'

'Tibet is a political hot potato,' Maggie said. 'It's now firmly a part of China, but it used to be a separate country. The whole region that used to be independent Tibet is the size of Alaska and Texas combined. That would make it the world's tenth largest nation. In 1951, Chinese communist forces invaded the then-sovereign region and annexed it, permanently.'

'Why?' Sarah asked. 'I was always led to believe that China didn't like to expand because of its culture.'

'That is correct,' Maggie replied. 'Throughout history, most Chinese believed that China was the center of the world, and everywhere else was the frontier, populated by barbarians.'

'Then why did China even invade Tibet?'

'The reason is as basic as you can get. They did it for water.'

'Water?' Sarah blurted.

Garcia looked up from his computer. 'Holy crap.'

Maggie smiled. 'Yes, Hector. Tell them how much.'

'Tibet is the source of fresh water for forty-seven percent of the world's population,' he said, reading from the screen of the laptop.

'That's correct,' Maggie said. 'When you have that much of a natural resource in the hands of a neighbor *and* you can justify your taking it by saying that you were simply retrieving what was once yours, you don't ask for permission. You just move in.'

Cobb shook his head. 'That's not all, though.'

'Unfortunately, no,' Maggie said. 'The Dalai Lama, the spiritual leader of Tibet, was just a boy when China invaded in 1951. He fled the country in '59 and has been living in exile in India ever since. The communists were incensed that he escaped. They set about persecuting the Buddhist leaders, and they eventually installed their own puppet as religious leader. Worst of all, they began a secret ethnic genocide, moving Han people into Tibet in order to displace and breed out the ethnic Tibetan population.'

McNutt sat up. 'Seriously?'

Maggie's face was grave. 'Two-hundred thousand people died in the atomic bombings at Hiroshima and Nagasaki. But close to a million Tibetans have died since China invaded. Of course, as a Chinese woman, I learned none of these things – even after the advent of the Internet – until I first traveled abroad. The region is one of the most oppressed in the world. Chinese troops have shut down ninety-nine percent of the monasteries around Tibet. Regardless of whoever attacked us in Guangzhou, we'll also have to face the People's Liberation Army in the capital city of Lhasa; especially around the Potala Palace. That's the former home of the Dalai Lama and a symbol of the Buddhist faith in Tibet.'

'Great,' McNutt muttered. 'Can't wait.'

'And what exactly are we looking for there?' Sarah asked.

Maggie shrugged. 'Unfortunately, this is where the conjecture begins. Professor Chu told us about a young woman Polo had met and fallen in love with. Her name was Yangchen, and she was a local girl who was assigned to Polo as a tour guide. He wanted to see the remnants of the Great Wall north of Lanzhou, and she was the one who led him. At that time, the Wall had fallen into total disrepair. Most of what was standing was in ruins. It wouldn't be until a hundred years later when serious reconstruction began.'

'What do the records say about Polo?' Sarah wondered. 'I'll bet a relationship between a "white ghost" and a local girl didn't go over too well.'

'Quite correct,' Maggie said. 'Many locals were incensed, and a few of the kinder folks tried to gently explain to Polo that their relationship would not be welcomed anywhere in China. But according to the scribes, he was determined to win over her family. By the end of his stay in the region, he was heading to Lhasa with Yangchen as his guide.'

'Were they going to the palace?' Cobb asked.

'Definitely not. The Potala Palace wasn't built yet. However, there was a different temple on the same spot, and the area was still run by the monasteries of the region. If they made it to Lhasa, the monks would have mentioned Polo in their records. And if those records survived, they would be at the Potala today. At least, I think that's where we'd find them. Again, a lot of this is guesswork.'

'It doesn't matter,' Cobb admitted. 'We could sit here for a month debating whether anyone kept records at the Potala, or whether they've turned to dust over the centuries. We won't know for sure unless we go there.'

Papineau cleared his throat. 'Won't going to Tibet open us up to further attacks – especially since we don't know who is after us?'

'Maybe. But we're not going to find the treasure in Tokyo.'

'Still,' Papineau argued, 'if they could track us from Hong Kong to Guangzhou, isn't it possible they will know of our arrival in Lhasa? It's imperative that we keep a low profile. I'm sure I don't need to elaborate on why a team of treasure hunters blowing up another city might be cause for alarm. Another incident like Alexandria would be very bad indeed.'

'First of all,' McNutt argued, 'we were the targets in Alexandria, so don't blame us for that. Secondly, the bomb in Panyu was barely a firecracker. It blew up one car, not an entire city.'

'What about Brighton Beach?'

McNutt smiled. 'Forgot about that one. Yeah, that was fun.'

Papineau rolled his eyes. 'Anyway, if we can avoid blowing up any more of China . . .'

'First things first,' Cobb said. 'If it's okay with you, I'd like to take the Gulfstream from Japan. I'm hoping we can get in and out of Tibet before anyone notices us.'

'No problem,' Papineau said.

Cobb looked at Garcia. 'Hector, if the monks did keep records, I'm assuming they won't be digitized. But don't let that stop you. Dig around and see what you can find. I want to know what you know the minute we touch down in Tibet.'

Garcia just nodded and tapped at his screen.

'Josh,' Cobb said, 'can you get us armed in Lhasa?'

'It'll be tougher than Hong Kong,' McNutt admitted. 'It's off the beaten path of the traditional smuggling routes. Plus, when you factor in the political upheaval in the area and combine that with the essentially peaceful Buddhists, the pickings will be slim. Even with Maggie's translation skills, I might only be able to get us some Chinese hand-me-downs.'

'It'll do,' Cobb said, as he headed for the door. 'But try to get something that goes boom, too. Just to be on the safe side.'

McNutt grinned. 'Whatever you say, chief.'

42

Corinthia Palace Hotel & Spa
Attard, Malta

Seymour Duggan sensed it was time to run.

He hadn't heard from any of his colleagues in almost two weeks. That wasn't just odd, it was downright disturbing. There were certainly days that went by without a source checking in, but a week was suspicious. And two was upsetting. John Sylvester and Jerry Westbrook were trusted operatives, yet neither had reached out to him since the end of March.

Warning bells sounded in Duggan's mind.

If it had been just one man, he wouldn't have been so concerned. Covert sleuthing was a cutthroat business, and he wasn't the only player in the game. Competitors had lured away associates of his on more than one occasion, the promise of shorter hours and larger paychecks too good to refuse. He was used to losing a person here and there; it came with the territory.

But when every agent on a case went dark, it usually meant one thing.

The hunted had become the hunter.

At times like this, he could either hunker down or flee.

Duggan had chosen the latter.

Any doubts he had about his choice had vanished the moment he heard the hotel's fire alarm. The sirens wailing in his ears only exacerbated the anxious buzzing in his head, reinforcing the decision to keep moving. He reasoned that the hotel's evacuation might slow his escape, but it would also afford him some cover if his pursuers already knew his location. If they were waiting for him, this might be his only opportunity to sneak past.

To Duggan, it was a stroke of good luck.

He knew it was now or never.

Duggan double-checked his pockets. His most important items – his phone, his money, and a selection of fake passports – were always on his person in a zipped inner compartment sewn into his coat. Satisfied that everything was in place, he grabbed his 'go bag', a stylish leather backpack that held his computer and a few days' worth of clothing, and bolted for the door.

Under normal circumstances he would have taken the time to carefully pack all of his belongings and wipe down the suite before he exited the hotel. He would have taken every precaution, leaving nothing that could be traced back to his real identity. But at the moment he feared that every second mattered. He needed to get ahead of whomever was coming for him.

Besides, he was convinced that they already knew his name.

He swung the backpack over his shoulders as he stepped into the third-floor hallway. Guests shuffled toward the exits at the opposite ends of the floor, guided by a bellman who continually shouted directions above the din. Even in the dead of night, the mood of the crowd was more curious than panicked, but it would still serve Duggan's needs. He quickly waded into the flow of humanity, trying to hide himself in the confusion.

As he reached the stairwell near the elevators, his confidence grew. The pace was slow, but steady, and he was surrounded on all sides by tourists with the same goal in mind: to get out of the building as safely as possible. Then he felt someone sidle up next to him.

Not just close, *too close*.

It was followed by the unmistakable pressure of a blade against the spine of his lower back.

'Seymour,' the pale man said in a hushed tone, 'if you scream or look at my face, you'll never walk again. One push, and you're paralyzed for life.'

For a fleeting moment Duggan considered challenging the man's pledge. He imagined that if he could only separate himself by a foot, he could move clear of the man's thrust and escape injury. He could also yell for help, and he reasoned the good Samaritans surrounding him would pummel his assailant before he could cause any harm.

Unfortunately, it wasn't meant to be.

The man was close enough that Duggan could suddenly feel the outline of his attacker's revolver pressing up against him. Duggan knew that he might be able to avoid the knife, but there was no way he could dodge a bullet.

'What do you want?' Duggan asked submissively.

'Not here,' the man replied. 'Keep walking.'

Duggan nodded. 'Fine. Just don't hurt anyone.'

Before they reached the lobby, the man shoved Duggan out a back door that led to the manicured grounds surrounding the scenic swimming pool. Duggan was ordered to sit on a blue lounge chair while the assailant hovered behind him, close enough to strike but allowing enough separation to dispel any suspicion from passersby.

For his own safety, Duggan kept his eyes focused on the water in front of him. He had no interest in looking at the man, much less studying his features. If he couldn't identify his attacker, there was still a chance he'd make it through the night alive.

'Answer my questions,' the man said, 'and I promise that I will walk away. Understood?'

Duggan nodded. 'Yes. I understand.'

'Good. Now, who hired you?'

Given the disappearances of Sylvester and Westbrook, Duggan knew which case the man was referring to. 'He is US military. Special Forces. Works with a covert unit. Well-built. Cropped hair. You know the type. Not to be trifled with.'

It was a calculated deception on Duggan's part. He hoped the mention of the US military would spook his attacker. Facing off against a civilian was one thing, but taking on the inexhaustible resources of the US armed forces was a different proposition altogether.

With any luck, Duggan hoped the implied threat would get him off the hook.

'What do you know?' the man demanded.

Duggan knew that lying wouldn't work. Not this time. He had learned a lot during his days working with the CIA, experiences he would not soon forget. He had seen evil, and he had come to know its traits. He knew that the man holding him hostage would not tolerate dishonesty.

'I know that Jean-Marc Papineau does not work alone. He is only the puppet; there is someone else pulling the strings. Whoever he is, he protects himself well. Much better than most. We know he lives on the West Coast, and we presume he has unlimited wealth – he has to, given the way he insulates himself. But that's as far as we got.'

'*We?* Who is *we?*'

'My associates,' Duggan answered. 'One in—'

'California. Another in Florida. Yes, we've already met.'

Duggan gulped hard. Any lingering doubts that this man had killed his colleagues instantly evaporated. The ghoul had traveled more than six thousand miles just to finish what he had started. Despite his predicament, guilt suddenly washed over Duggan. He felt responsible for their deaths. They were good men who were only doing what he had asked them to do.

'The soldier doesn't know?'

Duggan shook his head emphatically. 'I haven't given him my report yet. He's been off the grid on some mission. I haven't had the chance.'

'And you won't,' the man growled as he shoved Duggan from behind.

The push was so unexpected, Duggan tumbled off the lounge-chair and fell face-first onto the hard ground. The tan tile scraped his nose and knocked the breath from his lungs, but it was a hell of a lot better than a knife in his spine. Duggan stayed there for a moment, not knowing what was going to happen next.

A second turned to two and then it became five.

After ten full seconds, Duggan glanced back and realized no one was there.

The assailant had walked away, just as he had promised.

Relieved and exhausted, Duggan rolled over and stared at the dark sky above him. He didn't know why he had been allowed to live, but he was thankful nevertheless. The pounding in his chest slowly subsided, the thumping of his heart growing quieter.

A second later, it was replaced by a steady beeping from his backpack.

In his last moment of life, Duggan was overcome by a sense of clarity. Even without looking, he knew exactly what had happened. In the confusion on the stairwell, he hadn't felt the assassin slip a hand inside his pack. In the chair by the pool, he hadn't noticed the extra pound of Semtex, or C-4, or whatever plastic explosive his killer had chosen to burden him with.

He had spent his life noticing the details that others overlooked.

Yet he had missed the one thing that could have saved him.

The charge erupted like a volcano, only instead of lava and ash, blood and bone spewed into the air like grotesque fireworks. The parts of Duggan's torso that weren't vaporized in the blast rained back down, showering the three-foot crater with globs of charred skin and chunks of viscera that turned an eerie shade of red. Though his skull was shattered and his face torn to shreds, his legs still twitched despite their lack of a body. His suspenders and bow tie were nowhere to be seen, replaced by carnage and crimson in all directions.

A few guests who had exited the back door by mistake quickly scattered, some even running inside the possibly burning hotel in retreat from the explosion. Those who were brave enough to investigate the blast quickly regretted their actions. The site was a horror show of barbecued flesh. The smell alone was enough to turn even the most iron of stomachs.

Somewhere in the distance, the assassin moved in the shadows.

He pulled his ball cap low to hide his hairless features.

Then he smiled at a job well done.

43

Feng watched from his bedroom window as the sun slowly set on the harbor below. Soon the glowing orb would dip below the horizon of Lantau Island to the west, and the glittering skyscrapers of Hong Kong would light the city for the next ten hours.

Although Feng's true prowess lay in the business world, he did actually believe whole-heartedly in the stated mission of the Fists. For too many centuries the rest of the world had taken China for granted: intruding on Chinese territory, claiming Chinese property, and imposing their values and ideologies on the Chinese way of life.

The Yihequan Movement of 1898 – the Boxer Rebellion, as it was called in the West – was not the starting point of the Brotherhood of the Righteous and Harmonious Fists. It was merely the Fists' most well-known public event. The Fists had existed for centuries prior to the uprising, and their stated goal had always been to hold back the forces of industry and imperialism that constantly threatened the empire.

In simpler terms, to keep China for the Chinese.

It really wasn't until the 1980s that leaders of the organization began to realize the value of capitalism in achieving their goals. Money could move mountains. Mountains of money could move the world. Feng had thrown himself into the world of finance with the ultimate goal of freeing China from foreign oppression. He understood that most saw China, and particularly its communist government, as the problem. But he saw things with a different perspective. It was all well and good for the US and other Western countries to decry China for humanitarian abuses, but to do so while ignoring their own history of slavery and more recent atrocities like the treatment of prisoners in Guantanamo was downright laughable.

They were hypocrites, the lot of them.

They were happy to criticize China when the Chinese government wouldn't give them favorable trading status, and yet they were more than willing to send mercenaries in business suits to rape China's natural resources and to exploit its best asset – its people – while converting them into mindless consumers in order to keep Western commerce rolling along.

The thought sickened Feng.

So much so he decided to beat them at their own game.

At first, China would manufacture and sell products to Western companies, whose executives all had eyes on short-term profits. These fat cats didn't care about what would make their companies profitable in ten years, only what would earn them their bonuses this quarter.

And that would be their downfall.

Feng instead chose to focus on twenty years down the road. The shortsighted executives would be long gone, but he would still be around, buying shares here and shares there until he had accumulated so many shares that he would actually own their companies.

Of course, no one in the West was going to buy all of their products from China if they thought the Chinese were getting rich from it. But they were all too happy to shell out cash for products made in China – as long as the perception was that the companies were American.

They would be, but in name alone.

No one would know that he owned the Western companies, and by the time the tree-hugging, petition-signing rabble rousers figured it out, the general populace wouldn't care, provided he kept making the products that filled their lives with empty joy.

After that, he could move on to the next phase of his plan.

Americans have long discussed a wall to separate the US from Mexico, but Feng would actually have a wall to keep the world out of his homeland. In twenty years he would own most of the largest global companies. In thirty he would shut down the Chinese government and declare himself the new emperor of China. In forty, he would complete the Great Wall of China – and it would stretch all the way around his nation. It would be a symbol to the world: we don't need you, we don't want you, and you'll stay away . . . or else.

By then strife in American politics and the widening gulf between rich and poor would have caused at least two rebellions – or so the projections told him. Order would crumble, and their military might would wither. China already possessed enough battle-ready satellites to make any nuclear attacks from the US moot.

The great Eagle would finally be declawed.

Russia's Bear was in hibernation, perhaps for good.

All that would remain was China, and a new age of the Dragon.

The funny thing was that no one saw it coming. People talked about China as a rising economic giant and a potentially thorny political power, but no one grasped the truth. Most Chinese were culturally indoctrinated to believe that China was superior to everything and everywhere else. Feng laughed when he read articles speculating on Chinese expansion.

It would never happen.

We're happy right where we are.

We just want you bastards out.

The lights of the city twinkled brightly now, the sun having set in a spray of purple and pink across the sky like a Jackson Pollock painting.

Lim Bao rushed into the room, his face full of trepidation. Feng knew the man was incredibly devoted to the Fists' ideals. He was easy to read. He had news, but it wouldn't be good.

'Tell me, brother,' Feng encouraged him.

Lim bowed his head. 'We have news of the foreigners. They were foolish enough to return to China. This time they flew into Beijing. After refueling, they continued on toward Lhasa.'

'Lhasa?' Feng blurted. 'What are they doing now?'

'They're still in the air. They won't land for another hour.'

'What about our customs agents? I thought we had men at all the major airports looking for these people.'

'Yes, brother. An agent at the airport in Beijing just phoned me.'

'Now? After they've already continued on?'

'I'm afraid so. But our people to the west are being proactive. I've already sent a group ahead.' Lim presented this information – a small accomplishment, but a vital one – with pride. He recognized that the Fists held all the cards now. 'We can capture them there.'

'Don't capture them. *Follow* them. I want to know what they are doing as they do it. Who's running things in Tibet?'

'Chen,' Lim said.

'The same man from Xinjiang?' Feng asked, surprised.

Lim nodded. 'I took the initiative of sending him to Lhasa. He's quite determined to make up for his failures at the mine.'

'I bet he is,' Feng hissed. 'Tell Chen to keep a close eye on them. If it seems like they are about to damage anything of cultural value,

I want them stopped immediately. But if they are only collecting information, I want to know what they find. As soon as we have a location for the treasure they're seeking, we won't need them anymore. That's when I want them brought to me.'

44

Lhasa, Tibet

A forty-minute drive through the Yarlung Tsangpo River valley took the team from the airport to the city of Lhasa. At an elevation of nearly 11,000 feet, the city was so high up the Tibetan Plateau that pilots had to be specially trained in high-altitude maneuvers before they were allowed to fly planes into or out of the airport. Luckily, the weather had been extremely pleasant for early April, and the team had flown in on the private Gulfstream without incident.

Before leaving Tokyo, Sarah had dyed her hair dark brown and cut it much shorter. The effect was a stark change in appearance. She looked older and more serene, but still just as lovely. She heightened the change with dark eye shadow and loose-fitting clothes.

Garcia had shaved his head completely, which helped him blend in with the Buddhist monks that filled the area. Maggie had cut her hair short and spiky, and dressed in the jeans and T-shirt of a Taiwanese tourist. She had informed everyone on the team that she was using a Taiwanese accent as well, but to their untrained ears, she sounded just the same.

McNutt had cut his beard and trimmed his hair to a reasonable length, but he had avoided cutting it too short. He had suggested that if their unknown enemies had identified him, they might have done so from his Marine photos, so he didn't want to be shorn too closely. Cobb had trimmed his week's worth of stubble into a goatee. It wasn't much of a change, but it was enough to give a stranger pause – and sometimes that was all that was necessary.

Papineau had made minimal changes to his appearance too. Cobb was fairly certain the Frenchman wouldn't be on the radar of their unknown pursuers because he hadn't been in the field at all. Still, a different part to his perfectly coiffed hair and an outfit of khakis and a golf shirt changed his look enough to deflect average scrutiny.

Unfortunately, the new clothes did nothing to improve Papineau's mood.

They were all seated in a long minibus provided for transport into town. With no other arrivals at the tiny airport they had the vehicle to themselves, aside from the driver. It had not escaped Cobb's notice that Papineau had not let him out of sight since Tokyo, except in their hotel rooms at night. He had even sat next to Cobb on the flight into Tibet, and then again on the bus. He had been waiting for Cobb to open the conversation, but Cobb hadn't said a word to him the entire time. As the pristine blue water of the snaking river ran by outside the windows of the bus, the Frenchman could wait no longer.

'Why did you bring me along?' Papineau whispered to Cobb. 'Seriously, what was the point? And when were you going to tell me about the incident in Xinjiang? Am I that untrustworthy? Haven't I given you everything you asked for?'

Cobb often studied the way people talked with one another. He'd heard communication described as two monologues clashing, with each person waiting for their turn to speak instead of actively listening. He knew all of Papineau's complaints before the man voiced them, but he still allowed the man to spew, getting the anger out of his system, until he was ready to listen.

Finally Papineau fell silent, his face reddened.

Cobb waited an extra few seconds just to be sure. 'I didn't tell you about the rekky because I wasn't sure it was worth telling you about. As it was, the trip accomplished nothing other than arousing the wrath of the mine's security forces. And we still don't know if that was connected to the attack in Guangzhou. Could be two separate groups.'

Cobb spoke softly with an even tone, the pace of his response not leaving an opening for Papineau to object. 'And honestly, I didn't fully trust you. You've held things back from the team in the past. You've spied on us. You've been . . . difficult. But you're here now, and that counts for a lot. You've shown your willingness to get your hands dirty.'

Cobb knew the small compliment would go a long way toward disarming Papineau's indignant rage. 'Not everyone needs to know the whole plan. Compartmentalization helps if things turn south, and, as you've seen, that happens more often than we'd like. Sometimes I leave things out for Josh or Sarah, too.'

Papineau glanced at them, but they weren't listening.

Cobb continued. 'I've treated you as an equal member of this team since we got to Hong Kong. I understand why you might have been upset at being left out of things back in Florida, but I think maybe you've been letting your emotions cloud your viewpoint since Tokyo. I trust you now. We all do. We've just stopped treating you like our boss. After all, we're all wealthy now. We're not here for the money anymore – if any of us ever were.'

Cobb turned at last to face the Frenchman, and he saw his explanation had had the desired effect. Papineau was not only defused, but genuinely surprised, and maybe a bit honored to be treated as a member of the team. His face registered a variety of emotions, but anger was no longer one of them.

'And let's face it,' Cobb whispered. 'You were smart enough to hire us all for those things that drive us. You knew we weren't here for the money alone.'

Cobb had no idea whether his last statement was true or not, but it was an additional compliment that helped to further bury Papineau's anger.

'I don't know what to—' the Frenchman began, but his words died on his lips as the bus rounded the curve in the road and the picturesque valley of Lhasa opened up before them.

The second most populated city on the Tibetan Plateau at over half a million people, Lhasa's name literally meant 'place of the gods'.

The entire team could see why.

The city sits in a flat river valley, surrounded by 8,000-foot mountains. At this time of year, the snow had melted off parts of the slopes, revealing lush greenery. It looked like swirls of mint up the white hillsides. Below those slopes, but still raised above the city, was the white and brick-red Potala Palace.

As the bus continued around the bend, a ray of golden sunlight pierced the clouds overhead, illuminating the palace like a spotlight. The gilded canopies on the rooftop glittered in the light like diamonds. It was truly a sight to behold.

The rest of the city spread out below the palace looked dull by comparison, full of plain Chinese Communist architecture. The distinction between the stunning view of the mountains, the illuminated palace, and the drab city beneath it was a remarkable study of contrasts.

'It's amazing,' Sarah gasped.

'It is,' Maggie agreed. 'Let's try not to destroy it.'

45

Thursday, April 10th

Though construction of the Potala Palace did not begin until 1645 AD, it was built upon the remnants of an ancient temple that was more than a thousand years older.

Conceived as a seat of the Tibetan government, the purpose of the multi-leveled fortress has slowly transformed over the years. What used to be the home of the Dalai Lama, who abandoned the palace after the failed 1959 Tibetan Uprising, is now a museum, an archive, a monastery, and a cultural destination that caters to sixteen hundred visitors per day.

Tourists from around the world come to marvel at the functional decadence of the fortress that rises 384 feet above Red Mountain. They stare in awe at the gently sloping stairs, the multiple levels of wide, flat roofs, the expansive porticos, and rows upon rows of square windows, most of which are covered by fluttering drapes of embroidered tapestries.

Perched at a height of 12,000 feet above sea level, the complex spans a staggering 400 meters across the mountainside and includes thirteen stories of buildings containing over 1,000 rooms, 10,000 shrines, and 200,000 statues. The White Palace contains the main ceremonial hall with the throne of the Dalai Lama. His private rooms and audience hall are on the uppermost level. The palace contains 698 murals, almost 10,000 painted scrolls, and numerous objects of gold and silver, as well as a large collection of sutras and important historical documents.

The Red Palace lies to the west of the White Palace. Its main purpose is to house eight *stupa* – the entombed remains of prior Dalai Lamas – but it also serves as a center of religious study and prayer. It contains five distinct chapels, three galleries, and an expansive great hall. The interior of the palace is adorned with a variety of priceless gems, including one *mandala*, a geometric figure representing the universe that is made of nearly 200,000 pearls.

The sheer magnitude of the edifice was overwhelming. Massive stone walls dominated the landscape, each meticulously painted to match the color of its respective palace. The colossal temple climbed toward the heavens, its peaked, golden spires seemingly brushing against the clouds. The entire palace was simply a sight to behold.

Cobb looked at the structure in the distance and inhaled deeply, drawing in as much oxygen as he could. At their current altitude, he was breathing only sixty-eight percent of the oxygen he would have enjoyed in Florida, and his body knew it. They had stayed in a small, traditional Tibetan guesthouse instead of a hotel, and Cobb had woken several times throughout the night with his heart hammering in his chest from the rarefied atmosphere.

When he had seen the faces of the other team members at breakfast, he knew they had slept poorly as well. Maggie had bags under her eyes. Sarah had been extra irritable and distracted. Garcia had seemed to be half asleep – despite his four cups of coffee. Even Papineau had looked haggard. Only McNutt had looked alert and well rested, no doubt a result of his experience with high altitude in the mountains of Afghanistan.

Despite the effects of low oxygen, Cobb soldiered on.

The team would have to suck it up . . . *literally*.

It was a crisp morning with hardly any wind when Cobb, Sarah, and Maggie left their guesthouse on foot. Shops were just beginning to open on the winding streets and cobbled paths, but Maggie found one selling *khata*: small, white, ceremonial scarves that symbolized purity and compassion to the Tibetans. They bought several, including the most expensive ones available, which were made of white silk and embroidered with gold thread. Maggie explained that they would come in handy later with the monks, but she didn't explain why.

And Cobb and Sarah were too tired to ask.

Cobb had no idea what they might find in the palace, if anything, but Maggie had suggested that if Polo had been to Lhasa, there would be records of his stay inside. The Potala contained dozens of libraries where they might find such records. Unfortunately, it would take them days, if not weeks, to find what they were looking for on their own, and Cobb knew they didn't have that kind of time – not if their pursuers from Guangzhou were still on their trail.

'So . . .' Sarah said, pausing to suck in a breath as she looked up at the looming palace across the square. The image was broadcast to Garcia at the guesthouse via a pair of hi-tech glasses that used the same technology as Cobb's sunglasses in Loulan. 'Why are we taking a million stairs instead of driving to the top? I could've sworn you said something about a shuttle bus.'

'Contrition,' Maggie said as she glanced at the zigzagging staircases that made their way up the mountainside. 'The building doesn't officially open to tourists until later, but the monks will let us in early if we show respect. I've visited before with a distinguished Westerner.'

'Richard Gere?' Sarah asked. She knew of the actor's fondness for Tibet.

'It appears your definition of "distinguished" is quite different from mine,' Maggie said with a smile. 'Besides, if I was describing Richard Gere, I would have said "sexy".'

Cobb rolled his eyes. 'Ladies, if you don't mind . . .'

'Jealous?' Sarah teased.

Cobb started walking. 'Behind schedule.'

As they mounted the steps and began the long climb toward the main entrance, Cobb admired the lower white walls of the fortress. The top five stories made up the actual palace while the lower eight stories were built with defense in mind. The walls themselves were little more than stacked stones, but they were sixteen feet thick in some places. The bottom was wider and thicker than the top, so it could support the weight of the smaller red palace.

Despite the altitude, Cobb and Maggie had no problems scaling the gentle staircases. Meanwhile Sarah, who was in far better shape than anyone else on the team, was breathing heavily before they made it halfway up the incline.

'Altitude affects everyone differently,' Maggie said.

'Maybe so, but this is depressing,' Sarah croaked.

Cobb glanced back at her. 'Wheezing isn't sexy.'

'Yeah, well, neither is . . . shit! I can't think of anything.'

Cobb and Maggie both laughed; but not for long.

The second half of the journey wiped them out, too.

When they finally reached the main doorway, they could see that it was covered by a beautiful tapestry embroidered with symbols of good fortune and luck. A lone monk swept the threshold with a broom. His complexion was naturally darker than Maggie's, and it possessed a quality that Cobb and Sarah had rarely seen before. Having worked outdoors in high altitudes for nearly his entire life, his skin looked like the brown leather of a WWII bomber jacket: thick and rough, with plenty of creases.

His face erupted into a smile when he saw the *khata* draped over their necks.

Before the man had a chance to address them, Maggie raised her hands and pressed them together, as if in prayer. Though she didn't speak much Tibetan, she knew the traditional greeting that loosely translated to 'blessings and good luck'.

'*Tashi delek*,' she offered.

Cobb and Sarah quickly followed her lead.

The monk's smile widened. He returned the greeting before speaking to them in English. 'You have come early to see the palace.'

'The palace is stunning,' Maggie said. 'But we did not come to see it.'

The monk examined them again. His smile stayed in place, but the wattage dimmed slightly. 'Then why have you come?'

His English was excellent, with hardly a hint of an accent. Cobb suspected that the monk had been tasked with meeting the tourists who wandered up the mountain without a tour group. Cobb realized that the sweeping might have been just an act; the three of them surely would have been spotted and heard long before they got this far.

'We have come to give you these *khata*,' Maggie said with a bow. Then she lowered her voice to a whisper. 'And to talk of times long past.'

Cobb smiled at the precision of her answer.

He knew it was a calculated response.

Maggie had explained that most Tibetans would gladly speak to foreigners about the old days as long as there were no Chinese soldiers around to listen. He also knew that there were informers on both sides of the turmoil: Chinese in league with the Tibetans and discontented monks who simply wanted the struggle to end so that they might find peace.

The monk paused, considering her request.

Then he turned quietly and opened the door. 'Come in, please.'

46

The monk introduced himself as Thubten before leading them through a series of winding, twisting rooms and passageways, deep into the palace's interior. Most of the rooms were decorated with multi-colored carpets, white and gold tapestries with blue and red accents, and furniture made from dark wood. In most of the small chambers through which they passed, the scent of incense hung thick in the air, the smell deep and rich.

Eventually Thubten brought them to a small, sparse room. There were only four chairs and a wobbly tea table between them.

'Please wait here,' he said before scurrying behind the lone tapestry.

A hidden doorway, Cobb realized. He immediately closed his eyes and tried to remember how many tapestries he had passed along the way. There had been dozens of them. If only a quarter of them concealed doors, there was no telling how many people had seen them on their way to this room. For a man like Cobb, the thought was very unsettling.

'Well, things are going well so far,' Maggie whispered, partly as commentary for Cobb and Sarah, and partly to inform Garcia and the others who were undoubtedly listening in.

'As long as he doesn't come back with armed soldiers,' Cobb replied.

Sarah glanced at Maggie. 'Do you think he will?'

'No.'

'We'll find out soon enough,' Cobb said.

A few minutes later, a small fat monk in a red robe came into the room with a tray. On it was an antique tea set and an electric kettle. He set the tray down on the table and exited the room immediately.

Sarah looked to Maggie for guidance. 'Do you think we should have some or are we supposed to wait? I get the feeling that this is a test.'

'It probably is,' Maggie said. 'Truth be told, I didn't have tea at all the last time I was here, but we can assume it would be bad form to begin without our host.'

A minute later they heard Garcia's voice in their ears. 'I can't find anything specific on Tibetan tea etiquette, but I found a Buddhist proverb. It says—'

Maggie cut him off. 'We will wait.'

'Okay, okay.'

Several minutes later, a new monk entered the room. He moved in slow motion, as if his leg troubled him. He was visibly older than Thubten, with far more creases on his face.

'*Tashi delek*,' he said in greeting. 'My name is Kunchen.' As he studied the visitors, his face suddenly lit up in recognition. 'Miss Liu!'

Maggie stood. '*Tashi delek*, Kunchen. It has been a very long time.'

Kunchen turned to the others. 'Miss Liu has been here before, with guests who were very compassionate and understanding.'

Maggie smiled and nodded at the praise.

Cobb extended the traditional greeting before introducing himself and Sarah, using their first names only. Kunchen smiled and bowed.

'Are you the – I'm not sure of the correct word – the abbot of Potala?' Sarah asked.

Kunchen chuckled. 'No. I am merely a scholar and a historian. The highest ranking lamas in Lhasa are all lackeys to the Chinese government. I suspect you might already know some of this if Miss Liu is your guide.'

The monk showed none of Thubten's unease at discussing things in the open. Either the room was fantastically secure, or Kunchen just didn't care about possible reprisals.

'We know some,' Cobb said. 'Thank you for seeing us today.' He removed one of the white silk *khata* from his neck and held it out horizontally to Kunchen. 'Please accept this with good wishes and our thanks.'

The twinkle in Kunchen's eyes revealed his true happiness. He accepted the scarf that Cobb had offered and then the one Sarah held out in the same fashion, nodding his deep brown forehead at each of them in turn. Maggie presented hers last.

'They are lovely,' he gushed. 'Thank you. Shall we have some tea?'

'That would be great,' Cobb said. Normally he was in a hurry to get things done when he was in the field, but not today. As counterintuitive as it might seem, he sensed the quickest way to accomplish their goal at the palace was with patience.

Kunchen placed teabags in their cups and poured hot water on them.

'Is it green tea?' Sarah asked.

'Black, actually. From Assam, in India. I hope that is all right?' Kunchen looked worried, as if he might have offended his guests.

'It sounds delicious,' Sarah assured him, setting his mind at ease. 'It must be difficult for you to get. Thank you for sharing it with us.'

The monk's broad smile returned. 'It *is* quite difficult to get, as a matter of fact. But I have had a fondness for it since I was a child, which is when I first came to Lhasa.'

'When was that?' Cobb wondered.

'Let's just say that the Chinese were not yet here, and Tibet was a very different place.'

He handed them each a cup of tea, then stood slowly. The others did as well.

'Toasting is a Western custom, but I have always liked it since I first saw it in a motion picture. I think we should toast old friends, new ones, and lost times.'

Cobb grinned. 'Very appropriate.'

They sat and drank tea for a few moments. The monk continued smiling at them. Just as Cobb was about to break the silence, Maggie gently tapped him on his leg. He interpreted that to mean that it would be impolite to bring up business while sipping tea.

Sarah shifted in her seat, and Cobb could feel her impatience with the need for ceremony. She started looking around the room at the décor, and Cobb watched the monk watch her do it. Then, before her eyes were done scanning the small space, the monk's eyes met Cobb's again. The corner of the man's mouth twitched as if he was holding back a broader smile.

'You have a great stillness in you, Jack, like Miss Liu,' he said at last. 'But perhaps we should discuss the matter that brought you here today. I suspect you did not come solely to admire the architecture.'

Cobb nodded. 'I am afraid not. Nor did we come to discuss the tragic days of your youth when the Chinese came and Tenzin Gyatso fled.'

Cobb used the Fourteenth Dalai Lama's name as Maggie had told him to do. She knew it would elicit sympathy while also showing that he had taken the time to learn something of the plight of Tibet and the religious leader who had been living in exile since 1959.

'Instead,' Cobb continued, 'we came to speak with you about a much older time.'

The monk was intrigued. He clapped his hands and sat forward, like a giddy school boy. 'I have not spoken with a Westerner who was interested in more than a cursory glance at Tibet in many long years. In what era are you interested?'

Maggie answered for him 'We would be honored and privileged

244

to have the opportunity to examine any books the Potala might have dating from the thirteenth century.'

'Do you have a specific book in mind? We have many different libraries in this building, with hundreds of thousands of works. Many date from even earlier than the thirteenth century.'

'Do we trust this guy?' Garcia asked in Cobb's ear.

Cobb answered Garcia's question by providing the monk with additional information. 'We are interested in a story of a Westerner and a Chinese girl named Yangchen.'

Maggie picked up from there. 'We are particularly interested in any books you might possess that were stored here on the Red Hill, prior to the construction of the Potala Palace. Naturally, we only want to examine these documents and, with your kind permission, take some photos of them as well.'

Kunchen nodded his approval. 'You are correct: I could not allow you to take any books from the palace, but I can certainly arrange for you to see them.'

'Is this a common request?' Sarah wondered.

Kunchen laughed. 'Goodness, no. I've never heard of a Westerner coming here and asking to see any of our old books, as you have done. But you each have good hearts, and I believe you when you say you wish only to look. Plus, it has been many years since I have had this much fun practicing my English. Normally Americans want a photo and nothing more.'

He stood and walked toward the door, but before they had a chance to follow he stopped and turned back. 'Please understand our need for secrecy.'

Cobb nodded sharply. 'Yes. Of course.'

'Also, you should know that we have thousands of volumes from the era that you wish to study. It might take a long time to find what you seek.'

47

Chen Jie pulled his jacket closer to his chest, performing the twin tasks of cutting out the chill of the wind and further hiding his Chinese Type 95 rifle.

He had a team of five men with him, and each man wore a similarly long coat to hide the compact weapons. They were strange rifles to his eyes. He'd seen them before, but he personally had never used one. With its curved magazine set behind the pistol grip and trigger guard, the 'bullpup' style rifle looked to him like an American M-16 that had been squashed and put together with all its pieces in the wrong places. But when it came to taking lives, he had been assured the weapons would do the trick just fine.

Chen and his men ignored each other while they blended in with the tourists, who were checking out the lower reaches of the Potala's property. Knowing that the main part of the palace wasn't open yet, a few intrepid souls would always wander its lower slopes in the mornings, admiring the architecture and the view over the city. The monks were used to these early-morning visitors, and mostly ignored them until opening time. On occasion they allowed a few people in before the start of the day – as they had just done with the two Americans and the Chinese woman.

Chen reviewed his mental files on the intruders. Jackson Cobb was ex-military, and the biggest threat of the three. Maggie Liu was a tour guide for the rich and famous. She had cut her hair, but Chen still recognized her at once. The third woman, a dark-haired beauty, was clearly the blonde who had been spotted with the others in Hong Kong.

Another disguise, but a minimal attempt at concealment.

One of Chen's men had been in place to get a photograph of her in the market before the intruders had begun their ascent of the tiered stairs in front of the palace. Chen had sent the photo to Hong Kong for further research. It was the best picture they had taken of the woman so far, but he didn't expect to receive any information on her today.

These things took time.

In the meantime, his orders were odd. He was to shadow the intruders and see where their day led them. If at any point the Americans started to dig in Chinese soil, he was to kill them immediately and prevent anyone else – including the military or the police – from examining the site. On the other hand, if they merely moved about the city he was to simply record their behavior in hopes that their movements might hint at where they were headed next.

Based on these instructions and his observations from Xinjiang, he had a pretty good idea of what was going on. The Americans were seeking a treasure but were still looking for clues. Chen couldn't imagine what treasure might connect Lhasa with distant Loulan, but he was hardly a student of history. His specialty was beating up people who disobeyed the Fists or failed to pay their bills on time. When he wasn't doing that, he was running security at the potash mine.

He had come from humble beginnings in Xi'an, working his way up in the street gangs of that humid city until his father revealed that their family had been members of the Fists for decades and they had a higher purpose for him. Since then, he'd felt a kinship and a belonging – even after his father had passed away. He knew he was little more than a thug for the organization, but he was treated well, and that was what mattered most.

Today he was hoping his unusual orders would lead to an opportunity for revenge. His bosses had been lenient with his failure in the desert, but mostly because of the death of his friend, Zhang. Also, no one had expected the foreigners to be ex-military, and Feng He, the charismatic man who led the Fists, sounded intrigued by their incursion.

Chen noted with dismay the absence of the American sniper. The team, including the freshly shorn Marine, had been spotted entering a guesthouse the previous night. One of Chen's men had kept an eye on the place until dawn, when Chen's entire crew had dispersed through the neighborhood to wait for the foreigners to depart their guesthouse. But only Cobb, the American woman, and Liu had exited in the morning. The others had all stayed behind. Chen had a man there to keep an eye on them, but who knew if they were still inside?

Chen was suddenly haunted by a thought.

What if the sniper slipped out the back?

The man was responsible for Zhang's death from over a mile away. He was clearly one of the best snipers on Earth. The notion that he could be out there, perched in the surrounding mountains, made Chen's skin crawl. He imagined himself in the crosshairs of a scope, the barrel of a powerful rifle pointed at his back.

A cold shiver ran down his spine.

From his position on the whitewashed stairway, Chen started examining all the outlying structures around the base of the palace. He scrutinized every building, wall, and shed. Every bump and slope in the rocky ground. Every tree and scraggly bush on the hillside.

Was one of those a cleverly disguised American sniper?

It was only because of his paranoid search for an American boogeyman that he even noticed the convoy in the distance on Beijing East Road. The soldiers were still far off in the morning mist, but in his heart Chen knew the vehicles were coming to the Potala.

Probably for the same thing his men were supposed to find.

The same thing the intruders were after.

Treasure.

If the men in the convoy had heard about it – if they had even gotten a whiff of its scent – they would come crawling over everything like ants.

Suddenly patience was a luxury he no longer possessed.

Chen pulled out his phone and quickly dialed Hong Kong.

Lim Bao picked it up on the second ring. 'Yes?'

'The army is coming. They will be here soon. What should I do?'

48

Kunchen led them through a complex maze of twisting stairways down to the lower levels of the Potala. The original Tibetan art and décor had been replaced with plain concrete walls and dozens of cubicles with army cots in them. It was clear that the bulk of these floors had recently housed large numbers of Chinese troops.

'Are these still manned?' Cobb asked as the older man nimbly led them over raised doorframes and ducked under lowered lintels, sweeping aside tapestries covering each passageway as he went. His limp from earlier was no longer present.

'For the most part, no,' Kunchen answered, the breeziness in his voice absent when he spoke of the intrusion of Chinese troops into a religious structure. 'There are still over fifty soldiers stationed in the building at any given time, but I am leading you on a circuitous route that will help us to avoid them at this time of day. Some of the men are quite lazy, and therefore unpredictable, but most of them rigidly adhere to their rules and schedules, with the hopes of one day being promoted and relocated back to China proper.'

They fell silent as they entered a more traditional section of the building, where whitewashed walls gave way to brilliant colors, kaleidoscopic paintings of nature, and thousands of images of the Buddha. The passages grew tighter and lower, to the point where Cobb had to stoop and often turn sideways to make it through the tiny doorways, which were now protected by locked doors instead of just being covered by tapestries.

Looking like a high school janitor, Kunchen carried a huge brass ring filled with keys that unlocked most of the doors in the palace, but twice they stopped in front of hidden passageways that required the pressure of Kunchen's hands on the wall followed by a complex ballet of tiny movements. Cobb wondered if the old monk was being deliberately showy in order to hide the actual placement of his fingers needed to open the recessed doors.

'The Communists started ripping down walls that they felt were not load-bearing back in the 1950s.' Kunchen turned to them and grinned. 'They also took out a few that were, by mistake. Eventually they realized they should stop before the entire palace collapsed. Thankfully, many parts of these lower levels are still intact.'

They moved into a section with long narrow hallways that were lined with ancient codices. The dusty ends of the long wooden slats jutted out of the recesses in the walls. Maggie tried to ask how old the documents were, but the tiny monk was moving too fast for her to keep up.

As the passageway continued to narrow, another monk joined them from behind. He was obviously younger than Kunchen, but Cobb couldn't have guessed by how much. He smiled far less than their genial host and his skin was not nearly as weathered. The only thing that stood out about him was the ridiculous amount of prayer beads wrapped around his neck. If they had been made of gold, he would have looked like a Tibetan Mr T.

Finally, Kunchen unlocked a tiny doorway that was barely four feet in height. Even he had to contort his body to fit through the narrow frame. Despite the tiny door, the room was filled with bookcases that stretched from the floor to the twenty-foot-high ceiling, the upper levels of which were accessed by a narrow balcony. The shelves were designed as display cases, tilted at a forty-five-degree angle and covered over with glass. Each codex was splayed out slightly like a Chinese fan, so the monks could see the text of the first leaf between the wooden boards that bound it. As he continued to walk, Cobb could see varying scripts on the codices.

Although he could read none of them, he knew they were not all written in the blocky Tibetan language.

The massive room stretched on for forty feet before another hall branched to the left. Cobb could see more shelves in that corridor and another room at the end of the hallway. For all he knew, there were more halls and rooms beyond that. The glass over the shelves was clearly a recent addition, but the rest of the library appeared as if its current configuration might have been intact for hundreds of years. Surprisingly, the room did not have the thick cloying scent of incense that he had smelled upstairs. Then he realized why: to protect the fragile old books.

Kunchen was thrilled to see the look of amazement in Cobb's eyes. 'Mister Jack, do you know the volumes you are seeking?'

'I'm afraid not, but Maggie does,' he said.

Kunchen nodded. 'Then I will leave you for a while. I have other duties to attend to. Young Sonam here is the caretaker of this collection. The librarian, I suppose you would call him. Once you find a title you wish to inspect, inform him, and he will remove it from its case.'

'Kunchen,' Cobb said before the monk departed, 'you never asked for anything in return for allowing us access to your exquisite library. Is there something we can do for you?'

The monk looked at him, confused. 'Why should I require anything? You came with a smile on your face and several beautiful *khata* that you purchased in the market this morning. That was very thoughtful of you. Then you proved your humility by choosing the more arduous path to the doors of this palace when you could have easily taken the tour bus later in the day or driven your own vehicle here. You also showed patience with the tea.' Kunchen smiled. 'You have sought only knowledge, and you have asked politely. I require no further reward.'

'Nonetheless,' Cobb said with a bow. 'You strike me as a very intelligent man. I suspect you know what we are after ultimately involves more than simple knowledge.'

'Thank you for your appraisal. And yes, this is true.' His face was suddenly serious, showing no hint of his cheerfulness from earlier. 'However, I also know that whatever riches you seek, they are not Tibetan. I would ask only that you weigh the value of the journey against the value of the reward that you hope to obtain.'

Cobb pondered the advice before responding. 'Thank you for your wisdom. I promise we will. And whether we are successful or not, I will do whatever I can to help you and your brethren – even if that is nothing more than a shipment of black tea from abroad.'

Kunchen's grin returned in a flash, and Cobb knew it was genuine. The old monk smiled warmly at him, bowed once, then departed in silence.

Meanwhile the young librarian had wandered to the other end of the room, content to not peer over their shoulders like a hawk. If they were good enough for Kunchen's trust, they were good enough for his.

'So,' Sarah said as she glanced around the room, 'where do we start?'

Maggie explained. 'We are looking for the writing, not the shape of the book. All of the books from the time period we seek will be codices like these. If any of them were by Polo's hand, it will be written in a handful of languages: Mongolian, Turkish, Arabic, and, most importantly, Venetian.'

'That doesn't help much,' Sarah admitted. 'I can probably tell the difference between Arabic and East Asian scripts, but I have no idea what the others look like.'

'The Ottoman Turkish will look just like Arabic to you. Large, horizontally curvy letters, all written from right to left. The Mongolian will be easy to spot, too, because it will look like large dragons and jagged-edged knives, all written vertically. If you spot any of those, let me know. Those will most likely be written by Mongol invaders – men loyal to the Khan. There's a chance they would know something about Polo.'

'What about Venetian?' Cobb asked.

'Venetian used the Latin alphabet, the same letters as English.'

Cobb nodded. 'That's more in my wheelhouse.'

Maggie continued. 'But like I said this morning, it's unlikely we'll find anything written in Polo's hand. My guess is that I'll have to read several of these volumes to find a single mention of a white foreigner traveling in Lhasa.'

'What do you want us to look for first?' Sarah asked.

'Any books written in a language besides Tibetan script. If you find anything like that, let me know. And if we don't find anything useful, we'll ask the librarian for assistance. He might be able to help us with the Tibetan volumes that I can't read.'

Cobb and Sarah took opposite sides of the room from Maggie, working their way halfway down the hall and glancing at the scripts on the wide variety of pages, all contained in nearly identical wooden boards as covers. When they reached the end, they ascended a simple staircase and began searching the upper ten feet, walking back the way they had come, essentially segmenting the long hall into 'rooms' based on distance and the placement of the staircases to the upper balcony.

Nothing came close to the description Maggie had given.

They had been at it for nearly an hour when they reached the end of the collection with nothing to show for it. They had discovered a third hall after the second, but it contained more of the same. None of the documents were written in the characters they were hoping to find.

Sarah and Cobb met in the middle of the balcony, practically bumping into each other while their eyes rapidly scanned the hundreds of titles on shelves under glass.

'Nothing but Tibetan,' Sarah said.

'Same for me,' Cobb agreed.

'I was certain we'd find something here.'

'So was I,' Cobb said.

McNutt's voice suddenly squawked in his ear. 'Chief?'

Cobb was thankful for the interruption. 'Yeah, Josh. What is it?'

'Your search might have turned up empty, but someone found us.'

'What do you mean?' Cobb demanded.

McNutt stared at the approaching forces. 'I think someone tipped off the goddamned army. We've got an entire platoon headed our way.'

49

McNutt stared in horror as a line of Chinese ZBL-09s advanced toward the Potala Palace through a light mist. He knew the kind of damage that could be done by such vehicles, and he knew the peaceful monks in their red robes had no way of stopping it.

With four oversized wheels on each side, the 21-ton armored fighting vehicles (AFVs) were offensively minded personnel carriers. The AFVs could move at sixty mph on a flat road, were fully amphibious, and their heavy exterior was capable of repelling 7.62 mm armor-piercing rounds. In typical Chinese fashion, these four were painted in a high-gloss black, forest green, and white camouflage pattern that failed miserably to blend with the local terrain.

The AFVs had room for three crew members and an additional seven passengers. McNutt knew that they typically had a 30 mm cannon mounted on the front of the gun turret, but for reasons he couldn't explain the weapon had been removed from the first AFV in the four-vehicle convoy. The defanged turret was still menacing though, with a heavy machine gun mounted on a post and a gunner at the ready.

To McNutt, the AFVs resembled sharks on wheels. He quickly noted that while the first vehicle was missing its main gun, the other three sharks had their cannons intact. Worse still, their top hatches were battened down for business.

McNutt was seated at the foot of the main palace structure at the highest point on the eastern side of the building's base. He'd slipped out of the guesthouse hours before the others. On this mission, he'd be without a sniper rifle. They were too tough to acquire in

Tibet. Instead, he'd come out with just an automatic pistol and his wits. He figured if he couldn't keep an eye on things through a scope, the least he could do was get in position before dawn.

He had been on site when the first tourists began to wander around the property, and he'd been in place when Cobb, Maggie, and Sarah had made their long ascent up the steps to the front door. He'd already learned his way around, finding the blind corners – the perfect places for an ambush – and scoping out the points of ingress and egress. But what he was mostly looking for were more phony cops coming to mess with his team.

The last thing he'd expected was a military convoy.

That is, if these men were actually soldiers.

The guards in Loulan had been heavily armored, too.

McNutt watched as the first AFV turned off the mostly empty Beijing Middle Road onto a side road that ran parallel to the hillside and ended at the Potala's rear parking lot. He knew he would have to relocate if he wanted eyes on the winding route that led to the palace's back door.

He whispered into his microphone. 'Hey, Sanchez. You hear me?'

'Loud and clear,' Garcia said.

Before they had arrived in Tibet, McNutt had asked Garcia to check on local police and military personnel in the area. He knew the physical presence of soldiers on the ground was minimal in Lhasa – mostly to mollify protesters and civil rights groups in the international community, not to administer martial law – but he needed details on their positioning. Garcia had learned there was a small handful of men stationed inside the Potala and more in the eastern part of the city at a barracks not far from the team's guesthouse. Based on the direction from which the AFVs were arriving, McNutt figured that whole reserve group was headed their way. The next largest contingent of the People's Liberation Army was a garrison out at the airport.

McNutt continued to whisper. 'Just wondering if you can do your computer thingy and tell me if the army is mobilizing its troops out at the airport.'

'That's a negative. They haven't moved.'

'How do you know?'

'I'm staring at them.'

Shortly after Cobb, Sarah, and Maggie had left the guesthouse, Papineau and Garcia had slipped out the back to a waiting vehicle that whisked them out of town. Cobb had decided that it would be a good thing to have them both ready to go in case the team was attacked again. Garcia was in a private hangar at the airport keeping an eye on the PLA and the arriving flights while Papineau made arrangements with the jet's pilot to be ready at a moment's notice.

'Okay,' McNutt said, barely relieved. 'If they move at all, let me know ASAP. I have a bad feeling that this place is about to get rocked.'

McNutt left his post and ran along the base of the building, hoping to slip around the back where he could shadow the lone AFV if it started the ascent up the back road. There wasn't anything he could do against an armored vehicle with just a handgun, but if he stayed hidden long enough he could confront the soldiers when they climbed out of the personnel carrier.

He crouched low and raced along the rocky soil, keeping an eye on the AFV as it slowly trundled along the road toward the parking area. The idea had occurred to him that this was simply the vehicle used to ferry soldiers up and down from their living quarters at the palace, which would explain the missing cannon on the turret.

Then again, it wouldn't explain the other three AFVs out on the main road.

Just as he reached the end of the building, McNutt watched as the AFV turned away from the parking lot and up toward the winding road that led to the palace. His determination growing, he climbed over a low wall and dropped seven feet to the dirt on the other side before rushing around the edge of a curved tower to the back of the building. Staying in the shadows of the palace wall and partly cloaked by the morning mist, McNutt moved like a ghost nearer the AFV, which didn't seem to be in much of a hurry. It trudged along at a slow pace, getting closer and closer to the rear entrance of the palace, showing no signs of hostility.

For a brief moment, McNutt began to doubt his feelings of dread.

Are they merely transporting supplies to the palace?

Maybe the other three AFVs are simply running drills.

But those thoughts vanished when he heard the first shot.

McNutt instinctively dove to the rocky ground. With a gun in his hand, he looked up and couldn't believe what he saw. The gunner on the AFV was slumped forward, half-extended out of one of the twin hatches atop the vehicle. He was missing a sizeable chunk of his head.

A second later, automatic fire erupted from the hillside below and the armored sides of the AFV began sparking so much it looked like a fireworks display.

In a flash, McNutt realized he had gotten it all wrong.

The soldiers weren't firing at him or anything else.

Someone was shooting *at* the goddamned army.

50

Kunchen tried to suppress his alarm as he rushed into the library, but the look on his face gave away his emotions. He was quite concerned about the outbreak of violence.

Maggie pressed her palms together and apologized before he had a chance to catch his breath. 'I am so sorry, Kunchen. I understand from a friend of mine that soldiers are coming. We have brought suffering to your home and to your friends.'

The old man's eyes were kindly. 'Yes, they are most likely here for you, but we will do what we can to help. You have been a strong supporter in the past, Miss Maggie, and we know your heart is pure. The soldiers will shout and intimidate. They may even damage things. But they will not physically hurt my brothers. There was a time they would, but this younger generation is better. The soldiers do not know of this library at all, but the possibility exists that they will find it on one of their searches. For that reason and that reason alone, I suggest we move you.'

'Thank you,' Cobb said with a bow of his head.

'Come,' Kunchen said, and he led them through a hidden door they hadn't seen in their search of the library. It connected to a long narrow hallway.

'Chief,' McNutt said from outside the palace. 'You're not going to believe this, but I'm pretty sure the army isn't here for us.'

Cobb stopped at once. 'What do you mean?'

'The soldiers are exchanging fire with a bunch of tourists. Actually, the tourists opened fire on them. I think our Guangzhou bad guys are here. The front steps are turning into a war zone.'

'Shit,' Cobb said. 'The army will call in reinforcements to stop the gunfight.'

Garcia's voice cut in. 'That's confirmed. A large force just mobilized out of here at the airport, and they're hauling ass. You better get out of Lhasa before they arrive.'

Cobb nodded. 'We're going to need an exit, Josh.'

'I'm on it. Give me two,' McNutt replied.

Kunchen stopped when he realized Cobb, Sarah, and Maggie were no longer following him. He hurried back to see what was wrong.

'Papi, you listening?' Cobb asked, concern creeping into his voice. They were deep in the bowels of the building with a lot of troops bearing down on them.

'Yes, Jack,' came the Frenchman's reply.

'Get the plane in the air immediately. Pay what you have to pay.'

'Way ahead of you, Jack. Palms have been greased, so we can leave at a moment's notice. Are you sure we shouldn't wait around for you?'

'No,' Cobb growled. 'Leave now!'

'Wheels up in less than five,' Papineau assured him.

'Good,' Cobb said. 'Hector, how will this affect the comms?'

Garcia answered quickly. 'I amplified the field communications gear to handle the distance from the airport to the Potala, but your voice is faint on my end. Josh is much clearer than you. I'm hoping once you're outside, we'll be able to stay in touch from the air.'

Cobb turned to Kunchen and held up one hand, asking the man to wait. 'Josh? Which exit should we take? We need to move now.'

'Go to the western end of the building where the buses let off,' McNutt replied. 'Even if you're attacked, it will cause the least structural damage. I'm assuming that's a preference.'

Cobb, Sarah, and Maggie all said 'Yes' at the same time.

'Thought so,' McNutt said. 'Be there in one.'

Cobb turned to Kunchen. 'It's worse than I thought. Other men – *evil* men – are here for us. They're engaged in a gunfight on the front steps with the army. More troops are coming from the airport for ground support. This could get really bad, really fast.'

Kunchen frowned at the thought of a gunfight in front of the palace. They were too deep in the building's thick walls to even hear the sounds of automatic fire. 'How can I help?'

'We need to get to the western exit where the buses come up. If we're spotted, that should limit damage to the Potala.'

'Come.' Kunchen led them toward a spiral wooden staircase that took them several floors higher. The monk said nothing as he opened hidden doors and wound through darkened passageways that seemed to go on forever. Soon they could hear the automatic fire beyond the palace walls, as well as single isolated pops of handguns.

Kunchen started sprinting – something they had thought the old man was incapable of – down a long hallway that took them past several brightly decorated rooms. To their amazement, no one was present in any of the areas that they passed.

'Where are the other monks?' Cobb asked.

'They have gone to a special hiding place, deep in the bowels of the building. In the West, I believe you call it a "panic room".'

McNutt sighted his pistol on the Chinese gunman on the slope of the hill.

One of the men that he had pegged earlier as a harmless tourist had pulled a bullpup-style rifle from his coat and had sprayed the AFV with magazine after magazine of random shots. It had been sheer luck that the crazy bastard had killed the gunner in the turret. But with the dead soldier temporarily blocking access to the machine gun for crewmen inside the AFV, this idiot – gangster, tourist, whatever the hell he was – was a major threat.

McNutt shadowed him in silence, ready to dive for cover if one of the AFV's occupants managed to move the corpse and get control of the heavy mounted gun. McNutt waited until he had closed the distance to a hundred feet before he fired three shots from his pistol. Each hit the crazed gunman, spinning him in a semicircle before he had the good sense to fall down.

McNutt knew if the crewmen inside were watching, he only had a few seconds to get down to the vehicle before the Chinese troops came streaming out; and if that happened, chaos would ensue. He poured on the speed, leaping over large rocks on the hillside and sliding down loose stones while keeping his weapon up the entire time.

When he reached the bottom, he jumped onto the tire of the AFV, then scrambled up onto the top of the turret. Using the butt of his weapon, he banged on the metal surface twice, and waited, his gun trained on the twin side-by-side hatches: the opened one with the dead body, and the other, still closed. When nothing happened, he decided to change his tactic.

He knocked again, but this time he shouted out his favorite Chinese phrase. Other than 'thank you', it was the only one he knew. *'Wǒ néng yǒu yīgè píjiǔ ma?'*

Loosely translated, it meant: *Can I have a beer?*

A few seconds passed before the lock on the closed hatch clunked and rattled. McNutt tensed, ready for anything. The lid slowly opened, and a confused kid of barely eighteen raised his empty hands first before peeking out of the hole like a prairie dog looking for its mother. He was wearing a huge helmet with a headset that signified he was the driver.

'Where's my beer?' McNutt asked, stunned that his tactic had worked.

The kid stared at him, trembling.

'Out,' McNutt said as he motioned to the kid with his pistol. He scrambled out of the vehicle and onto the top of the turret. 'Anyone else in there?'

McNutt sensed the kid couldn't speak English, so he pointed at the military insignia on the young man's uniform then toward the AFV under their feet. The soldier understood the question and shook his head to indicate that he was alone.

'Good,' McNutt said with an exaggerated thumbs-up.

The teen grinned and mimicked the thumbs-up sign.

McNutt laughed and flipped him off, just for fun.

He mimicked the sign and flipped McNutt the bird.

McNutt laughed louder. 'Listen, kid. You're a riot. You'd be awesome at charades. But my friends are waiting for me, and I need to borrow your ride. I'm sorry about this next part.'

This time, McNutt stepped forward and punched him squarely in the jaw — an act of kindness that was done with the young soldier's welfare in mind. His helmet went flying and so did he. The unconscious youth bounced off the side of the AFV and rolled safely to the wet turf below where he would remain safe from harm for the rest of the skirmish.

Plus, he'd have a great story for the rest of his life.

McNutt was about to slip into the open hatch when the crazy gunman began to stir on the ground. He looked down at the man and saw he was bleeding from his shoulder and his leg.

'You're still alive,' McNutt said as he leaped off the AFV and hovered over the injured man. He quickly eyed the bullpup-style rifle that had fallen from his target's grasp. 'Either my aim is getting worse, or my pistol is a piece of shit. I'm betting on the latter. I'll tell you what: if you let me borrow your gun, I'll give you a lift in my fancy truck. What do you say?'

*　*　*

Cobb followed Kunchen through the palace until they reached an exterior door. Kunchen unlocked it, then stepped back until Cobb made sure the coast was clear. A light mist was falling, and the air was filling with smoke from the repeated small arms fire all around the Potala.

Their ears were assaulted by rapid fire in sustained bursts.

'Kunchen,' Cobb said, a deep sadness in his voice, 'I never would have come to Lhasa if I thought those men would be able to follow us here.'

The old monk started to accept his apology, but his eyes passed beyond Cobb, Sarah, and Maggie to the object behind them. His mouth hung open and he stuck out his tongue in a Tibetan gesture of shock or surprise, as automatic as Westerners widening their eyes.

Cobb turned to see what the fuss was about, and saw a Chinese armored vehicle racing up the road toward the palace. A blazing red star was painted on the front of the AFV, and a dead Chinese soldier was manning the machine gun.

Cobb smirked. 'That's something you don't see every day.'

51

The vehicle screeched to a stop at the top of the hill, right in front of Sarah and Maggie. When it did, the dead soldier in the gun turret flopped forward. A moment later, the driver's side door of the AFV opened, and McNutt stuck his head out.

'You three need an invitation, or what?' he asked.

Cobb turned to Kunchen. 'Will you be okay?'

The man reached out and grabbed Cobb's wrist. Then he pressed something into his hand. 'This drive contains digital photographs of what you seek. I took them as you searched the library. I wasn't sure I would give them to you, but I know that you are a good man. I can see it in your eyes and in your heart.'

'Thank you,' Cobb replied.

Kunchen tightened his grip. 'Remember what I told you, Mister Jack. Already the cost of your journey is high. Ensure that you are traveling down your path for the correct reasons. If you are on the wrong road, find another, or walk over the mountain instead.'

Then the man released his grasp and bolted inside the building.

Cobb turned and grabbed Maggie by the upper arm, ushering her toward the vehicle. 'You couldn't find something stealthier, Josh?'

McNutt snorted. 'I know, right? This thing is a pig to drive.'

Sarah climbed in next and Cobb piled in after her. He had no worries they might take a bullet inside the armored behemoth, but just to be safe, he pushed the dead soldier out of the turret and closed the top hatch. Only then did he spot another man in the rear of the passenger area. His wrists were bound with a zip tie, and he was bleeding in two places.

'Who's your friend?' Cobb shouted.

'I'll tell you later,' McNutt said as he backed up the vehicle quickly and cranked the wheel. 'Better buckle up. I'm still getting the hang of the steering.'

'The road is too narrow. You're not going to make the turn,' Maggie warned.

'Road? Where we're going, we don't need roads,' McNutt said with a laugh. 'Hold on to your spleens. Things are about to get bouncy.'

Sarah quickly realized that McNutt intended to bypass the winding path and drive straight down the side of the mountain. 'Oh, you crazy mother—'

Before she could finish, the AFV smashed into the retaining wall on the side of the road and plunged down the hillside. It mangled shrubs and saplings, crushing every obstacle in its path including small rises of soil and stone. When the AFV hit a solid patch of rock, it jounced and popped up and down, bouncing everyone violently in their restraints.

The side of the hill was a steep drop, and at times it felt like they were going straight down until the massive vehicle would buck toward the horizontal. Before they reached the lower switchback road, McNutt cranked hard on the controls, sending the vehicle into an impressive sideways drift. Sarah was certain the troop transport would flip and roll the rest of the way down the mountain, but McNutt whooped with joy.

The AFV demolished a white wall that marked the edge of the lower road. As it scrabbled across a field of basketball-sized stones, bouncing and jolting the entire time, McNutt stood on the accelerator. The vehicle suddenly finished its slide and gripped the asphalt of the road. An instant later, it lurched forward and started picking up speed.

'Nice,' Cobb said. 'Now worry about them.'

McNutt looked ahead down the steep hill to a crowd of six PLA soldiers in tan uniforms, all pointing Kalashnikov rifles at some target in the distance. A few shots pinged off the rocks near the squad, throwing puffs of grit and dust into the air, but the soldiers suddenly lost focus on their fight with the Chinese criminals. The sight of the AFV careening down the mountainside and then skidding onto the road had captured their collective attention.

McNutt laughed at their wimpy rifles and drove even faster. 'As long as they don't have a rocket-propelled grenade launcher, we're good.'

'Not them,' Cobb said as he pointed his finger. '*Them.*'

McNutt looked to where Cobb was pointing. Across from the massive concrete plaza at the base of the Potala was the main road out of town where there were three more AFVs – and each of them had their cannons intact. They sat side by side, waiting for anyone to try to escape.

'Oh,' McNutt grunted. 'I was wondering where they went.'

'I think you should slow down,' Cobb said.

'I think you're right.'

The vehicle shuddered to a full stop.

'Now what?' McNutt asked.

Cobb stared at him. 'Tell me about your friend.'

'Remember the dead guy in the turret? That *wasn't* my handiwork. The dude in the back shot him with this.' He handed the bullpup-style rifle to Cobb. 'I'm assuming he's one of the gunmen from Guangzhou. There's a few of them running around out there, and they opened fire on the soldiers without provocation. I popped the AFV driver in the jaw and left him behind. Kid was so young he still had diapers. The soldiers on foot must be from inside the palace.'

'Maggie,' Cobb called. 'Start asking that guy who he is and who he works for.'

'On it, Jack,' she said from the back.

Cobb waited until the questioning started in Mandarin before he turned his attention to Sarah. 'Do me a favor: make sure he doesn't die before I have a chance to talk to him.'

Sarah nodded and rushed to tend to their injured captive.

McNutt continued to stare at the roadblock ahead. 'Chief?'

'Yeah, Josh.'

'Sorry to bother you, but I'd feel a lot safer if we were moving.'

'I don't know about you, but I didn't feel real safe falling down that mountain.'

'That hurts, chief. It really does. I thought I stuck the landing.'

Cobb glanced at him. 'Where do you want to go?'

'Anywhere but here,' McNutt admitted. 'As far as I can tell, the only guns in the area that we need to worry about are the three cannons pointing at us. Based on the youth of the soldiers and their obvious inexperience, I'd feel a lot better if we were a moving target.'

'You raise a valid point.'

'Thank you, chief.'

Cobb pointed to the left. 'Drive over there. I want to see what they do.'

McNutt swung the wheel in that direction and pushed on the accelerator. The AFV chugged slowly toward ground level, well to the side of the waiting roadblock in the plaza. Suddenly one of the parked AFVs roared to life. It turned abruptly, then started on a course to intercept McNutt's AFV at the bottom of the hill.

'Interesting,' Cobb said. 'Jean-Marc, you listening?'

'I'm here,' Papineau assured him.

'Once we make it past the reception committee, we'll head south toward the airport.' He said it calmly, as if getting past the three AFVs would be a breeze. 'Obviously, we'll need a ride. It would be great if you could swing back around and pick us up.'

269

'No problem, Jack. Just tell us when.'

'Actually,' Cobb said, 'I'll need to tell you *where* – because we can't make it to the airport. There's an entire battalion headed our way. We'll need to be picked up on the highway.'

'You've got to be joking!'

'Do I sound like I'm joking?' Cobb growled. 'Trust me, the Gulfstream can land on the main road. I studied it on the way to Lhasa, and there's more than enough room. Seriously, why do you think I wanted you in the air so soon?'

The line went silent as Papineau panicked.

'Hector,' Cobb said, 'are you still there?'

'I sure am.'

'Did he pass out?'

Garcia smiled. 'Not yet.'

'Before he does, make sure he convinces the pilot to land on the road. In the meantime, I was hoping you could find us a different route out of town. Doesn't even have to be paved.'

'Sure, give me a second.' Garcia's fingers went to work on his ever-present keyboard. 'Okay, I think I found something that will work. Head northwest at the bottom of the hill. Go a little over a mile, then turn left. It'll give your pursuers the idea that you're making for the west, and they won't have a chance to cut you off from crossing the river at the south of the city.'

'Noted,' Cobb said.

'Once you're down there, let me know, and I'll talk you through the rest.'

'Just tell us now,' McNutt complained.

'Sure, Josh, grab a pen. All the road signs are in Tibetan.'

Before McNutt had a chance to reply, the hard-charging AFV fired its 30 mm cannon with a loud *boom*! McNutt cut the wheel sharply to the left, and their vehicle launched off the road again, tearing its way across rock and greenery. The fired shell passed them harmlessly and hit the side of a small ticket building beside an auxiliary parking lot at the bottom of the road. The force of the impact blew the tiny shed into smithereens.

'Heading back for the plaza,' McNutt announced.

'Veer right of it,' Garcia said in his ear. 'From there head for the park. It's a straight shot to the road north of the river.'

McNutt guided the AFV onto the road that ran in front of the Potala. Traffic had ceased at each end because of the gunfight on the hill. He angled across it, making for the park adjacent to the wide concrete plaza where McNutt steered around the large trees but went through smaller obstacles like benches and a shallow pond. The water didn't even slow the armored vehicle down.

The pursuing AFV lost precious time turning around after missing the opportunity to intercept McNutt. The drivers in the other AFVs noticed his escape attempt and decided to abandon their roadblock to give chase. They maneuvered the cumbersome vehicles around and came racing back down the road for the park.

'You should see a smaller building to your right and a larger one to the left behind a row of trees,' Garcia advised. 'Angle between them, then head for the center of the next large building on the left. There's a gateway through it.'

McNutt could see the trees Garcia had mentioned, and the smaller building to the right of the line of greenery, but the last tree, a stout oak with a gnarled, split trunk, was massive and way too close to the building to allow passage. Ironically, the tree had been planted there by the military for that very purpose: to prevent civilian vehicles from entering the park. It was a crowd and riot control tactic from fifty years ago that had finally come to fruition now.

In his gut, McNutt felt he could probably plow the huge tree down, but he doubted the vehicle would be drivable afterward.

With nowhere else to go, he made a risky choice.

271

'Hang on!' he shouted.

Cobb said nothing but his eyes doubled in size.

'Shit!' Sarah screamed from the back.

McNutt swerved the vehicle sharply to the right, bringing the armored vehicle into a perpendicular line with the front of the building. As he did, one of the pursuing AFVs fired its cannon. The shell missed its target but blasted the front façade of the building that McNutt was aiming for. The impact shattered the front wall as he hit the brakes in order to avoid the explosion. The blast sprayed concrete and glass in a maelstrom of smoke and debris.

Then McNutt sped up and smashed the AFV into the damaged structure.

He could only hope that no one was inside.

52

Brilliant spears of daylight pierced the white cloud of plaster dust as the AFV plowed through the far wall of the building. Debris slid away from the vehicle's clogged viewports as concrete ruptured all around it. When the haze cleared, they found themselves on a wide concrete walkway that led to a glassed-in breezeway between two much larger buildings.

The structures looked far too stout for the powerful AFV, but McNutt knew the glass breezeway would yield like tissue paper. He pulled a lever just before they hit, activating steel shields that dropped over the viewports. The sound of tinkling glass reverberated throughout the cabin as broken shards pinged off the vehicle's metal skin.

A second later, McNutt raised the viewport shields again and saw nothing but a straight concrete path for a thousand feet with a busy road at the end of it. He tramped on the accelerator, and the AFV charged ahead at full steam.

Maggie popped her head into the cockpit. 'Our guest won't talk.'

'No worries,' Cobb said. 'I figured he wouldn't.'

'Are we going to smash into more things? If so, I'd like to strap into a chair.'

'No, ma'am,' McNutt said. 'I'm done smashing things for now.'

A moment later, they heard a loud *thunk* sound behind them. One of the pursuing AFVs had fired its cannon. The shell smashed into a huge tree, just as they passed it. The top of the tree fell over on the roof of their AFV with a massive crunch, but it didn't stop them.

'For the record, that wasn't me,' McNutt said with a smile.

'Drive erratic,' Cobb ordered.

'I thought I was!'

'No,' Cobb stressed, 'remember the helicopter in Loulan?'

McNutt grinned at the memory. 'Gotcha, chief.'

Cobb hustled back into the passenger area then climbed the ladder up the gun turret, just as McNutt jerked the wheel again, swerving the AFV left and right in unpredictable patterns.

Cobb flung open the hatch, reached out for the handles on the machine gun, and quickly pulled himself halfway out. He hooked an ankle around the upright of the metal ladder for support and then swung around, leveling the machine gun back at the pursuing AFVs. He immediately realized that only two of their pursuers were behind him, and wondered if the third had taken a different route, attempting to cut them off.

The driver of the first vehicle had his head sticking out of a hatch in the cockpit, but he quickly dropped down when he saw Cobb level the machine gun. But Cobb wasn't trying to hit him. He aimed the weapon lower and blasted at the front tires of the first AFV.

Cobb waited just a tick as McNutt swerved violently across the concrete and onto the lawn on the right. They were heading for another tree, but Cobb knew the vehicle would swerve again in a second. Just as they hit the grass, the pursuing AFV fired its cannon again with a thunderous report that rattled Cobb's bones in his body like a subwoofer at a rock concert.

The shell passed harmlessly by as their AFV jerked again.

The move had put Cobb in the perfect position to target the front two wheels on the right side of the lead AFV. He opened fire with the heavy gun, the *chug-chug-chug* of the weapon rattling his body further. Cobb knew that AFVs were always equipped with eight run-flat tires, and most of them could actually lose multiple wheels and still roll on.

Unless, of course, the correct few were disabled.

The steady stream of 7.62 mm rounds shredded the first two tires on the right side with ease. The rubber split horizontally across the wheel and flipped off, like a blowout on a semi-truck on the interstate. With both tires blown, the front right corner of the vehicle tipped down to the ground, striking sparks off the concrete and wrenching the vehicle sideways.

As soon as the left side came into full view, helped by another of McNutt's wild turns, Cobb laid into the damaged vehicle's other front wheels. He destroyed the first tire under a volley of heavy fire, but he ran out of ammunition before he could get the second one. It didn't matter, though. The nose of the lead AFV mashed into the concrete walkway and the armor dug in deeply before the driver had the good sense to take his foot off the accelerator.

No way it could catch them now.

Cobb dropped down the hatch just before the second AFV swerved around the immobilized carcass of the first, their machine gunner spraying fire back. The volley of rounds hit the open hatch lid, denting it and clanging it shut just above his head.

Cobb breathed a sigh of relief after that one.

He had planned to come down for more ammunition, but the gunner above had changed his mind. As he made his way toward the cockpit, his ears were still ringing from the noise of the machine gun, but he clearly heard an argument as he neared the front of the vehicle.

'Trust me!' McNutt screamed.

Garcia shouted in their ears. 'That's not the bridge you want! The one you want is another mile west! That one takes you to an island in the middle of the river. You'll be trapped.'

McNutt pulled hard on the steering, sending the AFV onto the road that Garcia had warned him not to take. 'Just trust me, Rodrigo.'

Cobb looked to Sarah for an explanation.

She merely shrugged and grimaced.

Cobb noticed that Maggie was holding the back of Sarah's chair in a death grip, her knuckles turning white from the effort. He smiled at her and told her to relax before he turned his attention to McNutt.

'What are we doing, Josh?' Cobb asked.

'We won't make it to the next bridge,' McNutt said, jerking the vehicle unexpectedly to the left, and then quickly back to the right. 'Those guys are too close, and the road is too straight. One hit from that cannon, and we'll be cooked in here like scrambled eggs.'

The AFV was jolted hard from the rear, throwing everyone forward. Cobb realized the pursuing vehicle must have rammed them.

'Hang on,' McNutt said as he leaned into the steering wheel.

Cobb glanced ahead and saw they had only two hundred more feet of asphalt before they would hit a decorative fountain. There didn't seem to be any road after that.

'What's the plan?' Cobb demanded.

'Yeah,' Sarah said. 'We'd all love to know.'

McNutt grinned. 'I want to see if those teenagers in the RV fully understand the capabilities of their vehicle. I'm guessing they don't.'

'Guessing?' Sarah shouted as they neared the fountain. 'You're guessing?'

'What are you—' Cobb began as the Marine sped up more.

The AFV smashed through a wooden bench before hitting the fountain in a spray of water and rubble. A geyser erupted in the wreckage behind them as the AFV continued forward, barreling down a steep slope that led to the surging rapids ahead.

Sarah and Maggie screamed, but McNutt didn't stop.

He merely laughed as he drove straight into the river.

53

The nose of the AFV dipped and lurched suddenly, then the raging current of the spring thaw began to whisk the vehicle sideways in a slow, twisting motion.

'These things are amphibious,' McNutt said, grinning. 'They can only do about four knots, but it's enough to make do.'

'Won't they follow us?' Sarah asked. 'Their vehicle floats, too.'

'I doubt they ever field-tested it in water. Kids that young won't have the balls to try it. They'll be too scared to sink a million-dollar piece of machinery.'

Cobb moved back to the turret and cautiously peeked out. The island was already far behind, and he could see the AFV that had followed them to the river's edge was tilted at a strange angle with its nose in the air and its belly resting on the pile of rubble. Water from the smashed fountain shot in all directions. The soldiers might try to follow in the river once they got their vehicle unstuck, but his team was quickly widening the margin.

Cobb slipped back into the cockpit, where McNutt had corrected the lazy spin and was powering through the river, slow and steady, moving for the far shore. He mashed the nose into a wide sandy bank and ground the accelerator down until the front wheels chewed through the muck, dragging the AFV ashore inch by inch.

'How are we on fuel?' Cobb asked.

'We got plenty,' McNutt said, just as the wheels bit into solid rock and the AFV bolted forward, clunking up and down over the uneven ground.

'Great,' Sarah said. 'Now if we can just get some distance.'

'At this rate,' Garcia said in their ears, 'you're thirty minutes from the rendezvous point. The bad news is the army is, too. Do you think you can speed things up?'

'Ask me again in fifteen. Too many variables,' Cobb said.

'Just so you know,' Garcia added, 'they've scrambled a couple of MiGs out of Chengdu. Thankfully, it'll take them an hour to get to Lhasa. Probably nothing to worry about.'

'Keep us updated,' Cobb said.

The AFV could do sixty miles an hour in perfect conditions, but even a luxury SUV with brand-new shocks would have found that speed impossible on the rutted roads. McNutt pushed it as fast as he could without fear of shaking them all to death. When the road swept away from the direction he wanted, he drove off it, keeping a straight path for the point two miles further west where the main road turned due south to follow the river and head down to the airport. The roads in the region went where the mountains and the river allowed them, but with an amphibious assault vehicle the Marine was happy to just plow straight through, following the edge of the foothills on his left.

Five minutes later they were on the road heading south, and McNutt kicked the AFV to its top speed on the much smoother highway. No one spoke about the turmoil in Lhasa. They all understood the time for reflection would come later. The tension of whether they would make it to the rendezvous before the army had consumed them all.

Arriving first was the only thing that mattered.

If they didn't, they were headed to a military prison.

Unless, of course, they were killed at the scene.

'Hey chief,' McNutt said, 'I know you have a lot of stuff on your mind, but don't you think you should go back there and talk to our friend?'

'Let's worry about them first,' Cobb said, looking through the viewport. Far off in the distance, they could see a small line of trucks and cars at a standstill. Beyond them, they saw the glint of several white police cars blocking the road.

'The local fuzz,' McNutt said. 'Nothing to worry about.'

Maggie spoke up. 'They might have automatic weapons.'

'Nothing that can hurt us,' he replied.

As the AFV approached the stalled line of vehicles at the roadblock, McNutt swerved into the far-less-crowded oncoming lane and accelerated. Cobb could see six police officers in bluish-gray uniforms, all brandishing Chinese AK variant rifles.

Long before the AFV was in range, the police opened fire.

As the vehicle got closer, McNutt dropped the viewport shields again. They were blind now, but it didn't matter. In a second they would plow through the front end of one of the two sedans blocking the road, turning it into crumpled metal. Cobb hoped the men would have the sense to dive out of the way, or they might be injured.

When the crash came, Cobb was surprised how little it affected the AFV. The trees and the fountain back in Lhasa had made more noise than the police car. Ten seconds later, McNutt raised the shields again, and they were completely through the roadblock.

McNutt couldn't help but laugh. 'Whoooeeee! I'm starting to like this thing. Do you think Papi can buy me one? I'll park it next to his yacht.'

'First things first,' Sarah said. 'He still needs to pick us up.'

Cobb ignored the chatter. He once again climbed the turret and peeked behind them. No one was following the rogue AFV. Unfortunately, he knew why. The cops would have been informed that the army was on the way – on a direct collision course with the fleeing vehicle. The local police had done their part, now they would sit back and let the army take over.

Before closing the hatch, Cobb noticed a broken branch caught on the hinge. He reasoned it must have been there since their trip through the park. Smiling, he pulled the branch free and brought it inside with him.

'How long?' Cobb shouted.

'Ten minutes with no more speed bumps,' McNutt said.

'Hector, did you copy that?'

'Loud and clear,' Garcia replied. 'ETA is ten minutes.'

Cobb turned to Maggie. 'Come with me.'

They went into the back and found the bound prisoner. He looked miserable, and his leg was bleeding profusely. A puddle of his own blood had pooled beneath him on the floor of the vehicle. Any hope to flee had left the captive.

'Translate for me, please,' Cobb said.

Maggie nodded and waited.

'Three questions is all. Who do you work for? What do you want with us? And what do you know about us? If you answer all three to my satisfaction, you'll live. I'll wrap your wound, and we'll leave you on the side of the road in peace.'

Maggie translated everything in rapid Mandarin.

The man stared at Cobb the entire time, not flinching.

Cobb waited until she was done. 'If you don't answer my questions immediately, I'll be forced to show you a technique that was taught to me by this maniac friend of mine. It's called the Vietnam Stick Trick, and man, is it effective . . .'

Once again, Maggie translated everything.

'Here's how it works,' Cobb said with unblinking eyes. 'You take a stick, and you shove one end into a bullet hole, then you wiggle it around and around and around. The best part of all? It can't be called torture because all I'm trying to do is find the bullet inside the wound. So I keep doing it over and over again. I'm told it hurts like hell.'

Maggie, to her credit, didn't blanch. She translated everything.

As she did, Cobb pulled out his knife and started to sharpen one end of the branch that he had removed from above. With every swipe of his blade, the man's face grew more and more pale. Sweat trickled down his forehead and into his eyes. He blinked at the drops, unable to wipe away the fluid with his hands secured behind his back.

Cobb looked at his watch, as the seconds ticked past. For the safety of his team, he needed to know who was trying to kill them. It was the only way they would survive this mission. He yelled toward the cockpit, 'Do you have a lighter?'

McNutt fished in a pocket and tossed a stainless steel Zippo through the air.

Cobb caught it and admired the carved USMC insignia and the symbol of the US Embassy in Bishkek, Kyrgyzstan. He turned back to the captive, noting the man's panicked eyes following his every move before he flipped open the lighter with his free hand, then flicked the flint wheel to spark a flame.

The man's face melted in confusion and terror.

He spoke rapidly to Maggie in a tone of sheer panic.

She translated for Cobb. 'What are you doing?'

'Did I forget to tell you?' Cobb said as he held the fire under the branch, slowly moving the flame back and forth in full view of the prisoner. 'I heat up the stick to kill all the germs before I shove it into your wound . . . The smell of burning flesh is fantastic.'

Cobb lowered the lighter and stepped closer.

The man began to scream before Cobb even touched him.

54

Despite her calm demeanor, Maggie was thrilled that Cobb didn't touch the prisoner. He started screaming immediately, babbling answers to Cobb's three questions over and over again until his frightened pleas slowly but surely devolved into a single word.

'*Yihequan!*' he cried repeatedly. '*Yihequan! Yihequan!*'

'What does that mean?' Cobb asked.

Maggie answered as the vehicle slowed to a stop. 'He works for a criminal organization called *Yihequan* – the Brotherhood of Righteous and Harmonious Fists. They know we are after a treasure, but this man does not know which one.'

'And what do the brothers want?'

'They want the treasure, then they want us dead.'

'Yeah,' Cobb said. 'I kind of sensed that last part.'

Maggie continued. 'They were supposed to watch us and only confront us if we found the treasure. But the army showed up and spooked his colleagues. Once the shooting started, he had no choice but to fight back.'

'Do they know our names?'

'He doesn't, but they took our pictures and sent them to Hong Kong.'

Cobb groaned. 'That's not good.'

'What's not good?' McNutt asked as he left the cockpit. He had parked the AFV on the side of the road in anticipation of Papineau's jet and had missed some of the conversation.

'I'll tell you later. In the meantime, patch him up and gag him.'

'You got it, chief.'

Cobb climbed the ladder to the AFV's roof where Sarah was manning the machine gun, just in case they were attacked by unseen forces.

'So?' she asked. 'What are we facing?'

Cobb pointed to the sky behind her. 'A tricky landing.'

Low in the sky, the white Gulfstream G650 came in steadily, its landing gear already deployed. The small plane was one of the finest business aircraft in the world, designed for long flights of over 6,000 miles and able to top out at speeds just shy of Mach 1.

They watched as the plane swooped in lower and lower until the rear wheels gently tapped the road a moment before the nose gear settled. If everything went according to plan, the sleek jet would race on its wheels along the road and stop right next to them.

'Shit,' Cobb said as he stared to the south. Off in the distance, he could see the army convoy coming around a bend in the road behind the plane. The soldiers were less than a mile from the rendezvous point, and they were closing fast. Cobb immediately stuck his head in the hatch and shouted for his team. 'The troops are coming. Time to go!'

Sarah slid gracefully off the side of the AFV. 'Hector, keep those engines running. This is going to be close.'

'No shit!' Garcia replied. 'We just flew over them.'

To their left, snow-capped mountains rose up high. To their right, the muddy brown water of the surging river roared through a series of rapids, carrying tons of soil and debris along the way. Cobb knew they would be pinned by the geography if it came to a gunfight, but this was the only straightaway where the plane could safely land. Unfortunately, the road wasn't quite the recommended 6,000 feet they would need for takeoff, so getting airborne again would be dicey.

Still, it was the best chance they had.

With a rush of wind and the roar of the turbines, the plane rolled up next to the AFV. Papineau was at the door of the jet with the stairs already lowered; they cleared the ground by barely a foot. Sarah helped Maggie aboard first and nimbly hopped up the steps behind her.

McNutt was next, as Cobb ran alongside the still-moving aircraft to keep pace with it. He was about to catch up to the stairs when he heard the distinctive sound of one of the oncoming AFVs firing its 30 mm cannon in the distance. He dove forward and grabbed the handrail, holding on for his life as the round exploded on the other side of the jet.

'Go!' he shouted even though he wasn't inside the plane yet.

Immediately the engines revved louder as the plane picked up speed on the straight road. As it did, Cobb dragged on the asphalt next to the jet. Without his heavy-duty boots and reinforced cargo pants, he would have lost most of the skin on the lower half of his body, but they protected him until he was able to pull himself onto the stairs and into the plane itself.

Thankful to be inside, he pressed the control that should have retracted the stairs and closed the doorway on the Gulfstream, but nothing happened.

'You've got to be shitting me!' he blurted.

Cobb grabbed the handrail and tugged as hard as he could as the scenery whizzed by at an alarming rate, but he simply wasn't strong enough to pull the stairs inside while fighting the surging air. As Cobb pondered his options – and he didn't see many – Papineau joined him at the door. The Frenchman clamped onto the other rail and heaved with all his might until the steps flattened and the door swung shut. They collapsed to the floor completely out of breath as the pressure seals hissed their approval.

A moment later, the nose of the aircraft lifted up, tilting the cabin back as another round from the AFV's cannon hit the road nearby with a shuddering boom. Everyone held their breath as the plane lurched upward and then ripped into the sky at a steep angle. Cobb and Papineau rolled down the aisle in a tangle of limbs until McNutt reached out from his seat and grabbed them.

'I'll be damned: Papi saved the day,' McNutt said.

'In more ways than one,' Cobb admitted. He patted Papineau on the shoulder while untangling himself from the Frenchman. 'Thanks for coming back for us.'

'Happy to help,' Papineau said as he lay back on the floor. 'If it's okay with you, I'm just going to lie here a bit until I catch my breath.'

Cobb smiled. 'Take as long as you'd like.'

'I wouldn't advise it,' Garcia said, securely strapped into his seat while staring at his laptop. 'The jets are a lot closer than expected. I had guesstimated an hour. Turns out I was wrong.'

'How wrong?' Cobb asked as he helped Papineau to his feet. The Frenchman scrambled to the nearest seat and buckled himself in.

'Tough to say,' Garcia announced. 'We're sixty miles to the border of Bhutan. That's approximately six minutes at our top speed. But we're not there yet, so let's say seven.'

The pilot, who was fully aware of the incoming jets, abandoned his pursuit of altitude and punched the throttles. They needed speed, not height. The whine of the engines nearly doubled as Cobb buckled himself into the seat next to Sarah.

'What about the MiGs? Can they catch up to us?' McNutt asked.

Garcia answered. 'They're actually not MiGs. They're Chinese Chengdu J-10s, which is why my initial calculations were off. They can reach speeds of Mach 1.2.'

Cobb nodded. 'In other words, yes.'

'Definitely,' Garcia said. 'Here's the thing, though. They won't catch up to us until we're near the border. They might not fire on us that close to a sovereign nation. That is, *if* they're even coming after us. For all we know, they might be air support for the troops on the ground.'

'Give me some odds,' Cobb demanded.

'Fifty-fifty,' Garcia guessed.

Papineau pulled out his cell phone and made a frantic call, but the others couldn't hear what he was saying. Maggie was holding the armrests of her chair, her face drained of color. Garcia was tapping at the keys of his laptop and mumbling to himself. McNutt rested in his chair with his eyes closed. If he was worried, he didn't show it.

Their plane continued to gain speed.

Cobb glanced at Sarah, and she looked back at him. Their eyes locked for a few seconds, but there was nothing that needed to be said. The look alone expressed a range of emotions involving friendship, loyalty, concern, and lost possibilities.

Suddenly, a loud beeping noise emanated from Garcia's laptop like an alarm.

'What is it?' Cobb asked.

'The jets have altered course to chase us down. Two minutes out.'

From this point on, it was a race to the border.

Cobb felt each beat of his heart in his throat as the seconds ticked by slowly and painfully. When he closed his eyes he felt Sarah's hand slip into his, and he squeezed it tight.

Forty seconds later, Garcia spoke again. 'They've hit top speed.'

The Gulfstream's engines were already whining so loudly that Cobb didn't need to ask whether they had hit their maximum velocity. He knew the answer.

Almost a minute to go.

Cobb opened his eyes to look at Sarah, but she was in a trance of her own, her eyes closed in silent prayer. Papineau was off his phone, his eyes likewise shut.

'Thirty seconds,' Garcia called out.

Cobb closed his eyes again and started counting down.

At ten seconds, Garcia mumbled to himself. 'I think we're gonna make it.'

A moment later, another alarm shrieked – this time from the cockpit.

It was high-pitched and constant.

Cobb and McNutt knew the sound well.

One of the Chinese jets had missile lock.

'Shit!' Garcia shouted. 'They fired!'

55

The next few seconds in the Gulfstream were completely silent.

The pilot shut off the missile alarm, and team members each retreated into their own morbid thoughts as they waited to explode in a ball of fire. A split-second over the border, something whizzed past them on the left, fast enough to rock the plane. It was followed immediately by an explosion that lurched the Gulfstream forward.

Inexplicably, a third jet passed directly overhead, aiming back toward the Chinese border. Its wash forced them to dip suddenly, but then the Gulfstream corrected its course and continued deeper into Bhutan airspace unharmed.

'What was that?' Cobb shouted.

'Holy shit!' Garcia blurted as he stared at his screen. 'There's another jet up here. It took out the missiles with countermeasures. I don't know where it came from, but it certainly did the trick. The Chinese jets just turned back for home.'

The team let out a collective cheer, shocked by their good fortune.

'Where the hell did the reinforcements come from?' McNutt asked.

Papineau smiled. 'Some friends of mine from l'Armée de l'Air. They were in Sikkim on joint task-force training exercises with the Indian Air Force. I gave them a call.'

McNutt stared, open-mouthed.

'I wasn't always a businessman,' Papineau said.

Cobb realized he was talking about French mandatory military conscription, which would still have been in place when Papineau was graduating from high school. He probably would have served in North Africa or Lebanon. It wasn't something Cobb had ever thought to investigate, despite having Garcia look into Papineau's business dealings over the last decade.

The plane banked in an easy turn to the right, and Cobb could see the white Himalayas below the dipped wing through the small Plexiglas window. 'Where are we going?'

'Somewhere we can all decompress,' Papineau said as he pulled out a handkerchief and wiped his forehead. 'Then we need to examine what the monk gave to you.'

*   *   *

The Hyatt Regency in Katmandu, Nepal, was a luxury hotel that catered to the business set. With excellent restaurants, expensive decor, expansive meeting rooms, and a well-trained staff eager to please, it was a great place for the team to catch their second wind.

They had retired to their respective suites to rest for a few hours before regrouping and discussing their next move. Cobb had tried to sleep but failed miserably. He was too wound up. He knew Garcia would be, too, and that he would already be trying to decipher the contents of the USB drive the old monk had slipped to Cobb in the Potala.

Concerned for the monk and his brethren, Cobb had accessed the hotel's Wi-Fi to check the news about the palace, but the media hadn't gotten wind of the turmoil.

Or more likely, the Chinese had clamped down on all news coming out of Tibet.

Fed up with waiting, Cobb left his suite and headed down the hallway for Garcia's room. Just before he got to the door, he heard someone approaching from behind.

'Couldn't sleep?' McNutt called out to him.

Cobb shook his head. 'I thought I'd see if Hector is restless too.'

Cobb and McNutt knocked on the door in unison. Sarah opened it a moment later. She had changed her clothes, but she looked as tired as Cobb felt.

'Sorry, wrong room,' Cobb said. 'We were looking for—'

Sarah opened the door wide, and they could see Garcia at his desk, pounding away on his keyboard. Maggie was seated on the cream-colored sofa, looking at a tablet and swiping rapidly through images that Garcia streamed to her.

'Welcome to the party,' Sarah said, ushering them into the room.

Cobb and McNutt stepped inside and crossed the dark wooden floors. Exhausted from the day's events but too tired to sleep, they quickly grabbed chairs in the sitting area.

'No one else could sleep, either,' Garcia said, not looking up from his laptop. He had changed into cargo shorts and a T-shirt that read: I'M NOT ANTI-SOCIAL; I'M JUST NOT USER-FRIENDLY.

Cobb looked around the room. 'Papi must have been able to get some sleep, at least.'

'Actually,' Sarah said, 'he just went to get ice. He'll be right back.'

'How is it going with the USB?' Cobb asked.

Garcia kept typing. 'It wasn't encrypted. We're going through it now with the translation software. Maggie has a lot of stuff already.'

Maggie looked up from her tablet. 'Shall we wait for Jean-Marc?'

Just then they heard a knock at the door.

This time, Sarah made no move to get up. Instead, McNutt stood and quickly paced down the hallway to the door. Cobb noticed he did not look through the peephole in the thick wood, but rather stopped at the doorway to the bathroom and edged into it before calling out, 'Who's there?'

'It is I,' Papineau said.

As McNutt moved to open the door, Cobb was once again impressed with the sniper's ingrained security-consciousness. He would never use a peephole, alerting anyone on the other side of the door to his location via the shadow cast through to the front of the glass, and he knew well enough to stand aside from the door should shooters be waiting on the opposite side.

Papineau entered the suite carrying a silver tray with several cups of steaming coffee. 'I was going to have a Scotch,' he admitted sheepishly, 'but I thought perhaps coffee would be better for all concerned.'

'Thank you, sir,' McNutt said as he took the tray and set it on the coffee table in the center of the sitting area.

Papineau wasn't sure what stunned him more: the sniper's good manners, or the fact that McNutt called him 'sir' instead of 'Papi'.

Cobb noticed the change in McNutt as well, but the truth was Papineau had earned it with that miracle at the border. Cobb wondered idly whether the favor from the French Air Force was provided courtesy of loyalty or massive stacks of euros. He would have Garcia dig into Papineau's military days later. Not that he suspected he would find anything damning; he simply wanted all the pertinent information on the background of his people. If he had known about Papineau's military connections, he might have used them earlier instead of relying on Papineau to think of doing so at the last minute.

McNutt passed coffee around to everyone, and they all took sips of the imported brew before Papineau looked around expectantly. Cobb noticed he did not attempt to retake command of the room by asking everyone to begin. Cobb appreciated the gesture.

'Okay,' Cobb said. 'What do we have?'

Garcia answered first. 'We have a shit-ton of photos of two

separate books. We're running the translation program on the pages right now. It should be done any minute.'

Maggie took over from there. 'The first book is an official account from a clerical monk named Thokmay. He was basically the right-hand man to the Sakya lama, who was the head of the religious administration unit in Tibet during the thirteenth century. Thokmay's account will hopefully mention Marco Polo's visit to Lhasa. Unfortunately, I haven't found such a section yet. The book is a massive volume consisting of over three thousand pages. It will take some time to dig through everything.'

'Okay, not a problem,' Cobb said. 'And the other book?'

Maggie pointed at Garcia. 'Still waiting on that one.'

Cobb rubbed his tired eyes and thought back to the events at the Potala. Based on the urgency in the old monk's voice and the death grip that he'd had on his arm, Cobb had assumed that the contents of the USB drive would be staggering. Then again, maybe he had misread the situation. The palace was under attack and the monk was obviously scared. Maybe his superhuman kung fu grip had more to do with the adrenaline surging through his veins than anything else.

A ding on Garcia's computer pulled Cobb out of his thoughts.

It was soon followed by a shriek of feminine joy.

Strangely, the sound had come from Garcia.

'No way!' he shouted, his voice cracking in midsentence. 'Maggie! Take a look at this!'

She rushed to his side. 'At what?'

He pointed at the translation on his screen. 'Can this be right?'

She looked at the computer, then at Garcia, then back at the computer.

Sarah stood as well. 'What is it? Is it important?'

'Very important!' Garcia shouted.

Maggie's face broke into a huge grin as she turned to explain their discovery. 'Obviously I haven't had a chance to go through the data yet but, if this translation is correct, the second book on the drive is much more significant than the first.'

'Why? What is it?' Cobb demanded.

She smiled at him. 'It's the personal diary of Marco Polo.'

56

Papineau was the first to speak. 'Well done, everyone!'

The team celebrated with high fives and hugs, a moment of pure joy that temporarily made up for all they had been through in China.

Their efforts had paid off. They finally had a solid lead.

Despite her happiness, Maggie held up her hand and asked them to stop. She needed them to understand that their search was far from over.

'People,' she said, 'listen to me. There's still a lot of work to be done.'

Cobb agreed. 'Okay, guys. That's enough fun for today. There'll be plenty of time to celebrate after we find the treasure.'

'There'll be plenty to drink, too,' McNutt added.

Maggie shook her head. 'Joshua, don't plan your party quite yet. Just because we have his diary doesn't mean we'll find his treasure.'

'Why not?' McNutt asked. 'Seems pretty simple to me. "Dear Diary, Today I buried my treasure in the yard behind my house. I hope no one looks there. Signed, Marco."'

Maggie smiled at the comment. 'Obviously, I wish it were that easy, but the truth is I haven't had time to read the document yet. Assuming there are no maps or step-by-step directions to the prize, I will still have to search for details about the treasure. Also keep something in mind: this book was most likely left in Tibet *before* the Polos set out on their return journey. For all we know, it could have been toward the beginning of his trip – before he even had a treasure.'

'Understood,' Cobb said before McNutt could crack another

joke. 'But it will certainly give us a better picture of the man himself, even if it contains no direct clues.'

'True,' she said. 'That's why I'm smiling.'

'In the meantime, we have to worry about the Fists. What can you tell us about them?'

'Rumors, mostly,' she admitted. 'Their full name in English is The Brotherhood of Righteous and Harmonious Fists. They are quite famous in the south of China.'

'Famous for what?' Sarah asked.

'They are a secret society, well trained in the martial arts. But more than that, they are fiercely anti-Christian and against all involvement of foreigners in China. They became convinced – most likely through cult-like dogma from their leaders – that they were mystically imbued with a resistance to foreigners' weapons. They believed they were bulletproof.'

'Bulletproof? I proved that wrong,' McNutt bragged.

Maggie nodded. 'Disgusted with imperialist tactics by the Western nations and the wishy-washy politicians that allowed the West to interfere in Chinese issues, the Fists marched on Beijing. They started a siege that lasted for two months, while diplomats, foreigners, and Chinese Christians all took cover in the Dongcheng District near Tiananmen Square.'

'What happened?' Sarah wondered.

'What usually happens with such things,' Maggie said with a tinge of sadness. 'Politicians were divided, some throwing their support behind the Fists, and others claiming the desperate need to stamp out any public disobedience. They called for foreign aid: the exact thing the Fists were fighting against. The army split, half of them joining up with the Fists while the rest teamed up with international troops from Japan, Russia, five European countries, and the United States. There was chaos in the streets and rampant vandalism and plunder. Rioting, rapes, murder. Looting and atrocities of all sorts, until the uprising was crushed and the situation was brought under control. Then there were the inevitable recriminations and the prosecutions.'

'How come I've never heard of this?' McNutt asked.

'Because these events occurred in 1898. In the West, it is often called the Boxer Rebellion.'

'Oh yeah,' Garcia said. 'The Boxers were those dudes with the front of their heads shaved and the long braided ponytails that you always see in martial arts films.'

McNutt grinned, thinking back to the kung fu movies that he used to watch as a child. 'I loved those guys! Anyone who's willing to cut their hair like that is a badass in my eyes.'

'Actually,' Maggie said, 'that hairstyle was forced on the men of China by imperial edict, beginning in the seventeenth century. Those who refused were put to death.'

'That's insane!' Sarah blurted.

'Nevertheless, it lasted for centuries and was seen as a sign of loyalty to the Qing rulers. The Fists eventually rebelled by letting their hair grow.'

Cobb interrupted them. 'That's all well and good, but how are these guys still running around? And why are they after us?'

'I can answer the first question only,' Maggie said. 'They were clearly not eliminated, and they stayed underground. There were always whispers through the early part of the twentieth century that the Fists were still in operation. Whenever anything went wrong for foreigners or Christians in China, people claimed the Fists were responsible.'

'Regular boogeymen,' McNutt said.

'Indeed. Eventually they became gangsters, with hands in all manner of illicit activities. By the 1980s, they were mainstream enough that they were mentioned in the Western media.'

'And now?' Papineau asked.

'They diversified,' Maggie said. 'Rumors are that they moved a lot of their resources into legitimate enterprises like utilities and steel.'

Cobb suddenly made a connection. 'What about mining?'

'Probably,' Maggie conceded.

'Damn,' McNutt said, reaching the same conclusion as Cobb.

'They must have spotted me and Josh when we were in the desert,' Cobb said. 'If their helicopter had a camera, they could have taken our pictures without us knowing it.'

Papineau took a deep breath. 'So these men – these Fists – they spotted you in Loulan, and they again spotted you again in Hong Kong? Then they followed us to Guangzhou? And later to Tibet? Pardon me for saying so, but that seems unlikely at best.'

'Not really,' Maggie said. 'The Fists are fanatically opposed to foreigners being in China at all. If they thought Jack and Josh were looting the ruins in Loulan, they would have been very keen on stopping them. And clearly, at some point they put our locations together and figured out that we are looking for something valuable, something hidden in their homeland.'

Garcia seemed worried. 'Will they follow us here?'

Maggie pondered the question. 'Normally, I would have said "no" since the Fists are so focused on China. But with such a treasure on the line, who can say? These men will assume that the treasure is composed primarily of riches that originated in their homeland and they are violently hostile to the theft of resources and archeological artifacts from Chinese soil. If I had to guess, I'd say they're going to follow us to the ends of the Earth.'

57

Friday, April 11

Late the following day, they all met in Papineau's suite for a briefing.

This time Maggie had called the meeting.

Maggie and Garcia arrived together and were the last ones to show up. She carried a notebook and an iPad in her arms, while Garcia walked in with his laptop. She was dressed conservatively, but Garcia wore shorts, flip-flops, and yet another T-shirt. This one read: NERD? I PREFER THE TERM INTELLECTUAL BADASS.

The room was nearly identical to Garcia's suite, and the others had all taken the same positions they had occupied the day before. Garcia set his computer on the desk and flipped it open. His screen was split into six columns, each streaming different sets of data. Papineau glanced at the program but couldn't figure out what he was looking at.

'Okay,' Maggie said as she faced the group, 'we've finished the translation of Polo's journal. The software is terrible at colloquial expressions and outdated terms, but I've had a chance to skim through the diary a couple of times.'

'And?' Cobb asked.

'It's a tragic tale, really. Our Marco found the love of his life, the Chinese girl Yangchen, at a time when interracial relationships weren't just frowned upon, they were unheard of. As it was, Westerners themselves were pretty much unheard of in China, so you can imagine the furor that it caused.'

'I'll bet,' Sarah said.

'As Professor Chu told us, Yangchen acted as his guide in Lanzhou, and they quickly fell in love. Unfortunately, everyone they met in the province was full of hatred and scorn. No one was actually violent toward Marco – he possessed the golden tablet after all – but most people they encountered let them know how they felt. Worried for her emotional well-being, Polo decided to take Yangchen to Tibet where he hoped the Buddhist population would be more receptive.'

'Was it?' Papineau asked.

Maggie shook her head. 'Not really. Polo and Yangchen pretty much faced the same reaction that they had in Lanzhou. The lone exception was the clergy. They were a bit more open-minded.'

'Sounds like a first for clergy anywhere,' McNutt cracked.

Maggie smiled at the joke. 'Yangchen's brother, Lobsang, was a monk at the Songtem temple, which was on the same hill where the Potala sits today. On the couple's behalf, her brother begged his superior for permission to let them reside in Lhasa. If the lama approved of the interracial relationship, the locals would all come around eventually, and the couple would have been able to get married and live out their days peacefully in Tibet.'

'I'm guessing that didn't happen,' Sarah said.

'Afraid not,' Maggie said. 'The lama refused to give his blessing, but he did show some compassion by giving them sanctuary while they searched for a new place to live. By then, Polo had realized that his original plan of bringing Yangchen back to Italy would be met with even worse scorn and disapproval than he had encountered in China. After all, in Europe he would be just an ordinary man with a foreign bride, and he would no longer have the protection of the Khan. Not sure where to go or what to do, Polo turned to Lobsang for advice.'

'What did her brother say?' Cobb asked.

'He strongly recommended the island of Taprobane.'

'Taprobane?' McNutt said. 'Never heard of it.'

'Thankfully, Polo *had* – he had been there previously on a secret mission for the Khan. Nowadays the island goes by a different name: Sri Lanka.'

McNutt grinned. 'Now that's a name I know. Quite well, in fact. Did I ever tell you guys about the time that I took a live chicken and—'

'Hold on,' Cobb said, cutting McNutt off. 'Unless I'm mistaken, Sri Lanka wasn't on the list of countries that Polo had visited. Are you saying your initial list was wrong?'

Maggie didn't flinch. She knew Cobb was being thorough. 'I'm saying that my initial list needs to be updated based on new information from the diary. Although the island is mentioned twice in the Rustichello version of things, it's implied that Marco didn't personally visit. According to Rustichello, the king of the native people, known as the Sinhalese, had a ruby the size of a human fist. Polo and others in China had heard tales of the stone, and the Khan had sent an unknown emissary to the island to offer a city's worth of riches in exchange for the ruby, but the Sinhalese king had refused.'

'Let me guess: Polo was the emissary,' Sarah said.

Maggie nodded. 'In his diary, Polo mentions how impressed he had been with the island and how kind and generous he had found the people to be. That's in direct contrast to the account in many published versions of Rustichello's book, where Polo refused to go there because he had heard the Sinhalese were "paltry and mean-spirited creatures".'

'That doesn't add up,' McNutt said.

'You're right, Joshua. It doesn't. Polo was obviously lying to Rustichello about the people of Sri Lanka. My guess is he did so to throw him off the scent.'

'Either that,' Cobb said, 'or the descriptions are from different points in Polo's life. Maybe he was impressed by the Sinhalese when he first met them, but later when he took Yangchen to the island with hopes of settling down, they treated him poorly.'

'Yes,' Maggie admitted, 'that's another possibility, but a good one: it would mean Polo actually went to Sri Lanka.'

Papineau rejoined the conversation. 'What do we know about the brother? I'm assuming Polo trusted him if he left his diary at the temple for safekeeping?'

Maggie nodded. 'Marco spoke very highly of her brother. He mentioned that Lobsang was an academic who was studying the regional differences between Buddhism in Tibet and Buddhism in Sri Lanka. Much like Polo, he had done a lot of traveling himself. Back then, monasteries sent scholars abroad from time to time to bear gifts and good wishes. Based on Lobsang's travels, he felt that Sri Lanka was a place where the couple could spend the rest of their lives in peace.'

'Did Lobster mention anywhere specific? Sri Lanka's roughly the size of Scotland. A hell of a lot warmer, though,' McNutt said.

Maggie smiled. '*Lobsang* mentioned a few landmarks that impressed him, but nothing more than that.'

'Anything else?' Cobb asked.

'One more thing,' Maggie said. She held up her iPad and showed the others a picture of one of the pages in Polo's diary. It was mostly in Latin letters, with a few swirly, round symbols. 'The letters you can't read are Sinhala, one of the two major ethnic languages spoken in Sri Lanka. Although Polo doesn't say so explicitly, I believe Lobsang was teaching him the language.'

'Which makes sense if Polo was planning to move there,' Sarah said.

Cobb nodded in agreement. 'What's your next step?'

Maggie glanced at Garcia. 'I'll need Hector's help to narrow down any possible sites in Sri Lanka. I also need to finish the Thokmay manuscript. It might have further clues for us, but it will take some time.'

'Actually,' Cobb said, 'you can do your research in the air. As much as I like this hotel, I'd prefer to keep moving in case the Fists are closing in.'

'In the air to where?' Papineau asked.

Cobb smiled. 'I thought that was obvious. We're going to Sri Lanka.'

58

Saturday, April 12
Galle, Sri Lanka

Papineau dreaded the call he was about to make. He had received a simple text message from Maurice Copeland, which read: CALL NOW. It had been typed in all caps, which was undoubtedly his boss's way of shouting at him from halfway around the world. Delaying the moment for as long as he could, Papineau took a deep breath and glanced out from the deck of the *Wijarama Princess*, a rented yacht he had docked in the quiet waters of the harbor.

Just as Polo had claimed, it really was a beautiful country.

The walled city of Galle was eighty miles south of the capital city of Colombo. With a population just shy of 100,000 people, the fourth-largest city in Sri Lanka was a shining example of Portuguese and Dutch colonial artistry. The walled portion of the city was the largest standing fortress built anywhere in Asia by colonial hands. By day, the walls and ramparts were a sight to behold, but now that the sun had set, the sleepy city had little to offer.

Papineau tried his best to enjoy the moment.

Away from the chaos. Away from Copeland.

Even away from his team.

Separating had been Cobb's idea, but he happily went along with the plan.

McNutt had arrived first to secure weapons and other supplies on the island. Then Maggie and Garcia had flown to Colombo with a connecting flight to the Maldives that they simply didn't use. Instead, they had slipped off toward the interior of the country to a small guesthouse in the Hill Country capital of Kandy.

Sarah had flown commercial into Colombo and connected on a private charter up to Jaffna in the north, where she would make her way down to Trincomalee on the formerly beleaguered and war-torn east coast. She would attempt to secure freighters that could get the treasure out of the country – assuming they could pinpoint where it was.

Cobb, as usual, kept his own movements to himself.

Papineau was to fly from Chennai in India, which he had done, although he had refused to fly commercial. Still, he had left the Gulfstream and his pilot behind, instead renting a charter. He then took a helicopter down to Galle with the rental agent for the yacht, a small Tamil man with dark skin and an obnoxious sinus infection.

The idea was for Papineau to set sail in the morning, around the south of the island and up to Batticaloa in the east, which would put him a three-hour drive from the others in Kandy and only two from Sarah in 'Trinco', as it was called locally. With everyone spread out, they would be harder to find, and they had flexibility to get someone on site as soon as Maggie determined the hoard's exact location. Meanwhile, Garcia was feverishly trying to pinpoint key members of the Fist's hierarchy in order to see if any of them were headed to Sri Lanka.

The idea of having to face Copeland's wrath now, when they were *this* close, filled Papineau with unease. The man was mercurial, swinging from happy to furious over the slightest things, and Papineau hated to be on his bad side. He suspected the distance between his emotions could mean the difference between a stern lecture and a bullet in the back of the head.

Still, he needed to make the call or things would be worse. He pressed SEND on his phone and waited for it to connect. It was 6.30 a.m. in California, but he knew Copeland would be wide awake, following the strict boxing regimen of his youth.

The phone rang six times, and Papineau was about to hang up. The line had no voicemail, so Copeland would either accept the call or not. Those were the only options.

Just as his finger hovered over the red button, Papineau heard the call connect. Oddly, there was only silence on the other end.

'Hello,' Papineau said. 'Are you there?'

'I am, Jean-Marc. Just swallowing a glass of carrot juice and my daily vitamins. I'm also trying to hold on to my composure, but I'm losing the fight. Tell me, how do you expect me to stay calm after your latest fuckup in Tibet?'

Copeland took a deep breath to rein in his anger. 'Florence was bad enough. At least in Italy, they had nothing to tie us to the heist at the museum. But in Tibet, I'm hearing things about shootouts at the Potala Palace, car chases with some kind of armored Batmobile, and a border skirmish with an armed group of *brigands*. That's the word they used on CNN, Jean-Marc: *brigands*. The last time I heard that fucking word I was watching *Robin Hood*, yet you managed to find some in Lhasa. Unless I'm mistaken, I seem to recall having a talk with you after Egypt about your team keeping a low profile.'

'Yes, sir, you did—'

Copeland cut him off. 'I'm pretty sure I impressed upon you the need for secrecy. I believe the actual words I used were, "Keep your team out of the spotlight."' He took a deep, calming breath, then said in a softer voice, 'So, explain yourself.'

'It seems there is an organized criminal enterprise in China stretching back to before the start of the twentieth century. This brotherhood was the cause of the Boxer Rebellion in 1900. Today they have their hands in a number of legitimate enterprises. We only just learned their identity on the way out of Tibet. These were the same men that Cobb and McNutt skirmished with in Xinjiang. They also attempted to scuttle our operation in Guangzhou.'

'Jean-Marc,' he said as the tone of his voice began to rise, 'I hope you understand that this information is actually making it more difficult for me to maintain my poise. Please tell me you have some good news, or my arteries are going to burst.'

'We do,' Papineau said. 'We recently acquired a digital copy of Polo's diary.'

'Really?' Copeland's tone was markedly different. 'That's fucking brilliant.'

'Yes, sir, and we've narrowed the location to Sri Lanka – the land Polo referred to as Taprobane. We are already making plans to transport the hoard. We haven't located it yet, but with Polo's handwritten diary I expect it will be no time at all before we have our hands on the treasure.'

'And this Brotherhood?'

'If they actually follow us to Sri Lanka, Jack has a plan for smoking them out. They're a very xenophobic group. They might stay in China.'

'Or they might hire some mercenaries to wipe you out,' Copeland suggested.

Papineau noted a hint of glee in his voice. 'Again, sir, Jack has a plan.'

'So, to sum up,' Copeland said with a sarcastic chuckle, 'you have aroused the wrath of a criminal syndicate that may or may not chase you to Sri Lanka where you'll probably have to kill some people and, knowing your crew, probably blow up half the island. You know, they're just coming off a war that was, like, forty years long? I'm guessing they won't be keen on gunfire and explosions.'

'Yes, sir. I'm aware.'

'And even though you have Polo's personal diary, you can't narrow down the location to more than . . . what? A twenty-five-thousand-square-mile radius? Do I have all of these facts correct?'

Copeland paused, waiting for Papineau's response.

Just then, Papineau's phone beeped in his hand. He glanced at the screen and saw a text from Maggie that completely changed his mood. It read: *We found it: Sigiriya.*

'You have things nearly correct, sir,' Papineau said, a grin clawing its way across his face. 'There's just one last thing.'

'Really? And what would that be?'

'Maggie just texted me. The team has found the location.'

'That was fast,' Copeland said. 'And just in time, too. I was tempted to fire you. These pep talks are really paying off for you, aren't they? Maybe we should have them more often.'

'Does that mean I still have a job?' Papineau asked.

'I hope that's not sass, Jean-Marc.' Anger fueled Copeland's tone. 'Remember, you and your team are only as good to me as the next treasure.'

With that, the line went dead.

59

Before charging off to Sigiriya, the site of an ancient palace that sits upon a massive column of rock in central Sri Lanka, Cobb needed to know how Maggie had reached her conclusion. Stationed with McNutt at a tiny guesthouse in Colombo, they set up a secure, encrypted video chat through Cobb's computer.

Not surprisingly, Garcia answered the call.

'Cool news, huh?' he said as his face filled Cobb's screen.

'That depends on the details,' Cobb said. 'Is Maggie there?'

Garcia turned his computer so Maggie could be seen on the webcam, too.

'Hey guys,' she said, beaming. 'I think we found the site. We won't know for sure until we get there, but I'm fairly confident that the treasure is at Sigiriya, which is in the Matale district of the country near the town of Dambulla.'

'Tell us why,' Cobb said, sitting next to McNutt.

'The diary tells us of Polo's interest in a place that Lobsang described as a "heavenly monastery",' Maggie explained. 'I didn't catch it at first, but then it dawned on me—'

'Buddhists don't believe in heaven,' Cobb said. 'At least not in the same way that Polo would.'

Maggie smiled. 'Exactly. What Lobsang really meant was "elevated".'

'So the guy was high,' McNutt said. 'How does that help us?'

'*He* wasn't high,' Maggie said with a laugh, 'the monastery was.'

McNutt grimaced. 'So you're saying that *all* the monks were stoned?'

'Josh,' Cobb grunted, 'let her finish.'

Maggie was too excited to be offended by the interruptions. 'Anyway, I cross-referenced this new understanding with the Thokmay manuscript, and something jumped out at me. Thokmay explains that Lobsang spent a significant amount of time at a monastery on top of the giant rock known as Sigiriya.'

'An elevated monastery,' Cobb said. 'One near the heavens.'

'Precisely!' Maggie replied. 'And that's not all. Hector, if you would . . .'

The screen changed to an image from the Thokmay codex that Kunchen had given them at the Potala Palace. Cobb could see what looked like blueprints of a building or maybe a series of buildings. Rectangles and squares indicated rooms or plazas, and zigzagged lines resembled stairs. Based on the complexity of the drawing, it could have been a university or a small town.

'What am I looking at?' Cobb asked.

'It is a floor plan,' Maggie said. 'Lobsang created it during his stay on the island, as an architectural study.'

'And this floor plan matches Sigiriya?' Cobb guessed.

'Almost,' Garcia said. 'With one major exception.'

The image changed to a modern blueprint of the site with the Thokmay plans overlaid on top of it. A single discrepancy was circled in red.

'There's an extra room,' Maggie stressed. 'A *hidden* room.'

Cobb smiled at the significance. 'Nice work, you two.'

'Thanks,' Maggie said. 'Do you want us to head there now?'

'Not until Josh and I scope out the place,' Cobb said before shifting his gaze to Garcia. 'Hector, what have you learned about the Fists?'

'They started courting gang members from all over China in the 1990s. They lured them in with promises of better money, a better lifestyle, and a China for the Chinese – not foreigners. Most gang members were quick to take to the propaganda, since it meant an increase in income. I can find a lot of rumors about it in chat rooms and private forums until 2010 or so. After that, things started to go quiet. By that point, a lot of the former gangs were just gone, either absorbed or eradicated by the Brotherhood.'

Maggie spoke up. 'No one knows for sure who runs the Brotherhood, but a few key businessmen in Hong Kong are rumored to have gotten their start in the gangs.'

'Feng He is the most prominent businessman on the list – and the most secretive.' Garcia displayed a photo of Feng on the cover of a Chinese financial magazine on the screen. 'He owns both the mining operation in Loulan, and several steel factories throughout Gansu province, via holding companies. I had to hack through a shit-ton of firewalls and protected VPNs, but it looks like he's running the Brotherhood. And best of all . . .'

Garcia paused with a flourish as the screen changed once again, this time to a CCTV camera photo taken of a Chinese man in a dark suit, handing his passport to an immigration official. 'He just landed at Bandaranaike International Airport, two hours ago. So he's in Sri Lanka. We can assume he's not alone even though there was only one other person on the private flight with him. A man named Lim Bao.'

The screen changed to show a corporate photo of Lim.

'Anything on him?' McNutt asked.

'Just business stuff. He runs a lot of deals for Feng. He's seen in a lot of media photos with him. But nothing more than that.'

'Stick with it,' Cobb said. 'As for Feng, he's most likely going to converge on us at the site – *if* he's figured out where it is. So you should be safe in Kandy for the time being.'

'About that,' Maggie said, 'I'm not sure how he could know about the site without the information we possess. We've been very careful on our end.'

'Hector, any thoughts?' Cobb asked.

Garcia nodded. 'My guess is that they're hacking the CCTV feeds at airports and comparing the video stills to photos that they've taken of us. Once we leave the airport, they lose us until we pop up again on another camera. Thankfully, Sri Lanka doesn't have a huge number of cameras, at least not compared to Western countries.'

'Still,' Cobb said. 'If they're in country, they'll be coming for us eventually. Contact Papi and tell him to move tonight. I'll let Sarah know as well.'

'Wait,' Garcia said. 'We're out of the line of fire, and Sarah and Papi will have distance on their side. But what about you guys? The Fists will be coming, sooner or later.'

McNutt grinned at the thought. 'I'm hoping for sooner.'

60

Sigiriya, Sri Lanka

Cobb and McNutt had considered flying from Colombo, but the owner of the guesthouse had arranged a van and a driver. He didn't speak a word of English, but he smelled a hell of a lot better than their guide in China. It had been two hours and twenty minutes on roads quite similar to those they had driven in Xinjiang, but the surroundings were far different.

The vegetation was green, and lush, and full of wildlife.

With absolutely no camels in sight.

During their long, bumpy ride, Cobb had more than enough time to discuss his battle plans with McNutt and to make sure everyone had completed their tasks during the previous night. Shortly after speaking to Papineau, Cobb realized that he hadn't spoken to Seymour Duggan in quite some time. He wondered whether the New Zealander had fallen off the grid or if he had misjudged the man's reliability.

A moment later, his thoughts of Duggan vanished completely.

They were replaced by awe at the site that loomed ahead.

Cobb signaled for the driver to loop around the massive rock plateau before taking them to the main gate of the compound. When they looked through the bug-stained windshield of the van, all they could see was the multi-colored stone edifice rising high above the dense foliage. It stood 660 feet high and dwarfed everything in the area.

McNutt whistled softly. 'I'll be damned. That's a big fuckin' rock.'

*   *   *

The driver stopped the van at the western side of the complex. Cobb and McNutt got out, tucked handguns in their belts and some extra magazine in their cargo pockets, then started down a dirt path through sculptured gardens that led to the rock. They walked past long rectangular pools restored in the twentieth century and now filled with rainwater. The gardens were little more than dusty squares set off by low brick walls and seeded with scrub grass clawing for a tenuous hold in the dry soil.

At the far end of the path, they saw a man walk through a natural archway formed by two gigantic boulders leaning against each other. He wore a white business shirt, tan slacks, and leather sandals, just like most of the men they had passed at the airport. He had dark hair with just a touch of gray at the temples and the deep brown skin of the Sinhalese.

He smiled and reached out his hand. 'Mr Hall?'

Cobb stepped forward and shook the man's hand. In order to stay off the radar, the team was forced to use aliases at the site. 'Yes, and this is my associate, Mr Davidson.'

McNutt was tempted to say, 'Please, call me Harley.'

But he played it cool and merely nodded instead.

'I'm Doctor Nuwan Senanayake,' he said with a faint English accent. 'I'm the director here at Sigiriya. UNESCO told me to close the site immediately and await your arrival. They really didn't say why, but I did as instructed. I was hoping you could tell me more.'

The site was under the purview of UNESCO, the United Nations Educational, Scientific, and Cultural Organization. After serving as a fortified palace to a fifth-century king, the rock had been a monastery for centuries before it was eventually abandoned. In 1831, it had been rediscovered by British colonial officers, who

313

notified historians about the 'bush-covered summit'. More than a century and a half later, UNESCO had designated Sigiriya as a World Heritage Site, meaning it was a place of special cultural significance. Despite the crumbling state of the structures, the site fed a prosperous tourism business.

Thanks to an urgent phone call from Papineau and a follow-up call from Petr Ulster, who had worked closely with the organization on a number of his recent endeavors, UNESCO was willing to close the site to tourists for the foreseeable future.

Cobb nodded gravely. 'Yes, sorry we couldn't tell you more over the phone. We're with a private security firm that works with UNESCO from time to time. Unfortunately, we received a credible terrorist threat to the site. Not from the Tigers, but a foreign group.'

The Tigers were the Liberation Tigers of Tamil Eelam, a group of freedom fighters – or terrorists depending on one's perspective – that had thrown the nation into a civil war for decades. Cobb knew that Senanayake would be well versed in the Tigers and hoped the mere mention of their name would drive home the severity of the situation.

Cobb needed all the cooperation he could get.

'I see,' he said, suddenly concerned. 'What is it you need?'

'We just want to inspect the area as thoroughly as possible. Later today, we'll have more personnel on the site, including a helicopter to drop off some supplies. We'll assess the threat and then send a report back to headquarters in Paris. As long as we don't find anything wrong, you should be up for business in a few days . . . Can you show us how to get up top?'

'Of course.' Senanayake led them up several staircases while rambling on and on about the history of the site. Cobb slowly tuned him out and focused on military tactics. He needed to know the site's positions of strength and areas of weakness in case the Fists paid them a visit.

Next came a fenced-in cast-iron spiral staircase, leading up to a gallery carved into the rock. This was the home of the famous Sigiriya frescoes: over twenty paintings of half-naked buxom women. They were thought to be ladies from the King's harem, or possibly women taking part in some religious festival. At one time, nearly five hundred paintings covered the western face of the rock, an area 460 feet long and 130 feet high.

Needless to say, McNutt found them fascinating.

'Lovely, aren't they?' Senanayake asked.

'I guess it really was good to be the king,' McNutt replied.

Senanayake laughed. 'Indeed it was.'

He led them across a treacherous path of loose wooden planks resting on metal bars that protruded from the side of the rock just below the base of a manmade wall. The wall ran between ten and twenty feet high, its height changing as it marched up and down a natural rise in the rock. It reminded Cobb of the way the Great Wall had hugged the contours of the Chinese terrain.

'The Mirror Wall,' Senanayake explained. 'Constructed from brick and covered in plaster, it was eventually coated with honey and egg whites then buffed to a remarkable shine. It is said King Kashyapa could actually see his reflection in it.'

'Not so shiny now,' McNutt commented.

'Unfortunately, no,' Senanayake conceded. 'It has lost most of its luster over the years. Now it has a different reputation. At some point around the eighth century, tourists began to inscribe graffiti on the other side of the wall. Despite the historical verses from the eighth, ninth, and tenth centuries, people could not help but to add their own modern messages. We tried to stop them, but in the end we were forced to close this section entirely.'

McNutt grabbed Cobb's arm as Senanayake marched on.

'What's wrong?' Cobb asked.

'I'm so going to write my name on that wall,' McNutt whispered.

Cobb stared at him. 'No, Josh, you aren't.'

'My name's not Josh. It's Harley.'

'Well, neither of you can write your name on the wall.'

Eventually they came to a small plateau. Against the base of the rock stood the carved paws of a giant lion. They were nearly sixteen feet in length with a stairwell running between them that led up the side of the rock. Cobb walked around the plateau, putting on a good show as he examined the area and halfheartedly listened to Senanayake, who said there was once a head to the lion and the stairs used to pass right through the lion's mouth.

The steps were concrete for the first few flights, and then a series of black metal stairs had been bolted to the rock face like a fire escape. The treads of these were quite narrow, in some cases only wide enough for one foot. About halfway up, a metal cage had been placed around the stairs for safety purposes. Otherwise, people could fall or jump to their deaths.

Near the end of their climb, the stairs were concrete again. Cobb could see long grasses and trees growing on top of the rock. He also noted the weathered holes that paralleled the metal steps – the original hand-carved footholds. Water, sunlight, and ferrous minerals had streaked the cliff-like face with wide, vertical swaths of color in white, black, and orange.

'Doctor,' Cobb said, 'any other ways up or down?'

'Not without a rope,' Senanayake said. 'Or wings.'

'Good to know. Can we have a look around up top?'

The director nodded and started walking forward.

'Sir,' Cobb said, 'we'll need to ask you to wait down below for us. Between you and me, I don't think there's a bomb up there, but I have rules to follow. Can't endanger civilians.'

'Ah, of course,' Senanayake said. 'It's your show. If Paris says you're in charge, then you're in charge. I was about to head down to my office anyway. There are fences up near the edges. They're not terribly stable, and people have fallen, so don't get too close. When you're done, I trust you can find your way down. My office is on the edge of the car park at the south side of the compound. You can't miss it.'

Cobb and McNutt waited until the man was long gone before they started their final ascent. The director had said there were 1,200 steps to the top of the rock from the gardens below. It looked to Cobb like most of those were ahead of them.

As they made their way up the rock face, Cobb and McNutt didn't notice the sets of eyes that watched their every move from the shadows of the foliage below.

They had been there for several hours.

And they were ready to attack.

61

Having ascended the series of rusted steps that led to the rock's expansive top level, Cobb stopped and stared at the foliage below, admiring the view. The morning rains had collected the dust from the air, and the clear skies allowed him to see for miles in every direction. The distinct hills of the landscape were a quilt of lush forest interspersed with the occasional barren areas of dirt.

The top of the massive column of rock had been terraced centuries ago, the natural stone slopes replaced with a series of level areas of various heights and sizes. Each level had several staircases connecting it to the flat lawns, stone foundations, or shallow pools of the surrounding areas. Everywhere he looked Cobb could see reddish-brown bricks standing out against the grass and other creeping greenery that threatened to conceal the ruins. It reminded Cobb of photos he had seen of Machu Picchu in Peru.

McNutt stared at the murky brown water of the nearest pool, and at the dirty brown mutt basking in the sun at the water's edge. Despite its filth, the dog looked well fed and content. It certainly had far less concern for them than the men did for it.

'Will you look at that,' McNutt said. 'Snoopy looks perfectly at home up here.' He glanced back at the narrow staircase they had just climbed. 'Then again, maybe he's just making the most of a bad situation. That rickety fire escape is scary as hell.'

Cobb glanced at the dog. 'I highly doubt that he's stuck here. I bet he comes up here every day for handouts from tourists.'

McNutt grinned. 'I would, too, if people kept feeding me.'

Cobb smiled and pulled out his phone. He pressed a few buttons and brought up the image of the floor plan that Garcia had loaded into the device. He glanced back and forth between the blueprint on the screen and the landscape in front of him, trying to picture the buildings that once stood on the grounds. In his mind, he could see the lavish palace and the impenetrable ramparts, the stone courtyards and the exquisite gardens.

In reality, all that remained was little more than rubble.

'Where's the hidden room supposed to be?' McNutt asked.

Cobb oriented the image on the phone to match the landmarks in front of him, hoping it would give them a clearer picture of where to search. Cobb pointed up ahead. 'I think it's that way. Does that sound right to you, Hector?'

'I agree,' Garcia said in his ear. 'The palace was located on the highest ground.'

Thanks to the conveniences of technology, Garcia didn't need to make the climb to see the plateau. Instead, he and Maggie were watching Cobb and McNutt's video feeds from their hi-tech sunglasses. Garcia couldn't actually see the others atop the monument from the safety of the nearby Hotel Sigiriya – the distance was simply too far – but the unobstructed view gave their comms a clear path of transmission. Even though the devices had already proven that they could send and receive signals through several feet of solid rock, this wasn't the time to take unnecessary chances.

Not when they were so close to solving the mystery.

Not with Polo's treasure within their grasp.

They walked forward, traversing multiple levels on cracked stone stairs while avoiding a large retention pool in the center of the plateau. When they finally arrived at their destination, they were dripping in sweat from their long climb and the thick humidity. They took a moment to catch their breath and to enjoy the 360-degree vista of the surrounding terrain.

'I can see why he chose this place,' McNutt said.

'Polo?' Cobb asked.

'No, the king!' McNutt turned and imagined his personal kingdom. 'Got my palace here. My swimming pool there. And my naked ladies down below. What else would I need?'

'Electricity . . . Plumbing . . . Cable TV.'

'TV?' McNutt burst out laughing. 'Chief, I rarely have the opportunity to give you advice, but this is one of those times. If you have a harem, you don't need a TV.'

Cobb grinned. 'I'll try to remember that.'

'Trust me, you'll thank me later.'

'In the meantime, do you mind if we look for the treasure?'

McNutt shook his head. 'Just tell me what to do.'

Cobb walked along the edge of a low brown wall about two feet in height. He looked down at the bricks and wondered. Senanayake had confided in them that despite the site being a World Heritage location, restoration work had actually involved moving some of the bricks from one of the mostly ruined areas to another that was mostly intact. It was unthinkable from an archeological point of view, but it made perfect sense taken within the context of tourism.

Cobb's realization that damage had already been done to the site by the organization that was supposed to protect it eased his guilt considerably. He knew that they would have to damage some walls to look for the hidden room, but he also knew if they located Polo's treasure that the local government would make millions and the site would be inundated with tourists.

Still, he would do his best to limit damage.

'Hector,' Cobb said, 'I think we walked up too high. Based on this diagram, we have to go down a few levels to access the secret room.'

Garcia stared at the map on his screen. 'I tend to agree. The palace started at the top but sprawled down over multiple levels. You need to go a hundred feet south or so. You can access that area by taking the steps on your right.'

They followed his directions and climbed down two levels of stone steps to a grassy area below. They walked around in the flat space, peering at the brick walls on three sides of them. It wasn't an area most people bothered with; Cobb could tell from the overgrown grass, and the path behind him that ran parallel to the wall. People would walk down to this level and skirt around the base of the terrace, but they were on their way to or from the steps on either end of the stretch of grass.

Where Cobb and McNutt were standing, there was really nothing to see but the blocks of the wall in front of them. For some reason, the wall wasn't straight. It was canted in slightly, like the walls of the Potala. Upon closer inspection, Cobb realized that loose soil filled the spaces in between the stones instead of mortar. The wall stood simply because of the way the stones had been stacked, with gravity doing most of the work.

Cobb reached forward and pressed his palms against the rock. He felt the rough surface on his fingertips and tried to picture what the angled wall was protecting.

'Uh, chief? Do you two want to be left alone?'

Cobb ignored the comment. 'I think we're going to have to dig.'

'We're gonna need some shovels and picks then. Unless, of course, you give me permission to blow the wall. But, you know, not in a sexual way.'

Cobb pushed his fingers into the loose dirt around the nearest stone until he could grasp the brick with his hand. He wiggled it back and forth, his movements no more than an inch at first. Ever so slowly, he pulled the block free as soil spilled from the wall. He carefully set it in the grass at his feet, as if the brick was a part of the treasure itself.

'It's reinforced,' Cobb said. 'There's another wall inside the outer shell.'

Cobb stepped away and McNutt moved closer to see for himself.

True to Cobb's word, he saw a second layer of stonework on the other side of the first. The good news was that the layers would work in tandem, supporting each other as the men removed enough stones to pass through the wall. The bad news was that there was no way to pull the larger inner bricks out. McNutt could tell by looking at them that they were simply too heavy.

He put his hand through the opening and gently pushed on the inner stone. Much to his surprise, it moved.

'Chief, this is loose. I think I can push it in. But . . .'

Cobb knew what had given McNutt pause. Neither of them knew what might be damaged if the stone fell and ruptured. Maybe nothing. Or maybe the final clue to the treasure. Unfortunately, they had no way of knowing if they didn't get behind the wall.

'Do it,' Cobb ordered.

'Here goes nothing,' McNutt said as he leaned into the stone.

Surprisingly, it gave way quite easily, sliding out of position and dropping out of sight. They expected to hear it thump when it struck the ground at their feet a second later. Instead, they heard silence until it shattered at the bottom of a chasm somewhere deep inside the plateau.

'Holy hell, the mountain is hollow!' McNutt exclaimed.

Cobb nodded. 'Things just got a lot more interesting.'

McNutt removed his glasses and stuck them through the hole. Then he used his other arm to extend a small but powerful flashlight into the darkness. He hoped that he could cast enough light for Garcia to get some idea of what they had found. 'Diego, you see anything?'

'You were right,' Garcia replied. 'It's hollow. I'm guessing maybe thirty or forty feet down to the bottom. That's really all I can see.'

McNutt was disappointed. 'No gold? No silver? No dragon?'

'No, nothing like that,' Garcia replied. 'Just an empty chamber. It looks like a giant well.'

'Then let's throw something in and make a wish,' Sarah said as she joined the conversation. Her voice was backed by the rever-berating sound of a helicopter.

Cobb looked south and saw a small white chopper rising in the distance.

'Sure,' Cobb replied. 'What did you have in mind?'

'How about me?' Sarah said.

Cobb laughed. 'Copy that. See you in a few minutes.'

The helicopter made a beeline for the plateau as Cobb and McNutt cleared away several more of the outer blocks. By the time the gap was big enough for Sarah to climb through, the chopper was close enough for Cobb to make out the pale blue UN lettering on the side. Despite all the problems he'd had with Papineau, he really appreciated the man's efficiency.

Why rent a helicopter when you can convince the UN to let you use theirs for free?

62

As Cobb and McNutt watched from below, the side door of the helicopter slid open. A few seconds later, a thick coil of black nylon rope was pushed from the floor of the cargo bay and dropped to the ground between them.

Sarah looked down from the chopper. 'Heads up!'

'A little late, don't you think?' Cobb joked.

'I wasn't talking about the rope. I meant for *this*.'

McNutt's eyes lit up as she lifted the long plastic case to the edge of the doorway and secured it to a drop line. Despite the unmarked container, McNutt knew there was a cache of weapons inside. One of them was a Russian Dragunov sniper rifle. It was an older design, but it was still in wide use throughout the Sri Lankan Army. He raced forward to meet the package before it touched the dirt, cradling it in his arms as if it were a priceless Stradivarius.

When the line was free of McNutt's gift, Sarah grabbed a hold and stepped away from the safety of the cargo bay. She descended the rope without a harness, gliding down gracefully despite the oversized backpacks she had slung over each shoulder.

A moment later her feet touched down gently on the solid rock.

She dropped the packs to the ground and waved up at the crewman staring at her from the open helicopter door. She gave him the thumbs-up sign, inviting him to wind the rope back into the chopper, then watched as he returned the signal and began pulling in the drop line.

The pilot took his cue and lifted the aircraft higher into the sky.

A moment later, the team was alone on the mountaintop.

When the noise from the rotor had subsided, Cobb touched Sarah on the shoulder. 'Glad you could make it, Miss Ellis.'

'Me too, Mister Hall,' Sarah said, using his alias.

'Me three!' McNutt exclaimed as he caressed the weathered barrel of the rifle. The gun had seen better days, but he didn't care. To him, a well-used rifle meant an accurate gun; snipers didn't tolerate weapons that couldn't shoot straight.

Sarah focused on Cobb. 'If they had told me ahead of time that I couldn't land the Bell on the plateau, I would have brought the big lady from the start.'

Cobb and McNutt knew she was talking about the Boeing CH-47 Chinook dual-rotor helicopter that Sarah had temporarily procured from a construction company in India a few hundred miles away. The massive Boeing dwarfed the Bell 212 she had just ridden to the site and was capable of transporting roughly 28,000 pounds of freight or personnel. As long as the treasure didn't weigh more than fourteen tons, they could get it off the mountain in one trip.

'This is probably for the best,' Cobb said. 'You would have been forced to land the Chinook on the ground and then climb up. You'd get up here just fine, but there's no way we'd be able to hide that big sonofabitch.' He knew the pilot was waiting for their call in Trincomalee. It wasn't the best place for a gigantic cargo chopper to go unnoticed, but it was better than the open expanses at the base of the Sigiriya.

'Either way, there's no turning back now,' Sarah replied.

Not only had they removed and destroyed ancient rocks to expose the hidden chamber, they had just flown in reinforcements in broad daylight. Their cover story with the local authorities would last a few days, maybe even a week, but eventually someone would get suspicious if the site remained closed. More calls would be made, and their cover would be blown.

And they still had to worry about the Brotherhood.

If anyone was watching, the team just announced its arrival.

Cobb turned to McNutt. 'Josh, the only way up here is the stairs. Find some high ground and let me know if anyone tries to reach the summit.'

'No problem, chief.' McNutt pointed at the crate of weapons. 'Before I go, what do you want me to do with this?'

Cobb glanced around the plateau. 'See that heavy foliage in the southeast corner? Hide the crate in there. They'll never see it, and it'll be close by if we need it.'

'Sarah,' McNutt said, 'what are you carrying?'

'A Beretta, a knife, and several magazines.'

McNutt grimaced. 'Are you sure that's enough? I go to bed with more than that.'

Sarah smiled. 'Thanks for your concern, but I'll be fine.'

'Okay.' McNutt picked up the crate and carried it away.

'Hector,' Cobb said. 'Do you have anything on the Brotherhood?'

'Nothing yet,' Garcia replied from the hotel. 'But I have to tell you that there isn't a lot of help for us in this country. Closed-circuit cameras are virtually non-existent, and most of the security footage isn't hardwired to any sort of network. I mean, there are places here that are still using VHS systems! Besides, the Fists could walk from the coast to the Lion Rock and never leave the cover of the jungle. There's not even electricity out there, much less cameras!'

'Take a breath, Hector. No one's asking you to do the impossible.' Cobb was a bit concerned that the newly confident Garcia had somehow regressed into his former, doubting self.

'I know,' Garcia replied. 'I just want to help. And I can't do that if I'm blind.'

'Just keep trying. Check satellite coverage, ATM and traffic cameras, webcams, whatever you can find. Just keep looking. If they're out there, I'm sure you'll find them.'

'Okay, I'll keep digging around.'

'Good,' Cobb answered. 'Maggie, you're at the hotel?'

'Yes, I'm here,' she assured him.

'You might as well come over to the rock. I don't know what we're going to find inside, but I'd prefer if you were on site if we need you.'

'*When* we need you,' Sarah corrected. 'I've got a good feeling about this.'

'As do I,' Maggie agreed. 'I'm on my way.'

'You read that, Josh? Maggie is headed up the rock.'

'Copy that, chief. "Don't shoot Maggie." Got it.'

'Yes,' Maggie replied. 'Please don't shoot Maggie.'

Cobb glanced at Sarah. She was standing tall, with her hands planted firmly on her hips as she stared at the hole in the wall. Cobb could see her foot tapping impatiently, as if she were waiting for permission to dive inside.

'Hector,' he asked, 'are you recording?'

'Always,' Garcia said.

'Good – because Sarah and I are going in.'

*　　*　　*

It took them ten minutes to set the rigging that Sarah had pulled from the backpacks. They had anchored their lines around a ten-ton slab of stone near the wall's entrance. To ensure that they didn't pull any blocks down on top of themselves, they had extended the entry point all the way down to the ground. After securing a soft fabric mat at the lip of the crevasse to keep their ropes from rubbing against the abrasive stone, they had tossed an amber glow stick into the hole to help them judge the distance of their descent.

Sarah went first. 'You getting all of this, Hector?'

'I sure am. The rock looks similar to the rest of the mountain.'

Cobb rubbed his hand against the inner wall. 'It's too smooth to have been man-made. This cavern is natural. They just sealed it at the top.'

'But is there anything at the bottom?' Garcia asked.

'Let's find out,' Sarah replied. She leaned backward and dropped through the air, the black climbing rope zipping past her waist where her belay device was tethered to it. As she came within a few feet of the ground she thrust her right hand back behind her, quickly slowing her descent, and gently extended her legs until her toes touched the ground.

'The plot thickens,' Garcia announced as he stared at her footage.

She was facing a tunnel that ran parallel to the ground; one that had clearly been carved into the rock. She turned on her video flashlight and shined it back and forth. 'It looks like some sort of ancient mine shaft. The walls are braced with wood, and the ceiling is stained with soot.'

'I call dibs on the biggest nugget,' McNutt said in her ear.

'Sorry, Josh,' she said as Cobb landed behind her. 'There's nothing here.'

Maggie groaned as she made her way to the site. 'That can't be right. There has to be something. No symbols? No signs? No markers of any kind?'

'Hang on,' Sarah said as she and Cobb pushed deeper into the passageway. He turned on his flashlight as well. 'There's something on the floor up ahead.'

She could see a large wooden square on the ground, its frame having been cobbled together from scraps of the same sturdy timber that reinforced the tunnel. 'I think it's some sort of trap door. Jack, can you move that for me?'

'I can certainly try,' Cobb replied.

He dug his fingers into the gap at the edges of the wood and pulled with all his might. The door gave way with a groan, and a dry, dusty smell of ancient air escaped from the hole beneath. The opening was just wide enough for one person to squeeze through.

Sarah shined her flashlight down into the opening and spotted handholds carved into the side of the rock. She cracked another amber glow stick and dropped it into the hole; it fell a hundred feet straight down before it smacked some rock and rolled out of sight.

'What did you find?' Maggie asked.

'Another hole,' Cobb said as he peered below. 'This one's a lot deeper.'

'Deep enough to hide a treasure?' Garcia wondered.

Sarah nodded. 'Deep enough to hide a building.'

63

Lim Bao had watched the helicopter peel away nearly fifteen minutes ago, but his leader had yet to rise. Instead, Feng He lay perfectly still, as if literally frozen in place. Lim dared not budge until his mentor moved first.

They were both hidden among a plot of shrubberies that had grown near the lion's paws entrance to the plateau, waiting for their opportunity to surge ahead. During the arrival of the UN aircraft they had hunkered low, each of them wondering what new addition the aircraft had delivered above. They knew the American woman had been left atop the rock – they had seen her in the open door as the helicopter approached and noticed her absence during its departure – but assumed there was more to the story.

Finally, Feng spotted the missing piece to the puzzle.

'Ah, there you are,' he whispered as he stared up at the rock through high-powered binoculars.

'Sir?' Lim replied.

Feng slowly lowered the tinted lenses from his face and extended them toward his companion. 'See for yourself.'

Lim took the offering, but he had no idea what he was searching for.

Fortunately, Feng answered the question before Lim could even ask it.

'The soldier and the sniper took no weapons to the summit, but look now at the widest edge of the rock,' Feng whispered. 'Outside the fence line, in the trees that sprout horizontally from the stone. He's waiting there like a tiger. Do you see him?'

Lim moved his gaze to the spot that Feng had described and adjusted the focus. The sniper had somehow squeezed through the protective metal fence that encircled the top of the plateau and had crawled out and up the rounded trunk of one of the trees. From that vantage point, he could cover the entire series of zigzagging stairs that led from the lion's paws to the upper levels – and he could also fall to his death if the wind blew strongly.

'That man is crazy,' Lim said.

Feng sneered at the comment, wondering how many of his followers considered *him* crazy for battling gunmen in Sri Lanka instead of running his organization from the safety of his hotel penthouse. On the surface, it did seem rather foolish to risk his life for a pile of gold, but Feng valued something even more than the promise of wealth. He sought the political clout he would gain if he discovered Marco Polo's treasure and brought it back to China.

To Feng, that was priceless.

Though he was respected, even feared, in certain circles, Feng was not a household name in his homeland. He knew the only way to change that was to do something memorable; something the general populace viewed as heroic. That wouldn't happen by outfoxing telecom giants like Harold Ledner. Corporate deals weren't sexy to the working class. They weren't talked about in schools, in offices, or in rural villages, even though his efforts brought thousands of jobs and billions of dollars to his country.

But the recovery of gold, jewels, and artifacts from the time of Kublai Khan?

That would make front-page news around the globe.

'He's not crazy,' Feng assured Lim. 'He's *dedicated*. Never mistake the two.'

'I'm sorry, sir.' Lim handed the binoculars back to his boss. 'It appears he has us pinned down. I don't see how we can mount an assault from this direction.'

'We can't,' Feng agreed. 'Not yet.'

Feng knew that as long as the sniper held his location, there was little they could do. From his elevated position, the sniper could pick off anyone that approached from below.

'We need a diversion.'

*   *   *

Cobb had thought that the handholds in the cave wall would be smooth, shallow, and useless, just like the steps near the base of his initial ascent. But once they were inside the shaft, he realized that the scooped-out holes were actually quite deep, with pronounced lips that allowed for easy finger grip. Spared for centuries from the elements, the built-in ladder allowed them to make their way down without the need for a rappelling harness.

But, just to be safe, they tied a rope around their waists.

The floor was ten stories down into the rock. When Sarah reached the bottom, she shined her flashlight in all directions, illuminating a cavern that was eighty feet long and nearly half as wide. She remembered from Maggie's discourse that the entire Sigiriya rock was some four hundred and fifty feet long, so she assumed that there was plenty of solid stone around them on all sides to support the chamber. Still, the lack of any apparent bracing gave her a moment of pause.

'Amazing,' Cobb said. 'Hector?'

'Reading you loud and clear,' Garcia replied as he marveled at the video.

Cobb touched the walls. 'The surface is rough. Tools leave a smooth finish. This wasn't man-made.'

Sarah nodded. 'Polo and Lobsang found a natural cave inside the mountain.'

The 'natural cave', as she called it, was technically known as an igneous lava bubble. It was a hollow space that had been formed eons ago when the whole rock mountain had been shoved up from the bowels of the Earth.

'Do you see anything that looks out of place?' Maggie asked.

Cobb and Sarah walked carefully around the periphery of the space. At first, the room seemed completely empty, like an unused chamber in the world's biggest anthill. But as they moved deeper they spotted something in the farthest corner of the chamber. They were about to investigate when they heard a warning in their ears.

'Guys,' Garcia said, 'you might have a problem heading your way.'

'Explain,' Cobb demanded.

'A helicopter is coming,' Garcia said. 'It doesn't look like the UN chopper that brought Sarah. It's too early to tell if it's actually going to the rock, but it's headed in that direction.'

'You're watching via satellite?' Cobb asked.

'No. I won't have sat coverage of the rock for another ten minutes. I had to get creative. I'm using a UAV.'

'A what?' Sarah asked.

'An unmanned aerial vehicle,' Garcia said. 'The Pakistanis were testing it nearby, so I borrowed it for a few minutes.'

'What?' Sarah asked incredulously. 'You stole a military drone?'

'Relax,' Garcia answered. 'They have no idea what's going on. It's not like they're going to report a rogue UAV the moment they lose control of it. These things have to go through channels. Ain't that right, Josh?'

'Actually,' McNutt laughed, 'Guillermo the Kid has a point. The Pakis won't say a word to anyone until they know exactly what happened. No one will believe that they just lost it. They'll be accused of trying to start some shit in foreign airspace.'

'Jack,' Garcia pleaded. 'You told me to get you some eyes, and this was the only thing available. I made sure to swing well south of India, just in case they had an itchy trigger finger, but I'm telling you—'

'I'm sold,' Cobb said. 'We can worry about it later. What are you flying?'

'It's a US-made RQ-7.'

'Josh?' Cobb asked, searching for more information.

'RQ-7 Shadow,' McNutt explained. 'About eleven feet long, with a wingspan of fourteen feet against a height of only thirty-six inches. Top speed of, um, I honestly don't know, but the fucker moves really fast.'

'Armaments?' Cobb asked.

'It can be outfitted with a variety of toys, but I'm guessing an M134 minigun with a firing rate of about four thousand rounds per minute.' McNutt chuckled. 'Hey Guillermo, wanna trade?'

'Nope,' Garcia replied. 'And guys, the chopper is still headed your way.'

'That's not all,' McNutt said, his tone suddenly serious. 'Unless I'm seeing things, we've got hostiles on the ground.'

* * *

McNutt peered down into the thick undergrowth, scrutinizing even the slightest movement. He had already noticed a few monitor lizards – huge reptiles that stalked the lush vegetation looking for smaller prey – so he had grown accustomed to spotting things in the bushes. But the lizards were brown, and the flash of color he had just noticed was not. It was olive drab: the color of jungle camouflage.

McNutt was quite familiar with the hue.

He focused his scope on the suspect, waiting for any signs of movement. Instead, he saw a telltale burst of smoke and heard the whine of an RPG.

Unfortunately, he knew those, too.

In an instant, McNutt grabbed his Russian Dragunov sniper rifle and jumped from his perch in the tree. He hit the side of the rock and started a controlled slide toward the staircase below.

Behind him, the rocket-propelled grenade smashed into the surface of the rock only feet from where he had been lying. The impact of the warhead's tip against rock fired its piezoelectric fuse, transmitting a small electrical charge to the base of the projectile. The shaped charge exploded, forcing its way out the path of least resistance: the tiny opening at the nose of the cone-shaped rocket. The force of the blast was multiplied as it exited the cone.

McNutt felt the shards of razor-sharp rock tearing into his back and shoulders as he rolled nearly twenty feet down the rocky slope. He tried to grab the lip of the ledge but was unable to gather himself as he plunged an additional ten feet to the steps below. He hit the stairs with a meaty thud, but somehow managed to survive the fall without any broken bones.

He was bruised and battered, but very much alive.

'Josh!' Garcia shouted. 'Are you okay?'

'No, fuck-tard, I'm not okay. I just fell off a mountain.'

'I know, I mean . . . what can I do to help?'

McNutt rubbed his sore ribs and spat out some blood. The residue stained his teeth like a ravenous wolf's. 'Bring in the drone and start kicking ass.'

64

McNutt scrambled along the edge of the plateau, looking for the best position to return fire. He was determined to defend the Lion Gate against the enemy's advancement . . . or at least make them think twice about their assault. Adrenaline eased the pain of his superficial injuries as he rushed back up the stairs and onto the plateau's grassy surface.

He slowed his charge as he neared the six-hundred-foot drop to the base of the rock, diving onto his stomach then crawling the remaining few yards to the edge. Hidden in the tall grass, he raised his rifle and scanned the area from where the rocket had been launched. He could see several armed men, all Chinese, racing through the trees toward the stairs between the gate's stone paws.

'Sorry, folks. Park's closed,' he mumbled as he leveled the crosshairs on the nearest intruder. 'The moose out front should've told you.'

McNutt squeezed the trigger and unleashed the kind of fury that Clark Griswold couldn't have handled in *National Lampoon's Vacation*. The 7.62 mm round easily penetrated the foliage and sliced through his target's sternum like a laser beam, killing him instantly. The semi-automatic weapon readied itself for round two as McNutt adjusted his aim half a meter to the right. He fired again, and another man fell.

The remaining assailants took cover as they peppered the mountainside with spray from their assault rifles. These were pot shots, and McNutt knew it. They had no idea where he was hidden, and their only response to his aggression was to aimlessly fire in all directions. He knew he had been exposed in the tree – he had given up protection to find the best possible angle – but he wouldn't make that mistake again. Now he was nearly invisible in the overgrown grass near the edge.

He watched as the heads of his enemy randomly popped up from behind rocks, fallen trees, and bulbous shrubs. The men would peek for a few moments before diving back to the earth in fear. He chuckled as he thought back to the Whack-A-Mole game at the carnival that would visit his hometown every summer.

He was good then. He was better now.

Boom! A mole slumped over, dead.

Boom! A cloud of crimson mist erupted in his scope.

He picked them off one by one, until there was nothing left but bodies.

'The front door is officially closed,' McNutt informed his team.

'Great,' Garcia replied, 'but there's a party coming in the back door!'

McNutt grinned at the description. 'How many times have we told you not to watch porn when we're in the field?'

Garcia ignored the joke. 'Better check your six, Josh. You've got multiple hostiles inbound. There's a chopper landing on the opposite edge of the plateau. And you've got at least a dozen men trying to summit the southern face of the mountain.'

'How the hell are they doing that?' McNutt asked.

'They've got grappling hooks and some sort of reverse zip lines. They're literally *running* up the side of the rock!'

'Sneaky bastards,' McNutt said, impressed. 'I'm headed that way.'

'I'll meet you there,' Cobb said. He had been listening to their chatter and realized McNutt needed him more than Sarah. 'Hector, how good are you with the drone?'

'Very good. Why?'

'Good enough to take out that chopper?'

*   *   *

337

As a master of wing chun and a student of kung fu and tai chi, Maggie had learned how to move with stealth. She had showcased her ability on the day she had met the team in Florida – sneaking up on Sarah on more than one occasion – and she had used it again at the warehouse in Panyu. But those examples were child's play compared to her task at hand.

She needed to sneak up the mountain without getting shot.

'Joshua,' she whispered from the Lion Gate, 'I'm heading up the stairs right now. I'll let you know when I reach the top.'

'Be careful,' he said as he charged across the plateau.

She smiled at his concern. 'I always am.'

*　*　*

Piloting the RQ-7 was pretty simple for Garcia. After all, the hardest part had already been done for him: the Pakistanis had been kind enough to get the drone in the air before he had hijacked it. If all went according to plan, Garcia wouldn't need to land it either. He planned to return it to its original test-flight course and then relinquish control over it. The Pakistan Air Force would land it . . . and then they'd probably tear it apart.

Garcia knew that the military would most likely spend months trying to figure out why their drone had flitted off to central Sri Lanka, performed a variety of maneuvers, discharged its arsenal, and then headed back to home base. He suspected that they would disassemble the entire aircraft piece by piece, checking every bit of hardware and every line of code in its operating system in their search for the problem.

But they'd never really know why.

Back at the hotel, Garcia had turned his command center into a flight simulator. His three monitors displayed the video feed from the drone's nose and rear cameras, as well as providing him with up-to-the-second information on the aircraft's speed, elevation, fuel supply, and ammunition count. Garcia had even found a slim-line controller in his bag of random peripherals. He used it to fly the drone as if he were playing a video game.

And Garcia was very good at video games.

The image on his left-hand screen showed him that the helicopter, a commercial cargo bird, hadn't actually landed on the towering deck. Instead, it had pulled into a hover about twenty feet above the mountain. Four drop lines had been thrown from the stationary chopper, and the first two waves of unwelcome visitors had already deployed.

Four additional men appeared ready to join them below.

As the men stepped through the open bay doors, Garcia banked the drone and dive-bombed his target. With no missiles at his disposal, he activated the M134 minigun. The stream of bullets from the rotating barrels cut through the helicopter's engine hatch but, remarkably, didn't hit any vital components.

In response to the attack, the chopper's pilot jerked the stick, spinning the aircraft wildly. Three of the men at its sides dropped quickly to the dirt beneath them, but the fourth inexplicably held fast to his rope. The force of the chopper's sudden turn whipped him like a tetherball, causing him to lose his grip and fly helplessly over the edge.

The man plummeted several hundred feet to his death.

Feeling a surge of adrenaline from his first kill, Garcia pushed the drone's speed past 100 miles per hour as the helicopter gave chase. When he swung out wide of the rock, he could see a dozen more men climbing the face. They had launched grappling hooks to the summit and were using electric ascender units to propel themselves up their respective ropes. With the help of the mechanical gear, the men moved up the plateau with a fluid, almost serene grace.

'Nice try,' Garcia said as he sized up his opponents.

He brought the drone in line for a strafing run, fully prepared for what he had to do. He fired the weapon and a stream of deadly 7.62 mm rounds blurred out of the nose of the vehicle, slicing through the men and their ropes like a samurai sword splitting tender bamboo. Puffs of red and pink erupted from the rock face as the climbers were turned to chunky pulp before gravity claimed its hold and yanked their shattered remains to the ground.

Garcia watched as the video feed relayed the scene in real time.

'We need to get one of these for ourselves!' he said excitedly.

'A drone?' Cobb asked in his ear.

'No, a military-grade, hi-res camera,' Garcia answered. 'Gimbal-mounted. Digitally stabilized. Electro-optical infrared. This sucker is bad-ass.'

'Wow,' McNutt replied. 'You really are a geek.'

*　　*　　*

Unfortunately, McNutt had more to worry about than Garcia's seemingly odd fondness for hi-tech cameras over tactical weapon systems.

He had scampered across the mountaintop and revisited the case of firearms that he had hidden near the entrance to the secret tunnel, but the addition of an M-4 rifle hadn't made him completely at ease. Even the presence of Cobb – who had likewise armed himself with the compact assault rifle – didn't extinguish McNutt's anxiety.

It was still two against ten. Or more.

With an outer perimeter of free-falling death.

From a mile away, McNutt would have had a distinct advantage.

But close-quarters combat was a different story.

65

Cobb rolled to the ground behind a low wall of bricks, taking fire from one of the men the helicopter had ferried to the summit. They had scattered around the ruins, taking up cover around the corners of various terrace levels or diving behind small walls as Cobb had done.

McNutt had opened fire immediately, killing one of the men before return fire had forced him to flee and seek his own barricade. Cobb had no idea where he had gone, but he knew they needed to coordinate if they were going to survive.

'Josh, take north. I'll head south. Push them to the pond in the middle.'

The gunmen had arrived at the southeast corner of the pond on a small dirt trail that allowed passage around the rainwater-filled pool on that side. Cobb was already south of them, and two levels down, meaning the enemy had the high ground. He needed to make his way up the plateau before they converged on his position.

* * *

The helicopter was charging fast behind the drone.

Garcia started rocking the small craft back and forth, presenting a harder target, as he flew it out over the edge of the rock and away from the battle on the summit. The lone gunman still on board the pursuing chopper was leaning out the side door and trying to knock the drone from the sky with withering bursts of rifle fire.

Garcia had the advantage on maneuverability. He dropped the

nose on the RQ-7, flying the drone nearly vertical in a dive along the edge of the massive rock. The helicopter pilot dipped in pursuit, though not nearly as steeply as Garcia.

Showing off, he corkscrewed the drone, closer to the mountain as it fell. Then he abruptly brought it up and buzzed past the helicopter, the minigun blazing. Most of the rounds missed the helicopter, with just a few peppering the tail before the drone raced past.

But that wasn't the point of Garcia's maneuver.

The drone was unmanned and presented no danger to Garcia, whereas the buzzing minigun presented plenty of danger to the Chinese men in the helicopter. The gunman dove back into the passenger compartment, and the pilot banked hard and away from the drone, narrowly avoiding impact. The burst of fire had emptied the rotary-barrel gun on the drone after just the first few shots, but the Chinese pilot didn't know that. Garcia brought the UAV up in a steep climb, then twisted it in the air and dove down for the helicopter again.

The pilot reacted, banking away from the rock while trying to gain altitude. They were running scared, but they would soon realize the drone wasn't firing at them anymore.

Then Garcia had a crazy idea . . .

Who said I have to return the drone to Pakistan?

They're just going to tear it apart anyway.

The RQ-7 had a top speed of 127 mph, and Garcia cranked the accelerator, bringing the UAV toward the escaping helicopter as fast as it could go. A moment later, the pilot of the helicopter started to panic. Garcia could tell as he watched the craft zig and zag on his computer monitor. With every evasive maneuver the bird tried, Garcia's drone was able to match it. The much smaller UAV could turn on a dime and there was no worry about G-forces on human operators.

The pilot dropped the helicopter into a steep dive and banked hard back toward the massive stone rock. The gunman reappeared in the open door, firing again on the drone, but Garcia was able to jerk and twitch the smaller craft out of the way of each burst. The helicopter was heading straight for the side of the rock, half way up the plateau.

Garcia realized this was his chance to finish the job.

He pushed the drone to its maximum speed and steered the UAV straight at the top of the helicopter's rotor mount. Though he had no audio of the event, Garcia could've sworn that he heard the metallic *crunch* that it made when the drone impacted its target. He also imagined the scream that the gunman made when he fell out the cargo door and plummeted to his death.

His fall from the sky actually saved him from the massive fireball that consumed the interior of the cargo hold. The chopper's blades ripped loose from their mount and the tail boom swung in a full 180-degree arc before it smacked into the side of the rock wall. The whole technological mess crumpled together in a twisted hunk of metal before following the path of least resistance.

In this case, straight down to the jungle below.

*   *   *

Despite her age, Maggie was faster than she looked. She charged up the main stairs of the plateau, ran past the frescoes, the Mirror Wall, and many other sights on her way to the top. She stopped occasionally to make sure that gunmen weren't lurking nearby, but she quickly realized that the Brotherhood was focusing its assault on the other side of the plateau.

This allowed her to run without concern.

Before she knew it, she was cresting the top of the stairs, ducking behind ramparts, and eventually making her way inside the mouth of the tunnel.

*   *   *

Cobb rolled to the end of his terrace and dropped one level lower before moving back toward the west and the slightly higher ground. He assumed McNutt would already have gone that way, seeking the raised terraces and platforms that the western side of the summit provided. If McNutt could get back to the northern edge of the rock, he could cover all of it from the high ground there, which was easily thirty feet above the rest of the summit.

Garcia chimed in. 'I killed the drone, but I've got real-time satellite now.'

'Do you see me?' Cobb whispered.

'I do, and so does the gunman at your eleven o'clock. He's trying to belly-crawl his way west, just under the pond.'

Cobb sprang to his feet with the M-4 leveled, and sighted on the man. He fired a single round that hit the crawling man and sprayed his blood on the adjacent wall. Before return fire could come his way, Cobb dropped back down.

'Holy shit,' Garcia said. 'That was fast.'

A moment later, the wall in front of Cobb started to disintegrate under heavy fire from three directions. Cobb had no choice but to hunker down and ride out the storm.

'Josh!' Cobb called. 'They have me pinned.'

In response, he heard the sniper's rifle crack twice.

Each shot was punctuated with pink mist.

'Damn,' Garcia said, stunned by McNutt's efficiency. 'Two more down. And on the second guy, that was waaaaay down.'

McNutt grinned at the commentary. He wondered how many bodies had already plunged off the plateau. 'I've got eyes on the pond. As soon as they pop up, I'll take them out.'

'Hold up,' Garcia said as he watched the satellite feed on his screen. 'One of them is already north of your position. He's crawling behind a rampart along the eastern edge.'

'Where?' McNutt said. 'Describe the landmarks to me. I can

punch right through his cover with this rifle if I know where he is.'

'Umm, let me see. Go north of the pond by about fifteen feet. Maybe five feet out from the end of that terrace. There's a low wall running parallel to the edge.'

'I see it. Where's his head?' McNutt asked.

'His head? Umm, maybe six or seven feet from the corner. He's on his knees.'

McNutt processed the information instantly, then pulled the trigger. The round blasted a hole through the wall just a few inches in front of the crawling man, who immediately reversed direction and scrambled backward.

'South one meter,' Garcia said.

He corrected and fired again. This time the shot found its mark.

'I'll be damned. You got him right through the wall.'

McNutt grinned. 'Never had a satellite spotter before . . . Not bad, Manuel.'

* * *

Cobb stayed in position, waiting for a target to show or another update.

Before Garcia could warn him, one of the gunmen bolted toward Cobb's side of the plateau. He followed the same path the crawler had taken before him. Meanwhile, another two men broke cover and ran toward McNutt's most recent kill behind the rampart.

McNutt opened fire on his duo with his M-4, spraying a single continuous wave at the weaving men. He killed one and clipped the other in the shoulder. Cobb fired as well, just as Garcia started shouting in their ears.

'It's a diversion,' Garcia yelled. 'The others are running south under the cover of trees. They must've figured out that we have sat coverage.'

'Where are they heading?' Cobb demanded as he emptied his

magazine into the gunman rushing toward him. The man fell dead as Cobb scrabbled up the path behind him.

'Hang on,' Garcia said. 'Switching to infrared now. With all this running, their bodies are gonna be glowing bright red.'

'Hurry up, Hector. I'm kind of—'

'Jack,' Garcia said, cutting him off. 'Time to move to the western high ground. Your guys are going all the way south. They're going to try to outflank you.'

*   *   *

McNutt fired his assault rifle until the magazine ran dry. He casually tossed it aside and pulled out his pistol. The Beretta M-9 was one of a handful of available models easily found in Sri Lanka. The armed forces used a hodgepodge of weapons from different countries, so there were a lot floating around. He'd had his choice of Austrian, British, and German pistols, but McNutt opted for Italian since Polo – and their mission – had started in Italy.

'Where is he, Tito?' McNutt demanded.

'Who?'

'The guy I clipped in the shoulder.'

Garcia paused. 'He's heading for the stairs. Maybe he's bugging out.'

McNutt ran for the northwest corner, then veered to the east, spotting the man running for the edge. He fired his pistol on the move, hitting the fleeing man in the back and sending his body crashing to the dirt. McNutt kept running toward him with the barrel of the M-9 leveled, but the fallen man didn't move.

Still, he shot him again just to be sure.

It was time to go help Cobb.

*   *   *

Cobb exchanged fire with two men who had chosen the low ground in exchange for the series of terraces that provided cover when facing north. They were peppering the sides of the platform that he was lying on, but he couldn't see them well enough to aim.

346

They kept ducking behind the wall.

Even worse, Cobb realized they were near the opening to the cave.

'Jack,' Garcia said, 'one's moving for the stairs on your right.'

Cobb rolled to his side and saw the man pop up. With spare magazines in his pocket, Cobb didn't hold back. He fired seven rounds in a rapid grouping down the path, hitting the man in at least three places. Then he rolled back under cover, just as the other man returned fire from the middle of the rock. Cobb ejected his magazine and slapped another home.

Pinned down in his current position, Cobb cursed under his breath. Anytime he tried to move, the gunman fired in his general direction. Even though he kept missing, the edge of the rock platform kept spitting shards of brick and stone at Cobb. So far, he had suffered only a few scratches, but eventually one of the gunman's shots would do some damage.

'Are they flanking me?' Cobb whispered.

Garcia stared at his screen. 'I don't see anyone but that one guy. Josh is on his way down. He's using the east side.'

'Josh,' Cobb said. 'Hold your position.'

McNutt ducked behind a wall. 'Say again?'

'I can handle one guy. No need to bail me out. Worry about the rest of the mountain.'

'Copy that, chief.'

Cobb chanced a quick look. The guy was ducked down behind the terrace wall. He hadn't fired in several seconds. 'What's he doing? Is he reloading?'

Garcia nodded. 'Sure looks like it from outer space.'

Cobb got to his feet in a crouch. 'Tell me when he chambers.'

'Hang on . . . any second. And . . . now!'

Before Garcia had finished the vowel sound, Cobb was sprinting as fast as he could. He ran to the edge of his platform and leaped up and out into the air. His body sailed out over the square pond that was nearly thirty feet below him and he began his descent.

The Chinese man popped up and fired at the rock ledge where Cobb had been, but by then Cobb was already plunging through the air, his Beretta up, and sighting on the man. Cobb fired most of the magazine, hitting the man more than missing, before he landed feet-first into the rainwater, sending up a huge splash behind him.

Cobb knew the retention pond was over ten feet deep, so he had plenty of time to slow his acceleration before his boots hit the bottom. A few seconds later, his head broke free from the water and he swam to the edge of the pond just as gunfire broke out to his east. He raised his weapon from the murky water, ready to defend himself, but quickly realized it wasn't necessary.

McNutt was running forward with his pistol raised. On the turf in front of him was an injured gunman, who tried to get off one last shot. McNutt fired again and ended the threat.

'You're clear,' Garcia said in their ears.

Cobb crawled out of the murky brown water and immediately checked his magazine. He still had a few rounds left in his Beretta. Dripping wet and out of breath, he walked toward McNutt, who had crouched beside one of the dead gunmen.

'What are you doing?' Cobb asked.

McNutt rolled the man onto his back. As a former Marine, he was trained to study the faces of his victims, hoping upon hope that they had killed one of their top threats. 'Unless I'm mistaken, that's a guy from our briefing. Isn't he number two?'

Cobb nodded his confirmation. 'Sure looks like it.'

Garcia chimed in. 'Number two is Lim Bao. He's one of the men that we spotted at the airport and the right-hand man of Feng He, the leader of the Brotherhood.'

McNutt glanced at the nearby bodies. 'None of these are Feng.'

'I'm not surprised,' Cobb said. 'If he's as rich and powerful as Maggie claimed, there's a very good chance that he's sitting this one out. Just because he's in country, doesn't mean he's on site. I mean, Papi's on a yacht right now while we're getting dirty.'

McNutt grinned. 'You hear that, Franco? You better lock the door at the hotel. There's a damn good chance that the main dragon is hanging out near you.'

Garcia swallowed hard, then stood up to lock the door.

66

Maggie unclipped her rappelling harness and stepped into the narrow corridor. It was exactly as Sarah had described it earlier, so Maggie knew to look for the wooden covering on the floor that protected the lower levels. Fortunately, Cobb had left it open during his exit. She doubted that she could have moved it herself.

'I'm down the shaft and into the passageway,' Maggie reported to the others. 'I see the opening to the second descent.'

'Great,' Sarah replied. 'You're past the hard part already. You won't need climbing gear in the next shaft. Just use the ladder built into the wall. If it was strong enough to support Jack, it can definitely hold you.'

A few minutes later, Maggie had made the climb down to the expansive room at the base of the shaft. As she dropped to the solid rock, she marveled at the scope of the chamber. Despite its plain, natural features, the cavern seemed to be imbued with a sense of character. It was as if she could actually *feel* its importance.

'Fantastic,' Maggie said. 'Truly fantastic.'

'With hopefully a lot more to come,' Sarah answered from across the space. 'We just need to figure out how to get through this door.'

'What door?' Maggie asked.

Sarah popped another glow stick, further illuminating the massive doorway at the farthest corner of the room. Maggie walked over to find not only a wide wooden door, but also a four-foot-high pedestal that displayed a bound codex.

'Sarah,' she exclaimed, 'why didn't you mention that you found another book?'

'You were already headed my way, and anxious people tend to make mistakes. We needed you focused on the task in front of you.' She pointed at the codex. 'We still do.'

Maggie inspected the codex on its perch. The pages were bound with string that had almost fully decomposed with age. She wondered if the book could withstand even her most delicate investigation.

For all she knew, the text might disintegrate at the slightest touch.

Still, she had to try.

'It's written in Mongolian,' she said as she carefully examined the first page.

'Good,' Sarah said. 'I think the combination is, too.'

Maggie stopped reading. 'What combination?'

Sarah pointed to a small brass wheel at the center of the wooden door. It looked like a miniaturized version of a captain's wheel from an old steamship, with eight spokes passing through a solid ring. At the end of each spoke was a knob, and each knob had been etched with a passage in artful script. Though she was far from an expert in linguistics, Sarah realized the words in the book looked very similar to the symbols on the wheel.

'I'm betting that the hub spins,' Sarah explained. 'I haven't tried it yet – I didn't want the wrong movement to trigger defenses that would permanently lock us out – but nothing else fits. I've scoured every inch of this place looking for another exit, and this is the only one. I've been studying this door for long enough to know that it's sealed, as in airtight, and the only option I can see to open it is to dial that wheel to the right combination.'

Maggie moved away from the book and glanced at the symbols that had been carved around the wheel. 'This is known as the Noble Eightfold Path. They're teachings from the Buddha. A way to achieve a better sense of one's self. A spiritual awakening, if you will.'

'Great,' Sarah blurted as she put her hand on the wheel. 'Tell me which path comes first, and I'll spin this sucker open.'

Maggie shook her head. 'It's not that easy, Sarah. The achievements of the Noble Eightfold Path are to be reached simultaneously. There's no specific order to the sequence. Ideally, everything is to be done at the same time.'

Sarah stretched her neck in frustration. She hated feeling useless. And only one of them could read Mongolian. 'Check the book,' she insisted. 'Maybe it will tell us the order of the paths that we're supposed to walk.'

'Sarah, you don't actually walk—' Maggie stopped. She could see from the look on Sarah's face that she understood the concept of the Buddhist tenets. She could also tell that Sarah wasn't in the mood to argue over semantics. 'Right, the book.'

The codex was by no means thick, and Maggie scanned the pages quickly. Her eyes suddenly grew dark and mysterious as she squinted at the page, confirming her translation.

Sarah could see the resignation on her face. 'Nothing?'

'Nothing about the Noble Eightfold Path, but it tells us what we can find behind the door.'

'It does?' Sarah blurted.

'Yes, it does,' Maggie repeated. 'And it's not good.'

'It's not? What does it say?'

'The book says that Yangchen is buried inside.'

Sarah groaned. 'Polo's treasure is Yangchen's body? You've got to be shitting me!'

'No,' Maggie said sternly, 'you heard my words but didn't grasp their meaning. I said nothing about a treasure. This book is the last section of Polo's diary, and the mention of Yangchen's grave is meant to be a warning. Earlier entries describe the tough time that Marco and Yangchen had in Lhasa, often expressing that most saw Yangchen as only a "black mark". I thought it was a euphemism, but it wasn't. It was a diagnosis.'

'What do you mean?' Sarah asked.

'Yangchen had an actual black mark. It was on her face, and it was growing. She had *Yersinia pestis*. In the West, you know it as the Black Death.'

Sarah thought back to her studies in European history. 'I thought the plague hit Europe a century later.'

'It started in Asia, much earlier than that,' Maggie explained. 'This describes coming from Lhasa to Sri Lanka with Yangchen, but she didn't survive the journey. After her death, Polo spent many months at the monastery that sat upon Sigiriya at the time. At some point during his stay the monks offered to store his treasure on the mountain alongside Yangchen's remains.'

Sarah nodded in understanding. 'Who better to protect it than a group which had no interest in material wealth?'

'Agreed,' Maggie said. 'But I'm not sure he had protection in mind when he left. From the tone of his writing, I don't think he cared about riches anymore. The love of his life had been taken away from him, and that's all that truly mattered.'

Sarah thought things through. 'Then why withhold the exact location from Rustichello? If he didn't care about the treasure, why did Polo go to all the effort of describing his journey only to leave out the best part?'

Maggie laughed. 'The riches weren't the best part to Polo – the *journey* was. That's what led him to Yangchen, and she was the only prize he needed. He didn't keep details from Rustichello out of fear that someone else might find his treasure, he excluded certain elements because he was afraid that the same fate as hers might befall others.'

Sarah stared at the door that concealed a corpse of someone who had died from the Black Death. 'Thanks to antibiotics, I'll gladly take my chances. What's your best guess?'

'About what?'

'On how to open the door,' Sarah said. 'Buddhism is all about having faith and enlightenment, right? Well, have a little faith, and hopefully the enlightenment will follow.'

'I'm telling you, it doesn't work that way.'

Sarah shrugged. 'Maybe not, but if you don't figure something out by the time Josh comes down here, he will use an ax to open the door. Or C-4. Or both.'

'You can't be serious.'

'Have you met Josh? I'm *definitely* serious.'

Maggie closed her eyes, trying to recall everything she had ever learned about the religion. One thought stood out among the others. 'The canon of Chinese Buddhism speaks of the Noble Eightfold Path in turn. It stresses an original effort, with all the other tenets building upon that foundation.'

'Show me,' Sarah insisted.

Maggie opened her eyes and stepped to the door. She searched the knobs for a particular symbol then began to spin the wheel. 'One must first achieve *Right View*, an understanding of the natural world around you.' As she spoke she turned the wheel a complete revolution, stopping with the corresponding knob pointing directly upright near a notch on the door. She could feel the gears catch ever so slightly at the top of her turn. 'Sarah, I think I felt something.'

Sarah smiled. She had heard it, too. She was very experienced with locks and knew the oldest one ever found was over four thousand years old. By comparison, this one was fairly new. She pressed her ear to the wood and listened while Maggie continued. 'Keep going.'

'Next comes *Right Intention*, the will to change,' she said as she cranked the wheel in the opposite direction.

Sarah heard a soft ting of metal against metal as the next spoke came into position. 'It's working!'

'Then *Right Speech*, the use of proper words.' The wheel spun easier, as if centuries of cobwebs had just been cleaned from the mechanism concealed beneath the wood. '*Right Action*, ridding one's self from corruption . . . *Right Livelihood*, abstaining from doing harm . . . *Right Effort*, the banishment of negative thought . . . *Right Mindfulness*, understand the world's effect on the body . . .'

The gears seemed to click louder with each alignment. Both Sarah and Maggie were certain that their effort would soon be rewarded.

'And lastly,' Maggie said, '*Right Concentration*, the art of meditation.'

As the final turn was completed, Sarah heard the ancient tumblers fall into place.

The door popped open with a hiss, inviting them into Polo's chamber.

Sadly, only one of them would ever step inside.

67

Sarah heard the man before she saw him, and what she heard made her blood boil.

It was the unmistakable sound of laughter.

She turned around to see a lone Chinese gunman leveling a pistol at her and Maggie. As he stepped closer, she recognized the sharp features of his face. He was Feng He, the man that Garcia had said was now in charge of the Brotherhood.

He had come to do his dirty work personally.

'Your weapons,' he demanded, 'place them on the floor.'

Sarah slowly pulled her pistol out of the concealed holster and lowered it to the ground by her feet. As she straightened up again, she noticed Maggie had not done the same.

'I said "weapons".' Feng moved closer. 'That means both of you.'

Maggie took a defiant step forward. 'Why do you need *my* weapon? You never would have made it this far without me!'

The revelation struck Sarah like a sucker punch.

Her gut churned with disbelief.

Maggie was working with the Brotherhood?

'And neither would they,' Feng hissed, his delivery dripping with menace. 'If you had come to me in the beginning and told me of their quest, I would have kept my promise and paid you the sum of their millions combined. But instead, you betrayed your people by helping the foreigners raid our country and steal our history. The only reason you contacted me is because the Brotherhood was on your trail. You got scared like a weak-minded

Westerner and decided to hedge your bets. How could I reward someone like that?'

Everything that Feng had said about Maggie was true. In the beginning, she had never considered betraying her team. She enjoyed their company and had worked extremely hard to help them find the treasure. Unfortunately, her allegiance shifted when they interrogated one of the Fists in Tibet. Not because of their actions, but because of the captive's answers.

Under the threat of torture, he had revealed that several pictures of the team had been sent to the criminal organization's headquarters in Hong Kong, a city where Maggie was very well known. She knew it was only a matter of time before her friends and family were vigorously questioned about her whereabouts, and she couldn't let that happen. Although she liked her teammates, she would do anything to protect her loved ones.

While translating the anguished pleas of the captive, she had made her choice: she would give the Fists what they were missing. She would use her knowledge of Polo's treasure to bargain for her freedom and the safety of her family and, for a small percentage of the haul, she would reveal the location of the riches as soon as the team figured it out. Unfortunately for the hunters, the lateness of Maggie's betrayal had prevented the team from suspecting anything.

Which made it hurt even more.

Sarah faced Maggie, her lower back brushing against the top of the pedestal. 'You bitch! You sold us out! That's how these bastards found us here!'

Maggie slowly reached for the pistol inside her cargo pocket as Feng watched on.

He could only smile as he watched the inevitable creep into her mind.

He knew Maggie was going to make a move.

Sarah sensed it as well. She slid a hand behind her back and reached for the wooden-bound codex. She knew it wasn't much, but it was the only solid thing within reach. She was tempted to call out for help, hoping that Cobb or McNutt could come to her aid, but she quickly realized that she hadn't heard a transmission in several minutes. She wondered if the comms had gone down for everyone, or if Maggie or Feng were blocking the signal.

Then it happened.

Maggie spun to face her now-former teammate, the weapon still in hand.

Sarah reacted instantly, pulling the codex from behind her back and hurling the two-foot long wooden slats at Maggie's face. She hoped that the desecration of the sacred artifact would be the last thing that Maggie ever expected, and fortunately she was right.

Maggie's face registered a mix of shock and horror as she instinctively raised her arm to ward off the attack. The wooden boards slammed into her wrist, knocking her gun to the cavern floor with a clatter. Dismayed and disarmed, Maggie assumed a classic fighting pose and readied herself for Sarah's assault.

Sarah was happy to oblige.

She sprang across the room in a lightning-fast flurry of swinging limbs.

Maggie managed to sidestep the onslaught just at the last second. She retaliated with a flying sidekick, catching Sarah squarely in the ribs. The impact sent Sarah sprawling backwards, and she slammed into the cavern wall.

Determined to end the battle before her younger opponent could wear her down, Maggie rushed in but Sarah lunged upward with one fist outstretched. Her knuckles caught Maggie just under the chin, dropping her to the floor. Sarah tried to stomp on her while she was down, but Maggie lithely twisted away from the attack.

Maggie sprang up from the floor and wiped the trickle of blood from her split lip.

Sarah circled her wounded prey like a hungry predator.

The display delighted Feng, who simply stood nearby and watched as the two women squared off. In his chauvinistic mind, women were put on this planet for two reasons: to breed and to serve. Few things gave him greater joy than watching the un-restrained combat of the weaker sex. Not that he cared who actually won the fight.

Either way, he would end up victorious.

And that was the only thing that mattered.

Sarah danced to her right, and Maggie deftly shifted her weight to counter. Sarah kept moving, constantly adjusting her stance as she searched for the right opportunity to strike. When she sensed an opening, Sarah pounced forward with a series of rapid punches. When those failed to connect, she spun her body, using the torque to slam her elbow into Maggie's midsection as she passed by. She finished the 360-degree rotation by launching her trailing leg skyward and driving her knee into the bottom of Maggie's chin.

Maggie's head snapped back, and she staggered away.

In an attempt to press her advantage, Sarah swung her other leg up for a kick, but Maggie deflected the blow at the last possible instant.

Maggie rushed forward, raining lightning-fast blows upon the smaller Sarah. When she raised her hands in defense, Maggie lowered her aim and pounded away on Sarah's ribs.

Sarah doubled over to protect herself, and Maggie dropped back – but only for a second.

It wasn't a retreat; she simply needed room to use the full range of her leg.

Maggie leaped forward, swinging her hardened shin into the side of Sarah's head. The kick sent Sarah careening to the ground, but she rebounded beautifully. As Maggie moved in closer, Sarah sprang from her crouch and smashed the crown of her head into Maggie's oncoming face.

Blood sprayed from her ruptured eyebrow and gushed down Maggie's face. Snot dripped from her broken nose and mixed with the spit drooling down into the split in her chin. Her eyes were swollen and watery.

She staggered aimlessly, helpless against Sarah's advance.

Feng's chest pounded with excitement.

'Finish her,' he ordered. 'Kill her. Kill her now!'

Sarah's eyes glazed over with rage. Maggie's deception had unleashed a hornet's nest of pent-up frustration, a sea of simmering angst that had been bubbling since the catastrophic loss of their previous historian in the deserts of Egypt. Despite her opponent's defenseless condition, wrath overwhelmed her.

The roundhouse kick shattered Maggie's sternum.

The arm bar that followed collapsed her trachea and snapped her neck.

Maggie fell dead to the cavern floor as Sarah stood trembling above her.

She had won the fight, but the battle wasn't finished.

Feng didn't applaud her victory or wait for his enemy to regroup. He had never been interested in a fair fight; not when he could strike while his opponent was weakened. His sentiment toward life echoed his strategy in business: the strong prevail, while the feeble must be purged from existence.

The blow from him came silently, while her back was turned. Feng blasted a rock-hard fist into the flesh protecting her right kidney, dropping her to her knees as a wave of nauseating pain swept over her. She tried to stagger to her feet, but Feng delivered another vicious blow, this time catching her squarely on the backside of her lungs.

She gasped for breath, certain that at least two of her ribs had been shattered.

Feng grabbed her by the hair and slammed her face toward the floor. She desperately spun her head to keep her nose and teeth from breaking against the solid rock, but her temple still smashed against the unforgiving stone. She landed on her stomach, which drove the last of the air from her lungs in a tortured gasp. She rolled to her side in agony, trying to move further and faster to escape the deranged man about to kill her, but her body wouldn't respond.

She felt Feng's foot ram into her side, and another rib crumbled. She brought her knees up in a protective fetal curl, but the man's foot drove down onto her throat, squeezing off her air. Sarah clawed at his calf, but the man's leg was like granite, the muscles under his trousers corded and strong from years of training.

She tried to shove him off her, but it was like trying to move a tree.

Her eyes bulged from the sockets as her lungs sucked for fresh oxygen.

Slowly, her vision grew hazy around the edges.

A few moments more, and she would be gone.

In a last-ditch effort, she tried to swing her legs up behind the man and hook him with her heels, hoping that she could push him away, but he deflected each blow with a forearm. He leaned heavily into her, pressing his boot on her windpipe as if he were trying to ram his foot through her neck to the floor. She could feel herself losing consciousness, her resistance slipping with each passing second.

As her eyes rolled back, a final idea exploded in her mind.

The knife!

Sarah frantically dug into the folds of her pockets until her fingertips found her knife. Fighting the lack of air, she wrapped her fingers around the handle. With the last energy she could muster, she withdrew the blade and slashed the knife parallel to her throat. The only thing in her way was Feng's Achilles tendon.

She sliced through it like tender veal.

Feng roared in agony and jolted backward from the pain. Though he landed on his feet, the sliced tendon gave him no support. He immediately toppled backwards, the pistol from his holster sliding harmlessly across the floor.

Sarah rolled to her side and forced herself to her knees, still clutching the knife. Her bruised neck throbbed as she sucked in huge gulps of air, but she was oblivious to the pain.

She was just happy to be alive.

As she rose to her feet, Feng clawed desperately for his pistol, which had fallen just beyond his reach. His hand strained for the weapon, his limb extending back as his nails dug into the grip. The tips of his powerful fingers inched the gun closer, until it was finally within his grasp.

She saw the entire scene in slow motion.

In response, she cocked her arm backward, the knife still in hand.

As Feng raised the gun, she let the blade fly. The knife tumbled end over end through the air for what seemed like an eternity, but her aim was true.

And so was the pistol's.

The blade sank deep into his eye as a gunshot echoed through the chamber.

68

Sarah stared at the barrel of Feng's gun. There was no fire. There was no smoke. There was no projectile hurling its way toward her face at the speed of sound.

The knife had sunk securely into his left eye, the blade tunneling deeply into his skull and the handle lodging firmly up against his orbital bone. Yet it was the right half of his face that had left her in awe. It wasn't just damaged, it was shredded, the skull beneath having been pulverized into skeletal fragments.

The reality of the moment slowly crept into her brain.

Feng never got off a shot.

Someone else pulled the trigger.

Feng's body tipped over to the side, and Sarah glanced over her shoulder to see who had joined the fray. She breathed a sigh of relief at the sight of Cobb; she didn't have the strength to fight more of the Brotherhood.

'Nice timing,' Sarah croaked before dropping to the ground in exhaustion.

Cobb raced forward to catch her, but she held up a hand to signal that she was okay. He crouched beside her. 'I think what you meant to say was, "Thanks for saving my life."'

Sarah grinned as she gulped in air. 'Nah, I had him. The knife killed him first. You just made things messy.'

Cobb was about to laugh when he noticed Maggie's crumpled body near the other side of the room. He sprang up to investigate, but Sarah grabbed the cuff of his pant leg.

'Don't,' she pleaded. 'She's not worth it.'

Cobb's troubled stare told her that she needed to explain.

'She was working for Feng. She sold us out for a paycheck, then she turned on me.'

Cobb was confused. 'She couldn't have been in his pocket all along. Not with all the help she gave us. That doesn't make any sense.'

'I don't know when he flipped her,' Sarah admitted. 'All I can tell you is that she definitely wasn't working for us at the end. Xenophobia. Nationalistic fanaticism. I really don't know. But it was either her or me.'

'Well, you made the right choice,' Cobb said.

He went through Feng's pockets and found a small electronic device. He dropped it on the floor, then stomped on it with his boot. As he ground the remnants into dust with his heel, they heard Garcia in their ears.

'– repeat. Radio check. I have no audio. Jack? Sarah? Maggie?'

'Hector, we're here,' Cobb replied. 'Sarah and I are back on comms.'

'Any sign of Maggie?' Garcia asked.

'She's dead,' Sarah explained. 'So is Feng. They were working together. We don't know when or how, but he turned her.'

'Son of a bitch,' Garcia replied incredulously. 'That explains how they were able to tail us so relentlessly.'

'Everyone else is dead, too,' McNutt said as he entered the chamber. 'The bad guys, I mean. And Rodrigo still has the satellite keeping an eye on things up top.' McNutt looked down at Maggie's corpse. 'So Miss Maggie was a traitor, eh? And here I thought our luck was changing. I wonder if *anything* she said about Polo or his treasure was true.'

'It was,' Sarah assured him. She had caught a peek inside just before the confrontation with Feng. She walked over to the wooden door that was still ajar and pushed it open wide. 'I think we found it.'

On the other side of the door was a massive chamber, bigger than any of the natural caverns they had seen so far. The room was filled with ornate wooden chests, all of them bigger than a military footlocker. Cobb guessed there were as many as a hundred chests filling the space. He swept his flashlight around the room slowly so Garcia could record it all.

'You getting this, Hector?' he asked.

'That's a lot of chests,' Garcia replied.

Sarah moved to the nearest one. None of the chests were open, but their lids did not appear to be locked in any way. Instead of swinging upward on hinges, the tops had been seated straight down onto the crates, like the covers of cardboard file boxes. She set her flashlight on the ground and hefted a heavy wooden lid, using the light from the glow sticks to peek inside.

A moment later, she dropped the lid and grinned at the gold.

'Well?' Garcia asked.

Cobb could only smile as McNutt's boisterous laugh echoed throughout the chamber.

Epilogue

Sunday, April 13

Papineau had risen early to ensure his privacy. While the team continued to sleep – aided by more than a few celebratory libations from the previous evening – the Frenchman knew there was still work to be done. Finding Polo's fortune was only the beginning of his mission.

Papineau still needed to locate the true prize of the treasure.

A single item that Maurice Copeland had requested.

The air was warm in the pre-dawn hour, with a steady breeze that made for a pleasant morning. In the coming months the region would be blanketed by the rainstorms of monsoon season, but for the moment the humidity was still tolerable. The beads of sweat rolling down Papineau's brow were a result of his anxiety, not the weather.

As with everything his boss demanded, failure was not an option.

Approaching the base of the Lion Gate on foot, Papineau quickly noticed the squadron of patrolmen assigned to protect the mountain. He had half expected to see soldiers from the Sri Lankan Army, but he understood that it would take a day or two to mobilize the proper forces. In the meantime, the Ministry of Defence had used the local authorities to safeguard the rock against any and all visitors.

Officially, the historic site was closed because of a helicopter crash – the newspapers had even run notices describing possible damage to the site itself. Not even the men surrounding the structure knew the truth. Besides Papineau and his team, only a handful of select political officials were aware of the battle that had been fought there and the priceless discovery found within.

It would stay that way until they could devise a plan.

The last thing the country needed was a war with China.

In the meantime, Papineau flashed credentials identifying him as an engineer with UNESCO sent to inspect the damage and was immediately granted entry. As part of Copeland's deal with the heads of state, he – and he alone – was given unfettered access to the site. The paperwork he carried even included the Sri Lankan government's seal of approval.

The cover story was fake, but the president's signature was real.

The cops never questioned Papineau's arrival.

Nor did they help him climb down to the secret chambers.

Thankfully, the team's rappelling gear had been left behind.

When he reached the newly discovered cavern of riches, Papineau paused, taking it all in. As he moved the beam of his flashlight throughout the space, sparkling gems and precious metals glinted back at him in the darkness. The team had rooted through the chests to determine the extent of their find, and the disturbance to the tightly packed vessels had left it impossible to close many of their lids. The effect was that they now appeared to be bursting at the seams.

It was truly a sight to behold.

Papineau breathed a sigh of relief – his first moment of contentment in weeks – and stepped forward to inventory the haul. As he did, he felt a draft in the room as something took position behind him. A moment later, he felt the cold steel of a pistol barrel pressed against the base of his neck.

'That's far enough.'

Papineau recognized the voice. 'Jack? Is that you? How did—'

Cobb ground the barrel into Papineau's flesh. 'Shut your fucking mouth. I'm the one asking the questions here.' Cobb pressed hard on Papineau's shoulder. 'On your knees.'

Papineau dropped to the ground immediately. Behind him, he heard the distinct snap of a glow stick, followed by the eerie glow of the chemical reaction. Suddenly the cavern was filled with amber light. Papineau blinked as Cobb stepped forward, the shadows on his face exaggerating the bloodthirsty glare in his eyes. Papineau desperately wanted to speak, but he could see that the man staring back at him was in no mood to be tested.

This wasn't the leader of the hunters.

This was a killer, hell bent on punishment.

The previous evening Cobb had celebrated with his team, but he had never returned to his room. When the revelry was over he had made his way back to the Lion Gate and easily slipped past the preoccupied guards. He had found the cave in the darkness, and then he waited. The next person to enter would not leave until Cobb had answers . . . if Cobb let him leave at all.

'What are you doing here?' Cobb demanded.

Papineau tried to keep his cool. 'There is one item of special importance. I came to retrieve it before we surrendered the rest to the local government.'

'Which item is that?'

'A cross,' Papineau answered. 'A ruby cross, trimmed in gold. A gift from Kublai Khan to the Pope himself. It's known as the Blood Cross.'

'Bullshit!' Cobb growled. 'We're surrounded by gold and jewels. We didn't go through hell for a goddamn cross. Don't lie to me! Or I swear to God I'll kill you in this fucking tomb!'

'I swear, Jack! I'm telling you the truth! All I want is the cross!'

'Bullshit!' he yelled again. 'You didn't spend millions of dollars to get a single cross. Why are you here? What's your end game?'

The question caught Papineau off-guard. To him, the most obvious scenario had been that his boss had grown tired of him and had sent Cobb to permanently terminate his employment.

Papineau now understood the error of this assumption.

Cobb didn't know about Copeland.

Cobb was here for answers.

'I'm not in this for the riches,' Papineau assured him. It wasn't a lie. He actually didn't care about the money; he simply did as he was told to buy time.

Cobb grinned at him, the smile of the Devil as he confronts a sinner. 'Well, you're not in it for the fame. The train and the tomb were both discovered by anonymous parties. I know because I saw it on the news. And I'm willing to bet my entire paycheck that your name will never be linked to Marco Polo. So if you don't want the money, and you don't want the credit, then what's left? And don't you dare tell me a fucking cross.'

'The satisfaction,' Papineau answered defiantly. 'Knowing that you accomplished what no one else in history could achieve.'

Cobb laughed. 'What *you* accomplished? *You* didn't accomplish shit. All you did was foot the bill. My team made the discovery. *They* made this happen, not you.'

Papineau could feel the rage building inside his captor. He knew that Cobb had taken lives – he had seen it on multiple occasions; and he wondered if he was next.

'You don't understand that, do you?' Cobb continued. 'You see yourself as the king, and the rest of us as pawns. You'd replace us in a heartbeat if you could find better pieces to fit your needs; in fact, you did. Human life means nothing to you.' Cobb came closer to Papineau, bearing down on him like the Grim Reaper. 'You felt *nothing* when we lost Jasmine. I bet you felt the same when you had Seymour killed for following you.'

Papineau's emotion was instant. It couldn't be faked.

The look in his eyes told Cobb that he was wrong.

He could see the pain the Frenchman felt for Jasmine's death, and the anger he suppressed following Cobb's accusation. Even worse, Cobb could sense Papineau's surprise at the mention of Duggan's death. In a flash, Cobb knew that Papineau hadn't ordered his execution. In fact, Papineau didn't even know that Duggan had been following him.

A sickening mix of confusion and shame flooded Cobb's mind.

For the first time in a long time, he didn't know what to do.

'Seymour is dead?' Papineau dared to ask.

Cobb could only nod. He had been absolutely certain that Papineau was responsible for Duggan's death. He had convinced himself that Duggan's man in California had confessed Duggan's involvement and that Papineau had called for his grisly murder.

Now, he knew none of that was true.

'It wasn't you, was it?' Cobb asked.

Papineau said nothing. He was suddenly struck by the full magnitude of what he had learned. He had no idea that he was being tracked – by a former associate, no less. But Copeland knew. Copeland obviously knew. And when his boss sensed a threat, he took care of it immediately. Anyone who learned of Copeland's involvement would be silenced forever.

It was only a matter of time before Copeland would turn against him.

Papineau didn't have a choice. He had to strike first.

For that to happen, he would need help.

'It wasn't me,' Papineau finally answered. 'But I know who it was.'

'Who?' Cobb demanded.

Papineau had been given permission to string Cobb along, to lure him in with assurances that he would someday meet the man pulling the strings, but that timeline had changed. Papineau knew he would have to give up more information than that if he hoped to weather this storm.

Copeland pushed him from one direction.

Now Cobb pushed back from another.

The time had come to make a choice.

'I'll give you his name,' Papineau said, 'but you must promise me one thing.'

'Name it,' Cobb growled.

'When you meet him, you have to kill him.'

About Chris Kuzneski

Chris Kuzneski is the international bestselling author of numerous thrillers featuring the series characters Payne and Jones, including SIGN OF THE CROSS and THE SECRET CROWN. He is also the author of THE HUNTERS, the first novel in a new electrifying series that continues with THE FORBIDDEN TOMB and THE PRISONER'S GOLD. Chris's thrillers have been translated into more than twenty languages and are sold in more than forty countries. Chris grew up in Pennsylvania but currently lives on the Gulf Coast of Florida. To learn more, please visit his website: www.chriskuzneski.com